ESSAYS

FROM THE *RAMBLER, ADVENTURER,* AND *IDLER*

SAMUEL JOHNSON

Essays from the *Rambler*, *Adventurer*, and *Idler*

EDITED BY W. J. BATE

NEW HAVEN AND LONDON, YALE UNIVERSITY PRESS

1968

Library of Congress catalog card number: 68–27747

Designed by John O. C. McCrillis,
set in Baskerville type,
and printed in the United States of America by
The Carl Purington Rollins Printing-Office of
the Yale University Press, New Haven, Connecticut.

Distributed in Great Britain, Europe, Asia, and
Africa by Yale University Press Ltd., London; in
Canada by McGill University Press, Montreal; and
in Latin America by Centro Interamericano de Libros
Académicos, Mexico City.

PREFACE

This volume presents a substantial selection from the three series of periodical essays by Johnson, and is taken, with some modification in the commentary, from the relevant volumes of the Yale Edition of Johnson (Vols. II to V, for which I have served as general editor). Included are seventy-nine essays, sixty-nine of them complete.

The demand for a solid selection has increased sharply during the generation since World War II, and reflects the deepening interest of younger readers in the greater writing of the past on human nature and life. If plans for providing such a selection were deferred, this was because the lack of an established text and citation on which to draw naturally led an editor to hesitate, especially after the announcement of the new edition of the complete works. Like many others, I was eager to have a selection of this sort available as soon as possible, and began preparing it while the larger edition was still in the process of being printed. For years I had been assigning, in a college lecture course at Harvard on the Age of Johnson, from forty to fifty of the major essays, in which I felt—and hope my students agreed—that we were touching the heart of Johnson. But this meant that students were forced to compete for access, in the college library, to whatever copies were available of the 1825 and earlier editions of the complete works. The situation was obviously far from satisfactory. Nor was I consoled to think that the only future alternative, for students being introduced to Johnson, would be the four volumes of our new edition. For the necessary editorial machinery in those volumes and the abundant notes concerned with textual variants (especially in the *Rambler,* where there may be as many as three in a single line) would, I knew, be a serious distraction, constantly carrying the eye to the bottom of the page or, at the least, creating a sense of clutter.

This selection was originally announced as *The Moral Essays of Johnson*. It was later decided that the title might mislead, since about a third of the essays included are in one way or another concerned with literary criticism or the varied life, problems, and frustrations of the literary and learned world. Hence the straightforward title we now use for this by-product of the Yale Edition, Vols. II to V. But of course the word "moral"—broadly interpreted—subsumes almost all of the essays or, for that matter, almost everything Johnson wrote.

The text is that of the parent edition, with the textual—but not as a rule the other—notes removed. There have in some cases been expansions in the explanatory notes. The identification of mottoes and other indented quotations is editorial and simply inserted. The Introduction includes some of the introductory material I wrote for the Yale Edition, but is intended to be more general in character. Obligations are recorded in the Prefaces to the relevant volumes of the complete edition. But I should stress the indispensable work done on the text by my colleagues for those volumes—Professor Albrecht Strauss for the *Rambler,* Professor John Bullitt for the *Idler,* and, for the *Adventurer,* Dr. L. F. Powell.

W. J. BATE

Cambridge, Massachusetts.
September, 1967

CONTENTS

THE ADVENTURER

THE IDLER

INTRODUCTION

The most fertile decade of Johnson's writing begins with the publication of the *Vanity of Human Wishes* (1749), when he was nearly forty, continues through the *Rambler* (1750–52), the *Adventurer* (1753–54), and the publication of the *Dictionary* (1755), and then concludes with *Rasselas* (1759) and the *Idler* (1758–60).

With the works written during these years, Johnson emerges for us as one of the great moralists of modern times —one of a handful of men, during the last three centuries, whose writing on human life and destiny has become a permanent part of the conscience of mankind. Yet none of these works was composed with the leisure possessed by almost every other major moralist of whose life we know anything at all. The *Vanity of Human Wishes*—certainly one of the most powerfully distilled poems in the language—was composed at incredible speed. The deeply moving *Rasselas* was written by Johnson during the evenings of a week in order to defray the expenses of his mother's funeral. And three of the works—the essays in the *Rambler,* the *Adventurer,* and the *Idler*—were composed for periodical publication. The periodical form may have advantages, especially for a man of Johnson's temperament, who often responded best to the pressure of necessity. But there were liabilities which we might keep in mind when we compare these essays to those of writers whose circumstances were very different. When he began his first series, the *Rambler* and the *Adventurer,* he was also at work on the *Dictionary,* carrying out that heroic, pioneer work with a fitful dispatch that has always puzzled the historian of genius. He was in need of money, was often unwell, and was harassed by personal troubles. Such circumstances are by no means fatal even to so considered a form of writing as moral essays. But it helps to be at liberty to pick the opportune moment. And he who "condemns himself," as Johnson said in the final essay for the *Rambler* (No. 208),

> to compose on a stated day, will often bring to his task an attention dissipated, a memory overwhelmed, an imagination embarrassed, a mind distracted with anxieties, a body languishing with disease; he will labour on a barren topic till it is too late to change it; or . . . diffuse his thoughts into wild exuberance, which the pressing hour of publication cannot suffer judgment to examine or reduce.

But despite the circumstances, despite the fact that his essays, as his friend Sir John Hawkins said, were extemporaneous compositions, and hardly ever underwent a revision before they were sent to the press, Johnson gave the periodical essay a strength, an incisive insight, and at times a grandeur altogether new, with the result that Johnson transcends the *genre* of the periodical essay as we ordinarily think of it. The best of the *Rambler,* and of the two series that follow, is timeless. It is timeless because it is concerned with the fundamental questions of living; because its theme, like that of most of the greatest moral literature, is the purification of the motives and above all of the self-delusions that create most of the evil and unhappiness of the world; and because Johnson's honesty to experience, his immediacy in turning every thought to what can be "put to use"—to what can be brought directly to the aid of "helpless man"—is here as concentrated as in anything else he ever wrote.

I. The *Rambler* and the *Adventurer*

The first number of the *Rambler* appeared on Tuesday, March 20, 1750; and thereafter one was published every Saturday and Tuesday until the last day of publication,

Saturday, March 14, 1752. All but four of the *Ramblers,* and parts of three others, were written by Johnson himself.[1] He was paid two guineas for each paper. Though the sale of the *Rambler* was modest (probably never exceeding 500 copies per number), the series began to attract attention. It was a common practice for eighteenth-century periodicals to draw on each other; and many of them quickly began to swell their pages by reprinting entire numbers or selections from particular numbers of the *Ramblers.* Afterward, it was to go through ten numbered printings before Johnson died; and long before then, the *Rambler,* as much as the *Dictionary,* had permanently established his reputation.

It was in the wake of the *Rambler* that Johnson soon afterward began to contribute occasional essays (a total of twenty-nine) to John Hawkesworth's periodical, the *Adventurer,* for a period of a year (the first contribution appearing on March 3, 1753, about a year after the final number of the *Rambler,* and the last appearing on March 2, 1754). The *Adventurer* essays are so completely in the vein of the earlier series that discussion of them may be subsumed in our remarks on the *Rambler.*

Given the circumstances in which they were written, at stated times twice a week when he was often preoccupied with other matters, the 202 essays Johnson himself wrote for the *Rambler* are naturally uneven. But the majority of them—and of the essays that he later wrote for the *Adventurer*—are saturated with thought to an extent unexceeded by any other writer of English prose since Francis Bacon. Even though the *Rambler* and *Adventurer* essays were writ-

1. No. 30 was written by Catherine Talbot, No. 97 by Samuel Richardson, and Nos. 44 and 100 by Elizabeth Carter. No. 10 contains four billets by Hester Mulso (later Mrs. Chapone). According to Bishop Percy, the second letter in No. 15 was written by David Garrick, and the second letter in No. 107 by a former schoolfellow of Johnson, Joseph Simpson, of Lincoln's Inn.

ten with Johnson's usual haste and that impatience with which he faced any stated task, he brought to them a large internal fund of accumulated experience and reflection. It is typical that one of the best discussions in English of idleness and procrastination *(Rambler* 134) could be "hastily composed," according to Mrs. Thrale, "in Sir Joshua Reynolds's parlour, while the boy waited to carry it to the press."

Johnson's universality as a moralist stands in some contrast to the form that he took as readiest to hand—the eighteenth-century periodical essay. In the *Rambler,* as his first substantial effort in prose, he was especially on his guard against the usual—and expected—topicality of the periodical essay. (As he states in the last paper: "I have never complied with temporary curiosity, nor enabled my readers to discuss the topick of the day.") Johnson's range of reference and quotation is itself a reminder that we are dealing with a writer who disdained the "local and temporary": hardly more than a twentieth of the allusions are to eighteenth-century writers. Naturally, since Johnson is writing periodical essays, at least some of what Coleridge would call the "exterior" characteristics of the form are present.[2] Again, many of the *Ramblers* and the other two series may be classified as literary criticism; and for the insertion of such essays in a periodical series (however different Johnson's own critical premises), Addison was of course the great model.[3] In particular, we should remem-

2. Most obvious is the frequent (and not always too felicitous) use of the "letter to the editor" (63 of the *Ramblers* are written thus, in whole or in part). Johnson's impatience with this device—so trivially artificial and irrelevant to his interests and gifts as a moralist—is illustrated by the decline of its use in the *Adventurer.* For here he was actually contributing to the periodical series of another and might have been expected to use the letter-form. Yet only nine of 29 essays are couched as a letter. For the others, which become more common as time passes, one has the impression that Johnson simply forgot to inscribe them "To the *Adventurer.*"

3. Of the essays printed in this selection, almost a third (25) could be loosely classified as literary criticism. These would include general moral discussions *(Rambler,* Nos. 2, 14, 31), portraits concerned with the

ber that the *Rambler* and *Adventurer* essays, simply because they appeared in periodical form, would naturally differ in some ways from most of the traditional moral essays (such as those by Montaigne or Bacon) simply because a deadline had to be met and because the length of each number was roughly fixed.[4]

But the true literary ancestry of the *Rambler*—and of its sequel, the *Adventurer*—is overlooked, and our conception of it trivialized, if we concentrate merely on the periodical essay as it descended from Addison and Steele, or even if we confine ourselves too parochially to the eighteenth century itself. In one respect the nineteenth century was perfectly right when it contrasted the *Rambler* so unfavorably with the *Tatler* and the *Spectator*. It took Addison's *Spectator* as the prototype of one special form (the periodical essay), and then, finding the *Rambler* so much more serious in tone and weighty in thought, judged Johnson's work as failing to fulfill the special ideals and opportunities of that particular form. A more accurate statement is simply that he transcended that form.

If we are to use an historical framework, it should be far more capacious than the eighteenth-century periodical essay, and should extend from the Greek aphorists and the book of Ecclesiastes, through the Renaissance humanists and writers of *exempla,* and continue through the English seventeenth-century religious writers. Montaigne and Bacon, in particular, are the progenitors of the more straightforward moral essays. One of the quainter prejudices of the nineteenth

---

literary life *(Rambler,* Nos. 16, 101, 106, 146; *Idler,* Nos. 60 and 61); and, more specifically, *Rambler,* Nos. 4, 60, 90, 93, 121, 156, 158, 176; *Adventurer,* Nos. 95, 137; and *Idler,* Nos. 30, 36, 59, 65, 66, 84.

4. The *Ramblers* average about 1,450 words—ranging from 1,200 to 1,700 in the first 20 numbers, and gradually becoming shorter until, in the last 20, they average about 1,200 words. The *Adventurers* are somewhat longer (1,650 to 1,900 words). The much shorter *Idlers* begin at an average of about 1,050, and by the last 20 numbers are about 900 or less.

century that still linger on into the second half of our own is the belief that the eighteenth century was almost self-sealed as a unit of history—that, whatever men who lived in it might know about classical antiquity, they were relatively unaware of the periods immediately preceding their own. This assumption is especially grotesque in the case of Johnson. No major moralist of the past two centuries was or has been so deeply read in the writing of the period from the Renaissance through the seventeenth century. To begin with, his constant concern to discover what can be "put to use," to find and to share with others the means by which a thing can be achieved, led him sympathetically to the "Revival of Learning" in almost all of its aspects. One of Johnson's projected works, after all, was a

> "History of the Revival of Learning in Europe, containing an account of whatever contributed to the restoration of literature; such as controversies, printing, the destruction of the Greek empire, the encouragement of great men, with the lives of the most eminent patrons and most eminent early professors of all kinds of learning in different countries."
>
> (Boswell, *Life,* IV.382).

This deep sympathetic kinship with human effort, this close interest in the earlier stages of any achievement, is one of the principal characteristics of Johnson's mind. Above all we should recognize his close emotional affinity with the Renaissance humanist and with English writing generally—especially the great English religious and prudential prose—before 1700. Johnson, as Whitehead noticed a generation ago, is "still of the essence of the seventeenth century." His habitual citations (often showing, because of the speed with which he wrote, what was uppermost in his mind) offer a minor but convincing illustration.[5] Even if we leave these essays aside

5. See the discussion of the annotation of the three series in the Introductions to Vols. II and III of the Yale Edition of Johnson.

and consider only the narrative sketches and portraits, we could as justifiably cite an eighteenth-century influence other than the periodical essay itself—William Law's *Serious Call to a Devout and Holy Life* (1729), which Johnson had first read at Oxford, "expecting to find it a dull book . . . and perhaps to laugh at it. But I found Law quite an overmatch for me; and this was the first occasion of my thinking in earnest of religion."

Already, in Johnson's *Vanity of Human Wishes* (1749), we can see two strains combining, though with a good deal of tension. There is the satiric reductionism that unites him with Mandeville (and, for that matter, with Swift), further sharpened by the impatience and exasperation that we always find stirring in him. Even mere phrases in the essays exemplify it. Thus, of scientific research: "He that is growing great and happy by electrifying a bottle wonders how the world can be engaged by trifling prattle about war and peace." The whole frantic zeal of writing, scholarship, criticism, and reviewing is suddenly reduced in a phrase like the "epidemical conspiracy for the destruction of paper." And there is the good-natured man in *Rambler* 188, whose modest silence gives pleasure because his companions conclude that it results "not from inability to speak but from eagerness to hear." The tart, fidgety phrases are distilled from an unillusioned awareness of the frightening strength and sleepless craving of human egotism. In the *Vanity of Human Wishes* we have the hunger of the human ego presented in an almost savagely panoramic form, through the scramble for riches, for reputation, for advancement, for power (the "fawning" niece, "hot for a legacy"; the rising statesman whose "sinking" predecessor's "door / Pours in the morning worshipper no more"), on up to the rise and fall of entire nations. But at the same time this whole protest and all it distills are ultimately assimilated and morally directed as the *Vanity of Human Wishes* begins to follow the procedure of Law's *Serious Call*. One by one, Law (following in turn the prototype of Ecclesiastes) had touched on the ambitions and hungers of the human heart and imagination, disclosing how each new possession, each new achievement, soon ceases to fill the heart, which can ultimately find stability and purpose only through religion.

If we dwell for a moment on Johnson's powerful, condensed poem, it is because the great moral writing of the following decade, which begins with the *Rambler* and ends with *Rasselas* and the *Idler,* may be described as the prose explication of the *Vanity of Human Wishes.* (The difference is that here, in the prose writing, the religious answer is in general implied rather than stated.) One of the fascinations of Johnson is that he seemed to possess all the positive equipment for satire though he was himself ultimately incapable of writing it: his completely undeluded view of human nature; his strong aggressive instincts—above all his capacity for anger (not the cold anger of Swift, but, as in Juvenal, something heady, impetuous, even potentially violent); and, with it, his ingenious gift for inventing grotesque or ludicrous remarks and scenes, thrown off by an imagination that is often most fertile and concrete when it is stung by exasperation. Yet Johnson is not really a satirist, and in fact, as Mrs. Thrale said, had "an aversion" to general satire. We could put it more strongly and say that he had a hatred and fear of satire—a fear that led him to be notoriously unfair in his critical estimate of Swift. We do not explain the fact that he is not—could not be—a satirist by saying only that he feared to release the satiric impulse because it was too strong. We come closer to an explanation if we say that Johnson was unable merely to observe, but had to participate and share; and that his own participation sets a bar to satire. The result, time and again in all of his moral writing, is that we have anger, protest, even ridicule, always in the process of turning into something else. This creates a distinctive form of writing, from the *Rambler* through the *Adventurer* to *Rasselas* and the *Idler,* that we might describe as "satire manqué" or "satire foiled." From the portraits a single instance can be cited—the letter (No. 73) supposedly written by that stock figure in satire, the legacy hunter—an account quickly etched with a savage directness we might expect from Swift or Mandeville (but never Addison). As we read of this family sitting about and waiting for the death of three elderly, wealthy aunts, we also recall Johnson's affinity with Juvenal, the "angry" satirist. The story is both grotesque and ugly. But the anger and exasperation, before the short sketch is finished, are suffused by a sadness and a final charity that completely transform them. The aging nephew, who has waited so long and has consoled himself that "all are mortal," finds that he himself is altogether "mortal"—that he has become the helpless victim of time and habit. Having for so long become "corrupted with an inveterate disease of wishing," he is now "accustomed to give the future full power" over his mind, and to "start away" from the scene before him "to some expected enjoyment."

Though what we are saying applies most obviously to the portraits, the same spirit also pervades the direct moral essays, which comprise the bulk of the present volume. There too the subjects have to do with the self-defeating "snares" (to use the word in the *Vanity of Human Wishes*) that human beings are always creating for themselves and others in the short time that they have on the planet—the ceaseless jostle for position, for riches, for reassurance, for fame (that constantly defeated "desire of filling the minds of others"); the fanciful hope for relief through change of place; the frightening prevalence of envy as still another result of "the hunger of imagination which preys incessantly upon life." And if he is as unillusioned as Thomas Hobbes or Hobbes' modern descendants about the unsleeping strength of human egotism and man's almost infinite capacity to delude himself about his own motives, Johnson is constantly bringing to bear other considerations that are overlooked or forgotten by the reductionist who hastens to stratify human motivation under a few static labels. This is principally because Johnson probes more deeply, and is unable to forget the dynamic nature of the human imagination—its capacity to turn in so many different directions, its pliability as well as its restlessness, and its potential hunger (however confused, fitful, or distracted) for the "stability of truth." Those only, said Coleridge, "can acquire the philosophic imagination . . . who within themselves can interpret and understand the symbol, that the wings of the air-sylph are forming within the skin of the caterpillar. . . . They know and feel that the *potential* works in them." If this sense of process is so alive in Johnson, it is because he himself was so richly endowed with what Sir Walter Raleigh called an "experiencing nature." And whatever the awkwardnesses of expression in the writing of this period of his life, the tone of the style itself reflects this multiform consciousness, giving it the distinctive combination (hardly to be found in any other moralist) of psychological shrewdness and somber elevation, of impatience and the weight of experience, of irony and compassion. Hence the ring of authority even in single sentences that abound throughout the essays and are quoted time and again:

> Men seldom give pleasure where they are not pleased themselves. . . . We are more pained by ignorance than delighted by instruction. . . . The natural flights of the human mind are not from pleasure to pleasure, but from hope to hope. . . . Merit rather enforces respect than attracts fondness. . . . Many need no other provocation to enmity than that they find themselves excelled. . . . The vanity of being known to be trusted with a secret is generally one of the chief motives to disclose it. . . . Among other pleasing errors of young minds is the opinion of their own importance. He that has not yet remarked, how little attention his contemporaries can spare from themselves, conceives all eyes turned upon himself, and imagines everyone that approaches him to be an enemy or a follower, an admirer or a spy. . . . The cure for the

greatest part of human miseries is not radical, but
palliative. . . . Whatever is proposed, it is much easier
to find reasons for rejecting than embracing. . . . Ease, a
neutral state between pain and pleasure . . . if it is not
rising into pleasure, will be falling towards pain. . . . So
willing is every man to flatter himself, that the difference
between approving laws, and obeying them, is frequently
forgotten; he that acknowledges the obligations of
morality, and pleases his vanity with enforcing them
to others, concludes himself zealous in the cause of virtue.
. . . We have less reason to be surprised or offended when
we find others differ from us in opinion, because we very
often differ from ourselves.

If the direct moral essays carry us back to the seventeenth-
century sermon, to Jeremy Taylor, and especially to the
essays of Montaigne and Bacon, the mention of William
Law's *Serious Call* reminds us of the "Theophrastan character" of the seventeenth century, and, once again, of its classical sources (to which we should add the historical portraits
by Diogenes Laertius and Plutarch, especially in the *Moralia*).
And whether we are thinking either of the moral essays or
of the sketches and portraits, we are also led back—as we
suggested above—to Ecclesiastes, both directly and also
through the long tradition of Christian apologetics. We are
dealing, in short, with a mode of writing that in its amplitude
and essentialism cannot be dated, except in crudely obvious
stylistic ways.

Despite the speed with which he was forced to write and
however preoccupied he was with other matters during these
two years, he approached the *Rambler* at the start—and continued to do so until the end—with perhaps more deliberate
and self-conscious effort than anything he was to write afterward. There are the notes, for example, that he collected over
a period of time in preparation for the work *(Life,* I.204–06).

More revealing is Johnson's prayer on beginning the *Rambler* (*Diaries,* p. 43):

> Almighty God, . . . without whose grace all wisdom is folly, grant, I beseech Thee, that in this my undertaking thy Holy Spirit may not be withheld from me, but that I may promote thy glory, and the Salvation of both myself and others.

His belief that he had at least partly succeeded (expressed in the last paper, No. 208) remained with him as the years passed. Whatever else he wrote, he preserved a special fondness for the *Rambler.* Few writers have been less given to expressing self-approbation. Yet we recall the well-known remark recorded in Samuel Rogers' *Table-Talk:* "My other works are wine and water; but my *Rambler* is pure wine." Not that it can be called the "pure wine" of his style. The triumph of Johnson's style is to be found in the later works, especially the *Lives of the Poets.* However memorable many of the phrases—indeed whole paragraphs—the writing of the *Rambler,* as of the *Adventurer,* is often studded with the by-products of his struggle with expression in his early and middle years as a writer. In some respects these are even greater than they had been before. The work on the *Dictionary* was leaving its effect in the use of so many abstract nouns of Latin origin. But more important was the self-consciousness with which he approached the work—a self-consciousness which lack of leisure never permitted him to turn to profit, and which therefore, in these almost extemporaneous writings, remains in an earlier, rawer state than would otherwise have been the case.

The sense of dedication expressed in the prayer on beginning the *Rambler,* and with it a deeply uneasy sense of humility, is revealed in another way altogether typical of Johnson. This was his decision to keep the authorship secret—to keep himself, in fact, as completely out of the picture as possible. To begin with, he did not wish to disrupt the series with the unsolicited contributions that the periodical writer was expected to ask for and accept. But he had a deeper, less obvious reason. No moralist has been so acutely aware of the inevitable disparity between a writer's moral precepts and the temptations and unpredictable accidents, the divided feelings and mixed motives, of the writer's life as an individual. The subject recurs constantly in Johnson's writing, and especially throughout the dark middle years of his life. True enough, his general tendency is to defend the frailty of human nature, in this as in other ways:

> Nothing is more unjust, however common, than to charge with hypocrisy him that expresses zeal for those virtues, which he neglects to practise; since he may be sincerely convinced of the advantages of conquering his passions, without having yet obtained the victory, as a man may be confident of the advantages of a voyage, or a journey, without having courage or industry to undertake it, and may honestly recommend to others, those attempts which he neglects himself.
>
> *(Rambler, No. 14)*

But "reasonable with regard to others," said Mrs. Thrale, Johnson "had formed vain hopes of performing impossibilities himself." At no point in his life was he pleased with the result, least of all in the years that preceded and followed the *Rambler*. And he was only too aware of the way in which he appeared to others as well as to himself. It was less than six years earlier that, invited to dinner by Edward Cave after the *Life of Savage* was published, Johnson had eaten behind a screen because of the shabbiness of his clothes. Though some of the finest observations in the *Rambler* were to be concerned with the value of good nature and good humor, he once despondently told Henry Thrale that he had never even "sought to please till past thirty years old, considering the matter as hopeless." As he prepared to begin the *Rambler,* he deeply wished the purity and soundness of the

work to be free from the prejudices the reader might bring
to it if he knew the author.[6] Finally, a deliberate effort not to
claim too much appears in the title, the *Rambler,* that he
selected after some hesitation—a title, as Boswell said, that
seems singularly inappropriate to the moral elevation of so
many of the essays. Arthur Murphy wondered whether it had
been "suggested by the *Wanderer;* a poem which he mentions
with the warmest praise in the *Life of Savage.*" Murphy was
probably right. Years after Johnson had written the *Rambler*
he told Oliver Edwards that he considered himself something
of a "straggler"—"I may leave this town and go to Grand
Cairo without being missed here or observed there"; and
there was an important part of Johnson that was sympathetically identified with writers, like Savage, who lacked
opportunities and hung on the fringes of literary as well as
other society. From Johnson himself we have only the following account of the title, which he later gave to Sir Joshua
Reynolds: He was "at a loss how to name it." Finally, "I sat
down at night upon my bedside, and resolved that I would
not go to sleep till I had fixed its title. The *Rambler* seemed
the best that occurred, and I took it."

II.   The *Idler*

Four preoccupied years after he wrote his last contribution
to the *Adventurer,* Johnson began his third and final peri-

6. Early in the series, said Samuel Richardson, and before the name
of the writer was known, "Mr. Doddington sent a letter to the *Rambler,*
inviting him to his house, when he should be disposed to enlarge his
acquaintance." Johnson, plainly a little embarrassed, did not accept the
invitation, and "in a subsequent number a kind of excuse was made,
with a hint that a good writer might not appear to advantage in conversation." Richardson here refers to No. 14, in which occurs the passage
quoted above. Needless to say, Johnson's hope to keep the authorship
secret was doomed from the start. David Garrick and others who were
closely acquainted with Johnson recognized his style and mode of
thought, and within a short time the authorship of the *Rambler* was
widely known.

odical series, the *Idler*. The new essays, which continued for two years (April 15, 1758 to April 5, 1760), were in a far lighter vein, and were intended to be so.

One of the interesting things about Johnson as a professional writer is that he so rarely took the initiative in planning a work, especially as he grew older. No other major writer of the past three centuries has excelled him in speed and fluency of writing—if occasion really demanded. But years of anxiety, and the constant association of writing with drudgery and need, had given him a settled dislike of the act of composition. It is unlikely that he would have begun another periodical series unless he had been persuaded by others. He was becoming much more widely known than when he had started the *Rambler*. It was proposed that he now contribute essays to a new weekly newspaper, which was to be called the *Universal Chronicle*. The proposal seemed attractive for at least two reasons: the chance to earn some badly needed money; and the fact that the effort involved was expected to be comparatively light. For because the essays were to be published as part of a newspaper, and not (like the *Rambler*) as a self-contained periodical number, there was the hope that they would have a wider circulation, while at the same time they would have to be much shorter in order to leave room for the other parts of the newspaper. Moreover, they were to be written only once a week, whereas the *Rambler* had to be published twice a week. A third attraction, reflected in Johnson's self-amused choice of the title, was the opportunity the new series gave him to defer other and more demanding work. According to Thomas Tyers, Johnson himself said that the *Rambler* had been written "by way of relief" from his work on the *Dictionary;* and Sir John Hawkins was probably justified in saying that, when Johnson began the *Idler,* "his motive . . . was aversion to a labour he had undertaken"—the great edition of Shakespeare, the *Proposals* for which had been issued two years before (1756).

Agreeing to write essays for the weekly newspaper, the

Universal Chronicle, and to share directly in whatever financial profits might accrue, Johnson, for the first time in his periodical essays, deliberately tried to catch the easy tone of Addison and Steele and of the eighteenth-century periodical essay that descended from them. The first twenty or so of the *Idlers* are in marked contrast to the deeply reflective essays that usher in the *Rambler*—so much so that the confirmed Johnsonian finds them rather thin. Then, with Nos. 23 and 27, the *Idler* begins to recapture some of the habitual qualities that Johnson at first had apparently tried to avoid. But some of the general differences in tone and style, as well as length, remain. The *Idlers* not only continue short but grow still shorter as Johnson's habitual indolence reappears.[7] Polysyllabic words, frequent in the *Rambler,* appear rarely. The sentences are brief; and, when the subject is not trivial (as it occasionally is in the earlier papers), they become pithy and anticipate the style of the *Lives of the Poets.* Literary citations are far less frequent. The critical essays are less analytic than those in the *Rambler.* Equally important, as a difference from the earlier series, is the tone of the portraits. Very few of the character portraits in the *Rambler* or *Adventurer* are favorable, despite the searching, even touching remarks on the need for "good-humour" throughout the *Ramblers,* and despite the union of charity and sadness that modifies the impatience and exasperation we feel stirring in them. But in the *Idler* the portraits are almost uniformly either favorable or, at least, gentle. Significantly, a fair number of the *Idler* portraits appear to have been based on actual people. Several of the earlier *Idlers* are also concerned with topical problems, or at least filled with allusions to contemporary events. These, as Johnson would have been the first to predict, have for a century and a half been the least read of the *Idler* essays.

It is apparent that Johnson wrote the *Idlers* with less commitment than he had felt to the earlier series. He was far

---

7. See above, note 4.

more eager, for example, to secure help in writing the *Idler*.[8]
He extensively revised the *Ramblers,* but showed no desire to
revise the *Idlers* to even a faintly comparable degree. There
are several explanations. The *Rambler* was altogether his
own; the *Idler* was part of a newspaper. Again, he had tail-
ored the *Idler* essays (especially at the start) to what others
considered the acceptable way of gaining an increased circulation. The deliberate topicality of many of them and the
equally deliberate simplicity of subject may possibly have
lowered them in his own estimation. But the principal explanation is that the periodical essay had by now become an
old story to him. The appeal of novelty had evaporated.

But this in no way reflects on the value of the *Idler*. When
a shorter work is written in the wake of an earlier, larger effort, habits of thought and expression will not only remain
but may have become even sharper in focus and readiness.
The best of the *Idlers* contain some of the finest proverbial
wisdom in the language:

> He that never labours may know the pains of idleness,
> but not the pleasure. . . . The great differences that dis-
> turb the peace of mankind are not about ends, but
> means. . . . Pain is less subject than pleasure to caprices
> of expression . . . Man has from nature a mode of utter-
> ance peculiar to pain, but he has none peculiar to plea-
> sure, because he never has pleasure but in such degrees
> as the ordinary use of language may equal or surpass. . . .
> Nothing is more hopeless than a scheme of merriment.

8. Twelve of the *Idlers,* as Johnson stated in the first collected edition (1761), were written by others (Nos. 9, 15, 33, 42, 54, 67, 76, 79, 82,
93, 96, and 98). Three were by Reynolds (Nos. 76, 79, and 82), three by
Thomas Warton (Nos. 33, 93, and 96), and one (No. 67) by Bennet
Langton. The authors of two more have been learned from the marginal
notes in Bishop Percy's copy: Bonnell Thornton wrote No. 15, and
William Emerson No. 98. The authorship of Nos. 9, 42, and 54, if unknown to us, was also unknown to Johnson, who wrote beside them "Ign."
in Percy's copy. Johnson does not appear to have troubled greatly to find
out the authors of these three numbers.

... Reformation is seldom the work of pure virtue or un-assisted reason. ... Much of the pain and pleasure of mankind arises from the conjectures which everyone makes of the thoughts of others. ... There are few things not purely evil, of which we can say, without some emotion of uneasiness, *this is the last*. ... All envy would be extinguished, if it were universally known that there are none to be envied, and surely none can be much envied who are not pleased with themselves ... Such is our desire of abstraction from ourselves, that very few are satisfied with the quantity of stupefaction which the needs of the body force upon the mind. Alexander himself added intemperance to sleep, and solaced with the fumes of wine the sovereignty of the world; and almost every man has some art by which he steals his thoughts away from his present state.

It can even be argued that the principal reason he did not revise the *Idler* as he had the *Rambler* is that the *Idler* (for what it attempted to do) was in less need of it—that his style had profited from his work on the earlier series. In any case the appeal of the *Idler* was almost immediate. Not simply did the *Idler* sustain the modest circulation of the *Universal Chronicle*—a newspaper of such meager attractions that it would have otherwise quickly died—but the essays were "seized on," as Boswell said, "with avidity by various publishers of newspapers and magazines to enrich their publications." (These numerous reprintings—a common practice at the time, as we noted above—brought nothing financially to Johnson.)

With the close of the *Idler,* and the poignant farewell (No. 103) to the entire *genre* of the periodical essay, we come to a central turning-point in Johnson's career. It is the Johnson of the next 24 years who was to pass into legend, and who was also to achieve a mastery of expression that places him, at his best, among the half-dozen greatest prose stylists in English. Moreover, he was to turn increasingly to the criticism of literature. But the later Johnson is very much the product of these crucial middle years during which—against immense odds both of temperament and circumstance—he emerged as the most sympathetic of the great prudential moralists, and as probably the most shrewdly practical and psychologically clairvoyant of modern religious moralists. If he is almost unique among critics of literature, for example, it is because no one else with a comparable grasp of the most exacting technical criteria has at the same time been so closely aware of the basic claims and interests of human nature—so constantly concerned with "what comes near to ourselves, what we can put to use." His greatness as a critic is inseparable from his greatness as a moralist.

III.   Note on the Annotation and Text

Many of the references are placed in the text after quotations rather than as notes. All of these are editorial insertions. For the convenience of students who may wish to read further in Johnson, some of the notes refer to essays (and other works of Johnson) not included in the present volume.

The basic text of the *Rambler* is the fourth edition (1756); that of the *Adventurer* is the folio edition of 1753–54; and that of the *Idler* is the second edition (1761)—the first collected edition.

For details, including discussions of collation, and also for further discussion of the annotation, the reader is referred to the Introductions to the three periodical essays in the relevant volumes (II–V) of the complete edition.

SHORT TITLES OF WORKS CITED IN NOTES

Life—Boswell's *Life of Johnson,* ed. G. B. Hill, rev. by L. F. Powell, 6 vols., 1934–50.
Lives—*Lives of the English Poets,* ed. G. B. Hill, 3 vols., 1905.
Miscellanies—*Johnsonian Miscellanies,* ed. G. B. Hill, 2 vols., 1897; reprinted 1966.

THE *RAMBLER*

No. 2. Saturday, 24 March 1750.

Stare loco nescit, pereunt vestigia mille
Ante fugam, absentemque ferit gravis ungula campum.
Statius, THEBAID, VI.400–01.

Th' impatient courser pants in ev'ry vein,
And pawing seems to beat the distant plain;
Hills, vales, and floods, appear already crost,
And, ere he starts, a thousand steps are lost.

Pope.

That the mind of man is never satisfied with the objects immediately before it, but is always breaking away from the present moment,[1] and losing itself in schemes of future felicity; and that we forget the proper use of the time now in our power, to provide for the enjoyment of that which, perhaps, may never be granted us, has been frequently remarked; and as this practice is a commodious subject of raillery to the gay, and of declamation to the serious, it has been ridiculed with all the pleasantry of wit, and exaggerated with all the amplifications of rhetoric. Every instance, by which its absurdity might appear most flagrant, has been studiously collected; it has been marked with every epithet of contempt, and all the tropes and figures have been called forth against it.

Censure is willingly indulged, because it always implies some superiority; men please themselves with imagining

1. "So few of the hours of life are filled up with objects adequate to the mind of man . . . that we are forced to have recourse every moment to the past and future for supplemental satisfactions, and relieve the vacuities of our being, by recollection of former passages, or anticipation of events to come" (*Rambler* 41, par. 1). Cf. *Rasselas,* ch. 30 ("No mind is much employed upon the present; recollection and anticipation fill up almost all our moments"), and *Rambler,* Nos. 5 (par. 1) and 104 (par. 3).

that they have made a deeper search, or wider survey, than others, and detected faults and follies, which escape vulgar observation. And the pleasure of wantoning in common topicks is so tempting to a writer, that he cannot easily resign it; a train of sentiments generally received enables him to shine without labour, and to conquer without a contest. It is so easy to laugh at the folly of him who lives only in idea, refuses immediate ease for distant pleasures, and, instead of enjoying the blessings of life, lets life glide away in preparations to enjoy them. It affords such opportunities of triumphant exultation, to exemplify the uncertainty of the human state, to rouse mortals from their dream, and inform them of the silent celerity of time, that we may believe authors willing rather to transmit than examine so advantageous a principle, and more inclined to pursue a track so smooth and so flowery, than attentively to consider whether it leads to truth.

This quality of looking forward into futurity seems the unavoidable condition of a being, whose motions are gradual, and whose life is progressive: as his powers are limited, he must use means for the attainment of his ends, and intend first what he performs last; as, by continual advances from his first stage of existence, he is perpetually varying the horizon of his prospects, he must always discover new motives of action, new excitements of fear, and allurements of desire.

The end therefore which at present calls forth our efforts will be found, when it is once gained, to be only one of the means to some remoter end. The natural flights of the human mind are not from pleasure to pleasure, but from hope to hope.[2]

2. Cf. Nekayah's remark, *Rasselas*, ch. 47: "Such is the state of life, that none are happy but by the anticipation of change: the change

He that directs his steps to a certain point, must frequently turn his eyes to that place which he strives to reach; he that undergoes the fatigue of labour, must solace his weariness with the contemplation of its reward. In agriculture, one of the most simple and necessary employments, no man turns up the ground but because he thinks of the harvest, that harvest which blights may intercept, which inundations may sweep away, or which death or calamity may hinder him from reaping.

Yet as few maxims are widely received or long retained but for some conformity with truth and nature, it must be confessed, that this caution against keeping our view too intent upon remote advantages is not without its propriety or usefulness, though it may have been recited with too much levity, or enforced with too little distinction: for, not to speak of that vehemence of desire which presses through right and wrong to its gratification, or that anxious inquietude which is justly chargeable with distrust of heaven, subjects too solemn for my present purpose; it frequently happens that, by indulging early the raptures of success, we forget the measures necessary to secure it, and suffer the imagination to riot in the fruition of some possible good, till the time of obtaining it has slipped away.

There would however be few enterprises of great labour or hazard undertaken, if we had not the power of magnifying the advantages which we persuade ourselves to expect from them. When the knight of La Mancha gravely recounts to his companion the adventures by which he is to signalize himself in such a manner that he shall be summoned to the support of empires, solicited

---

itself is nothing; when we have made it, the next wish is to change again."

to accept the heiress of the crown which he has preserved, have honours and riches to scatter about him, and an island to bestow on his worthy squire,[3] very few readers, amidst their mirth or pity, can deny that they have admitted visions of the same kind; though they have not, perhaps, expected events equally strange, or by means equally inadequate. When we pity him, we reflect on our own disappointments; and when we laugh, our hearts inform us that he is not more ridiculous than ourselves, except that he tells what we have only thought.

The understanding of a man, naturally sanguine, may, indeed, be easily vitiated by the luxurious indulgence of hope, however necessary to the production of every thing great or excellent, as some plants are destroyed by too open exposure to that sun which gives life and beauty to the vegetable world.

Perhaps no class of the human species requires more to be cautioned against this anticipation of happiness, than those that aspire to the name of authors. A man of lively fancy no sooner finds a hint moving in his mind, than he makes momentaneous excursions to the press, and to the world, and, with a little encouragement from flattery, pushes forward into future ages, and prognosticates the honours to be paid him, when envy is extinct, and faction forgotten, and those, whom partiality now suffers to obscure him, shall have given way to other triflers of as short duration as themselves.

Those, who have proceeded so far as to appeal to the tribunal of succeeding times, are not likely to be cured of their infatuation; but all endeavours ought to be used for the prevention of a disease, for which, when it has attained its height, perhaps no remedy will be found in

3. *Don Quixote*, pt. I, chs. 7, 15, 21.

the gardens of philosophy, however she may boast her physick of the mind, her catharticks of vice, or lenitives of passion.

I shall, therefore, while I am yet but lightly touched with the symptoms of the writer's malady, endeavour to fortify myself against the infection, not without some weak hope, that my preservatives may extend their virtue to others, whose employment exposes them to the same danger:

> *Laudis amore tumes? Sunt certa piacula, quae te*
> *Ter pure lecto poterunt recreare libello.*
>
> Horace, EPISTLES, I.1.36–37.

Is fame your passion? Wisdom's pow'rful charm,
If thrice read over, shall its force disarm.

Francis.

It is the sage advice of Epictetus, that a man should accustom himself often to think of what is most shocking and terrible, that by such reflexions he may be preserved from too ardent wishes for seeming good, and from too much dejection in real evil.[4]

There is nothing more dreadful to an author than neglect, compared with which reproach, hatred, and opposition, are names of happiness; yet this worst, this meanest fate every man who dares to write has reason to fear.

> *I nunc, et versus tecum meditare canoros.*
>
> Horace, EPISTLES, II.2.76.

Go now, and meditate thy tuneful lays.

Elphinston.

---

4. *Enchiridion*, c. 21; Cf. *Ramblers* 17 (pars. 3–4) and 52 (par. 2). On the other hand, for Johnson's misgivings about Stoicism, see, e.g. *Ramblers* 6 (pars. 1–2), 32 (pars. 2–3), 89 (par. 6), and *Rasselas*, ch. 18.

It may not be unfit for him who makes a new entrance
into the lettered world, so far to suspect his own powers as
to believe that he possibly may deserve neglect; that nature may not have qualified him much to enlarge or
embellish knowledge, nor sent him forth entitled by
indisputable superiority to regulate the conduct of the
rest of mankind; that, though the world must be granted
to be yet in ignorance, he is not destined to dispel the
cloud, nor to shine out as one of the luminaries of life.
For this suspicion, every catalogue of a library will furnish
sufficient reason;[5] as he will find it crouded with names
of men, who, though now forgotten, were once no less
enterprising or confident than himself, equally pleased
with their own productions, equally caressed by their
patrons, and flattered by their friends.

But, though it should happen that an author is capable
of excelling, yet his merit may pass without notice,
huddled in the variety of things, and thrown into the
general miscellany of life. He that endeavours after fame
by writing, solicits the regard of a multitude fluctuating
in pleasures, or immersed in business, without time for intellectual amusements; he appeals to judges prepossessed
by passions, or corrupted by prejudices, which preclude
their approbation of any new performance. Some are too
indolent to read any thing, till its reputation is established; others too envious to promote that fame, which
gives them pain by its increase. What is new is opposed,
because most are unwilling to be taught; and what is
known is rejected, because it is not sufficiently considered,
that men more frequently require to be reminded than
informed. The learned are afraid to declare their opinion

5. Cf. esp. *Ramblers* 106 (par. 3, "No place affords a more striking
conviction of the vanity of human hopes, than a public library . . .");
21 (pars. 2–7), and 146 (pars. 6–7).

early, lest they should put their reputation in hazard; the ignorant always imagine themselves giving some proof of delicacy, when they refuse to be pleased: and he that finds his way to reputation, through all these obstructions, must acknowledge that he is indebted to other causes besides his industry, his learning, or his wit.

No. 4. Saturday, 31 March 1750.[1]

Simul et jucunda et idonea dicere vitae.
Horace, ARS POETICA, l. 334.

And join both profit and delight in one.
Creech.

The works of fiction, with which the present generation seems more particularly delighted, are such as exhibit life in its true state, diversified only by accidents that daily happen in the world, and influenced by passions and qualities which are really to be found in conversing with mankind.

This kind of writing may be termed not improperly the comedy of romance, and is to be conducted nearly by the rules of comic poetry. Its province is to bring about natural events by easy means, and to keep up curiosity without the help of wonder: it is therefore precluded from the machines and expedients of the heroic romance, and can neither employ giants to snatch away a lady from the nuptial rites, nor knights to bring her back from captivity; it can neither bewilder its personages in desarts, nor lodge them in imaginary castles.[2]

1. This paper was occasioned by the popularity of Smollett's *Roderick Random* (1748) and Fielding's *Tom Jones* (1749).

2. Cf. *Preface to Shakespeare*, par. 13 (". . . as the writers of barbarous romances invigorated the reader by a giant and a dwarf"). For Johnson's

I remember a remark made by Scaliger upon Pontanus, that all his writings are filled with the same images; and that if you take from him his lillies and his roses, his satyrs and his dryads, he will have nothing left that can be called poetry.[3] In like manner, almost all the fictions of the last age will vanish, if you deprive them of a hermit and a wood, a battle and a shipwreck.

Why this wild strain of imagination found reception so long, in polite and learned ages, it is not easy to conceive; but we cannot wonder that, while readers could be procured, the authors were willing to continue it: for when a man had by practice gained some fluency of language, he had no further care than to retire to his closet, let loose his invention, and heat his mind with incredibilities; a book was thus produced without fear of criticism, without the toil of study, without knowledge of nature, or acquaintance with life.

The task of our present writers is very different; it requires, together with that learning which is to be gained from books, that experience which can never be attained by solitary diligence, but must arise from general converse, and accurate observation of the living world. Their performances have, as Horace expresses it, *plus oneris quantum veniae minus,*[4] little indulgence, and therefore more difficulty. They are engaged in portraits of which every one knows the original, and can detect any deviation from exactness of resemblance. Other writings are safe, except from the malice of learning, but these are in danger from every common reader; as the slipper ill exe-

---

attraction to romances, see the account told Boswell by Bishop Percy (*Life*, I.49). Cf. *Life*, IV.17.

   3. Scaliger's *Poetics*, VI.4.

   4. *Epistles*, II.1.70.

cuted was censured by a shoemaker who happened to stop in his way at the Venus of Apelles.[5]

But the fear of not being approved as just copyers of human manners, is not the most important concern that an author of this sort ought to have before him. These books are written chiefly to the young, the ignorant, and the idle, to whom they serve as lectures of conduct, and introductions into life. They are the entertainment of minds unfurnished with ideas, and therefore easily susceptible of impressions; not fixed by principles, and therefore easily following the current of fancy; not informed by experience, and consequently open to every false suggestion and partial account.

That the highest degree of reverence should be paid to youth, and that nothing indecent should be suffered to approach their eyes or ears; are precepts extorted by sense and virtue from an ancient writer, by no means eminent for chastity of thought.[6] The same kind, tho' not the same degree of caution, is required in every thing which is laid before them, to secure them from unjust prejudices, perverse opinions, and incongruous combinations of images.

In the romances formerly written, every transaction and sentiment was so remote from all that passes among men, that the reader was in very little danger of making any applications to himself; the virtues and crimes were equally beyond his sphere of activity; and he amused himself with heroes and with traitors, deliverers and persecutors, as with beings of another species, whose actions were regulated upon motives of their own, and who had neither faults nor excellencies in common with himself.

But when an adventurer is levelled with the rest of the world, and acts in such scenes of the universal drama, as

5. Pliny, *Natural History*, XXXV.36.85.
6. Juvenal, XIV.

may be the lot of any other man; young spectators fix their eyes upon him with closer attention, and hope by observing his behaviour and success to regulate their own practices, when they shall be engaged in the like part.

For this reason these familiar histories may perhaps be made of greater use than the solemnities of professed morality, and convey the knowledge of vice and virtue with more efficacy than axioms and definitions. But if the power of example is so great, as to take possession of the memory by a kind of violence, and produce effects almost without the intervention of the will, care ought to be taken that, when the choice is unrestrained, the best examples only should be exhibited; and that which is likely to operate so strongly, should not be mischievous or uncertain in its effects.

The chief advantage which these fictions have over real life is, that their authors are at liberty, tho' not to invent, yet to select objects, and to cull from the mass of mankind, those individuals upon which the attention ought most to be employ'd; as a diamond, though it cannot be made, may be polished by art, and placed in such a situation, as to display that lustre which before was buried among common stones.

It is justly considered as the greatest excellency of art, to imitate nature; but it is necessary to distinguish those parts of nature, which are most proper for imitation: greater care is still required in representing life, which is so often discoloured by passion, or deformed by wickedness. If the world be promiscuously described, I cannot see of what use it can be to read the account; or why it may not be as safe to turn the eye immediately upon mankind, as upon a mirror which shows all that presents itself without discrimination.

It is therefore not a sufficient vindication of a character, that it is drawn as it appears, for many characters ought never to be drawn; nor of a narrative, that the train of events is agreeable to observation and experience, for that observation which is called knowledge of the world, will be found much more frequently to make men cunning than good. The purpose of these writings is surely not only to show mankind, but to provide that they may be seen hereafter with less hazard; to teach the means of avoiding the snares which are laid by Treachery for Innocence, without infusing any wish for that superiority with which the betrayer flatters his vanity; to give the power of counteracting fraud, without the temptation to practise it; to initiate youth by mock encounters in the art of necessary defence, and to increase prudence without impairing virtue.

Many writers, for the sake of following nature, so mingle good and bad qualities in their principal personages, that they are both equally conspicuous; and as we accompany them through their adventures with delight, and are led by degrees to interest ourselves in their favour, we lose the abhorrence of their faults, because they do not hinder our pleasure, or, perhaps, regard them with some kindness for being united with so much merit.

There have been men indeed splendidly wicked, whose endowments threw a brightness on their crimes, and whom scarce any villainy made perfectly detestable, because they never could be wholly divested of their excellencies; but such have been in all ages the great corrupters of the world, and their resemblance ought no more to be preserved, than the art of murdering without pain.

Some have advanced, without due attention to the consequences of this notion, that certain virtues have their correspondent faults, and therefore that to exhibit either apart is to deviate from probability. Thus men

are observed by Swift to be "grateful in the same degree
as they are resentful."[7] This principle, with others of the
same kind, supposes man to act from a brute impulse,
and persue a certain degree of inclination, without any
choice of the object; for, otherwise, though it should be
allowed that gratitude and resentment arise from the
same constitution of the passions, it follows not that they
will be equally indulged when reason is consulted; yet
unless that consequence be admitted, this sagacious
maxim becomes an empty sound, without any relation
to practice or to life.

Nor is it evident, that even the first motions to these
effects are always in the same proportion. For pride, which
produces quickness of resentment, will obstruct gratitude,
by unwillingness to admit that inferiority which obligation implies; and it is very unlikely, that he who cannot
think he receives a favour will acknowledge or repay it.

It is of the utmost importance to mankind, that positions of this tendency should be laid open and confuted;
for while men consider good and evil as springing from
the same root, they will spare the one for the sake of the
other, and in judging, if not of others at least of themselves, will be apt to estimate their virtues by their vices.
To this fatal error all those will contribute, who confound
the colours of right and wrong, and instead of helping to
settle their boundaries, mix them with so much art, that
no common mind is able to disunite them.

In narratives, where historical veracity has no place. I
cannot discover why there should not be exhibited the
most perfect idea of virtue; of virtue not angelical, nor
above probability, for what we cannot credit we shall
never imitate, but the highest and purest that humanity
can reach, which, exercised in such trials as the various

7. Swift-Pope *Miscellanies* (1727), II.354.

revolutions of things shall bring upon it, may, by conquering some calamities, and enduring others, teach us
what we may hope, and what we can perform. Vice, for
vice is necessary to be shewn, should always disgust; nor
should the graces of gaiety, or the dignity of courage, be
so united with it, as to reconcile it to the mind. Wherever
it appears, it should raise hatred by the malignity of its
practices, and contempt by the meanness of its stratagems; for while it is supported by either parts or spirit,
it will be seldom heartily abhorred. The Roman tyrant
was content to be hated, if he was but feared;[8] and there
are thousands of the readers of romances willing to be
thought wicked, if they may be allowed to be wits. It is
therefore to be steadily inculcated, that virtue is the
highest proof of understanding, and the only solid basis
of greatness; and that vice is the natural consequence of
narrow thoughts, that it begins in mistake, and ends in
ignominy.

No. 6. Saturday, 7 April 1750.

Strenua nos exercet inertia, navibus atque
Quadrigis petimus bene vivere: quod petis, hic est;
Est Ulubris, animus si te non deficit aequus.

Horace, EPISTLES, I.11.28–30.

Active in indolence, abroad we roam
In quest of happiness, which dwells at home:
With vain persuits fatigu'd, at length you'll find,
No place excludes it from an equal mind.

Elphinston.

That man should never suffer his happiness to depend
upon external circumstances, is one of the chief precepts

8. Suetonius, *Lives,* "Caligula," 30.1.

of the Stoical philosophy; a precept, indeed, which that lofty sect has extended beyond the condition of human life, and in which some of them seem to have comprised an utter exclusion of all corporal pain and pleasure, from the regard or attention of a wise man.

Such *sapientia insaniens*, as Horace calls the doctrine of another sect,[1] such extravagance of philosophy, can want neither authority nor argument for its confutation; it is overthrown by the experience of every hour, and the powers of nature rise up against it. But we may very properly enquire, how near to this exalted state it is in our power to approach, how far we can exempt ourselves from outward influences, and secure to our minds a state of tranquillity: For, though the boast of absolute independence is ridiculous and vain, yet a mean flexibility to every impulse, and a patient submission to the tyranny of casual troubles, is below the dignity of that mind, which, however depraved or weakened, boasts its derivation from a celestial original, and hopes for an union with infinite goodness, and unvariable felicity.

Ni vitiis pejora fovens
  Proprium deserat ortum.

                          Boethius, CONSOLATIO, III. metr. 6.9

Unless the soul, to vice a thrall,
Desert her own original.

The necessity of erecting ourselves to some degree of intellectual dignity, and of preserving resources of pleasure, which may not be wholly at the mercy of accident, is never more apparent than when we turn our eyes upon those whom fortune has let loose to their own conduct; who not being chained down by their condition to a regu-

1. *Odes,* 1.34.2.

lar and stated allotment of their hours, are obliged to find themselves business or diversion, and having nothing within that can entertain or employ them, are compelled to try all the arts of destroying time.

The numberless expedients practised by this class of mortals to alleviate the burthen of life, is not less shameful, nor, perhaps, much less pitiable, than those to which a trader on the edge of bankruptcy is reduced. I have seen melancholy overspread a whole family at the disappointment of a party for cards; and when, after the proposal of a thousand schemes; and the dispatch of the footman upon a hundred messages, they have submitted, with gloomy resignation, to the misfortune of passing one evening in conversation with each other, on a sudden, such are the revolutions of the world, an unexpected visiter has brought them relief, acceptable as provision to a starving city, and enabled them to hold out till the next day.

The general remedy of those, who are uneasy without knowing the cause, is change of place; they are willing to imagine that their pain is the consequence of some local inconvenience, and endeavour to fly from it, as children from their shadows; always hoping for more satisfactory delight from every new scene, and always returning home with disappointment and complaints.

Who can look upon this kind of infatuation, without reflecting on those that suffer under the dreadful symptom of canine madness, termed by physicians the hydrophobia, or "dread of water"? These miserable wretches, unable to drink, though burning with thirst, are sometimes known to try various contortions, or inclinations of the body, flattering themselves that they can swallow in one posture that liquor, which they find in another to repel their lips.

Yet such folly is not peculiar to the thoughtless or ig-norant, but sometimes seizes those minds which seem most exempted from it, by the variety of attainments, quickness of penetration, or severity of judgment; and, indeed, the pride of wit and knowledge is often mortified by finding, that they confer no security against the com-mon errors, which mislead the weakest and meanest of mankind.

These reflexions arose in my mind upon the remem-brance of a passage in Cowley's preface to his poems,[2] where, however exalted by genius, and enlarged by study, he informs us of a scheme of happiness to which the im-agination of a girl, upon the loss of her first lover, could have scarcely given way; but which he seems to have indulged till he had totally forgotten its absurdity, and would probably have put in execution, had he been hin-dered only by his reason.

"My desire," says he, "has been for some years past, though the execution has been accidentally diverted, and does still vehemently continue, to retire myself to some of our American plantations, not to seek for gold, or en-rich myself with the traffic of those parts, which is the end of most men that travel thither; but to forsake this world for ever, with all the vanities and vexations of it, and to bury myself there in some obscure retreat, but not with-out the consolation of letters and philosophy."

Such was the chimerical provision which Cowley had made, in his own mind, for the quiet of his remaining life, and which he seems to recommend to posterity, since there is no other reason for disclosing it. Surely no stronger instance can be given of a persuasion that con-tent was the inhabitant of particular regions, and that a

2. *Works* (1707), I.lvii. Cf. "Cowley," *Lives,* I.15–17.

man might set sail with a fair wind, and leave behind him all his cares, incumbrances, and calamities.

If he travelled so far with no other purpose than to "bury himself in some obscure retreat," he might have found, in his own country, innumerable coverts sufficiently dark to have concealed the genius of Cowley; for, whatever might be his opinion of the importunity with which he should be summoned back into publick life, a short experience would have convinced him, that privation is easier than acquisition, and that it would require little continuance to free himself from the intrusion of the world. There is pride enough in the human heart to prevent much desire of acquaintance with a man by whom we are sure to be neglected, however his reputation for science or virtue may excite our curiosity or esteem; so that the lover of retirement needs not be afraid lest the respect of strangers should overwhelm him with visits. Even those to whom he has formerly been known will very patiently support his absence, when they have tried a little to live without him, and found new diversions for those moments which his company contributed to exhilarate.

It was, perhaps, ordained by providence, to hinder us from tyrannising over one another, that no individual should be of such importance, as to cause, by his retirement or death, any chasm in the world. And Cowley had conversed to little purpose with mankind, if he had never remarked, how soon the useful friend, the gay companion, and the favoured lover, when once they are removed from before the sight, give way to the succession of new objects.

The privacy, therefore, of his hermitage might have been safe enough from violation, though he had chosen it within the limits of his native island; he might have found here preservatives against the "vanities" and "vexa-

tions" of the world, not less efficacious than those which
the woods or fields of America could afford him: but
having once his mind imbittered with disgust, he conceived it impossible to be far enough from the cause of
his uneasiness; and was posting away with the expedition
of a coward, who, for want of venturing to look behind
him, thinks the enemy perpetually at his heels.

When he was interrupted by company, or fatigued with
business, he so strongly imaged to himself the happiness
of leisure and retreat, that he determined to enjoy them
for the future without interruption, and to exclude for
ever all that could deprive him of his darling satisfaction.
He forgot, in the vehemence of desire, that solitude and
quiet owe their pleasures to those miseries, which he was
so studious to obviate; for such are the vicissitudes of the
world, through all its parts, that day and night, labour
and rest, hurry and retirement, endear each other; such
are the changes that keep the mind in action; we desire,
we pursue, we obtain, we are satiated; we desire something else, and begin a new persuit.

If he had proceeded in his project, and fixed his habitation in the most delightful part of the new world, it may
be doubted, whether his distance from the "vanities" of
life would have enabled him to keep away the "vexations." It is common for a man, who feels pain, to fancy
that he could bear it better in any other part. Cowley
having known the troubles and perplexities of a particular condition, readily persuaded himself that nothing
worse was to be found, and that every alteration would
bring some improvement; he never suspected that the
cause of his unhappiness was within, that his own passions
were not sufficiently regulated, and that he was harrassed
by his own impatience, which could never be without
something to awaken it, would accompany him over the

sea, and find its way to his American elysium. He would, upon the tryal, have been soon convinced, that the fountain of content must spring up in the mind; and that he, who has so little knowledge of human nature, as to seek happiness by changing any thing, but his own dispositions, will waste his life in fruitless efforts, and multiply the griefs which he purposes to remove.

No. 8. Saturday, 14 April 1750.

—Patitur poenas peccandi sola voluntas;
Nam scelus intra se tacitum qui cogitat ullum,
Facti crimen habet.

Juvenal, XIII.208–10.

For he that but conceives a crime in thought,
Contracts the danger of an actual fault.

Creech.

If the most active and industrious of mankind was able, at the close of life, to recollect distinctly his past moments, and distribute them, in a regular account, according to the manner in which they have been spent, it is scarcely to be imagined how few would be marked out to the mind, by any permanent or visible effects, how small a proportion his real action would bear to his seeming possibilities of action, how many chasms he would find of wide and continued vacuity, and how many interstitial spaces unfilled, even in the most tumultuous hurries of business, and the most eager vehemence of persuit.

It is said by modern philosophers, that not only the great globes of matter are thinly scattered thro' the universe, but the hardest bodies are so porous, that, if all matter were compressed to perfect solidity, it might be contained in a cube of a few feet. In like manner, if all the employment of life were crowded into the time which it really occupied, perhaps a few weeks, days, or hours, would be sufficient for its accomplishment, so far as the mind was engaged in the performance. For such is the inequality of our corporeal to our intellectual faculties, that we contrive in minutes what we execute in years, and the soul often stands an idle spectator of the labour of the hands, and expedition of the feet.

For this reason, the antient generals often found themselves at leisure to persue the study of philosophy in the camp; and Lucan, with historical veracity, makes Caesar relate of himself, that he noted the revolutions of the stars in the midst of preparations for battle.

————————*Media inter proelia semper*
Siberibus, coelique plagis, superisque vacavi.

PHARSALIA, X.185–86.

Amid the storms of war, with curious eyes
I trace the planets and survey the skies.

That the soul always exerts her peculiar powers, with greater or less force, is very probable, though the common occasions of our present condition require but a small part of that incessant cogitation; and by the natural frame of our bodies, and general combination of the world, we are so frequently condemned to inactivity, that as through all our time we are thinking, so for a great part of our time we can only think.

Lest a power so restless should be either unprofitably, or hurtfully employed, and the superfluities of intellect run to waste, it is no vain speculation to consider how we may govern our thoughts, restrain them from irregular motions, or confine them from boundless dissipation.[1]

How the understanding is best conducted to the knowledge of science, by what steps it is to be led forwards in its persuit, how it is to be cured of its defects, and habituated to new studies, has been the inquiry of many acute and learned men, whose observations I shall not either adopt or censure; my purpose being to consider the moral discipline of the mind, and to promote the increase of virtue rather than of learning.

This inquiry seems to have been neglected for want of remembering that all action has its origin in the mind, and that therefore to suffer the thoughts to be vitiated, is to poison the fountains of morality: Irregular desires will produce licentious practices; what men allow themselves to wish they will soon believe, and will be at last incited to execute what they please themselves with contriving.

For this reason the casuists of the Romish church, who gain, by confession, great opportunities of knowing human nature, have generally determined that what it is a crime to do, it is a crime to think.[2] Since by revolving with pleasure, the facility, safety or advantage of a wicked deed, a man soon begins to find his constancy relax, and his detestation soften; the happiness of success glittering before him, withdraws his attention from the atrociousness of the guilt, and acts are at last confidently perpetrated, of which the first conception only crept into the mind, disguised in pleasing complications, and permitted rather than invited.

No man has ever been drawn to crimes, by love or

1. For other remarks on our freedom to control our thinking, cf. *Ramblers* 7 (pars. 13–15), 78 (par. 4), and 151 (final par.).

2. Aquinas, *Summa*, I–II, Q. 74, a. 8; Q. 108, a. 3.

jealousy, envy or hatred, but he can tell how easily he might at first have repelled the temptation, how readily his mind would have obeyed a call to any other object, and how weak his passion has been after some casual avocation, 'till he has recalled it again to his heart, and revived the viper by too warm a fondness.

Such, therefore, is the importance of keeping reason a constant guard over imagination, that we have otherwise no security for our own virtue, but may corrupt our hearts in the most recluse solitude, with more pernicious and tyrannical appetites and wishes, than the commerce of the world will generally produce;[3] for we are easily shocked by crimes which appear at once in their full magnitude, but the gradual growth of our own wickedness, endeared by interest, and palliated by all the artifices of self-deceit, gives us time to form distinctions in our own favour, and reason by degrees submits to absurdity, as the eye is in time accommodated to darkness.

In this disease of the soul, it is of the utmost importance to apply remedies at the beginning; and, therefore, I shall endeavour to shew what thoughts are to be rejected or improved, as they regard the past, present, or future; in hopes that some may be awakened to caution and vigilance, who, perhaps, indulge themselves in dangerous dreams, so much the more dangerous, because being yet only dreams they are concluded innocent.

The recollection of the past is only useful by way of provision for the future; and therefore, in reviewing all occurrences that fall under a religious consideration, it is proper that a man stop at the first thoughts, to remark how he was led thither, and why he continues the reflexion. If he is dwelling with delight upon a stratagem of successful

---

3. Cf. the hermit in *Rasselas*, ch. 21 (pars. 8–9).

fraud, a night of licentious riot, or an intrigue of guilty pleasure, let him summon off his imagination as from an unlawful persuit, expel those passages from his remembrance, of which, though he cannot seriously approve them, the pleasure overpowers the guilt, and refer them to a future hour, when they may be considered with greater safety. Such an hour will certainly come; for the impressions of past pleasure are always lessening, but the sense of guilt, which respects futurity, continues the same.

The serious and impartial retrospect of our conduct is indisputably necessary to the confirmation or recovery of virtue, and is, therefore, recommended under the name of self-examination, by divines, as the first act previous to repentance. It is, indeed, of so great use, that without it we should always be to begin life, be seduced for ever by the same allurements, and misled by the same fallacies. But in order that we may not lose the advantage of our experience, we must endeavour to see every thing in its proper form, and excite in ourselves those sentiments which the great author of nature has decreed the concomitants or followers of good or bad actions.

> Μηδ' ὕπνον μαλακοῖσιν ἐπ' ὄμμασι προσδέξασθαι,
> Πρὶν τῶν ἡμερινῶν ἔργων τρὶς ἕκαστον ἐπελθεῖν·
> Πῇ παρέβην; τί δ'ἔρεξα; τί μοι δέον οὐκ ἐτελέσθη;
> Ἀρξάμενος δ' ἀπὸ πρώτου ἐπέξιθι· καὶ μετέπειτα,
> Δειλὰ μὲν ἐκπρήξας, ἐπιπλήσσεο, χρηστὰ δὲ, τέρπου.[4]

Let not sleep, says Pythagoras, fall upon thy eyes till thou hast thrice reviewed the transactions of the past day. Where have I turned aside from rectitude? What have I been doing? What have I left undone, which I

4. *Aurea Carmina*, ll. 40–44.

ought to have done? Begin thus from the first act, and proceed; and in conclusion, at the ill which thou hast done be troubled, and rejoice for the good.

Our thoughts on present things being determined by the objects before us, fall not under those indulgences, or excursions, which I am now considering. But I cannot forbear, under this head, to caution pious and tender minds, that are disturbed by the irruptions of wicked imaginations, against too great dejection, and too anxious alarms; for thoughts are only criminal, when they are first chosen, and then voluntarily continued.

> Evil into the mind of god or man
> May come and go, so unapprov'd, and leave
> No spot or stain behind.
>
> PARADISE LOST, V.117–19.

In futurity chiefly are the snares lodged, by which the imagination is intangled. Futurity is the proper abode of hope and fear, with all their train and progeny of subordinate apprehensions and desires. In futurity events and chances are yet floating at large, without apparent connexion with their causes, and we therefore easily indulge the liberty of gratifying ourselves with a pleasing choice. To pick and cull among possible advantages is, as the civil law terms it, *in vacuum venire,* to take what belongs to nobody; but it has this hazard in it, that we shall be unwilling to quit what we have seized, though an owner should be found. It is easy to think on that which may be gained, till at last we resolve to gain it, and to image the happiness of particular conditions till we can be easy in no other. We ought, at least, to let our desires fix upon nothing in another's power for the sake of our quiet, or in another's possession for the sake of our innocence. When a man finds himself led, though by a train of honest sentiments, to a wish for that to which he has no right, he should start back as from a pitfal covered with flowers. He that fancies he should benefit the publick more in a great station than the man that fills it, will in time imagine it an act of virtue to supplant him; and, as opposition readily kindles into hatred, his eagerness to do that good, to which he is not called, will betray him to crimes, which in his original scheme were never purposed.

He therefore that would govern his actions by the laws of virtue, must regulate his thoughts by those of reason; he must keep guilt from the recesses of his heart, and remember that the pleasures of fancy, and the emotions of desire are more dangerous as they are more hidden, since they escape the awe of observation, and operate equally in every situation, without the concurrence of external opportunities.

No. 9. Tuesday, 17 April 1750.

Quod sis esse velis, nihilque malis.

Martial, X.47.12.

Chuse what you are; no other state prefer.

Elphinston.

It is justly remarked by Horace, that, howsoever every man may complain occasionally of the hardships of his condition, he is seldom willing to change it for any other on the same level:[1] for whether it be that he, who follows an employment, made choice of it at first on account of its suitableness to his inclination; or that when accident,

1. *Satires,* I.1.16–19.

or the determination of others, have placed him in a
particular station, he, by endeavouring to reconcile himself to it, gets the custom of viewing it only on the fairest
side; or whether every man thinks that class to which he
belongs the most illustrious, merely because he has
honoured it with his name; it is certain that, whatever be
the reason, most men have a very strong and active
prejudice in favour of their own vocation, always working
upon their minds, and influencing their behaviour.

This partiality is sufficiently visible in every rank of
the human species; but it exerts itself more frequently
and with greater force among those who have never
learned to conceal their sentiments for reasons of policy,
or to model their expressions by the laws of politeness;
and therefore the chief contests of wit among artificers
and handicraftsmen arise from a mutual endeavour to
exalt one trade by depreciating another.

From the same principle are derived many consolations
to alleviate the inconveniences to which every calling is
peculiarly exposed. A blacksmith was lately pleasing himself at his anvil, with observing that, though his trade was
hot and sooty, laborious and unhealthy, yet he had the
honour of living by his hammer, he got his bread like a
man, and if his son should rise in the world, and keep his
coach, no body could reproach him that his father was a
taylor.

A man, truly zealous for his fraternity, is never so
irresistibly flattered, as when some rival calling is mentioned with contempt. Upon this principle a linen-draper
boasted that he had got a new customer, whom he could
safely trust, for he could have no doubt of his honesty,
since it was known, from unquestionable authority, that
he was now filing a bill in chancery to delay payment for
the cloaths which he had worn the last seven years; and

he himself had heard him declare, in a publick coffee-house, that he looked upon the whole generation of woollen-drapers to be such despicable wretches, that no gentleman ought to pay them.

It has been observed that physicians and lawyers are no friends to religion; and many conjectures have been formed to discover the reason of such a combination between men who agree in nothing else, and who seem less to be affected, in their own provinces, by religious opinions, than any other part of the community. The truth is, very few of them have thought about religion; but they have all seen a parson, seen him in a habit different from their own, and therefore declared war against him. A young student from the inns of court, who has often attacked the curate of his father's parish with such arguments as his acquaintances could furnish, and returned to town without success, is now gone down with a resolution to destroy him; for he has learned at last how to manage a prig, and if he pretends to hold him again to syllogism, he has a catch in reserve, which neither logic nor metaphysics can resist.

> I laugh to think how your unshaken Cato
> Will look aghast, when unforeseen destruction
> Pours in upon him thus.
> ADDISON, CATO, II.VI.48–50.

The malignity of soldiers and sailors against each other has been often experienced at the cost of their country; and, perhaps, no orders of men have an enmity of more acrimony, or longer continuance. When, upon our late successes at sea,[2] some new regulations were concerted for establishing the rank of the naval commanders, a

2. During the War of the Austrian Succession.

captain of foot very acutely remarked, that nothing was more absurd than to give any honorary rewards to seamen, "for honour," says he, "ought only to be won by bravery, and all the world knows that in a sea-fight there is no danger, and therefore no evidence of courage."

But although this general desire of aggrandizing themselves by raising their profession, betrays men to a thousand ridiculous and mischievous acts of supplantation and detraction, yet as almost all passions have their good as well as bad effects, it likewise excites ingenuity, and sometimes raises an honest and useful emulation of diligence. It may be observed in general that no trade had ever reached the excellence to which it is now improved, had its professors looked upon it with the eyes of indifferent spectators; the advances, from the first rude essays, must have been made by men who valued themselves for performances, for which scarce any other would be persuaded to esteem them.

It is pleasing to contemplate a manufacture rising gradually from its first mean state by the successive labours of innumerable minds; to consider the first hollow trunk of an oak, in which, perhaps, the shepherd could scarce venture to cross a brook swelled with a shower, enlarged at last into a ship of war, attacking fortresses, terrifying nations, setting storms and billows at defiance, and visiting the remotest parts of the globe. And it might contribute to dispose us to a kinder regard for the labours of one another, if we were to consider from what unpromising beginnings the most useful productions of art have probably arisen. Who, when he saw the first sand or ashes, by a casual intenseness of heat melted into a metalline form, rugged with excrescences, and clouded with impurities, would have imagined, that in this shapeless lump lay concealed so many conveniencies of life, as would in time constitute a great part of the happiness of the world? Yet by some such fortuitous liquefaction was mankind taught to procure a body at once in a high degree solid and transparent, which might admit the light of the sun, and exclude the violence of the wind; which might extend the sight of the philosopher to new ranges of existence, and charm him at one time with the unbounded extent of the material creation, and at another with the endless subordination of animal life; and, what is yet of more importance, might supply the decays of nature, and succour old age with subsidiary sight. Thus was the first artificer in glass employed, though without his own knowledge or expectation. He was facilitating and prolonging the enjoyment of light, enlarging the avenues of science, and conferring the highest and most lasting pleasures; he was enabling the student to contemplate nature, and the beauty to behold herself.

This passion for the honour of a profession, like that for the grandeur of our own country, is to be regulated not extinguished.[3] Every man, from the highest to the lowest station, ought to warm his heart and animate his endeavours with the hopes of being useful to the world, by advancing the art which it is his lot to exercise; and for that end he must necessarily consider the whole extent of its application, and the whole weight of its importance. But let him not too readily imagine that another is ill employed, because, for want of fuller knowledge of his business, he is not able to comprehend its dignity. Every man ought to endeavour at eminence, not by pulling others down, but by raising himself, and enjoy the pleasure of his own superiority, whether imaginary or real, without interrupting others in the same felicity. The

3. Cf. *Rambler* 49 (par. 8): "the love of fame is to be regulated rather than extinguished."

philosopher may very justly be delighted with the extent
of his views, and the artificer with the readiness of his
hands; but let the one remember, that, without mechanical performances, refined speculation is an empty dream,
and the other, that, without theoretical reasoning, dex-
terity is little more than a brute instinct.

No. 13. Tuesday, 1 May 1750.

Commissumque teges & vino tortus & irâ.
                                          Horace, EPISTLES, I.18.38.

And let not wine or anger wrest
Th' intrusted secret from your breast.
                                          Francis.

It is related by Quintus Curtius,[1] that the Persians always
conceived an invincible contempt of a man, who had violated the laws of secrecy; for they thought, that, however
he might be deficient in the qualities requisite to actual
excellence, the negative virtues at least were in his power,
and though he perhaps could not speak well if he was to
try, it was still easy for him not to speak.

   In forming this opinion of the easiness of secrecy, they
seem to have consider'd it as opposed, not to treachery,
but loquacity, and to have conceived the man, whom they
thus censured, not frighted by menaces to reveal, or
bribed by promises to betray, but incited by the mere
pleasure of talking, or some other motive equally trifling,
to lay open his heart without reflection, and to let whatever he knew slip from him, only for want of power to
retain it. Whether, by their settled and avowed scorn of

---

1. *History of Alexander,* IV.6.5–6.

thoughtless talkers, the Persians were able to diffuse to any great extent the virtue of taciturnity, we are hindered by the distance of those times from being able to discover, there being very few memoirs remaining of the court of Persepolis, nor any distinct accounts handed down to us of their office clerks, their ladies of the bed-chamber, their attorneys, their chamber-maids, or their footmen.

In these latter ages, though the old animosity against a prattler is still retained, it appears wholly to have lost its effects upon the conduct of mankind; for secrets are so seldom kept, that it may with some reason be doubted, whether the antients were not mistaken in their first postulate, whether the quality of retention be so generally bestowed, and whether a secret has not some subtle volatility, by which it escapes imperceptibly at the smallest vent, or some power of fermentation, by which it expands itself so as to burst the heart that will not give it way.

Those that study either the body or the mind of man, very often find the most specious and pleasing theory falling under the weight of contrary experience; and instead of gratifying their vanity by inferring effects from causes, they are always reduced at last to conjecture causes from effects. That it is easy to be secret the speculatist can demonstrate in his retreat, and therefore thinks himself justified in placing confidence; the man of the world knows, that, whether difficult or not, it is uncommon, and therefore finds himself rather inclined to search after the reason of this universal failure in one of the most important duties of society.

The vanity of being known to be trusted with a secret is generally one of the chief motives to disclose it; for however absurd it may be thought to boast an honour by an act which shews that it was conferred without merit, yet

most men seem rather inclined to confess the want of
virtue than of importance, and more willingly shew their
influence, though at the expense of their probity, than
glide through life with no other pleasure than the private
consciousness of fidelity; which, while it is preserved,
must be without praise, except from the single person who
tries and knows it.

There are many ways of telling a secret, by which a man
exempts himself from the reproaches of his conscience,
and gratifies his pride without suffering himself to believe
that he impairs his virtue. He tells the private affairs of
his patron, or his friend, only to those from whom he
would not conceal his own; he tells them to those, who
have no temptation to betray the trust, or with a denunciation of a certain forfeiture of his friendship, if he
discovers that they become public.

Secrets are very frequently told in the first ardour of
kindness, or of love, for the sake of proving, by so important a sacrifice, sincerity, or tenderness; but with this
motive, though it be strong in itself, vanity concurs, since
every man desires to be most esteemed by those whom he
loves, or with whom he converses, with whom he passes
his hours of pleasure, and to whom he retires from business and from care.[2]

When the discovery of secrets is under consideration,
there is always a distinction carefully to be made between
our own and those of another; those of which we are fully
masters as they affect only our own interest, and those
which are reposited with us in trust, and involve the
happiness or convenience of such as we have no right to
expose to hazard. To tell our own secrets is generally folly,
but that folly is without guilt; to communicate those with

2. Cf. "Pope," *Lives*, III.207 (par. 274).

which we are intrusted is always treachery, and treachery
for the most part combined with folly.

There have, indeed, been some enthusiastick and
irrational zealots for friendship, who have maintained,
and perhaps believed, that one friend has a right to all
that is in possession of another; and that therefore it is a
violation of kindness to exempt any secret from this
boundless confidence. Accordingly a late female minister
of state has been shameless enough to inform the world,
that she used, when she wanted to extract any thing from
her sovereign, to remind her of Montaigne's reasoning,
who has determined, that to tell a secret to a friend is no
breach of fidelity, because the number of persons trusted
is not multiplied, a man and his friend being virtually the
same.[3]

That such a fallacy could be imposed upon any human
understanding, or that an author could have advanced a
position so remote from truth and reason, any otherwise than as a declaimer, to shew to what extent he could
stretch his imagination, and with what strength he could
press his principle, would scarcely have been credible, had
not this lady kindly shewn us how far weakness may be
deluded, or indolence amused. But since it appears, that
even this sophistry has been able, with the help of a strong
desire to repose in quiet upon the understanding of
another, to mislead honest intentions, and an understanding not contemptible, it may not be superfluous to
remark, that those things which are common among
friends are only such as either possesses in his own right,
and can alienate or destroy without injury to any other
person. Without this limitation, confidence must run on

3. *Account of the Conduct of the Dowager Duchess of Marlborough*
(1742), p. 221; Montaigne, "De l'Amitié," *Essais,* ed. Pierre Michel (1957),
I.228–229.

without end, the second person may tell the secret to the third upon the same principle as he received it from the first, and the third may hand it forward to a fourth, till at last it is told in the round of friendship to them from whom it was the first intention chiefly to conceal it.

The confidence which Caius has of the faithfulness of Titius is nothing more than an opinion which himself cannot know to be true, and which Claudius, who first tells his secret to Caius may know to be false; and therefore the trust is transferred by Caius, if he reveal what has been told him, to one from whom the person originally concerned would have withheld it; and, whatever may be the event, Caius has hazarded the happiness of his friend, without necessity and without permission, and has put that trust in the hand of fortune which was given only to virtue.

All the arguments upon which a man who is telling the private affairs of another may ground his confidence of security, he must upon reflection know to be uncertain, because he finds them without effect upon himself. When he is imagining that Titius will be cautious from a regard to his interest, his reputation, or his duty, he ought to reflect that he is himself at that instant acting in opposition to all these reasons, and revealing what interest, reputation, and duty direct him to conceal.

Every one feels that in his own case he should consider the man incapable of trust, who believed himself at liberty to tell whatever he knew to the first whom he should conclude deserving of his confidence; therefore Caius, in admitting Titius to the affairs imparted only to himself, must know that he violates his faith, since he acts contrary to the intention of Claudius, to whom that faith was given. For promises of friendship are, like all others, useless and vain, unless they are made in some known sense, adjusted and acknowledged by both parties.

I am not ignorant that many questions may be started relating to the duty of secrecy, where the affairs are of publick concern; where subsequent reasons may arise to alter the appearance and nature of the trust; that the manner in which the secret was told may change the degree of obligation; and that the principles upon which a man is chosen for a confident may not always equally constrain him. But these scruples, if not too intricate, are of too extensive consideration for my present purpose, nor are they such as generally occur in common life; and though casuistical knowledge be useful in proper hands, yet it ought by no means to be carelessly exposed, since most will use it rather to lull than awaken their own consciences; and the threads of reasoning, on which truth is suspended, are frequently drawn to such subtility, that common eyes cannot perceive, and common sensibility cannot feel them.

The whole doctrine as well as practice of secrecy, is so perplexing and dangerous, that, next to him who is compelled to trust, I think him unhappy who is chosen to be trusted; for he is often involved in scruples without the liberty of calling in the help of any other understanding; he is frequently drawn into guilt, under the appearance of friendship and honesty; and sometimes subjected to suspicion by the treachery of others, who are engaged without his knowledge in the same schemes; for he that has one confident has generally more, and when he is at last betrayed, is in doubt on whom he shall fix the crime.

The rules therefore that I shall propose concerning secrecy, and from which I think it not safe to deviate, without long and exact deliberation, are——Never to solicit the knowledge of a secret. Not willingly, nor without many limitations, to accept such confidence when it is offered. When a secret is once admitted, to consider the trust as of a very high nature, important as society, and sacred as truth, and therefore not to be violated for any incidental convenience, or slight appearance of contrary fitness.

No. 14. Saturday, 5 May 1750.

_____ *Nil fuit unquam*

Sic dispar sibi _____

Horace, SATIRES, I.3.18–19.

Sure such a various creature ne'er was known.

Francis.

Among the many inconsistencies which folly produces, or infirmity suffers in the human mind, there has often been observed a manifest and striking contrariety between the life of an author and his writings; and Milton, in a letter to a learned stranger, by whom he had been visited, with great reason congratulates himself upon the consciousness of being found equal to his own character, and having preserved in a private and familiar interview that reputation which his works had procured him.[1]

Those whom the appearance of virtue, or the evidence of genius, have tempted to a nearer knowledge of the writer in whose performances they may be found, have indeed had frequent reason to repent their curiosity; the bubble that sparkled before them has become common

1. To Emeric Bigot, 24 March, 1656/1657.

water at the touch; the phantom of perfection has vanished when they wished to press it to their bosom. They have lost the pleasure of imagining how far humanity may be exalted, and, perhaps, felt themselves less inclined to toil up the steeps of virtue, when they observe those who seem best able to point the way, loitering below, as either afraid of the labour, or doubtful of the reward.

It has been long the custom of the oriental monarchs to hide themselves in gardens and palaces, to avoid the conversation of mankind, and to be known to their subjects only by their edicts. The same policy is no less necessary to him that writes, than to him that governs; for men would not more patiently submit to be taught, than commanded, by one known to have the same follies and weaknesses with themselves. A sudden intruder into the closet of an author would perhaps feel equal indignation with the officer, who having long solicited admission into the presence of Sardanapalus, saw him not consulting upon laws, enquiring into grievances, or modelling armies, but employed in feminine amusements, and directing the ladies in their work.[2]

It is not difficult to conceive, however, that for many reasons a man writes much better than he lives.[3] For, without entering into refined speculations, it may be shown much easier to design than to perform. A man proposes his schemes of life in a state of abstraction and disengagement, exempt from the enticements of hope, the solicitations of affection, the importunities of appetite, or the depressions of fear, and is in the same state with him that teaches upon land the art of navigation, to whom the sea is always smooth, and the wind always prosperous.

2. Diodorus Siculus, II.23.
3. Cf. *Rambler* 77 (pars. 7–9), and *Tour to the Hebrides*, 14 September, 1773.

The mathematicians are well acquainted with the difference between pure science, which has to do only with ideas, and the application of its laws to the use of life, in which they are constrained to submit to the imperfection of matter and the influence of accidents. Thus, in moral discussions it is to be remembred that many impediments obstruct our practice, which very easily give way to theory. The speculatist is only in danger of erroneous reasoning, but the man involved in life has his own passions, and those of others, to encounter, and is embarrassed with a thousand inconveniences, which confound him with variety of impulse, and either perplex or obstruct his way. He is forced to act without deliberation, and obliged to choose before he can examine; he is surprised by sudden alterations of the state of things, and changes his measures according to superficial appearances; he is led by others, either because he is indolent, or because he is timorous; he is sometimes afraid to know what is right, and sometimes finds friends or enemies diligent to deceive him.

We are, therefore, not to wonder that most fail, amidst tumult, and snares, and danger, in the observance of those precepts, which they laid down in solitude, safety, and tranquillity, with a mind unbiassed, and with liberty unobstructed. It is the condition of our present state to see more than we can attain; the exactest vigilance and caution can never maintain a single day of unmingled innocence, much less can the utmost efforts of incorporated mind reach the summits of speculative virtue.

It is, however, necessary for the idea of perfection to be proposed, that we may have some object to which our endeavours are to be directed; and he that is most deficient in the duties of life, makes some atonement for his faults, if he warns others against his own failings, and hinders, by the salubrity of his admonitions, the contagion of his example.

Nothing is more unjust, however common, than to charge with hypocrisy him that expresses zeal for those virtues, which he neglects to practise; since he may be sincerely convinced of the advantages of conquering his passions, without having yet obtained the victory, as a man may be confident of the advantages of a voyage, or a journey, without having courage or industry to undertake it, and may honestly recommend to others, those attempts which he neglects himself.

The interest which the corrupt part of mankind have in hardening themselves against every motive to amendment, has disposed them to give to these contradictions, when they can be produced against the cause of virtue, that weight which they will not allow them in any other case. They see men act in opposition to their interest, without supposing, that they do not know it; those who give way to the sudden violence of passion, and forsake the most important persuits for petty pleasures, are not supposed to have changed their opinions, or to approve their own conduct. In moral or religious questions alone, they determine the sentiments by the actions, and charge every man with endeavouring to impose upon the world, whose writings are not confirmed by his life. They never consider that they themselves neglect, or practise something every day, inconsistently with their own settled judgment, nor discover that the conduct of the advocates for virtue can little increase, or lessen, the obligations of their dictates; argument is to be invalidated only by argument, and is in itself of the same force, whether or not it convinces him by whom it is proposed.

Yet since this prejudice, however unreasonable, is always likely to have some prevalence, it is the duty of

every man to take care lest he should hinder the efficacy of
his own instructions. When he desires to gain the belief of
others, he should shew that he believes himself; and when
he teaches the fitness of virtue by his reasonings, he
should, by his example, prove its possibility: Thus much
at least may be required of him, that he shall not act worse
than others because he writes better, nor imagine that, by
the merit of his genius, he may claim indulgence beyond
mortals of the lower classes, and be excused for want of
prudence, or neglect of virtue.

Bacon, in his History of the winds, after having offered
something to the imagination as desirable, often proposes
lower advantages in its place to the reason as attainable.[4]
The same method may be sometimes pursued in moral endeavours, which this philosopher has observed in natural
enquiries; having first set positive and absolute excellence
before us, we may be pardoned though we sink down to
humbler virtue, trying, however, to keep our point always
in view, and struggling not to lose ground, though we
cannot gain it.

It is recorded of Sir Matthew Hale, that he, for a long
time, concealed the consecration of himself to the stricter
duties of religion, lest, by some flagitious and shameful
action, he should bring piety into disgrace.[5] For the same
reason, it may be prudent for a writer, who apprehends
that he shall not inforce his own maxims by his domestic
character, to conceal his name that he may not injure
them.

There are, indeed, a greater number whose curiosity to
gain a more familiar knowledge of successful writers, is
not so much prompted by an opinion of their power to im-

4. *Historia Naturalis, Works,* ed. Spedding, Ellis, and Heath (1857–
1874), IX.377, 464.
5. Gilbert Burnet, *Life and Death of Sir Matthew Hale* (1700), p. 74.

prove as to delight, and who expect from them not arguments against vice, or dissertations on temperance or
justice, but flights of wit, and sallies of pleasantry, or, at
least, acute remarks, nice distinctions, justness of sentiment, and elegance of diction.

This expectation is, indeed, specious and probable, and
yet, such is the fate of all human hopes, that it is very often
frustrated, and those who raise admiration by their books,
disgust by their company. A man of letters for the most
part spends, in the privacies of study, that season of life in
which the manners are to be softened into ease, and polished into elegance, and, when he has gained knowledge
enough to be respected, has neglected the minuter acts by
which he might have pleased. When he enters life, if his
temper be soft and timorous, he is diffident and bashful,
from the knowledge of his defects; or if he was born with
spirit and resolution, he is ferocious and arrogant from
the consciousness of his merit: he is either dissipated by
the awe of company, and unable to recollect his reading,
and arrange his arguments; or he is hot, and dogmatical,
quick in opposition, and tenacious in defence, disabled by
his own violence, and confused by his haste to triumph.

The graces of writing and conversation are of different
kinds, and though he who excels in one might have been
with opportunities and application equally successful in
the other, yet as many please by extemporary talk, though
utterly unacquainted with the more accurate method, and
more laboured beauties, which composition requires; so
it is very possible that men, wholly accustomed to works of
study, may be without that readiness of conception, and
affluence of language, always necessary to colloquial
entertainment. They may want address to watch the hints
which conversation offers for the display of their particular attainments, or they may be so much unfurnished with

matter on common subjects, that discourse not pro-
fessedly literary glides over them as heterogeneous bodies,
without admitting their conceptions to mix in the circulation.

A transition from an author's books to his conversation,
is too often like an entrance into a large city, after a
distant prospect. Remotely, we see nothing but spires of
temples, and turrets of palaces, and imagine it the residence of splendor, grandeur, and magnificence; but,
when we have passed the gates, we find it perplexed with
narrow passages, disgraced with despicable cottages, embarrassed with obstructions, and clouded with smoke.

No. 16. Saturday, 12 May 1750.

—————————*Multis dicendi copia torrens,*
Et sua mortifera est facundia—————————

                                              Juvenal, x.9–10.

Some who the depths of eloquence have found,
In that unnavigable stream were drown'd.

                                              Dryden.

SIR,

I am the modest young man whom you favoured with
your advice, in a late paper; and, as I am very far from
suspecting that you foresaw the numberless inconveniences which I have, by following it, brought upon myself, I will lay my condition open before you, for you
seem bound to extricate me from the perplexities, in
which your counsel, however innocent in the intention,
has contributed to involve me.

You told me, as you thought, to my comfort, that a

writer might easily find means of introducing his genius
to the world, for the "presses of England were open." This
I have now fatally experienced; the press is, indeed, open.

——————————*Facilis descensus Averni,*
Noctes atque dies patet atri janua Ditis.

AENEID, VI.126–27.

The gates of hell are open night and day;
Smooth the descent, and easy is the way.

Dryden.

The means of doing hurt to ourselves are always at
hand. I immediately sent to a printer, and contracted with
him for an impression of several thousands of my pam-
phlet. While it was at the press, I was seldom absent from
the printing-house, and continually urged the workmen
to haste, by solicitations, promises, and rewards. From the
day all other pleasures were excluded, by the delightful
employment of correcting the sheets; and from the night
sleep was generally banished, by anticipations of the
happiness, which every hour was bringing nearer.

At last the time of publication approached, and my
heart beat with the raptures of an author. I was above all
little precautions, and, in defiance of envy or of criticism,
set my name upon the title, without sufficiently considering, that what has once passed the press is irrevocable,
and that though the printing-house may properly be
compared to the infernal regions, for the facility of its
entrance, and the difficulty with which authors return
from it; yet there is this difference, that a great genius can
never return to his former state, by a happy draught of the
waters of oblivion.

I am now, Mr. Rambler, known to be an author, and
am condemned, irreversibly condemned, to all the

miseries of high reputation.[1] The first morning after
publication my friends assembled about me; I presented
each, as is usual, with a copy of my book. They looked
into the first pages, but were hindered, by their admiration, from reading farther. The first pages are, indeed,
very elaborate. Some passages they particularly dwelt
upon, as more eminently beautiful than the rest; and
some delicate strokes, and secret elegancies, I pointed out
to them, which had escaped their observation. I then
begged of them to forbear their compliments, and invited them, I could not do less, to dine with me at a tavern.
After dinner, the book was resumed; but their praises
very often so much overpowered my modesty, that I was
forced to put about the glass, and had often no means of
repressing the clamours of their admiration, but by
thundering to the drawer for another bottle.

Next morning another set of my acquaintance con-
gratulated me upon my performance, with such importunity of praise, that I was again forced to obviate their
civilities by a treat. On the third day I had yet a greater
number of applauders to put to silence in the same manner; and, on the fourth, those whom I had entertained
the first day came again, having, in the perusal of the
remaining part of the book, discovered so many forcible
sentences and masterly touches, that it was impossible for
me to bear the repetition of their commendations. I,
therefore, persuaded them once more to adjourn to the
tavern, and choose some other subject, on which I might
share in the conversation. But it was not in their power
to withold their attention from my performance, which
had so entirely taken possession of their minds, that no

1. Cf. the remarks on the illusions of those who are "oppressed by
their own reputation" (*Rambler* 159, final par.), and the sketch of the wit
whose invention collapses because of it (*Rambler* 101, pars. 7 to end).

intreaties of mine could change their topick, and I was obliged to stifle, with claret, that praise, which neither my modesty could hinder, nor my uneasiness repress.

The whole week was thus spent in a kind of literary revel, and I have now found that nothing is so expensive as great abilities, unless there is join'd with them an insatiable eagerness of praise; for to escape from the pain of hearing myself exalted above the greatest names dead and living of the learned world, it has already cost me two hogsheads of port, fifteen gallons of arrack, ten dozen of claret, and five and forty bottles of champagne.

I was resolved to stay at home no longer, and, therefore, rose early and went to the coffee-house; but found that I had now made myself too eminent for happiness, and that I was no longer to enjoy the pleasure of mixing, upon equal terms, with the rest of the world. As soon as I enter the room, I see part of the company raging with envy, which they endeavour to conceal, sometimes with the appearance of laughter, and sometimes with that of contempt; but the disguise is such, that I can discover the secret rancour of their hearts, and as envy is deservedly its own punishment, I frequently indulge myself in torment- ing them with my presence.

But, though there may be some slight satisfaction received from the mortification of my enemies, yet my benevolence will not suffer me to take any pleasure in the terrors of my friends. I have been cautious, since the appearance of my work, not to give myself more pre- meditated airs of superiority, than the most rigid humility might allow. It is, indeed, not impossible that I may sometimes have laid down my opinion, in a manner that shewed a consciousness of my ability to maintain it, or interrupted the conversation, when I saw its tendency, without suffering the speaker to waste his time in explain-

ing his sentiments; and, indeed, I did indulge myself for
two days in a custom of drumming with my fingers, when
the company began to lose themselves in absurdities, or
to encroach upon subjects which I knew them unqualified
to discuss. But I generally acted with great appearance of
respect, even to those whose stupidity I pitied in my heart.
Yet, notwithstanding this exemplary moderation, so universal is the dread of uncommon powers, and such the
unwillingness of mankind to be made wiser, that I have
now for some days found myself shunned by all my
acquaintance. If I knock at a door, no body is at home; if
I enter a coffee-house, I have the box to myself. I live in
the town like a lion in his desart, or an eagle on his rock,
too great for friendship or society, and condemned to
solitude, by unhappy elevation, and dreaded ascendency.

Nor is my character only formidable to others, but
burdensome to myself. I naturally love to talk without
much thinking, to scatter my merriment at random, and
to relax my thoughts with ludicrous remarks and fanciful
images; but such is now the importance of my opinion,
that I am afraid to offer it, lest, by being established too
hastily into a maxim, it should be the occasion of error to
half the nation; and such is the expectation with which I
am attended, when I am going to speak, that I frequently
pause to reflect whether what I am about to utter is
worthy of myself.

This, Sir, is sufficiently miserable, but there are still
greater calamities behind. You must have read in Pope
and Swift how men of parts have had their closets rifled,
and their cabinets broke open at the instigation of pirati-
cal booksellers, for the profit of their works,[2] and it is

2. Preface to *Miscellanies* (1727), jointly signed but actually by Pope.
Cf. Johnson on the "pleasing errors of young minds" who consider those
they meet as "an enemy or a follower, an admirer or a spy" (*Rambler*
196, par. 8).

apparent, that there are many prints now sold in the shops, of men whom you cannot suspect of sitting for that purpose, and whose likenesses must have been certainly stolen when their names made their faces vendible. These considerations at first put me on my guard, and I have, indeed, found sufficient reason for my caution, for I have discovered many people examining my countenance, with a curiosity that shewed their intention to draw it; I immediately left the house, but find the same behaviour in another.

Others may be persecuted, but I am haunted; I have good reason to believe that eleven painters are now dogging me, for they know that he who can get my face first will make his fortune. I often change my wig, and wear my hat over my eyes, by which I hope somewhat to confound them; for you know it is not fair to sell my face, without admitting me to share the profit.

I am, however, not so much in pain for my face as for my papers, which I dare neither carry with me nor leave behind. I have, indeed, taken some measures for their preservation, having put them in an iron chest, and fixed a padlock upon my closet. I change my lodgings five times a week, and always remove at the dead of night.

Thus I live, in consequence of having given too great proofs of a predominant genius, in the solitude of a hermit, with the anxiety of a miser, and the caution of an outlaw; afraid to shew my face, lest it should be copied; afraid to speak, lest I should injure my character, and to write lest my correspondents should publish my letters; always uneasy lest my servants should steal my papers for the sake of money, or my friends for that of the publick. This it is to soar above the rest of mankind; and this representation I lay before you, that I may be informed how to divest myself of the laurels which are so cumbersome to the wearer, and descend to the enjoyment of that quiet from which I find a writer of the first class so fatally debarred.

MISELLUS.

No. 17. Tuesday, 15 May 1750.

—————————*Me non oracula certum,*
Sed mors certa facit.

Lucan, PHARSALIA, IX.582–83.

Let those weak minds, who live in doubt and fear,
To juggling priests for oracles repair;
One certain hour of death to each decreed,
My fixt, my certain soul from doubt has freed.

Rowe.

It is recorded of some eastern monarch, that he kept an officer in his house, whose employment it was to remind him of his mortality, by calling out every morning, at a stated hour: "Remember, prince, that thou shalt die."[1] And the contemplation of the frailness and uncertainty of our present state appeared of so much importance to Solon of Athens, that he left this precept to future ages: "Keep thine eye fixed upon the end of life."[2]

---

1. Johnson possibly recalls, or combines in memory, any of the following: the familiar account from Herodotus, II.78, of the image of death at the Egyptian feasts, where the servant cried, "When you die, such will you be"; the accounts (see esp. Tertullian, *Apologeticus*, XXXIII.4), of the man behind the Emperor in the triumphal chariot, whispering *"Respice post te! Hominem te memento";* the common motto, *"Memento mori";* the injunction, "Remember the end" (e.g. Plutarch, "Solon," *Lives,* XXVIII.4) quoted by Solon to Croesus.

2. *Greek Anthology,* IX.366.

A frequent and attentive prospect of that moment, which must put a period to all our schemes, and deprive us of all our acquisitions, is, indeed, of the utmost efficacy to the just and rational regulation of our lives; nor would ever any thing wicked, or often any thing absurd, be undertaken or prosecuted by him who should begin every day with a serious reflection, that he is born to die.

The disturbers of our happiness, in this world, are our desires, our griefs, and our fears, and to all these, the consideration of mortality is a certain and adequate remedy. Think, says Epictetus, frequently on poverty, banishment, and death, and thou wilt then never indulge violent desires, or give up thy heart to mean sentiments, οὐδὲν οὐδέποτε ταπεινὸν ἐνθυμήσῃ, οὔτε ἄγαν ἐπιθυμήσεις τινός.[3]

That the maxim of Epictetus is founded on just observation will easily be granted, when we reflect, how that vehemence of eagerness after the common objects of persuit is kindled in our minds. We represent to ourselves the pleasures of some future possession, and suffer our thoughts to dwell attentively upon it, till it has wholly ingrossed the imagination, and permits us not to conceive any happiness but its attainment, or any misery but its loss; every other satisfaction which the bounty of providence has scattered over life is neglected as inconsiderable, in comparison of the great object which we have placed before us, and is thrown from us as incumbering our activity, or trampled under foot as standing in our way.

Every man has experienced, how much of this ardour has been remitted, when a sharp or tedious sickness has set death before his eyes. The extensive influence of great-

3. *Enchiridion* c. 21; cf. *Rambler* 2, n. 4.

ness, the glitter of wealth, the praises of admirers, and the attendance of supplicants, have appeared vain and empty things, when the last hour seemed to be approaching; and the same appearance they would always have, if the same thought was always predominant. We should then find the absurdity of stretching out our arms incessantly to grasp that which we cannot keep, and wearing out our lives in endeavours to add new turrets to the fabrick of ambition, when the foundation itself is shaking, and the ground on which it stands is mouldering away.

All envy is proportionate to desire; we are uneasy at the attainments of another, according as we think our own happiness would be advanced by the addition of that which he witholds from us; and, therefore, whatever depresses immoderate wishes, will, at the same time, set the heart free from the corrosion of envy, and exempt us from that vice which is, above most others, tormenting to ourselves, hateful to the world, and productive of mean artifices, and sordid projects. He that considers how soon he must close his life, will find nothing of so much importance as to close it well; and will, therefore, look with indifference upon whatever is useless to that purpose. Whoever reflects frequently upon the uncertainty of his own duration, will find out, that the state of others is not more permanent, and that what can confer nothing on himself very desirable, cannot so much improve the condition of a rival, as to make him much superior to those from whom he has carried the prize, a prize too mean to deserve a very obstinate opposition.[4]

Even grief, that passion to which the virtuous and

4. Cf. *Rambler* 29 (par. 10); *Idlers* 32 (pars. 9–10) and 50 (par. 6); *Adventurers* 111 (pars. 2–3) and 120 (par. 6); *Rasselas*, ch. 16 (par. 9).

tender mind is particularly subject, will be obviated, or alleviated, by the same thoughts. It will be obviated, if all the blessings of our condition are enjoyed with a constant sense of this uncertain tenure. If we remember, that whatever we possess is to be in our hands but a very little time, and that the little, which our most lively hopes can promise us, may be made less, by ten thousand accidents; we shall not much repine at a loss, of which we cannot estimate the value, but of which, though we are not able to tell the least amount, we know, with sufficient certainty, the greatest, and are convinced that the greatest is not much to be regretted.

But, if any passion has so much usurped our understanding, as not to suffer us to enjoy advantages with the moderation prescribed by reason, it is not too late to apply this remedy, when we find ourselves sinking under sorrow, and inclined to pine for that which is irrecoverably vanished. We may then usefully revolve the uncertainty of our own condition, and the folly of lamenting that from which, if it had stayed a little longer, we should ourselves have been taken away.

With regard to the sharpest and most melting sorrow, that which arises from the loss of those whom we have loved with tenderness, it may be observed, that friendship between mortals can be contracted on no other terms, than that one must sometime mourn for the other's death: And this grief will always yield to the surviver one consolation proportionate to his affliction; for the pain, whatever it be, that he himself feels, his friend has escaped.

Nor is fear, the most overbearing and resistless of all our passions, less to be temperated by this universal medicine of the mind. The frequent contemplation of death, as it shows the vanity of all human good, discovers likewise the lightness of all terrestrial evil,[5] which, certainly, can last no longer than the subject upon which it acts, and, according to the old observation, must be shorter, as it is more violent. The most cruel calamity, which misfortune can produce, must, by the necessity of nature, be quickly at an end. The soul cannot long be held in prison, but will fly away, and leave a lifeless body to human malice.

——————— *Ridetque sui ludibria trunci.*

Lucan, PHARSALIA, IX.14.

And soaring mocks the broken frame below.

The utmost that we can threaten to one another is that death, which, indeed, we may precipitate, but cannot retard, and from which, therefore, it cannot become a wise man to buy a reprieve at the expence of virtue, since he knows not how small a portion of time he can purchase, but knows that, whether short or long, it will be made less valuable by the remembrance of the price at which it has been obtained. He is sure that he destroys his happiness, but is not sure that he lengthens his life.

The known shortness of life, as it ought to moderate our passions, may likewise, with equal propriety, contract our designs. There is not time for the most forcible genius, and most active industry, to extend its effects beyond a certain sphere. To project the conquest of the world, is the madness of mighty princes; to hope for excellence in every science, has been the folly of literary heroes; and both have found, at last, that they have panted for a height of eminence denied to humanity,

5. Cf. *Rambler* 29 (par. 9).

and have lost many opportunities of making themselves useful and happy, by a vain ambition of obtaining a species of honour, which the eternal laws of providence have placed beyond the reach of man.[6]

The miscarriages of the great designs of princes are recorded in the histories of the world, but are of little use to the bulk of mankind, who seem very little interested in admonitions against errors which they cannot commit.[7] But the fate of learned ambition is a proper subject for every scholar to consider; for who has not had occasion to regret the dissipation of great abilities in a boundless multiplicity of persuits, to lament the sudden desertion of excellent designs, upon the offer of some other subject, made inviting by its novelty, and to observe the inaccuracy and deficiencies of works left unfinished by too great an extension of the plan?

It is always pleasing to observe, how much more our minds can conceive, than our bodies can perform; yet it is our duty, while we continue in this complicated state, to regulate one part of our composition by some regard to the other. We are not to indulge our corporeal appetites with pleasures that impair our intellectual vigour, nor gratify our minds with schemes which we know our lives must fail in attempting to execute. The uncertainty of our duration ought at once to set bounds to our designs, and add incitements to our industry; and when we find ourselves inclined either to immensity in our schemes, or sluggishness in our endeavours, we may either check, or animate, ourselves, by recollecting, with the father of physic, "that art is long, and life is short."[8]

6. Cf. *Rambler* 134 (esp. pars. 9–10).
7. Cf. *Idler* 84 (pars. 3–4).
8. Hippocrates, *Aphorisms* I.1.

From No. 24. Saturday, 9 June 1750.

Nemo in sese tentat descendere.

Persius, SATIRES, IV.23

None, none descends into himself.

Dryden.

Among the precepts, or aphorisms, admitted by general consent, and inculcated by frequent repetition, there is none more famous among the masters of antient wisdom, than that compendious lesson, Γνῶθι σεαυτὸν, "Be acquainted with thyself"; ascribed by some to an oracle,. and by others to Chilo of Lacedemon.[1]

This is, indeed, a dictate, which, in the whole extent of its meaning, may be said to comprise all the speculation requisite to a moral agent. For what more can be necessary to the regulation of life, than the knowledge of our original, our end, our duties, and our relation to other beings?

It is however very improbable that the first author, whoever he was, intended to be understood in this unlimited and complicated sense; for of the inquiries, which, in so large an acceptation, it would seem to recommend, some are too extensive for the powers of man, and some require light from above, which was not yet indulged to the heathen world.

We might have had more satisfaction concerning the original import of this celebrated sentence, if history had informed us, whether it was uttered as a general instruction to mankind, or as a particular caution to some pri-

1. *Greek Anthology*, IX.366 (cited *Rambler* 11, n. 1), where Chilo is said to be the author; and Plato, *Protagoras*, 343A, where he is one of seven sages responsible for the inscription at Delphi.

vate inquirer; whether it was applied to some single occasion, or laid down as the universal rule of life.

There will occur, upon the slightest consideration, many possible circumstances, in which this monition might very properly be inforced; for every error in human conduct must arise from ignorance in ourselves, either perpetual or temporary; and happen either because we do not know what is best and fittest, or because our knowledge is at the time of action not present to the mind.

When a man employs himself upon remote and unnecessary subjects, and wastes his life upon questions, which cannot be resolved, and of which the solution would conduce very little to the advancement of happiness; when he lavishes his hours in calculating the weight of the terraqueous globe, or in adjusting successive systems of worlds beyond the reach of the telescope; he may be very properly recalled from his excursions by this precept, and reminded that there is a nearer being with which it is his duty to be more acquainted; and from which, his attention has hitherto been witheld, by studies, to which he has no other motive, than vanity or curiosity.

The great praise of Socrates is, that he drew the wits of Greece, by his instruction and example, from the vain persuit of natural philosophy to moral inquiries, and turned their thoughts from stars and tides, and matter and motion, upon the various modes of virtue, and relations of life.[2] All his lectures were but commentaries upon this saying; if we suppose the knowledge of ourselves recommended by Chilo, in opposition to other inquiries less suitable to the state of man.

The great fault of men of learning is still, that they of-

2. Cf. "Milton," *Lives,* I.99–100.

fend against this rule, and appear willing to study any thing rather than themselves; for which reason they are often despised by those, with whom they imagine themselves above comparison; despised, as useless to common purposes, as unable to conduct the most trivial affairs, and unqualified to perform those offices by which the concatenation of society is preserved, and mutual tenderness excited and maintained.

*   *   *   *

No. 25. Tuesday, 12 June 1750.

Possunt quia posse videntur.

AENEID, V.231.

For they can conquer who believe they can.

Dryden.

There are some vices and errors, which, though often fatal to those in whom they are found, have yet, by the universal consent of mankind, been considered as entitled to some degree of respect, or have, at least, been exempted from contemptuous infamy, and condemned by the severest moralists with pity rather than detestation.

A constant and invariable example of this general partiality will be found in the different regard which has always been shown to rashness and cowardice, two vices, of which, though they may be conceived equally distant from the middle point, where true fortitude is placed, and may equally injure any publick or private interest, yet the one is never mentioned without some kind of veneration, and the other always considered as a topick of unlimited and licentious censure, on which all the virulence of reproach may be lawfully exerted.

The same distinction is made, by the common suffrage, between profusion and avarice, and, perhaps, between many other opposite vices: and, as I have found reason to pay great regard to the voice of the people, in cases where knowledge has been forced upon them by experience,[1] without long deductions or deep researches, I am inclined to believe that this distribution of respect, is not without some agreement with the nature of things; and that in the faults, which are thus invested with extraordinary privileges, there are generally some latent principles of merit, some possibilities of future virtue, which may, by degrees, break from obstruction, and by time and opportunity be brought into act.

It may be laid down as an axiom, that it is more easy to take away superfluities than to supply defects; and, therefore, he that is culpable, because he has passed the middle point of virtue, is always accounted a fairer object of hope, than he who fails by falling short.[2] The one has all that perfection requires, and more, but the excess may be easily retrenched; the other wants the qualities requisite to excellence, and who can tell how he shall obtain them? We are certain that the horse may be taught to keep pace with his fellows, whose fault is that he leaves them behind. We know that a few strokes of the axe will lop a cedar; but what arts of cultivation can elevate a shrub?

To walk with circumspection and steadiness in the right path,[3] at an equal distance between the extremes of error, ought to be the constant endeavour of every reasonable being; nor can I think those teachers of moral wis-

---

1. Cf. *Ramblers* 23 (par. 8), 52 (par. 2); *Adventurer* 138 (par. 15); and *Lives*, II.132, III.441.
2. Cf. *Rambler* 129 (pars. 7–8).
3. Cf. Horace, *Epistles*, I.18.9.

dom much to be honoured as benefactors to mankind, who are always enlarging upon the difficulty of our duties, and providing rather excuses for vice, than incentives to virtue.

But, since to most it will happen often, and to all sometimes, that there will be a deviation towards one side or the other, we ought always to employ our vigilance, with most attention, on that enemy from which there is greatest danger, and to stray, if we must stray, towards those parts from whence we may quickly and easily return.

Among other opposite qualities of the mind, which may become dangerous, though in different degrees, I have often had occasion to consider the contrary effects of presumption and despondency; of heady confidence, which promises victory without contest, and heartless pusillanimity, which shrinks back from the thought of great undertakings, confounds difficulty with impossibility, and considers all advancement towards any new attainment as irreversibly prohibited.

Presumption will be easily corrected. Every experiment will teach caution, and miscarriages will hourly shew, that attempts are not always rewarded with success. The most precipitate ardour will, in time, be taught the necessity of methodical gradation, and preparatory measures; and the most daring confidence be convinced that neither merit, nor abilities, can command events.

It is the advantage of vehemence and activity, that they are always hastening to their own reformation; because they incite us to try whether our expectations are well grounded, and therefore detect the deceits which they are apt to occasion. But timidity is a disease of the mind more obstinate and fatal; for a man once persuaded, that any impediment is insuperable, has given it, with respect to himself, that strength and weight which it had not before.

He can scarcely strive with vigour and perseverance, when he has no hope of gaining the victory; and since he never will try his strength, can never discover the unreasonableness of his fears.

There is often to be found in men devoted to literature, a kind of intellectual cowardice, which whoever converses much among them, may observe frequently to depress the alacrity of enterprise, and, by consequence, to retard the improvement of science. They have annexed to every species of knowledge some chimerical character of terror and inhibition, which they transmit, without much reflexion, from one to another; they first fright themselves, and then propagate the panic to their scholars and acquaintance. One study is inconsistent with a lively imagination, another with a solid judgment; one is improper in the early parts of life, another requires so much time, that it is not to be attempted at an advanced age; one is dry and contracts the sentiments, another is diffuse and overburdens the memory; one is insufferable to taste and delicacy, and another wears out life in the study of words, and is useless to a wise man, who desires only the knowledge of things.

But of all the bugbears by which the *Infantes barbati*,[4] boys both young and old, have been hitherto frighted from digressing into new tracts of learning, none has been more mischievously efficacious than an opinion that every kind of knowledge requires a peculiar genius, or mental constitution, framed for the reception of some ideas, and the exclusion of others;[5] and that to him whose genius is

4. Johnson is playing with the phrase which can mean both "bearded infants" and also "philosophers [because of long beards] unable to speak."

5. Cf. Johnson's favorite idea of genius as "a mind of large general powers, accidentally determined to some particular direction" ("Cowley," *Lives*, I.2; *Life*, V.34–35 [*Hebrides*, 15 August]; *Miscellanies*, II.287).

not adapted to the study which he prosecutes, all labour shall be vain and fruitless, vain as an endeavour to mingle oil and water, or, in the language of chemistry, to amalgamate bodies of heterogeneous principles.

This opinion we may reasonably suspect to have been propagated, by vanity, beyond the truth. It is natural for those who have raised a reputation by any science, to exalt themselves as endowed by heaven with peculiar powers, or marked out by an extraordinary designation for their profession; and to fright competitors away by representing the difficulties with which they must contend, and the necessity of qualities which are supposed to be not generally conferred, and which no man can know, but by experience, whether he enjoys.

To this discouragement it may be possibly answered, that since a genius, whatever it be, is like fire in the flint, only to be produced by collision with a proper subject,[6] it is the business of every man to try whether his faculties may not happily co-operate with his desires; and since they whose proficiency he admires, knew their own force only by the event, he needs but engage in the same undertaking, with equal spirit, and may reasonably hope for equal success.

There is another species of false intelligence, given by those who profess to shew the way to the summit of knowledge, of equal tendency to depress the mind with false distrust of itself, and weaken it by needless solicitude and dejection. When a scholar, whom they desire to animate, consults them at his entrance on some new study, it is common to make flattering representations of its pleasant-

6. "Great powers cannot be exerted, but when great exigencies make them necessary" (*Idler* 51, par. 8).

ness and facility. Thus they generally attain one of two ends almost equally desirable; they either incite his industry by elevating his hopes, or produce a high opinion of their own abilities, since they are supposed to relate only what they have found, and to have proceeded with no less ease than they promise to their followers.

The student, inflamed by this encouragement, sets forward in the new path,[7] and proceeds a few steps with great alacrity, but he soon finds asperities and intricacies of which he has not been forewarned, and imagining that none ever were so entangled or fatigued before him, sinks suddenly into despair, and desists as from an expedition in which fate opposes him. Thus his terrors are multiplied by his hopes, and he is defeated without resistance, because he had no expectation of an enemy.

Of these treacherous instructors, the one destroys industry, by declaring that industry is vain, the other by representing it as needless; the one cuts away the root of hope, the other raises it only to be blasted. The one confines his pupil to the shore, by telling him that his wreck is certain, the other sends him to sea, without preparing him for tempests.

False hopes and false terrors are equally to be avoided. Every man, who proposes to grow eminent by learning, should carry in his mind, at once, the difficulty of excellence, and the force of industry; and remember that fame is not conferred but as the recompense of labour, and that labour, vigorously continued, has not often failed of its reward.

7. Cf. the student in the *Vanity of Human Wishes:* "Through all his veins the fever of renown/ Spreads from the strong contagion of the gown" (ll. 137–38).

From No. 28. Saturday, 23 June 1750.

Illi mors gravis incubat,
Qui, notus nimis omnibus,
Ignotus moritur sibi.

Seneca, THYESTES, ll. 401–03.

To him, alas, to him, I fear,
The face of death will terrible appear,
Who in his life, flatt'ring his senseless pride,
By being known to all the world beside,
Does not himself, when he is dying know,
Nor what he is, nor whither he's to go.

Cowley.[1]

• • • •

One sophism by which men persuade themselves that they have those virtues which they really want, is formed by the substitution of single acts for habits. A miser who once relieved a friend from the danger of a prison, suffers his imagination to dwell for ever upon his own heroick generosity; he yields his heart up to indignation at those who are blind to merit, or insensible to misery, and who can please themselves with the enjoyment of that wealth, which they never permit others to partake. From any censures of the world, or reproaches of his conscience, he has an appeal to action and to knowledge; and though his whole life is a course of rapacity and avarice, he concludes himself to be tender and liberal, because he has once performed an act of liberality and tenderness.

As a glass which magnifies objects by the approach of one end to the eye, lessens them by the application of the other, so vices are extenuated by the inversion of that

1. Cowley's translation appears in "Of Solitude," *Several Discourses by Way of Essay* in *Works* (1668), p. 98.

fallacy, by which virtues are augmented. Those faults which we cannot conceal from our own notice, are considered, however frequent, not as habitual corruptions, or settled practices, but as casual failures, and single lapses. A man who has, from year to year, set his country to sale, either for the gratification of his ambition or resentment, confesses that the heat of party now and then betrays the severest virtue to measures that cannot be seriously defended. He that spends his days and nights in riot and debauchery, owns that his passions oftentimes overpower his resolution. But each comforts himself that his faults are not without precedent, for the best and the wisest men have given way to the violence of sudden temptations.

There are men who always confound the praise of goodness with the practice,[2] and who believe themselves mild and moderate, charitable and faithful, because they have exerted their eloquence in commendation of mildness, fidelity, and other virtues. This is an error almost universal among those that converse much with dependents, with such whose fear or interest disposes them to a seeming reverence for any declamation, however enthusiastick, and submission to any boast, however arrogant. Having none to recall their attention to their lives, they rate themselves by the goodness of their opinions, and forget how much more easily men may shew their virtue in their talk than in their actions.

The tribe is likewise very numerous of those who regulate their lives, not by the standard of religion, but the measure of other men's virtue; who lull their own remorse with the remembrance of crimes more atrocious

2. Cf. *Rambler* 76 (par. 2), and "Savage," *Lives*, II.380 (par. 169) ("The reigning error of his life was, that he mistook the love for the practice of virtue . . .").

than their own, and seem to believe that they are not bad while another can be found worse.

For escaping these and a thousand other deceits, many expedients have been proposed. Some have recommended the frequent consultation of a wise friend, admitted to intimacy, and encouraged to sincerity.[3] But this appears a remedy by no means adapted to general use: for in order to secure the virtue of one, it presupposes more virtue in two than will generally be found.[4] In the first, such a desire of rectitude and amendment, as may incline him to hear his own accusation from the mouth of him whom he esteems, and by whom, therefore, he will always hope that his faults are not discovered; and in the second such zeal and honesty, as will make him content for his friend's advantage to lose his kindness.

A long life may be passed without finding a friend in whose understanding and virtue we can equally confide, and whose opinion we can value at once for its justness and sincerity. A weak man, however honest, is not qualified to judge. A man of the world, however penetrating, is not fit to counsel. Friends are often chosen for similitude of manners, and therefore each palliates the other's failings, because they are his own. Friends are tender and unwilling to give pain, or they are interested, and fearful to offend.

These objections have inclined others to advise, that he who would know himself, should consult his enemies, remember the reproaches that are vented to his face, and listen for the censures that are uttered in private.[5] For his

3. Bacon, "Of Friendship."

4. Cf. "Pope," *Lives*, III.207 (par. 274) ("Friendship has no tendency to secure veracity . . .").

5. So Jeremy Taylor urges that we use an enemy as an "impartial relator of our faults" (*Holy Living*, ch. II, sec. 6, "Instruments or Exercises to procure contentedness," par. 1).

great business is to know his faults, and those malignity will discover, and resentment will reveal. But this precept may be often frustrated; for it seldom happens that rivals or opponents are suffered to come near enough to know our conduct with so much exactness as that conscience should allow and reflect the accusation. The charge of an enemy is often totally false, and commonly so mingled with falsehood, that the mind takes advantage from the failure of one part to discredit the rest, and never suffers any disturbance afterward from such partial reports.

Yet it seems that enemies have been always found by experience the most faithful monitors; for adversity has ever been considered as the state in which a man most easily becomes acquainted with himself, and this effect it must produce by withdrawing flatterers, whose business it is to hide our weaknesses from us, or by giving loose to malice, and licence to reproach; or at least by cutting off those pleasures which called us away from meditation on our conduct, and repressing that pride which too easily persuades us, that we merit whatever we enjoy.

Part of these benefits it is in every man's power to procure to himself, by assigning proper portions of his life to the examination of the rest, and by putting himself frequently in such a situation by retirement and abstraction, as may weaken the influence of external objects. By this practice he may obtain the solitude of adversity without its melancholy, its instructions without its censures, and its sensibility without its perturbations.

The necessity of setting the world at a distance from us, when we are to take a survey of ourselves, has sent many from high stations to the severities of a monastick life; and indeed, every man deeply engaged in business, if all regard to another state be not extinguished, must have the conviction, tho', perhaps, not the resolution of Valdesso, who, when he solicited Charles the Fifth to dismiss him, being asked, whether he retired upon disgust, answered that he laid down his commission, for no other reason but because "there ought to be some time for sober reflection between the life of a soldier and his death."[6]

There are few conditions which do not entangle us with sublunary hopes and fears, from which it is necessary to be at intervals disencumbered, that we may place ourselves in his presence who views effects in their causes, and actions in their motives; that we may, as Chillingworth expresses it, consider things as if there were no other beings in the world but God and ourselves;[7] or, to use language yet more awful, "may commune with our own hearts, and be still."[8]

．　　．　　．　　．

No. 29. Tuesday, 26 June 1750.

Prudens futuri temporis exitum
Caliginosa nocte premit deus,
　　Ridetque si mortalis ultra
　　Fas trepidet ————

Horace, ODES, III.29.29–32.

But God has wisely hid from human sight
　　The dark decrees of future fate,

6. Alfonso de Valdés (1490–1532), Latin Secretary to Charles V (1526–1532), often confused with his brother, Juan de Valdés, until the late nineteenth century. Johnson's source was probably Izaak Walton, "Herbert," *Lives* (1805), II.95–96.

7. Johnson may refer to Sermon IV, secs. 12 and 15, in *Works* (10th ed., 1742), pp. 43–44.

8. Psalms, iv.4.

And sown their seeds in depth of night;
He laughs at all the giddy turns of state,
When mortals search too soon, and fear too late.

                                        Dryden.

There is nothing recommended with greater frequency
among the gayer poets of antiquity, than the secure possession of the present hour, and the dismission of all the
cares which intrude upon our quiet, or hinder, by importunate perturbations, the enjoyment of those delights
which our condition happens to set before us.

The antient poets are, indeed, by no means unexcep-
tionable teachers of morality; their precepts are to be
always considered as the sallies of a genius, intent rather
upon giving pleasure than instruction, eager to take every
advantage of insinuation, and provided the passions can
be engaged on its side, very little solicitous about the
suffrage of reason.

The darkness and uncertainty through which the
heathens were compelled to wander in the persuit of
happiness, may, indeed, be alleged as an excuse for many
of their seducing invitations to immediate enjoyment,
which the moderns, by whom they have been imitated,
have not to plead. It is no wonder that such as had no
promise of another state should eagerly turn their
thoughts upon the improvement of that which was before
them; but surely those who are acquainted with the
hopes and fears of eternity, might think it necessary to
put some restraint upon their imagination, and reflect
that by echoing the songs of the ancient bacchanals, and
transmitting the maxims of past debauchery, they not
only prove that they want invention, but virtue, and submit to the servility of imitation only to copy that of which
the writer, if he was to live now, would often be ashamed.

Yet as the errors and follies of a great genius are seldom without some radiations of understanding, by which meaner minds may be enlightened, the incitements to pleasure are, in these authors, generally mingled with such reflections upon life, as well deserve to be considered distinctly from the purposes for which they are produced, and to be treasured up as the settled conclusions of extensive observation, acute sagacity, and mature experience.

It is not without true judgment that on these occasions they often warn their readers against enquiries into futurity, and solicitude about events which lie hid in causes yet unactive, and which time has not brought forward into the view of reason. An idle and thoughtless resignation to chance, without any struggle against calamity, or endeavour after advantage, is indeed below the dignity of a reasonable being, in whose power providence has put a great part even of his present happiness; but it shews an equal ignorance of our proper sphere, to harrass our thoughts with conjectures about things not yet in being. How can we regulate events, of which we yet know not whether they will ever happen? And why should we think, with painful anxiety, about that on which our thoughts can have no influence?

It is a maxim commonly received, that a wise man is never surprised;[1] and perhaps, this exemption from astonishment may be imagined to proceed from such a prospect into futurity, as gave previous intimation of those evils which often fall unexpected upon others that have less foresight. But the truth is, that things to come, except when they approach very nearly, are equally hidden from men of all degrees of understanding; and if a wise man is not amazed at sudden occurrences, it is not that

1. See Horace, *Epistles*, I.6.1 et seq.

he has thought more, but less upon futurity. He never considered things not yet existing as the proper objects of his attention; he never indulged dreams till he was deceived by their phantoms, nor ever realized nonentities to his mind. He is not surprised because he is not disappointed, and he escapes disappointment because he never forms any expectations.

The concern about things to come, that is so justly censured, is not the result of those general reflections on the variableness of fortune, the uncertainty of life, and the universal insecurity of all human acquisitions, which must always be suggested by the view of the world; but such a desponding anticipation of misfortune, as fixes the mind upon scenes of gloom and melancholy, and makes fear predominate in every imagination.

Anxiety of this kind is nearly of the same nature with jealousy in love, and suspicion in the general commerce of life; a temper which keeps the man always in alarms, disposes him to judge of every thing in a manner that least favours his own quiet, fills him with perpetual stratagems of counteraction, wears him out in schemes to obviate evils which never threatened him, and at length, perhaps, contributes to the production of those mischiefs of which it had raised such dreadful apprehensions.

It has been usual in all ages for moralists to repress the swellings of vain hope by representations of the innumerable casualties to which life is subject, and by instances of the unexpected defeat of the wisest schemes of policy, and sudden subversions of the highest eminences of greatness. It has, perhaps, not been equally observed, that all these examples afford the proper antidote to fear as well as to hope, and may be applied with no less efficacy as consolations to the timorous, than as restraints to the proud.

Evil is uncertain in the same degree as good, and for
the reason that we ought not to hope too securely, we
ought not to fear with too much dejection. The state of
the world is continually changing, and none can tell the
result of the next vicissitude. Whatever is afloat in the
stream of time, may, when it is very near us, be driven
away by an accidental blast, which shall happen to cross
the general course of the current. The sudden accidents
by which the powerful are depressed, may fall upon those
whose malice we fear; and the greatness by which we
expect to be overborn, may become another proof of the
false flatteries of fortune. Our enemies may become weak,
or we grow strong before our encounter, or we may advance against each other without ever meeting. There
are, indeed, natural evils which we can flatter ourselves
with no hopes of escaping, and with little of delaying;
but of the ills which are apprehended from human malignity, or the opposition of rival interests, we may always
alleviate the terror by considering that our persecutors
are weak and ignorant, and mortal like ourselves.

The misfortunes which arise from the concurrence of
unhappy incidents should never be suffered to disturb
us before they happen; because, if the breast be once laid
open to the dread of mere possibilities of misery, life
must be given a prey to dismal solicitude, and quiet must
be lost for ever.

It is remarked by old Cornaro, that it is absurd to be
afraid of the natural dissolution of the body; because it
must certainly happen, and can, by no caution or artifice,
be avoided.[2] Whether this sentiment be entirely just, I
shall not examine; but certainly, if it be improper to fear

2. Luigi Cornaro (c. 1464–1566), the Venetian centenarian, in *La Vita
Sobria* (1558), Disc. I, II, and IV (trans. and ed. William F. Butler [1905],
pp. 65, 74, 107). Cf. Addison, *Spectator* 195 (13 October 1711).

events which must happen, it is yet more evidently contrary to right reason to fear those which may never happen, and which, if they should come upon us, we cannot resist.

As we ought not to give way to fear any more than indulgence to hope, because the objects both of fear and hope are yet uncertain, so we ought not to trust the representations of one more than of the other, because they are both equally fallacious; as hope enlarges happiness, fear aggravates calamity. It is generally allowed, that no man ever found the happiness of possession proportionate to that expectation which incited his desire, and invigorated his pursuit; nor has any man found the evils of life so formidable in reality, as they were described to him by his own imagination; every species of distress brings with it some peculiar supports, some unforeseen means of resisting, or power of enduring. Taylor justly blames some pious persons, who indulge their fancies too much, set themselves, by the force of imagination, in the place of the ancient martyrs and confessors, and question the validity of their own faith because they shrink at the thoughts of flames and tortures. It is, says he, sufficient that you are able to encounter the temptations which now assault you; when God sends trials, he may send strength.[3]

All fear is in itself painful, and when it conduces not to safety is painful without use. Every consideration, therefore, by which groundless terrors may be removed, adds something to human happiness. It is likewise not unworthy of remark, that in proportion as our cares are imployed upon the future, they are abstracted from the present, from the only time which we can call our own, and of which if we neglect the duties, to make provision

3. *The Worthy Communicant,* ch. 2, sec. 3 *(Works,* ed. Heber and Eden [1854], VIII.70).

against visionary attacks, we shall certainly counteract our own purpose; for he, doubtless, mistakes his true interest, who thinks that he can increase his safety, when he impairs his virtue.

No. 31. Tuesday, 3 July 1750.

Non ego mendosos ausim defendere mores,
  Falsaque pro vitiis arma tenere meis.

Ovid, AMORES, II.4.1–2.

Corrupted manners I shall ne'er defend,
Nor, falsely witty, for my faults contend.

Elphinston.

Though the fallibility of man's reason, and the narrowness of his knowledge, are very liberally confessed, yet the conduct of those who so willingly admit the weakness of human nature, seems to discern that this acknowledgment is not altogether sincere; at least, that most make it with a tacit reserve in favour of themselves, and that with whatever ease they give up the claims of their neighbours, they are desirous of being thought exempt from faults in their own conduct, and from error in their opinions.

The certain and obstinate opposition, which we may observe made to confutation, however clear, and to reproof however tender, is an undoubted argument, that some dormant privilege is thought to be attacked; for as no man can lose what he neither possesses, nor imagines himself to possess, or be defrauded of that to which he has no right, it is reasonable to suppose that those who break out into fury at the softest contradiction, or the slightest censure, since they apparently conclude themselves injured, must fancy some antient immunity violated, or some natural prerogative invaded. To be mistaken, if they thought themselves liable to mistake, could not be considered as either shameful or wonderful, and they would not receive with so much emotion intelligence which only informed them of what they knew before, nor struggle with such earnestness against an attack that deprived them of nothing to which they held themselves entitled.

It is related of one of the philosophers, that when an account was brought him of his son's death, he received it only with this reflexion,[1] "I knew that my son was mortal." He that is convinced of an error, if he had the same knowledge of his own weakness, would, instead of straining for artifices, and brooding malignity, only regard such oversights as the appendages of humanity, and pacify himself with considering that he had always known man to be a fallible being.

If it be true that most of our passions are excited by the novelty of objects,[2] there is little reason for doubting that to be considered as subject to fallacies of ratiocination, or imperfection of knowledge, is to a great part of mankind entirely new; for it is impossible to fall into any company where there is not some regular and established subordination, without finding rage and vehemence produced only by difference of sentiments about things in which neither of the disputants have any other interest than what proceeds from their mutual unwillingness to give way to any opinion that may bring upon them the disgrace of being wrong.

I have heard of one that, having advanced some erro-

1. Said by Lochagus the Spartan, Plutarch, *Moralia,* 225F. Cf. the satiric sketch of the stoic who loses his daughter, in *Rasselas,* ch. 18 (pars. 7–9).
2. "Novelty is the great source of pleasure" ("Prior," *Lives,* II.206, par. 67); cf. *Ramblers* 78 (par. 1) and 80 (par. 1).

neous doctrines in philosophy, refused to see the experiments by which they were confuted:[3] and the observation of every day will give new proofs with how much industry subterfuges and evasions are sought to decline the pressure of resistless arguments, how often the state of the question is altered, how often the antagonist is wilfully misrepresented, and in how much perplexity the clearest positions are involved by those whom they happen to oppose.

Of all mortals none seem to have been more infected with this species of vanity, than the race of writers, whose reputation arising solely from their understanding, gives them a very delicate sensibility of any violence attempted on their literary honour.[4] It is not unpleasing to remark with what solicitude men of acknowledged abilities will endeavour to palliate absurdities and reconcile contradictions, only to obviate criticisms to which all human performances must ever be exposed, and from which they can never suffer, but when they teach the world by a vain and ridiculous impatience to think them of importance.

Dryden, whose warmth of fancy, and haste of composition very frequently hurried him into inaccuracies, heard himself sometimes exposed to ridicule for having said in one of his tragedies,

I follow fate, which does too fast persue.

INDIAN EMPEROR, IV.iii.3.

3. Julius Libri, professor at Pisa, who refused to look through a telescope and, with Cesare Cremonino, professor at Padua and colleague of Galileo, rejected *a priori* Galileo's discoveries. (J. J. Fahie, *Galileo* [1903], p. 101.)

4. Cf. *Rambler* 40 (par. 4). Hence Johnson's amusing comparison of the rivalries and antagonisms of scholars to those of celebrated "beauties," since "both depend for happiness on the regard of others" (*Adventurer* 45, pars. 13–14).

That no man could at once follow and be followed was, it may be thought, too plain to be long disputed; and the truth is, that Dryden was apparently betrayed into the blunder by the double meaning of the word "fate," to which in the former part of the verse he had annexed the idea of "fortune," and in the latter that of "death"; so that the sense only was, "though persued by 'death,' I will not resign myself to despair, but will follow 'fortune,' and do and suffer what is appointed." This however was not completely expressed, and Dryden being determined not to give way to his critics, never confessed that he had been surprised by an ambiguity; but finding luckily in *Virgil* an account of a man moving in a circle, with this expression, *Et se sequiturque fugitque*,[5] "Here," says he, "is the passage in imitation of which I wrote the line that my critics were pleased to condemn as nonsense; not but I may sometimes write nonsense, though they have not the fortune to find it."[6]

Every one sees the folly of such mean doublings to escape the persuit of criticism; nor is there a single reader of this poet, who would not have paid him greater veneration, had he shewn consciousness enough of his own superiority to set such cavils at defiance, and owned that he sometimes slipped into errors by the tumult of his imagination, and the multitude of his ideas.

---

5. Actually Ovid, *Metamorphoses*, IV.461.

6. Preface to *Tyrannick Love, Prose Works*, ed. Edmond Malone (1800), I (pt. II).353. Johnson, as usual, quotes from memory, substituting, for Dryden's quotation from Virgil *(Aeneid,* XI.65), a somewhat similar one from Ovid (n. 5, above). Dryden actually says: "Some fool before them had charged me in *The Indian Emperor* with nonsense, in these words: 'And follow Fate, which does too fast pursue;' which was borrowed from Virgil in the eleventh of his Aeneids: *Eludit gyro interior, sequiturque sequentem.* I quote not these to prove that I never writ nonsense, but only to shew that they are so unfortunate as not to have found it."

It is happy when this temper discovers itself only in little things, which may be right or wrong without any influence on the virtue or happiness of mankind. We may, with very little inquietude, see a man persist in a project, which he has found to be impracticable, live in an inconvenient house because it was contrived by himself, or wear a coat of a particular cut, in hopes by perseverance to bring it into fashion. These are indeed follies, but they are only follies, and, however wild or ridiculous, can very little affect others.

But such pride, once indulged, too frequently operates upon more important objects, and inclines men not only to vindicate their errors, but their vices; to persist in practices which their own hearts condemn, only lest they should seem to feel reproaches, or be made wiser by the advice of others; or to search for sophisms tending to the confusion of all principles, and the evacuation of all duties, that they may not appear to act what they are not able to defend.

Let every man, who finds vanity so far predominant, as to betray him to the danger of this last degree of corruption, pause a moment to consider what will be the consequences of the plea which he is about to offer for a practice to which he knows himself not led at first by reason, but impelled by the violence of desire, surprized by the suddenness of passion, or seduced by the soft approaches of temptation, and by imperceptible gradations of guilt. Let him consider what he is going to commit by forcing his understanding to patronise those appetites, which it is its chief business to hinder and reform.

The cause of virtue requires so little art to defend it, and good and evil, when they have been once shewn, are so easily distinguished, that such apologists seldom gain proselytes to their party, nor have their fallacies power to deceive any but those whose desires have clouded their discernment. All that the best faculties thus employed can perform is, to persuade the hearers that the man is hopeless whom they only thought vitious, that corruption has passed from his manners to his principles, that all endeavours for his recovery are without prospect of success, and that nothing remains but to avoid him as infectious, or hunt him down as destructive.

But if it be supposed that he may impose on his audience by partial representations of consequences, intricate deductions of remote causes, or perplexed combinations of ideas, which having various relations appear different as viewed on different sides; that he may sometimes puzzle the weak and well-meaning, and now and then seduce, by the admiration of his abilities, a young mind still fluctuating in unsettled notions, and neither fortified by instruction nor enlightened by experience; yet what must be the event of such a triumph? A man cannot spend all this life in frolick: age, or disease, or solitude will bring some hours of serious consideration, and it will then afford no comfort to think, that he has extended the dominion of vice, that he has loaded himself with the crimes of others, and can never know the extent of his own wickedness, or make reparation for the mischief that he has caused. There is not perhaps in all the stores of ideal anguish, a thought more painful, than the consciousness of having propagated corruption by vitiating principles, of having not only drawn others from the paths of virtue, but blocked up the way by which they should return, of having blinded them to every beauty but the paint of pleasure, and deafened them to every call but the alluring voice of the syrens of destruction.

There is yet another danger in this practice: men who cannot deceive others, are very often successful in deceiving themselves; they weave their sophistry till their own reason is entangled, and repeat their positions till they are credited by themselves; by often contending they grow sincere in the cause, and by long wishing for demonstrative arguments they at last bring themselves to fancy that they have found them. They are then at the uttermost verge of wickedness, and may die without having that light rekindled in their minds, which their own pride and contumacy have extinguished.

The men who can be charged with fewest failings, either with respect to abilities or virtue, are generally most ready to allow them; for not to dwell on things of solemn and awful consideration, the humility of confessors, the tears of saints, and the dying terrors of persons eminent for piety and innocence, it is well known that Caesar wrote an account of the errors committed by him in his wars of Gaul, and that Hippocrates, whose name is perhaps in rational estimation greater than Caesar's, warned posterity against a mistake into which he had fallen. "So much," says Celsus, "does the open and artless confession of an error become a man conscious that he has enough remaining to support his character."[7]

As all error is meanness, it is incumbent on every man who consults his own dignity, to retract it as soon as he discovers it, without fearing any censure so much as that of his own mind. As justice requires that all injuries should be repaired, it is the duty of him who has seduced others by bad practices, or false notions, to endeavour that such as have adopted his errors should know his retraction, and that those who have learned vice by his example, should by his example be taught amendment.

7. *De Medicina*, VIII.4.4.

No. 32. Saturday, 7 July 1750.

"Οσσά τε δαιμονίησι τύχαις βροτοὶ ἄλγε' ἔχουσιν,
Ὧν ἄν μοῖραν ἔχης, πράως φέρε, μηδ' ἀγανάκτει·
Ἰᾶσθαι δὲ πρέπει κάθοσον δύνη.

Pythagoras, AUREA CARMINA, II.17–19.

Of all the woes that load the mortal state,
Whate'er thy portion, mildly meet thy fate;
But ease it as thou can'st ————————
                                    Elphinston.

So large a part of human life passes in a state contrary to
our natural desires, that one of the principal topics of
moral instruction is the art of bearing calamities. And
such is the certainty of evil, that it is the duty of every
man to furnish his mind with those principles that may
enable him to act under it with decency and propriety.

The sect of ancient philosophers, that boasted to have
carried this necessary science to the highest perfection,
were the stoics, or scholars of Zeno, whose wild enthusiastick virtue pretended to an exemption from the sensi-
bilities of unenlightened mortals, and who proclaimed
themselves exalted, by the doctrines of their sect, above
the reach of those miseries, which embitter life to the rest
of the world. They therefore removed pain, poverty, loss
of friends, exile, and violent death, from the catalogue
of evils; and passed, in their haughty stile, a kind of ir-
reversible decree, by which they forbad them to be
counted any longer among the objects of terror or
anxiety, or to give any disturbance to the tranquillity of
a wise man.

This edict was, I think, not universally observed, for
though one of the more resolute, when he was tortured
by a violent disease, cried out, that let pain harrass him

to its utmost power, it should never force him to consider it as other than indifferent and neutral; yet all had not stubbornness to hold out against their senses: for a weaker pupil of Zeno is recorded to have confessed in the anguish of the gout, that "he now found pain to be an evil."[1]

It may however be questioned, whether these philosophers can be very properly numbered among the teachers of patience; for if pain be not an evil, there seems no instruction requisite how it may be borne; and therefore when they endeavour to arm their followers with arguments against it, they may be thought to have given up their first position. But, such inconsistencies are to be expected from the greatest understandings, when they endeavour to grow eminent by singularity, and employ their strength in establishing opinions opposite to nature.

The controversy about the reality of external evils is now at an end. That life has many miseries, and that those miseries are, sometimes at least, equal to all the powers of fortitude, is now universally confessed; and therefore it is useful to consider not only how we may escape them, but by what means those which either the accidents of affairs, or the infirmities of nature must bring upon us, may be mitigated and lightened; and how we may make those hours less wretched, which the condition of our present existence will not allow to be very happy.

The cure for the greatest part of human miseries is not radical, but palliative. Infelicity is involved in corporeal nature, and interwoven with our being; all attempts therefore to decline it wholly are useless and vain: the armies of pain send their arrows against us on every side, the choice is only between those which are more or less sharp, or tinged with poison of greater or less malignity;

1. Possibly Dionysius of Heraclea. See Diogenes Laertius, *Lives*, VII.37, ch. 1; 166, ch. 4.

and the strongest armour which reason can supply, will only blunt their points, but cannot repel them.

The great remedy which heaven has put in our hands is patience, by which, though we cannot lessen the torments of the body, we can in a great measure preserve the peace of the mind, and shall suffer only the natural and genuine force of an evil, without heightening its acrimony, or prolonging its effects.

There is indeed nothing more unsuitable to the nature of man in any calamity than rage and turbulence, which, without examining whether they are not sometimes impious, are at least always offensive, and incline others rather to hate and despise than to pity and assist us. If what we suffer has been brought upon us by ourselves, it is observed by an ancient poet, that patience is eminently our duty, since no one should be angry at feeling that which he has deserved.

Leniter ex merito quicquid patiare ferendum est.
Ovid, HEROIDES, V.7.

Let pain deserv'd without complaint be borne.

And surely, if we are conscious that we have not contributed to our own sufferings, if punishment fall upon innocence, or disappointment happens to industry and prudence, patience, whether more necessary or not, is much easier, since our pain is then without aggravation, and we have not the bitterness of remorse to add to the asperity of misfortune.

In those evils which are allotted to us by providence, such as deformity, privation of any of the senses, or old age, it is always to be remembered, that impatience can have no present effect, but to deprive us of the consolations which our condition admits, by driving away from us those by whose conversation or advice we might be amused or helped; and that with regard to futurity it is yet less to be justified, since, without lessening the pain, it cuts off the hope of that reward, which he by whom it is inflicted will confer upon them that bear it well.

In all evils which admit a remedy, impatience is to be avoided, because it wastes that time and attention in complaints, that, if properly applied, might remove the cause. Turenne, among the acknowledgments which he used to pay in conversation to the memory of those by whom he had been instructed in the art of war, mentioned one with honour, who taught him not to spend his time in regretting any mistake which he had made, but to set himself immediately and vigorously to repair it.[2]

Patience and submission are very carefully to be distinguished from cowardice and indolence. We are not to repine, but we may lawfully struggle; for the calamities of life, like the necessities of nature, are calls to labour, and exercises of diligence. When we feel any pressure of distress, we are not to conclude that we can only obey the will of heaven by languishing under it, any more than when we perceive the pain of thirst we are to imagine that water is prohibited. Of misfortune it never can be certainly known whether, as proceeding from the hand of God, it is an act of favour, or of punishment: but since all the ordinary dispensations of providence are to be interpreted according to the general analogy of things, we may conclude, that we have a right to remove one inconvenience as well as another; that we are only to take care lest we purchase ease with guilt; and that our Maker's purpose, whether of reward or severity, will be answered by the labours which he lays us under the necessity of performing.

2. Andrew Ramsay, *Histoire du Vicomte de Turenne* (1736), I.109. The "one" mentioned is the Duc de Weymar.

This duty is not more difficult in any state, than in diseases intensely painful, which may indeed suffer such exacerbations as seem to strain the powers of life to their utmost stretch, and leave very little of the attention vacant to precept or reproof. In this state the nature of man requires some indulgence, and every extravagance but impiety may be easily forgiven him. Yet, lest we should think ourselves too soon entitled to the mournful privileges of irresistible misery, it is proper to reflect that the utmost anguish which human wit can contrive, or human malice can inflict, has been borne with constancy; and that if the pains of disease be, as I believe they are, sometimes greater than those of artificial torture, they are therefore in their own nature shorter, the vital frame is quickly broken, or the union between soul and body is for a time suspended by insensibility, and we soon cease to feel our maladies when they once become too violent to be born. I think there is some reason for questioning whether the body and mind are not so proportioned, that the one can bear all which can be inflicted on the other, whether virtue cannot stand its ground as long as life, and whether a soul well principled will not be separated sooner than subdued.

In calamities which operate chiefly on our passions, such as diminution of fortune, loss of friends, or declension of character, the chief danger of impatience is upon the first attack, and many expedients have been contrived, by which the blow may be broken. Of these the most general precept is, not to take pleasure in any thing, of which it is not in our power to secure the possession to ourselves. This counsel, when we consider the enjoyment of any terrestrial advantage, as opposite to a constant and habitual solicitude for future felicity, is undoubtedly just, and delivered by that authority which cannot be disputed; but in any other sense, is it not like

advice, not to walk lest we should stumble, or not to see
lest our eyes should light upon deformity?[3] It seems to
me reasonable to enjoy blessings with confidence as well
as to resign them with submission, and to hope for the
continuance of good which we possess without insolence
or voluptuousness, as for the restitution of that which we
lose without despondency or murmurs.

The chief security against the fruitless anguish of impatience, must arise from frequent reflection on the wisdom and goodness of the God of nature, in whose hands
are riches and poverty, honour and disgrace, pleasure and
pain, and life and death. A settled conviction of the tendency of every thing to our good, and of the possibility
of turning miseries into happiness, by receiving them
rightly, will incline us to "bless the name of the Lord,
whether he gives or takes away."[4]

No. 41. Tuesday, 7 August 1750.

Nulla recordanti lux est ingrata gravisque,
   Nulla fuit cujus non meminisse velit.
Ampliat aetatis spatium sibi vir bonus, hoc est
   Vivere bis, vitâ posse priore frui.

Martial, x.23.5–8.

No day's remembrance shall the good regret,
Nor wish one bitter moment to forget;
They stretch the limits of this narrow span,
And, by enjoying, live past life again.

F. Lewis.

3. Cf. Swift's remarks about the Stoics, "Thoughts on Various Subjects," *Works*, ed. Temple Scott (1897–1908), I.277.
4. Job, i.21.

So few of the hours of life are filled up with objects adequate to the mind of man, and so frequently are we in
want of present pleasure or employment, that we are
forced to have recourse every moment to the past and
future for supplemental satisfactions, and relieve the
vacuities of our being, by recollection of former passages,
or anticipation of events to come.[1]

I cannot but consider this necessity of searching on
every side for matter on which the attention may be employed, as a strong proof of the superior and celestial
nature of the soul of man. We have no reason to believe
that other creatures have higher faculties, or more extensive capacities, than the preservation of themselves, or
their species, requires; they seem always to be fully employed, or to be completely at ease without employment,
to feel few intellectual miseries or pleasures, and to have
no exuberance of understanding to lay out upon curiosity or caprice, but to have their minds exactly adapted
to their bodies, with few other ideas than such as corporal
pain or pleasure impress upon them.

Of memory, which makes so large a part of the excellence of the human soul, and which has so much influence
upon all its other powers, but a small portion has been
allotted to the animal world. We do not find the grief,
with which the dams lament the loss of their young, proportionate to the tenderness with which they caress, the
assiduity with which they feed, or the vehemence with
which they defend them. Their regard for their offspring,
when it is before their eyes, is not, in appearance, less
than that of a human parent; but when it is taken away,
it is very soon forgotten, and, after a short absence, if
brought again, wholly disregarded.

1. See *Rambler* 2, above, n. 1.

That they have very little remembrance of any thing once out of the reach of their senses, and scarce any power of comparing the present with the past, and regulating their conclusions from experience, may be gathered from this, that their intellects are produced in their full perfection. The sparrow that was hatched last spring makes her first nest the ensuing season, of the same materials, and with the same art, as in any following year; and the hen conducts and shelters her first brood of chickens with all the prudence that she ever attains.

It has been asked by men who love to perplex any thing that is plain to common understandings, how reason differs from instinct; and Prior has with no great propriety made Solomon himself declare, that, to distinguish them is "the fool's ignorance, and the pedant's pride."[2] To give an accurate answer to a question, of which the terms are not compleatly understood, is impossible; we do not know in what either reason or instinct consist, and therefore cannot tell with exactness how they differ; but surely he that contemplates a ship and a bird's nest, will not be long without finding out, that the idea of the one was impressed at once, and continued through all the progressive descents of the species, without variation or improvement; and that the other is the result of experiments compared with experiments, has grown, by accumulated observation, from less to greater excellence, and exhibits the collective knowledge of different ages, and various professions.

Memory is the purveyor of reason, the power which places those images before the mind upon which the judgment is to be exercised, and which treasures up the determinations that are once passed, as the rules of future action, or grounds of subsequent conclusions.

2. *Solomon*, I.236.

It is, indeed, the faculty of remembrance, which may be said to place us in the class of moral agents. If we were to act only in consequence of some immediate impulse, and receive no direction from internal motives of choice, we should be pushed forward by an invincible fatality, without power or reason for the most part to prefer one thing to another, because we could make no comparison but of objects which might both happen to be present.

We owe to memory not only the increase of our knowledge, and our progress in rational enquiries, but many other intellectual pleasures. Indeed, almost all that we can be said to enjoy is past or future; the present is in perpetual motion, leaves us as soon as it arrives, ceases to be present before its presence is well perceived, and is only known to have existed by the effects which it leaves behind. The greatest part of our ideas arises, therefore, from the view before or behind us, and we are happy or miserable, according as we are affected by the survey of our life, or our prospect of future existence.

With regard to futurity, when events are at such a distance from us, that we cannot take the whole concatenation into our view, we have generally power enough over our imagination to turn it upon pleasing scenes, and can promise ourselves riches, honours, and delights, without intermingling those vexations and anxieties, with which all human enjoyments are polluted. If fear breaks in on one side, and alarms us with dangers and disappointments, we can call in hope on the other, to solace us with rewards, and escapes, and victories; so that we are seldom without means of palliating remote evils, and can generally sooth ourselves to tranquillity, whenever any troublesome presage happens to attack us.

It is therefore, I believe, much more common for the solitary and thoughtful, to amuse themselves with schemes of the future, than reviews of the past. For the future is pliant and ductile, and will be easily moulded by a strong fancy into any form. But the images which memory presents are of a stubborn and untractable nature, the objects of remembrance have already existed, and left their signature behind them impressed upon the mind, so as to defy all attempts of rasure, or of change.

As the satisfactions, therefore, arising from memory are less arbitrary, they are more solid, and are, indeed, the only joys which we can call our own. Whatever we have once reposited, as Dryden expresses it, "in the sacred treasure of the past,"[3] is out of the reach of accident, or violence, nor can be lost either by our own weakness, or another's malice:

——————— *Non tamen irritum*
Quodcunque retro est efficiet, neque
  Diffinget, infectumque reddet,
  Quod fugiens semel hora vexit.

Horace, ODES, III.29.45–48.[4]

Be fair or foul or rain or shine,
The joys I have possess'd in spite of fate are mine.
Not heav'n itself upon the past has pow'r,
But what has been has been, and I have had my hour.

Dryden.

There is certainly no greater happiness, than to be able to look back on a life usefully and virtuously employed,

3. Johnson apparently misquotes "The Hind and the Panther," pt. I, ll. 56–58 (*Poems*, ed. Kinsley, I.476): "The god-head took a deep consid'ring space:/ And, to distinguish man from all the rest,/ Unlock'd the sacred treasures of his breast."

4. For the translation, see Dryden's "The Twenty-ninth Ode of the Third Book of Horace: paraphrased in Pindaric Verse," st. 8, in *Original Poems and Translations* (London, 1743), I.75.

to trace our own progress in existence, by such tokens as excite neither shame nor sorrow. Life, in which nothing has been done or suffered to distinguish one day from another, is to him that has passed it, as if it had never been, except that he is conscious how ill he has husbanded the great deposit of his Creator. Life, made memorable by crimes, and diversified thro' its several periods by wickedness, is indeed easily reviewed, but reviewed only with horror and remorse.

The great consideration which ought to influence us in the use of the present moment, is to arise from the effect, which, as well or ill applied, it must have upon the time to come; for though its actual existence be inconceivably short, yet its effects are unlimited, and there is not the smallest point of time but may extend its consequences, either to our hurt or our advantage, through all eternity, and give us reason to remember it for ever, with anguish or exultation.

The time of life, in which memory seems particularly to claim predominance over the other faculties of the mind, is our declining age. It has been remarked by former writers, that old men are generally narrative, and fall easily into recitals of past transactions, and accounts of persons known to them in their youth.[5] When we approach the verge of the grave it is more eminently true;

Vitae summa brevis spem nos vetat inchoare longam.
                                        Horace, ODES, I.4.15.

Life's span forbids thee to extend thy cares,
    And stretch thy hopes beyond thy years.
                                        Creech.

5. For example, in Pope's *Iliad* (III.200): "But, wise thro' time, and narrative with age." Cf. *Rambler* 203 (par. 2).

We have no longer any possibility of great vicissitudes in our favour; the changes which are to happen in the world will come too late for our accommodation; and those who have no hope before them, and to whom their present state is painful and irksome, must of necessity turn their thoughts back to try what retrospect will afford. It ought, therefore, to be the care of those who wish to pass the last hours with comfort, to lay up such a treasure of pleasing ideas, as shall support the expences of that time, which is to depend wholly upon the fund already acquired.

———— *Petite hinc juvenesque senesque*
Finem animo certum, miserisque viatica canis.

Persius, SATIRES, V.64–65.

Seek here, ye young, the anchor of your mind;
Here, suff'ring age, a bless'd provision find.

Elphinston.

In youth, however unhappy, we solace ourselves with the hope of better fortune, and, however vicious, appease our consciences with intentions of repentance; but the time comes at last, in which life has no more to promise, in which happiness can be drawn only from recollection, and virtue will be all that we can recollect with pleasure.

No. 45. Tuesday, 21 August 1750.

Ἥπερ μεγίστη γίγνεται σωτηρία,
Ὅταν γύνη πρὸς ἄνδρα μὴ διχοστατῇ,
Νῦν δ' ἐκθρὰ πάντα.

Euripides, MEDEA, ll. 14–16.

This is the chief felicity of life,
That concord smile on the connubial bed;
But now 'tis hatred all ————————————

TO THE RAMBLER.

SIR,

Though, in the dissertations which you have given us on marriage,[1] very just cautions are laid down against the common causes of infelicity, and the necessity of having, in that important choice, the first regard to virtue is carefully inculcated; yet I cannot think the subject so much exhausted, but that a little reflection would present to the mind many questions in the discussion of which great numbers are interested, and many precepts which deserve to be more particularly and forcibly impressed.

You seem, like most of the writers that have gone before you, to have allowed, as an uncontested principle, that "Marriage is generally unhappy": but I know not whether a man who professes to think for himself, and concludes from his own observations, does not depart from his character when he follows the crowd thus implicitly, and receives maxims without recalling them to a new examination, especially when they comprise so wide a circuit of life, and include such variety of circumstances. As I have an equal right with others to give my opinion of the objects about me, and a better title to determine concerning that state which I have tried, than many who talk of it without experience, I am unwilling to be restrained by mere authority from advancing what, I believe, an accurate view of the world will confirm, that marriage is not commonly unhappy, otherwise than as life is unhappy; and that most of those who complain of connubial miseries, have as much satisfaction as their nature would have admitted, or their conduct procured in any other condition.

1. *Ramblers* 18 (pars. 4 ff.), 35, and 39. For later ones, see Nos. 113, 115, 119, and 167. Cf. *Rasselas*, chs. 28–29.

It is, indeed, common to hear both sexes repine at their change, relate the happiness of their earlier years, blame the folly and rashness of their own choice, and warn those whom they see coming into the world against the same precipitance and infatuation. But it is to be remembred, that the days which they so much wish to call back, are the days not only of celibacy but of youth, the days of novelty and improvement, of ardour and of hope, of health and vigour of body, of gayety and lightness of heart. It is not easy to surround life with any circumstances in which youth will not be delightful; and I am afraid that whether married or unmarried, we shall find the vesture of terrestrial existence more heavy and cumbrous, the longer it is worn.

That they censure themselves for the indiscretion of their choice, is not a sufficient proof that they have chosen ill, since we see the same discontent at every other part of life which we cannot change. Converse with almost any man, grown old in a profession, and you will find him regretting that he did not enter into some different course, to which he too late finds his genius better adapted, or in which he discovers that wealth and honour are more easily attained. "The merchant," says Horace, "envies the soldier, and the soldier recounts the felicity of the merchant; the lawyer when his clients harrass him, calls out for the quiet of the countryman; and the countryman, when business calls him to town, proclaims that there is no happiness but amidst opulence and crouds."[2] Every man recounts the inconveniencies of his own station, and thinks those of any other less, because he has not felt them.[3] Thus the married praise the ease and freedom of a single state, and the single fly to marriage

2. *Satires,* I.1.4–12.
3. Cf. *Rasselas,* ch. 22 (par. 3).

from the weariness of solitude. From all our observations we may collect with certainty, that misery is the lot of man, but cannot discover in what particular condition it will find most alleviations; or whether all external appendages are not, as we use them, the causes either of good or ill.

Whoever feels great pain naturally hopes for ease from change of posture;[4] he changes it, and finds himself equally tormented: and of the same kind are the expedients by which we endeavour to obviate or elude those uneasinesses, to which mortality will always be subject. It is not likely that the married state is eminently miserable, since we see such numbers, whom the death of their partners has set free from it, entering it again.

Wives and husbands are, indeed, incessantly complaining of each other; and there would be reason for imagining that almost every house was infested with perverseness or oppression beyond human sufferance, did we not know upon how small occasions some minds burst out into lamentations and reproaches, and how naturally every animal revenges his pain upon those who happen to be near, without any nice examination of its cause. We are always willing to fancy ourselves within a little of happiness, and when, with repeated efforts, we cannot reach it, persuade ourselves that it is intercepted by an ill-paired mate, since, if we could find any other obstacle, it would be our own fault that it was not removed.

Anatomists have often remarked, that though our diseases are sufficiently numerous and severe, yet when we enquire into the structure of the body, the tenderness of some parts, the minuteness of others, and the immense multiplicity of animal functions that must concur to the healthful and vigorous exercise of all our powers, there

4. Cf. *Rambler* 6 (final par.).

appears reason to wonder rather that we are preserved so long, than that we perish so soon, and that our frame subsists for a single day, or hour, without disorder, rather than that it should be broken or obstructed by violence of accidents, or length of time.

The same reflection arises in my mind, upon observation of the manner in which marriage is frequently contracted. When I see the avaricious and crafty taking companions to their tables, and their beds, without any enquiry, but after farms and money; or the giddy and thoughtless uniting themselves for life to those whom they have only seen by the light of tapers at a ball; when parents make articles for their children, without enquiring after their consent; when some marry for heirs to disappoint their brothers, and others throw themselves into the arms of those whom they do not love, because they have found themselves rejected where they were more solicitous to please; when some marry because their servants cheat them, some because they squander their own money, some because their houses are pestered with company, some because they will live like other people, and some only because they are sick of themselves, I am not so much inclined to wonder that marriage is sometimes unhappy, as that it appears so little loaded with calamity; and cannot but conclude that society has something in itself eminently agreeable to human nature, when I find its pleasures so great that even the ill choice of a companion can hardly over-balance them.

By the ancient custom of the Muscovites the men and women never saw each other till they were joined beyond the power of parting.[5] It may be suspected that by this

5. See Capt. John Perry, *The State of Russia under the Present Czar* (1716), pp. 200–02.

method many unsuitable matches were produced, and many tempers associated that were not qualified to give pleasure to each other. Yet, perhaps, among a people so little delicate, where the paucity of gratifications, and the uniformity of life gave no opportunity for imagination to interpose its objections, there was not much danger of capricious dislike, and while they felt neither cold nor hunger they might live quietly together, without any thought of the defects of one another.

Amongst us, whom knowledge has made nice, and affluence wanton, there are, indeed, more cautions requisite to secure tranquillity; and yet if we observe the manner in which those converse, who have singled out each other for marriage, we shall, perhaps, not think that the Russians lost much by their restraint. For the whole endeavour of both parties, during the time of courtship, is to hinder themselves from being known, and to disguise their natural temper, and real desires, in hypocritical imitation, studied compliance, and continued affectation. From the time that their love is avowed, neither sees the other but in a mask, and the cheat is managed often on both sides with so much art, and discovered afterwards with so much abruptness, that each has reason to suspect that some transformation has happened on the wedding-night, and that by a strange imposture one has been courted, and another married.

I desire you, therefore, Mr. Rambler, to question all who shall hereafter come to you with matrimonial complaints, concerning their behaviour in the time of courtship, and inform them that they are neither to wonder nor repine, when a contract begun with fraud has ended in disappointment.

I am, &c.

No. 47. Tuesday, 28 August 1750.

Quanquam his solatiis acquiescam, debilitor & frangor
eadem illa humanitate quae me, ut hoc ipsum per-
mitterem, induxit, non ideo tamen velim durior fieri:
nec ignoro alios hujusmodi casus nihil amplius vo-
care quam damnum; eoque sibi magnos homines &
sapientes videri. Qui an magni sapientesque sint,
nescio: homines non sunt. Hominis est enim affici
dolore, sentire: resistere tamen, & solatia admittere;
non solatiis non egere.

Pliny, EPISTLES, VIII.16.

These proceedings have afforded me some comfort in
my distress; notwithstanding which, I am still dis-
pirited, and unhinged by the same motives of humanity that induced me to grant such indulgences.
However, I by no means wish to become less susceptible of tenderness. I know these kind of misfortunes
would be estimated by other persons only as common
losses, and from such sensations they would conceive
themselves great and wise men. I shall not determine
either their greatness or their wisdom; but I am certain they have no humanity. It is the part of a man to
be affected with grief; to feel sorrow, at the same time,
that he is to resist it, and to admit of comfort.

Earl of Orrery.[1]

Of the passions with which the mind of man is agitated, it
may be observed, that they naturally hasten towards their
own extinction by inciting and quickening the attainment of their objects. Thus fear urges our flight, and
desire animates our progress; and if there are some which
perhaps may be indulged till they out-grow the good

1. Translated by John Boyle, Earl of Orrery, *Letters of Pliny the
Younger* (1751), II.231.

appropriated to their satisfaction, as is frequently observed of avarice and ambition, yet their immediate tendency is to some means of happiness really existing, and generally within the prospect. The miser always imagines that there is a certain sum that will fill his heart to the brim; and every ambitious man, like king Pyrrhus, has an acquisition in his thoughts that is to terminate his labours, after which he shall pass the rest of his life in ease or gayety, in repose or devotion.[2]

Sorrow is perhaps the only affection of the breast that can be excepted from this general remark, and it therefore deserves the particular attention of those who have assumed the arduous province of preserving the balance of the mental constitution. The other passions are diseases indeed, but they necessarily direct us to their proper cure. A man at once feels the pain, and knows the medicine, to which he is carried with greater haste as the evil which requires it is more excruciating, and cures himself by unerring instinct, as the wounded stags of Crete are related by Ælian to have recourse to vulnerary herbs.[3] But for sorrow there is no remedy provided by nature; it is often occasioned by accidents irreparable, and dwells upon objects that have lost or changed their existence; it requires what it cannot hope, that the laws of the universe should be repealed; that the dead should return, or the past should be recalled.

Sorrow is not that regret for negligence or error which may animate us to future care or activity, or that repentance of crimes for which, however irrevocable, our Creator has promised to accept it as an attonement; the pain which arises from these causes has very salutary effects, and is every hour extenuating itself by the reparation of

2. Plutarch, *Lives,* "Pyrrhus," xiv.
3. Claudius Aelianus, *Varia Historia,* I (par. 10).

those miscarriages that produce it. Sorrow is properly that state of the mind in which our desires are fixed upon the past, without looking forward to the future, an incessant wish that something were otherwise than it has been, a tormenting and harrassing want of some enjoyment or possession which we have lost, and which no endeavours can possibly regain. Into such anguish many have sunk upon some sudden diminution of their fortune, an un-expected blast of their reputation, or the loss of children or of friends. They have suffered all sensibility of pleasure to be destroyed by a single blow, have given up for ever the hopes of substituting any other object in the room of that which they lament, resigned their lives to gloom and despondency, and worn themselves out in unavailing misery.

Yet so much is this passion the natural consequence of tenderness and endearment, that, however painful and however useless, it is justly reproachful not to feel it on some occasions; and so widely and constantly has it always prevailed, that the laws of some nations, and the customs of others, have limited a time for the external appearances of grief caused by the dissolution of close alliances, and the breach of domestic union.

It seems determined, by the general suffrage of man-kind, that sorrow is to a certain point laudable, as the offspring of love, or at least pardonable as the effect of weakness; but that it ought not to be suffered to increase by indulgence, but must give way, after a stated time, to social duties, and the common avocations of life. It is at first unavoidable, and therefore must be allowed, whether with or without our choice; it may afterwards be admitted as a decent and affectionate testimony of kindness and esteem; something will be extorted by nature, and some-thing may be given to the world. But all beyond the bursts of passion, or the forms of solemnity, is not only useless, but culpable; for we have no right to sacrifice, to the vain longings of affection, that time which providence allows us for the task of our station.

Yet it too often happens that sorrow, thus lawfully entering, gains such a firm possession of the mind, that it is not afterwards to be ejected; the mournful ideas, first violently impressed, and afterwards willingly received, so much engross the attention, as to predominate in every thought, to darken gayety, and perplex ratiocination. An habitual sadness seizes upon the soul, and the faculties are chained to a single object, which can never be contemplated but with hopeless uneasiness.

From this state of dejection it is very difficult to rise to chearfulness and alacrity, and therefore many who have laid down rules of intellectual health, think preservatives easier than remedies, and teach us not to trust ourselves with favourite enjoyments, not to indulge the luxury of fondness, but to keep our minds always suspended in such indifference, that we may change the objects about us without emotion.

An exact compliance with this rule might, perhaps, contribute to tranquillity, but surely it would never produce happiness. He that regards none so much as to be afraid of losing them, must live for ever without the gentle pleasures of sympathy and confidence; he must feel no melting fondness, no warmth of benevolence, nor any of those honest joys which nature annexes to the power of pleasing. And as no man can justly claim more tenderness than he pays, he must forfeit his share in that officious and watchful kindness which love only can dictate, and those lenient endearments by which love only can soften life. He may justly be overlooked and neglected by such as have more warmth in their heart; for who would be the friend of him, whom, with whatever assiduity he may be courted, and with whatever services obliged, his principles will not suffer to make equal returns, and who, when you have exhausted all the instances of good will, can only be prevailed on not to be an enemy?

An attempt to preserve life in a state of neutrality and indifference, is unreasonable and vain. If by excluding joy we could shut out grief, the scheme would deserve very serious attention; but since, however we may debar ourselves from happiness, misery will find its way at many inlets, and the assaults of pain will force our regard, though we may withhold it from the invitations of pleasure, we may surely endeavour to raise life above the middle point of apathy at one time, since it will necessarily sink below it at another.

But though it cannot be reasonable not to gain happiness for fear of losing it, yet it must be confessed, that in proportion to the pleasure of possession, will be for some time our sorrow for the loss; it is therefore the province of the moralist to enquire whether such pains may not quickly give way to mitigation. Some have thought, that the most certain way to clear the heart from its embarrassment is to drag it by force into scenes of merriment. Others imagine, that such a transition is too violent, and recommend rather to sooth it into tranquillity, by making it acquainted with miseries more dreadful and afflictive, and diverting to the calamities of others the regard which we are inclined to fix too closely upon our own misfortunes.

It may be doubted whether either of those remedies will be sufficiently powerful. The efficacy of mirth it is not always easy to try, and the indulgence of melancholy may be suspected to be one of those medicines, which will destroy, if it happens not to cure.

The safe and general antidote against sorrow, is employment. It is commonly observed, that among soldiers and seamen, though there is much kindness, there is little grief; they see their friend fall without any of that lamentation which is indulged in security and idleness, because they have no leisure to spare from the care of themselves; and whoever shall keep his thoughts equally busy, will find himself equally unaffected with irretrievable losses.

Time is observed generally to wear out sorrow, and its effects might doubtless be accelerated by quickening the succession, and enlarging the variety of objects.

> *Si tempore longo*
> *Leniri poterit luctus, tu sperne morari,*
> *Qui sapiet sibi tempus erit.* ————
>
> Grotius.[4]

> 'Tis long e'er time can mitigate your grief;
> To wisdom fly, she quickly brings relief.
>
> F. Lewis.

Sorrow is a kind of rust of the soul, which every new idea contributes in its passage to scour away. It is the putrefaction of stagnant life, and is remedied by exercise and motion.

No. 49. Tuesday, 4 September 1750.

> *Non omnis moriar, multaque pars mei*
> *Vitabit Libitinam, usque ego posterâ*
> *Crescam laude recens.*
>
> Horace, ODES, III.30.6–8.

---

4. Grotius, "Consolatoria ad Patrem," ll. 55–57, in *Poemata Omnia* (Leyden, 1595), p. 332.

Whole Horace shall not die; his songs shall save
The greatest portion from the greedy grave.

Creech.

The first motives of human actions are those appetites
which providence has given to man, in common with the
rest of the inhabitants of the earth. Immediately after our
birth, thirst and hunger incline us to the breast, which we
draw by instinct, like other young creatures, and, when
we are satisfied, we express our uneasiness by importunate
and incessant cries, till we have obtained a place or
posture proper for repose.

The next call that rouses us from a state of inactivity,
is that of our passions; we quickly begin to be sensible of
hope and fear, love and hatred, desire and aversion; these
arising from the power of comparison and reflexion,
extend their range wider, as our reason strengthens, and
our knowledge enlarges. At first we have no thought of
pain, but when we actually feel it; we afterwards begin to
fear it, yet not before it approaches us very nearly; but by
degrees we discover it at a greater distance, and find it
lurking in remote consequences. Our terror in time
improves into caution, and we learn to look round with
vigilance and solicitude, to stop all the avenues at which
misery can enter, and to perform or endure many things
in themselves toilsome and unpleasing, because we know
by reason, or by experience, that our labour will be overbalanced by the reward, that it will either procure some
positive good, or avert some evil greater than itself.

But as the soul advances to a fuller exercise of its
powers, the animal appetites, and the passions immediately arising from them, are not sufficient to find it employment; the wants of nature are soon supplied, the fear of

their return is easily precluded, and something more is
necessary to relieve the long intervals of inactivity, and to
give those faculties, which cannot lie wholly quiescent,
some particular direction. For this reason, new desires,
and artificial passions are by degrees produced; and, from
having wishes only in consequence of our wants, we begin
to feel wants in consequence of our wishes; we persuade
ourselves to set a value upon things which are of no use,
but because we have agreed to value them; things which
can neither satisfy hunger, nor mitigate pain, nor secure
us from any real calamity, and which, therefore, we find
of no esteem among those nations whose artless and
barbarous manners keep them always anxious for the
necessaries of life.

This is the original of avarice, vanity, ambition, and
generally of all those desires which arise from the comparison of our condition with that of others. He that
thinks himself poor, because his neighbour is richer; he
that, like Caesar, would rather be the first man of a village,
than the second in the capital of the world,[1] has apparently kindled in himself desires which he never received
from nature, and acts upon principles established only by
the authority of custom.

Of those adscititious passions, some, as avarice and
envy, are universally condemned; some, as friendship and
curiosity, generally praised; but there are others about
which the suffrages of the wise are divided, and of which
it is doubted, whether they tend most to promote the
happiness, or increase the miseries of mankind.

Of this ambiguous and disputable kind is the love of
fame, a desire of filling the minds of others with admira-

---

1. Plutarch, *Moralia*, 206B, and *Lives*, "Caesar," XI.2.

tion, and of being celebrated by generations to come with praises which we shall not hear. This ardour has been considered by some, as nothing better than splendid madness, as a flame kindled by pride, and fanned by folly; for what, say they, can be more remote from wisdom, than to direct all our actions by the hope of that which is not to exist till we ourselves are in the grave? To pant after that which can never be possessed, and of which the value thus wildly put upon it, arises from this particular condition, that, during life, it is not to be obtained? To gain the favour, and hear the applauses of our contemporaries, is indeed equally desirable with any other prerogative of superiority, because fame may be of use to smooth the paths of life, to terrify opposition, and fortify tranquillity; but to what end shall we be the darlings of mankind, when we can no longer receive any benefits from their favour? It is more reasonable to wish for reputation, while it may yet be enjoyed, as Anacreon calls upon his companions to give him for present use the wine and garlands which they purpose to bestow upon his tomb.[2]

The advocates for the love of fame allege in its vindication, that it is a passion natural and universal; a flame lighted by heaven, and always burning with greatest vigour in the most enlarged and elevated minds. That the desire of being praised by posterity implies a resolution to deserve their praises, and that the folly charged upon it, is only a noble and disinterested generosity, which is not felt, and therefore not understood by those who have been always accustomed to refer every thing to themselves, and whose selfishness has contracted their understandings. That the soul of man, formed for eternal life, naturally springs forward beyond the limits of corporeal existence,

2. *Anacreonta,* Ode IV.

and rejoices to consider herself as cooperating with future ages, and as co-extended with endless duration. That the reproach urged with so much petulance, the reproach of labouring for what cannot be enjoyed, is founded on an opinion which may with great probability be doubted; for since we suppose the powers of the soul to be enlarged by its separation, why should we conclude that its knowledge of sublunary transactions is contracted or extinguished?

Upon an attentive and impartial review of the argument, it will appear that the love of fame is to be regulated, rather than extinguished; and that men should be taught not to be wholly careless about their memory, but to endeavour that they may be remembered chiefly for their virtues, since no other reputation will be able to transmit any pleasure beyond the grave.

It is evident that fame, considered merely as the immortality of a name, is not less likely to be the reward of bad actions than of good; he therefore has no certain principle for the regulation of his conduct, whose single aim is not to be forgotten. And history will inform us, that this blind and undistinguishing appetite of renown has always been uncertain in its effects, and directed by accident or opportunity, indifferently to the benefit or devastation of the world. When Themistocles complained that the trophies of Miltiades hindered him from sleep, he was animated by them to perform the same services in the same cause.[3] But Caesar, when he wept at the sight of Alexander's picture, having no honest opportunities of action, let his ambition break out to the ruin of his country.[4]

3. Plutarch, *Lives*, "Themistocles," III.3-4, and *Moralia*, 185A.

4. Johnson here coalesces the story of Plutarch ("Caesar," XI.3, and *Moralia*, 206B), that Caesar "burst into tears" when reading a history of Alexander, with that of either Dio Cassius or Suetonius. Dio Cassius says

If, therefore, the love of fame is so far indulged by the
mind as to become independent and predominant, it is
dangerous and irregular; but it may be usefully employed
as an inferior and secondary motive, and will serve sometimes to revive our activity, when we begin to languish
and lose sight of that more certain, more valuable, and
more durable reward, which ought always to be our first
hope and our last. But it must be strongly impressed upon
our minds, that virtue is not to be persued as one of the
means to fame, but fame to be accepted as the only
recompence which mortals can bestow on virtue; to be
accepted with complacence, but not sought with eagerness. Simply to be remembered is no advantage; it is a
privilege which satire as well as panegyric can confer, and
is not more enjoyed by Titus or Constantine, than by
Timocreon of Rhodes, of whom we only know from his
epitaph, "that he had eaten many a meal, drunk many a
flaggon, and uttered many a reproach."[5]

> Πολλὰ φαγὼν, καὶ πολλὰ πιὼν, καὶ πολλὰ κακ' εἰπὼν
> Ἀνθρώπους, κεῖμαι Τιμοκρέων Ῥόδιος.

The true satisfaction which is to be drawn from the
consciousness that we shall share the attention of future
times, must arise from the hope, that, with our name, our
virtues will be propagated; and that those whom we cannot benefit in our lives, may receive instruction from our
examples, and incitement from our renown.

---

that "on seeing an image of Alexander," Caesar "groaned aloud"
(XXXVII.52.2); Suetonius, that, on seeing a "statue of Alexander," he
sighed ("The Deified Julius," VII.1).
  5. Simonides, in *Greek Anthology*, VII.348.

No. 60. Saturday, 13 October 1750.

———— *Quid sit pulchrum, quid turpe, quid utile, quid non,*
Plenius et melius Chrysippo et Crantore dicit.

Horace, EPISTLES, I.2.3–4.

Whose works the beautiful and base contain;
Of vice and virtue more instructive rules,
Than all the sober sages of the schools.

Francis.

All joy or sorrow for the happiness or calamities of others is produced by an act of the imagination, that realises the event however fictitious, or approximates it however remote, by placing us, for a time, in the condition of him whose fortune we contemplate; so that we feel, while the deception lasts, whatever motions would be excited by the same good or evil happening to ourselves.

Our passions are therefore more strongly moved, in proportion as we can more readily adopt the pains or pleasures proposed to our minds, by recognising them as once our own, or considering them as naturally incident to our state of life. It is not easy for the most artful writer to give us an interest in happiness or misery, which we think ourselves never likely to feel, and with which we have never yet been made acquainted. Histories of the downfal of kingdoms, and revolutions of empires, are read with great tranquillity; the imperial tragedy pleases common auditors only by its pomp of ornament, and grandeur of ideas; and the man whose faculties have been engrossed by business, and whose heart never fluttered but at the rise or fall of stocks, wonders how the attention can be seized, or the affection agitated by a tale of love.

Those parallel circumstances, and kindred images, to which we readily conform our minds, are, above all other writings, to be found in narratives of the lives of particular persons; and therefore no species of writing seems more worthy of cultivation than biography, since none can be more delightful or more useful, none can more certainly enchain the heart by irresistible interest, or more widely diffuse instruction to every diversity of condition.

The general and rapid narratives of history, which involve a thousand fortunes in the business of a day, and complicate innumerable incidents in one great transaction, afford few lessons applicable to private life, which derives its comforts and its wretchedness from the right or wrong management of things which nothing but their frequency makes considerable, *Parva, si non fiant quotidie,* says Pliny,[1] and which can have no place in those relations which never descend below the consultation of senates, the motions of armies, and the schemes of conspirators.

I have often thought that there has rarely passed a life of which a judicious and faithful narrative would not be useful. For, not only every man has, in the mighty mass of the world, great numbers in the same condition with himself, to whom his mistakes and miscarriages, escapes and expedients, would be of immediate and apparent use; but there is such an uniformity in the state of man, considered apart from adventitious and separable decorations and disguises, that there is scarce any possibility of good or ill, but is common to human kind. A great part of the time of those who are placed at the greatest distance by fortune, or by temper, must unavoidably pass in the same manner; and though, when the claims of

1. *Epistles,* III.1.

nature are satisfied, caprice, and vanity, and accident, begin to produce discriminations and peculiarities, yet the eye is not very heedful, or quick, which cannot discover the same causes still terminating their influence in the same effects, though sometimes accelerated, sometimes retarded, or perplexed by multiplied combinations. We are all prompted by the same motives, all deceived by the same fallacies, all animated by hope, obstructed by danger, entangled by desire, and seduced by pleasure.

It is frequently objected to relations of particular lives, that they are not distinguished by any striking or wonderful vicissitudes. The scholar who passed his life among his books, the merchant who conducted only his own affairs, the priest, whose sphere of action was not extended beyond that of his duty, are considered as no proper objects of publick regard, however they might have excelled in their several stations, whatever might have been their learning, integrity, and piety. But this notion arises from false measures of excellence and dignity, and must be eradicated by considering, that, in the esteem of uncorrupted reason, what is of most use is of most value.

It is, indeed, not improper to take honest advantages of prejudice, and to gain attention by a celebrated name; but the business of the biographer is often to pass slightly over those performances and incidents, which produce vulgar greatness, to lead the thoughts into domestick privacies, and display the minute details of daily life, where exterior appendages are cast aside, and men excel each other only by prudence and by virtue. The account of Thuanus is, with great propriety, said by its author to have been written, that it might lay open to posterity the private and familiar character of that man, *cujus ingenium et candorem ex ipsius scriptis sunt olim semper miraturi,* whose candour and genius will to the end of time be by his writings preserved in admiration.[2]

There are many invisible circumstances which, whether we read as enquirers after natural or moral knowledge, whether we intend to enlarge our science, or increase our virtue, are more important than publick occurrences. Thus Salust, the great master of nature, has not forgot, in his account of Catiline, to remark that "his walk was now quick, and again slow," as an indication of a mind revolving something with violent commotion.[3] Thus the story of Melancthon affords a striking lecture on the value of time, by informing us, that when he made an appointment, he expected not only the hour, but the minute to be fixed, that the day might not run out in the idleness of suspense;[4] and all the plans and enterprizes of De Witt are now of less importance to the world, than that part of his personal character which represents him as "careful of his health, and negligent of his life."[5]

But biography has often been allotted to writers who seem very little acquainted with the nature of their task, or very negligent about the performance. They rarely afford any other account than might be collected from publick papers, but imagine themselves writing a life when they exhibit a chronological series of actions or preferments; and so little regard the manners or behaviour of their heroes, that more knowledge may be

2. *Historiarum Sui Temporis* (1733), VII, pt. IV, p. 3, n. (col. 2), printing the commentary of Nicolaus Rigaltius. A few days before his death, Johnson told John Nichols he "seriously entertained the thought of translating Thuanus" *(Life,* IV.410).

3. *De Coniuratione Catilinae,* XV.5.

4. Joachim Camerarius (1500–1574), *Vita Melanchthonis* (1777), p. 62.

5. Sir William Temple, "Essay on the Cure of Gout," *Works* (1770), III.244.

gained of a man's real character, by a short conversation with one of his servants, than from a formal and
studied narrative, begun with his pedigree, and ended
with his funeral.

If now and then they condescend to inform the world
of particular facts, they are not always so happy as to select the most important. I know not well what advantage
posterity can receive from the only circumstance by
which Tickell has distinguished Addison from the rest
of mankind, "the irregularity of his pulse"[6]: nor can I
think myself overpaid for the time spent in reading the
life of Malherb, by being enabled to relate, after the
learned biographer, that Malherb had two predominant
opinions; one, that the looseness of a single woman might
destroy all her boast of ancient descent; the other, that
the French beggars made use very improperly and bar-
barously of the phrase "noble Gentleman," because either
word included the sense of both.[7]

There are, indeed, some natural reasons why these
narratives are often written by such as were not likely to
give much instruction or delight, and why most accounts
of particular persons are barren and useless. If a life be
delayed till interest and envy are at an end, we may hope
for impartiality, but must expect little intelligence; for
the incidents which give excellence to biography are of a
volatile and evanescent kind, such as soon escape the
memory, and are rarely transmitted by tradition. We
know how few can portray a living acquaintance, except
by his most prominent and observable particularities, and
the grosser features of his mind; and it may be easily
imagined how much of this little knowledge may be

6. Preface, Addison, *Works* (1721), I.xvi.

7. Honorat de Bueil, Marquis de Racan, "Mémoirs pour la vie de
Malherbe," *Oeuvres Complètes* (1857), I.258–59, 265.

lost in imparting it, and how soon a succession of copies will lose all resemblance of the original.

If the biographer writes from personal knowledge, and makes haste to gratify the publick curiosity, there is danger lest his interest, his fear, his gratitude, or his tenderness, overpower his fidelity, and tempt him to conceal, if not to invent. There are many who think it an act of piety to hide the faults or failings of their friends, even when they can no longer suffer by their detection; we therefore see whole ranks of characters adorned with uniform panegyrick, and not to be known from one another, but by extrinsick and casual circumstances. "Let me remember," says Hale, "when I find myself inclined to pity a criminal, that there is likewise a pity due to the country."[8] If we owe regard to the memory of the dead, there is yet more respect to be paid to knowledge, to virtue, and to truth.

From No. 63. Tuesday, 23 October 1750.

―――――― *Habebat saepe ducentos,*
Saepe decem servos; modò reges atque tetrarchas,
Omnia magna loquens: modò, sit mihi mensa tripes, et
Concha salis puri, et toga, quae defendere frigus,
Quamvis crassa, queat.

Horace, SATIRES, I.3.11–15.

Now with two hundred slaves he crowds his train;
Now walks with ten. In high and haughty strain
At morn, of kings and governors he prates:
At night ―――――― "A frugal table, O ye fates,
A little shell the sacred salt to hold,
And clothes, tho' coarse, to keep me from the cold."

Francis.

8. Gilbert Burnet, *Life and Death of Sir Matthew Hale* (1805), p. 39.

.   .   .   .

Irresolution and mutability are often the faults of men, whose views are wide, and whose imagination is vigorous and excursive, because they cannot confine their thoughts within their own boundaries of action, but are continually ranging over all the scenes of human existence, and consequently, are often apt to conceive that they fall upon new regions of pleasure, and start new possibilities of happiness. Thus they are busied with a perpetual succession of schemes, and pass their lives in alternate elation and sorrow, for want of that calm and immoveable acquiescence in their condition, by which men of slower understandings are fixed for ever to a certain point, or led on in the plain beaten track, which their fathers, and grandsires, have trod before them.

Of two conditions of life equally inviting to the prospect, that will always have the disadvantage which we have already tried; because the evils which we have felt we cannot extenuate; and tho' we have, perhaps from nature, the power as well of aggravating the calamity which we fear, as of heightening the blessing we expect, yet in those meditations which we indulge by choice, and which are not forced upon the mind by necessity, we have always the art of fixing our regard upon the more pleasing images, and suffer hope to dispose the lights by which we look upon futurity.

The good and ill of different modes of life are sometimes so equally opposed, that perhaps no man ever yet made his choice between them upon a full conviction, and adequate knowledge; and therefore fluctuation of will is not more wonderful, when they are proposed to the election, than oscillations of a beam charged with equal weights. The mind no sooner imagines itself determined by some prevalent advantage, than some convenience of equal weight is discovered on the other side, and the resolutions which are suggested by the nicest examination, are often repented as soon as they are taken.

* * * *

From No. 64. Saturday, 27 October 1750.[1]

Idem velle, et idem nolle, ea demum firma amicitia est.
Sallust, DE CONIURATIONE CATILINAE, xx.4.

To live in friendship, is to have the same desires and
the same aversions.

* * * *

That friendship may be at once fond and lasting, there must not only be equal virtue on each part, but virtue of the same kind; not only the same end must be proposed, but the same means must be approved by both. We are often, by superficial accomplishments and accidental endearments, induced to love those whom we cannot esteem; we are sometimes, by great abilities and incontestable evidences of virtue, compelled to esteem those whom we cannot love. But friendship, compounded of esteem and love, derives from one its tenderness, and its permanence from the other; and therefore requires not only that its candidates should gain the judgement, but that they should attract the affections; that they should not only be firm in the day of distress, but gay in the hour of jollity; not only useful in exigences, but pleasing in familiar life; their presence should give chearfulness as well as courage, and dispel alike the gloom of fear and of melancholy.

1. Cf. *Idler* 23, on friendship.

•   •   •   •   •

That man will not be long agreeable, whom we see only in times of seriousness and severity; and therefore, to maintain the softness and serenity of benevolence, it is necessary that friends partake each others pleasures as well as cares, and be led to the same diversions by similitude of taste. This is, however, not to be considered as equally indispensable with conformity of principles, because any man may honestly, according to the precepts of Horace,[2] resign the gratifications of taste to the humour of another, and friendship may well deserve the sacrifice of pleasure, though not of conscience.

It was once confessed to me, by a painter, that no professor of his art ever loved another. This declaration is so far justified by the knowledge of life, as to damp the hopes of warm and constant friendship, between men whom their studies have made competitors, and whom every favourer and every censurer are hourly inciting against each other. The utmost expectation that experience can warrant, is, that they should forbear open hostilities and secret machinations, and when the whole fraternity is attacked, be able to unite against a common foe. Some however, though few, may perhaps be found, in whom emulation has not been able to overpower generosity, who are distinguished from lower beings by nobler motives than the love of fame, and can preserve the sacred flame of friendship from the gusts of pride, and the rubbish of interest.

Friendship is seldom lasting but between equals, or where the superiority on one side is reduced by some equivalent advantage on the other. Benefits which cannot be repaid, and obligations which cannot be discharged,

2. *Epistles*, II.2.111–13.

are not commonly found to increase affection; they excite gratitude indeed, and heighten veneration, but commonly take away that easy freedom, and familiarity of intercourse, without which, though there may be fidelity, and zeal, and admiration, there cannot be friendship. Thus imperfect are all earthly blessings; the great effect of friendship is beneficence, yet by the first act of uncommon kindness it is endangered, like plants that bear their fruit and die. Yet this consideration ought not to restrain bounty, or repress compassion; for duty is to be preferred before convenience, and he that loses part of the pleasures of friendship by his generosity, gains in its place the gratulation of his conscience.

No. 71. Tuesday, 20 November 1750.

Vivere quod propero pauper, nec inutilis annis
Da veniam, properat vivere nemo satis.

Martial, II.90.3–4.

True, sir, to live I haste, your pardon give,
For tell me, who makes haste enough to live?

F. Lewis.

Many words and sentences are so frequently heard in the mouths of men, that a superficial observer is inclined to believe, that they must contain some primary principle, some great rule of action, which it is proper always to have present to the attention, and by which the use of every hour is to be adjusted. Yet, if we consider the conduct of those sententious philosophers, it will often be found, that they repeat these aphorisms, merely because they have somewhere heard them, because they have nothing else to say, or because they think veneration gained by such appearances of wisdom, but that no ideas are annexed to the words, and that, according to the old blunder of the followers of Aristotle, their souls are mere pipes or organs, which transmit sounds, but do not understand them.[1]

Of this kind is the well known and well attested position, "that life is short," which may be heard among mankind by an attentive auditor, many times a day, but which never yet within my reach of observation left any impression upon the mind; and perhaps if my readers will turn their thoughts back upon their old friends, they will find it difficult to call a single man to remembrance, who appeared to know that life was short till he was about to lose it.

It is observable that Horace, in his account of the characters of men, as they are diversified by the various influence of time, remarks, that the old man is *dilator, spe longus*, given to procrastination, and inclined to extend his hopes to a great distance.[2] So far are we, generally, from thinking what we often say of the shortness of life, that at the time when it is necessarily shortest, we form projects which we delay to execute, indulge such expectations as nothing but a long train of events can gratify, and suffer those passions to gain upon us, which are only excusable in the prime of life.

These reflections were lately excited in my mind, by an evening's conversation with my friend Prospero, who at the age of fifty-five, has bought an estate, and is now

1. The allusion is unclear. He may possibly be thinking of Swift's burlesque of the Aeolists *(Tale of a Tub,* sec. 8, esp. pars. 1–3). The passage in Aristotle, on which this sort of mechanism could be based, is the description of the soul not as simple or self-contained, but as the entelechy or "first actuality of a natural body furnished with organs" *(De Anima* II.1.412b, 5–6).

2. *Ars Poetica,* l. 172.

contriving to dispose and cultivate it with uncommon elegance. His great pleasure is to walk among stately trees, and lye musing in the heat of noon under their shade; he is therefore maturely considering how he shall dispose his walks and his groves, and has at last determined to send for the best plans from Italy, and forbear planting till the next season.

Thus is life trifled away in preparations to do what never can be done, if it be left unattempted till all the requisites which imagination can suggest are gathered together. Where our design terminates only in our own satisfaction, the mistake is of no great importance; for the pleasure of expecting enjoyment, is often greater than that of obtaining it, and the completion of almost every wish is found a disappointment; but when many others are interested in an undertaking, when any design is formed, in which the improvement or security of mankind is involved, nothing is more unworthy either of wisdom or benevolence, than to delay it from time to time, or to forget how much every day that passes over us, takes away from our power, and how soon an idle purpose to do an action, sinks into a mournful wish that it had once been done.

We are frequently importuned, by the bacchanalian writers, to lay hold on the present hour, to catch the pleasures within our reach, and remember that futurity is not at our command.

Τὸ ῥόδον ἀκμάζει βαιὸν χρόνον· ἤν δὲ παρέλθῃ,
Ζητῶν εὑρήσεις οὐ ῥόδον, ἀλλὰ βάτον.[3]

Soon fades the rose; once past the fragrant hour,
The loiterer finds a bramble for a flow'r.

3. *Greek Anthology*, XI.53. Johnson's translation *(Poems,* p. 133).

But surely these exhortations may, with equal propriety, be applied to better purposes; it may be at least inculcated, that pleasures are more safely postponed than virtues, and that greater loss is suffered by missing an opportunity of doing good, than an hour of giddy frolick and noisy merriment.

When Baxter had lost a thousand pounds, which he had laid up for the erection of a school, he used frequently to mention the misfortune, as an incitement to be charitable while God gives the power of bestowing, and considered himself as culpable in some degree for having left a good action in the hands of chance, and suffered his benevolence to be defeated for want of quickness and diligence.[4]

It is lamented by Hearne, the learned antiquary of Oxford, that this general forgetfulness of the fragility of life, has remarkably infected the students of monuments and records; as their employment consists first in collecting and afterwards in arranging or abstracting what libraries afford them, they ought to amass no more than they can digest; but when they have undertaken a work, they go on searching and transcribing, call for new supplies, when they are already overburdened, and at last leave their work unfinished. "It is," says he, "the business of a good antiquary, as of a good man, to have mortality always before him."

Thus, not only in the slumber of sloth, but in the dissipation of ill directed industry, is the shortness of life generally forgotten. As some men lose their hours in laziness, because they suppose, that there is time enough for the reparation of neglect; others busy themselves in pro-

---

4. Edmund Calamy, *Abridgement of Mr. Baxter's . . . Life and Times* (1702), pp. 596–97. Richard Baxter (1615–91), an eloquent, high-minded Puritan minister, was the author of *Saint's Everlasting Rest* (1650).

viding that no length of life may want employment; and it often happens, that sluggishness and activity are equally surprised by the last summons, and perish not more differently from each other, than the fowl that received the shot in her flight, from her that is killed upon the bush.

Among the many improvements, made by the last centuries in human knowledge, may be numbered the exact calculations of the value of life; but whatever may be their use in traffick, they seem very little to have advanced morality. They have hitherto been rather applied to the acquisition of money, than of wisdom; the computer refers none of his calculations to his own tenure, but persists, in contempt of probability, to foretel old age to himself, and believes that he is marked out to reach the utmost verge of human existence, and see thousands and ten thousands fall into the grave.

So deeply is this fallacy rooted in the heart, and so strongly guarded by hope and fear against the approach of reason, that neither science nor experience can shake it, and we act as if life were without end, though we see and confess its uncertainty and shortness.

Divines have, with great strength and ardour, shewn the absurdity of delaying reformation and repentance; a degree of folly indeed, which sets eternity to hazard. It is the same weakness in proportion to the importance of the neglect, to transfer any care, which now claims our attention, to a future time; we subject ourselves to needless dangers from accidents which early diligence would have obviated, or perplex our minds by vain precautions, and make provision for the execution of designs, of which the opportunity once missed never will return.

As he that lives longest lives but a little while, every man may be certain that he has no time to waste. The duties of life are commensurate to its duration, and every day brings its task, which if neglected, is doubled on the morrow. But he that has already trifled away those months and years, in which he should have laboured, must remember that he has now only a part of that of which the whole is little; and that since the few moments remaining are to be considered as the last trust of heaven, not one is to be lost.

No. 72. Saturday, 24 November 1750.

Omnis Aristippum decuit status, et color, et res,
Sectantem majora fere; presentibus aequum.

Horace, EPISTLES, I.17.23–24.

Yet Aristippus ev'ry dress became;
In ev'ry various change of life the same:
And though he aim'd at things of higher kind,
Yet to the present held an equal mind.

Francis.

TO THE RAMBLER.

SIR,

Those who exalt themselves into the chair of instruction, without enquiring whether any will submit to their authority, have not sufficiently considered how much of human life passes in little incidents, cursory conversation, slight business, and casual amusements;[1] and therefore they have endeavoured only to inculcate the more awful virtues, without condescending to regard those petty qualities, which grow important only by their frequency, and which though they produce no single acts of heroism, nor astonish us by great events, yet are every moment exerting their influence upon us, and make the draught

1. Cf. *Ramblers* 68 (par. 3) and 98 (par. 1).

of life sweet or bitter by imperceptible instillations. They operate unseen and unregarded, as change of air makes us sick or healthy, though we breathe it without attention, and only know the particles that impregnate it by their salutary or malignant effects.

You have shewn yourself not ignorant of the value of those subaltern endowments, yet have hitherto neglected to recommend good humour to the world, though a little reflection will shew you that it is the "balm of being,"[2] the quality to which all that adorns or elevates mankind must owe its power of pleasing. Without good humour, learning and bravery can only confer that superiority which swells the heart of the lion in the desart, where he roars without reply, and ravages without resistance. Without good humour, virtue may awe by its dignity, and amaze by its brightness; but must always be viewed at a distance, and will scarcely gain a friend or attract an imitator.[3]

Good humour may be defined a habit of being pleased;[4] a constant and perennial softness of manner, easiness of approach, and suavity of disposition; like that which every man perceives in himself, when the first transports of new felicity have subsided, and his thoughts are only kept in motion by a slow succession of soft impulses. Good humour is a state between gayety and

2. *Paradise Lost*, XI.

3. Johnson told Mr. Thrale that he had never even "sought to please till past thirty years old, considering the matter as hopeless" (*Miscellanies*, I.318). Caustic remarks on the negative quality of "good humor" are frequent; cf. *Rambler* 188 (esp. pars. 4–6, 10–11) and the sketches of Gulosulus in *Rambler* 206 and Phil Gentle in *Idler* 83. The sentiment in *Ramblers* 74, 76, and 112 is more significant because it is hard-earned, represents a quality he himself increasingly struggled to attain, and in later years hoped he had acquired (cf. e.g. *Life*, II.362).

4. "Men seldom give pleasure, where they are not pleased themselves" (*Rambler* 74, par. 1).

unconcern; the act or emanation of a mind at leisure to regard the gratification of another.

It is imagined by many, that whenever they aspire to please, they are required to be merry, and to shew the gladness of their souls by flights of pleasantry, and bursts of laughter. But, though these men may be for a time heard with applause and admiration, they seldom delight us long. We enjoy them a little, and then retire to easiness and good humour, as the eye gazes a while on eminences glittering with the sun, but soon turns aching away to verdure and to flowers.

Gayety is to good humour as animal perfumes to vegetable fragrance; the one overpowers weak spirits, and the other recreates and revives them. Gayety seldom fails to give some pain; the hearers either strain their faculties to accompany its towerings, or are left behind in envy and despair. Good humour boasts no faculties which every one does not believe in his own power, and pleases principally by not offending.[5]

It is well known that the most certain way to give any man pleasure, is to persuade him that you receive pleasure from him,[6] to encourage him to freedom and confidence, and to avoid any such appearance of superiority as may overbear and depress him. We see many that by this art only, spend their days in the midst of caresses, invitations, and civilities; and without any extraordinary qualities or attainments, are the universal favourites of both sexes, and certainly find a friend in every place. The darlings of the world will, indeed, be generally found such as excite neither jealousy nor fear, and are not considered as candidates for any eminent degree of reputation, but

5. Cf. *Life,* III.149, and *Rambler* 160 (par. 10).

6. "We naturally endear to ourselves those to whom we impart any kind of pleasure" (*Rambler* 148, par. 5).

content themselves with common accomplishments, and endeavour rather to solicit kindness than to raise esteem; therefore in assemblies and places of resort it seldom fails to happen, that though at the entrance of some particular person every face brightens with gladness, and every hand is extended in salutation, yet if you persue him beyond the first exchange of civilities, you will find him of very small importance, and only welcome to the company, as one by whom all conceive themselves admired, and with whom any one is at liberty to amuse himself when he can find no other auditor or companion, as one with whom all are at ease, who will hear a jest without criticism, and a narrative without contradiction, who laughs with every wit, and yields to every disputer.[7]

There are many whose vanity always inclines them to associate with those from whom they have no reason to fear mortification; and there are times in which the wise and the knowing are willing to receive praise without the labour of deserving it, in which the most elevated mind is willing to descend, and the most active to be at rest. All therefore are at some hour or another fond of companions whom they can entertain upon easy terms, and who will relieve them from solitude, without condemning them to vigilance and caution. We are most inclined to love when we have nothing to fear, and he that encourages us to please ourselves, will not be long without preference in our affection to those whose learning holds us at the distance of pupils, or whose wit calls all attention from us, and leaves us without importance and without regard.

It is remarked by Prince Henry, when he sees Falstaff lying on the ground, that "he could have better spared

7. Cf. *Rambler* 188.

a better man."[8] He was well acquainted with the vices and follies of him whom he lamented, but while his conviction compelled him to do justice to superior qualities, his tenderness still broke out at the remembrance of Falstaff, of the chearful companion, the loud buffoon, with whom he had passed his time in all the luxury of idleness, who had gladded him with unenvied merriment, and whom he could at once enjoy and despise.

You may perhaps think this account of those who are distinguished for their good humour, not very consistent with the praises which I have bestowed upon it. But surely nothing can more evidently shew the value of this quality, than that it recommends those who are destitute of all other excellencies, and procures regard to the trifling, friendship to the worthless, and affection to the dull.

Good humour is indeed generally degraded by the characters in which it is found; for being considered as a cheap and vulgar quality, we find it often neglected by those that having excellencies of higher reputation and brighter splendor, perhaps imagine that they have some right to gratify themselves at the expence of others, and are to demand compliance, rather than to practise it. It is by some unfortunate mistake that almost all those who have any claim to esteem or love, press their pretensions with too little consideration of others. This mistake my own interest as well as my zeal for general happiness makes me desirous to rectify, for I have a friend, who because he knows his own fidelity, and usefulness, is never willing to sink into a companion. I have a wife whose beauty first subdued me, and whose wit confirmed her conquest, but whose beauty now serves no other purpose

8. *Henry IV*, pt. I, v.4.104.

than to entitle her to tyranny, and whose wit is only used to justify perverseness.

Surely nothing can be more unreasonable than to lose the will to please, when we are conscious of the power, or show more cruelty than to chuse any kind of influence before that of kindness. He that regards the welfare of others, should make his virtue approachable, that it may be loved and copied; and he that considers the wants which every man feels, or will feel of external assistance, must rather wish to be surrounded by those that love him, than by those that admire his excellencies, or sollicit his favours; for admiration ceases with novelty,[9] and interest gains its end and retires. A man whose great qualities want the ornament of superficial attractions, is like a naked mountain with mines of gold, which will be frequented only till the treasure is exhausted.

I am, &c.

PHILOMIDES.

No. 73. Tuesday, 27 November 1750.

Stulte quid heu votis frustra puerilibus optas
Quae non ulla tulit, fertve, feretve dies.

Ovid, TRISTIA, III.8.11–12.

Why thinks the fool with childish hope to see
What neither is, nor was, nor e'er shall be?

Elphinston.

TO THE RAMBLER.

SIR,

If you feel any of that compassion, which you recommend to others, you will not disregard a case which I have

9. "Admiration begins where acquaintance ceases . . ." (*Rambler* 77, par. 9).

reason from observation to believe very common, and which I know by experience to be very miserable. And though the querulous are seldom received with great ardour of kindness, I hope to escape the mortification of finding that my lamentations spread the contagion of impatience, and produce anger rather than tenderness. I write not merely to vent the swelling of my heart, but to enquire by what means I may recover my tranquillity; and shall endeavour at brevity in my narrative, having long known that complaint quickly tires, however elegant, or however just.

I was born in a remote county, of a family that boasts alliances with the greatest names in English history, and extends its claims of affinity to the Tudors and Plantagenets. My ancestors, by little and little, wasted their patrimony, till my father had not enough left for the support of a family, without descending to the cultivation of his own grounds, being condemned to pay three sisters the fortunes allotted them by my grandfather, who is suspected to have made his will when he was incapable of adjusting properly the claims of his children, and who, perhaps without design, enriched his daughters by beggaring his son. My aunts being, at the death of their father, neither young nor beautiful, nor very eminent for softness of behaviour, were suffered to live unsolicited, and by accumulating the interest of their portions grew every day richer and prouder. My father pleased himself with foreseeing that the possessions of those ladies must revert at last to the hereditary estate, and, that his family might lose none of its dignity, resolved to keep me untainted with a lucrative employment; whenever therefore I discovered any inclination to the improvement of my condition, my mother never failed to put me in mind of my birth, and charged me to do nothing with which I might be reproached, when I should come to my aunts' estate.

In all the perplexities or vexations which want of money brought upon us, it was our constant practice to have recourse to futurity. If any of our neighbours surpassed us in appearance, we went home and contrived an equipage, with which the death of my aunts was to supply us. If any purse-proud upstart was deficient in respect, vengeance was referred to the time in which our estate was to be repaired. We registered every act of civility and rudeness, enquired the number of dishes at every feast, and minuted the furniture of every house, that we might, when the hour of affluence should come, be able to eclipse all their splendor, and surpass all their magnificence.

Upon plans of elegance and schemes of pleasure the day rose and set, and the year went round unregarded, while we were busied in laying out plantations on ground not yet our own, and deliberating whether the manor-house should be rebuilt or repaired. This was the amusement of our leisure, and the solace of our exigencies; we met together only to contrive how our approaching fortune should be enjoyed; for in this our conversation always ended, on whatever subject it began. We had none of the collateral interests, which diversify the life of others with joys and hopes, but had turned our whole attention on one event, which we could neither hasten nor retard, and had no other object of curiosity, than the health or sickness of my aunts, of which we were careful to procure very exact and early intelligence.

This visionary opulence for a while soothed our imagination, but afterwards fired our wishes, and exasperated our necessities, and my father could not always restrain himself from exclaiming, that "no creature had so many

lives as a cat and an old maid." At last upon the recovery
of his sister from an ague, which she was supposed to
have caught by sparing fire, he began to lose his stomach,
and four months afterwards sunk into the grave.

My mother, who loved her husband, survived him but
a little while, and left me the sole heir of their lands,
their schemes, and their wishes. As I had not enlarged
my conceptions either by books or conversation, I dif-
fered only from my father by the freshness of my cheeks,
and the vigour of my step; and, like him, gave way to no
thoughts but of enjoying the wealth which my aunts were
hoarding.

At length the eldest fell ill. I paid the civilities and
compliments which sickness requires with the utmost
punctuality. I dreamed every night of escutcheons and
white gloves, and enquired every morning at an early
hour, whether there were any news of my dear aunt. At
last a messenger was sent to inform me that I must come
to her without the delay of a moment. I went and heard
her last advice, but opening her will found that she had
left her fortune to her second sister.

I hung my head; the younger sister threatened to be
married, and every thing was disappointment and discontent. I was in danger of losing irreparably one third
of my hopes, and was condemned still to wait for the
rest. Of part of my terror I was soon eased; for the youth,
whom his relations would have compelled to marry the
old lady, after innumerable stipulations, articles, and
settlements, ran away with the daughter of his father's
groom; and my aunt, upon this conviction of the perfidy
of man, resolved never to listen more to amorous
addresses.

Ten years longer I dragged the shackles of expectation, without ever suffering a day to pass, in which I did

not compute how much my chance was improved of being rich tomorrow. At last the second lady died, after a short illness, which yet was long enough to afford her time for the disposal of her estate, which she gave to me after the death of her sister.

I was now relieved from part of my misery; a larger fortune, though not in my power, was certain and unalienable; nor was there now any danger, that I might at last be frustrated of my hopes by a fret of dotage, the flatteries of a chambermaid, the whispers of a tale-bearer, or the officiousness of a nurse. But my wealth was yet in reversion, my aunt was to be buried before I could emerge to grandeur and pleasure; and there were yet, according to my father's observation, nine lives between me and happiness.

I however lived on, without any clamours of discontent, and comforted myself with considering, that all are mortal, and they who are continually decaying, must at last be destroyed.

But let no man from this time suffer his felicity to depend on the death of his aunt. The good gentlewoman was very regular in her hours, and simple in her diet, and in walking or sitting still, waking or sleeping, had always in view the preservation of her health. She was subject to no disorder but hypochondriac dejection; by which, without intention, she encreased my miseries, for whenever the weather was cloudy, she would take her bed and send me notice that her time was come. I went with all the haste of eagerness, and sometimes received passionate injunctions to be kind to her maid, and directions how the last offices should be performed; but if before my arrival the sun happened to break out, or the wind to change, I met her at the door, or found her in the garden, bustling and vigilant, with all the tokens of long life.

Sometimes however she fell into distempers, and was thrice given over by the doctor, yet she found means of slipping through the gripe of death, and after having tortured me three months at each time with violent alternations of hope and fear, came out of her chamber without any other hurt than the loss of flesh, which in a few weeks she recovered by broths and jellies.

As most have sagacity sufficient to guess at the desires of an heir, it was the constant practice of those who were hoping at second hand, and endeavoured to secure my favour against the time when I should be rich, to pay their court, by informing me that my aunt began to droop, that she had lately a bad night, that she coughed feebly, and that she could never climb May hill; or at least, that the autumn would carry her off. Thus was I flattered in the winter with the piercing winds of March, and in summer, with the fogs of September. But she lived through spring and fall, and set heat and cold at defiance, till after near half a century, I buried her on the fourteenth of last June, aged ninety-three years, five months, and six days.

For two months after her death I was rich, and was pleased with that obsequiousness and reverence which wealth instantaneously procures. But this joy is now past, and I have returned again to my old habit of wishing. Being accustomed to give the future full power over my mind, and to start away from the scene before me to some expected enjoyment, I deliver up myself to the tyranny of every desire which fancy suggests, and long for a thousand things which I am unable to procure. Money has much less power, than is ascribed to it by those that want it. I had formed schemes which I cannot execute, I had supposed events which do not come to pass, and the rest of my life must pass in craving solicitude, unless you can find some remedy for a mind, corrupted with an inveterate disease of wishing, and unable to think on any thing but wants, which reason tells me will never be supplied.

I am, &c.
CUPIDUS.

No. 76. Saturday, 8 December 1750.

——————— Silvis ubi passim
Palantes error certo de tramite pellit,
Ille sinistrorsum, hic dextrorsum abit, unus utrique
Error, sed variis illudit partibus.

Horace, SATIRES, II.3.48–51.

While mazy error draws mankind astray
From truth's sure path, each takes his devious way:
One to the right, one to the left recedes,
Alike deluded, as each fancy leads.

Elphinston.

It is easy for every man, whatever be his character with others, to find reasons for esteeming himself, and therefore censure, contempt, or conviction of crimes, seldom deprive him of his own favour. Those, indeed, who can see only external facts, may look upon him with abhorrence, but when he calls himself to his own tribunal, he finds every fault, if not absolutely effaced, yet so much palliated by the goodness of his intention, and the cogency of the motive, that very little guilt or turpitude remains; and when he takes a survey of the whole complication of his character, he discovers so many latent excellencies, so many virtues that want but an opportunity to exert themselves in act, and so many kind wishes for universal happiness, that he looks on himself as suffering unjustly under the infamy of single failings, while the general temper of his mind is unknown or unregarded.

It is natural to mean well, when only abstracted ideas of virtue are proposed to the mind, and no particular passion turns us aside from rectitude;[1] and so willing is every man to flatter himself, that the difference between approving laws, and obeying them, is frequently forgotten;[2] he that acknowledges the obligations of morality, and pleases his vanity with enforcing them to others, concludes himself zealous in the cause of virtue, though he has no longer any regard to her precepts, than they conform to his own desires; and counts himself among her warmest lovers, because he praises her beauty, though every rival steals away his heart.

There are, however, great numbers who have little recourse to the refinements of speculation, but who yet live at peace with themselves, by means which require less understanding, or less attention. When their hearts are burthened with the consciousness of a crime, instead of seeking for some remedy within themselves, they look round upon the rest of mankind, to find others tainted with the same guilt: they please themselves with observing, that they have numbers on their side; and that though they are hunted out from the society of good men, they are not likely to be condemned to solitude.

It may be observed, perhaps without exception, that none are so industrious to detect wickedness, or so ready to impute it, as they whose crimes are apparent and confessed. They envy an unblemished reputation, and what

1. Cf. "Pope," *Lives,* III.207–08 (par. 275).
2. Cf. *Rambler* 28, above, and n. 2.

they envy they are busy to destroy: they are unwilling
to suppose themselves meaner, and more corrupt than
others, and therefore willingly pull down from their elevations those with whom they cannot rise to an equality.
No man yet was ever wicked without secret discontent,
and according to the different degrees of remaining virtue, or unextinguished reason, he either endeavours to
reform himself, or corrupt others; either to regain the
station which he has quitted, or prevail on others to
imitate his defection.

It has been always considered as an alleviation of
misery not to suffer alone, even when union and society
can contribute nothing to resistance or escape; some comfort of the same kind seems to incite wickedness to seek
associates, though indeed another reason may be given,
for as guilt is propagated the power of reproach is diminished, and among numbers equally detestable every individual may be sheltered from shame, though not from
conscience.

Another lenitive by which the throbs of the breast are
assuaged, is, the contemplation, not of the same, but
of different crimes. He that cannot justify himself by his
resemblance to others, is ready to try some other expedient, and to enquire what will rise to his advantage from
opposition and dissimilitude. He easily finds some faults
in every human being, which he weighs against his own,
and easily makes them preponderate while he keeps the
balance in his own hand, and throws in or takes out at
his pleasure circumstances that make them heavier or
lighter. He then triumphs in his comparative purity, and
sets himself at ease, not because he can refute the charges
advanced against him, but because he can censure his
accusers with equal justice, and no longer fears the arrows

of reproach, when he has stored his magazine of malice with weapons equally sharp and equally envenomed.

This practice, though never just, is yet specious and artful, when the censure is directed against deviations to the contrary extreme. The man who is branded with cowardice, may, with some appearance of propriety, turn all his force of argument against a stupid contempt of life, and rash precipitation into unnecessary danger. Every recession from temerity is an approach towards cowardice, and though it be confessed that bravery, like other virtues, stands between faults on either hand, yet the place of the middle point may always be disputed; he may therefore often impose upon careless understandings, by turning the attention wholly from himself, and keeping it fixed invariably on the opposite fault; and by shewing how many evils are avoided by his behaviour, he may conceal for a time those which are incurred.

But vice has not always opportunities or address for such artful subterfuges; men often extenuate their own guilt, only by vague and general charges upon others, or endeavour to gain rest to themselves, by pointing some other prey to the persuit of censure.

Every whisper of infamy is industriously circulated, every hint of suspicion eagerly improved, and every failure of conduct joyfully published, by those whose interest it is, that the eye and voice of the publick should be employed on any rather than on themselves.

All these artifices, and a thousand others equally vain and equally despicable, are incited by that conviction of the deformity of wickedness, from which none can set himself free, and by an absurd desire to separate the cause from the effects, and to enjoy the profit of crimes without suffering the shame. Men are willing to try all methods

of reconciling guilt and quiet, and when their understandings are stubborn and uncomplying, raise their passions against them, and hope to over-power their own
knowledge.

It is generally not so much the desire of men, sunk into
depravity, to deceive the world as themselves, for when
no particular circumstances make them dependant on
others, infamy disturbs them little, but as it revives their
remorse, and is echoed to them from their own hearts.
The sentence most dreaded is that of reason and conscience, which they would engage on their side at any
price but the labours of duty, and the sorrows of repentance. For this purpose every seducement and fallacy is
sought, the hopes still rest upon some new experiment till
life is at an end; and the last hour steals on unperceived,
while the faculties are engaged in resisting reason, and
repressing the sense of the divine disapprobation.

No. 79. Tuesday, 18 December 1750.

*Tam saepe nostrum decipi Fabullum, quid
Miraris, Aule? Semper bonus homo tiro est.*

> Martial, XII.51.

You wonder I've so little wit,
Friend John, so often to be bit,—
None better guard against a cheat
Than he who is a knave compleat.

> F. Lewis.

Suspicion, however necessary it may be to our safe passage through ways beset on all sides by fraud and malice,
has been always considered, when it exceeds the common
measures, as a token of depravity and corruption; and a
Greek writer of sentences has laid down as a standing

maxim, that "he who believes not another on his oath, knows himself to be perjured."[1]

We can form our opinions of that which we know not, only by placing it in comparison with something that we know: whoever therefore is over-run with suspicion, and detects artifice and stratagem in every proposal, must either have learned by experience or observation the wickedness of mankind, and been taught to avoid fraud by having often suffered or seen treachery, or he must derive his judgment from the consciousness of his own disposition, and impute to others the same inclinations which he feels predominant in himself.

To learn caution by turning our eyes upon life, and observing the arts by which negligence is surprised, timidity overborne, and credulity amused, requires either great latitude of converse and long acquaintance with business, or uncommon activity of vigilance, and acuteness of penetration. When therefore a young man, not distinguished by vigour of intellect, comes into the world full of scruples and diffidence; makes a bargain with many provisional limitations; hesitates in his answer to a common question, lest more should be intended than he can immediately discover; has a long reach in detecting the projects of his acquaintance; considers every caress as an act of hypocrisy, and feels neither gratitude nor affection from the tenderness of his friends, because he believes no one to have any real tenderness but for himself; whatever expectations this early sagacity may raise of his future eminence or riches, I can seldom forbear to consider him as a wretch incapable of generosity or benevolence, as a villain early completed beyond the need of common opportunities and gradual temptations.

1. Antiphanes, frag. 241 (*Comicorum Atticorum Fragmenta*, ed. K. T. Kock [1884], II.117). Johnson probably read it in Stobaeus, XXVII.5.

Upon men of this class instruction and admonition are generally thrown away, because they consider artifice and deceit as proofs of understanding; they are misled at the same time by the two great seducers of the world, vanity and interest, and not only look upon those who act with openness and confidence, as condemned by their principles to obscurity and want, but as contemptible for narrowness of comprehension, shortness of views, and slowness of contrivance.

The world has been long amused with the mention of policy in publick transactions, and of art in private affairs; they have been considered as the effects of great qualities, and as unattainable by men of the common level: yet I have not found many performances either of art, or policy, that required such stupendous efforts of intellect, or might not have been effected by falshood and impudence, without the assistance of any other powers. To profess what he does not mean, to promise what he cannot perform, to flatter ambition with prospects of promotion, and misery with hopes of relief, to sooth pride with appearances of submission, and appease enmity by blandishments and bribes, can surely imply nothing more or greater than a mind devoted wholly to its own purposes, a face that cannot blush, and a heart that cannot feel.

These practices are so mean and base, that he who finds in himself no tendency to use them, cannot easily believe that they are considered by others with less detestation; he therefore suffers himself to slumber in false security, and becomes a prey to those who applaud their own subtilty, because they know how to steal upon his sleep, and exult in the success which they could never have obtained, had they not attempted a man better than themselves, who was hindered from obviating their stratagems, not by folly, but by innocence.

Suspicion is, indeed, a temper so uneasy and restless, that it is very justly appointed the concomitant of guilt. It is said, that no torture is equal to the inhibition of sleep long continued; a pain, to which the state of that man bears a very exact analogy, who dares never give rest to his vigilance and circumspection, but considers himself as surrounded by secret foes, and fears to entrust his children, or his friend, with the secret that throbs in his breast, and the anxieties that break into his face. To avoid, at this expence, those evils to which easiness and friendship might have exposed him, is surely to buy safety at too dear a rate, and, in the language of the Roman satirist, to save life by losing all for which a wise man would live.[2]

When in the diet of the German empire, as Camerarius relates, the princes were once displaying their felicity, and each boasting the advantages of his own dominions, one who possessed a country not remarkable for the grandeur of its cities, or the fertility of its soil, rose to speak, and the rest listened between pity and contempt, till he declared, in honour of his territories, that he could travel through them without a guard, and if he was weary, sleep in safety upon the lap of the first man whom he should meet; a commendation which would have been ill exchanged for the boast of palaces, pastures, or streams.[3]

Suspicion is not less an enemy to virtue than to happiness: he that is already corrupt is naturally suspicious, and he that becomes suspicious will quickly be corrupt. It is too common for us to learn the frauds by which ourselves have suffered; men who are once persuaded that

2. Juvenal, VIII.84.
3. We have not found the story in Camerarius. But Johnson refers to the fifteenth-century Graf Eberhard im Bart—also the subject of the well-known German poem by Justinus Kerner. The Diet in question was probably that of Worms (1495), a year before Eberhard's death.

deceit will be employed against them, sometimes think the same arts justified by the necessity of defence. Even they whose virtue is too well established to give way to example, or be shaken by sophistry, must yet feel their love of mankind diminished with their esteem, and grow less zealous for the happiness of those by whom they imagine their own happiness endangered.

Thus we find old age, upon which suspicion has been strongly impressed by long intercourse with the world, inflexible and severe, not easily softened by submission, melted by complaint, or subdued by supplication. Frequent experience of counterfeited miseries, and dissembled virtue, in time overcomes that disposition to tenderness and sympathy, which is so powerful in our younger years, and they that happen to petition the old for compassion or assistance, are doomed to languish without regard, and suffer for the crimes of men who have formerly been found undeserving or ungrateful.

Historians are certainly chargeable with the depravation of mankind, when they relate without censure those stratagems of war by which the virtues of an enemy are engaged to his destruction. A ship comes before a port, weather-beaten and shattered, and the crew implore the liberty of repairing their breaches, supplying themselves with necessaries, or burying their dead. The humanity of the inhabitants inclines them to consent, the strangers enter the town with weapons concealed, fall suddenly upon their benefactors, destroy those that make resistance, and become masters of the place; they return home rich with plunder, and their success is recorded to encourage imitation.

But surely war has its laws, and ought to be conducted with some regard to the universal interest of man. Those may justly be pursued as enemies to the community of nature, who suffer hostility to vacate the unalterable laws of right, and pursue their private advantage by means, which, if once established, must destroy kindness, cut off from every man all hopes of assistance from another, and fill the world with perpetual suspicion and implacable malevolence. Whatever is thus gained ought to be restored, and those who have conquered by such treachery may be justly denied the protection of their native country.

Whoever commits a fraud is guilty not only of the particular injury to him whom he deceives, but of the diminution of that confidence which constitutes not only the ease but the existence of society. He that suffers by imposture has too often his virtue more impaired than his fortune. But as it is necessary not to invite robbery by supineness, so it is our duty not to suppress tenderness by suspicion; it is better to suffer wrong than to do it, and happier to be sometimes cheated than not to trust.

From No. 85. Tuesday, 8 January 1751.

Otia si tollas periere Cupidinis arcus
  Contemptaeque jacent, et sine luce faces.
                           Ovid, REMEDIA AMORIS, ll. 139–40.

At busy hearts in vain love's arrows fly;
Dim, scorn'd, and impotent, his torches lie.

.   .   .   .

Such is the constitution of man, that labour may be stiled its own reward; nor will any external incitements be requisite, if it be considered how much happiness is gained, and how much misery escaped by frequent and violent agitation of the body.

Ease is the utmost that can be hoped from a sedentary and unactive habit; ease, a neutral state between pain and pleasure. The dance of spirits, the bound of vigour, readiness of enterprize, and defiance of fatigue, are reserved for him that braces his nerves, and hardens his fibres, that keeps his limbs pliant with motion, and by frequent exposure fortifies his frame against the common accidents of cold and heat.

With ease, however, if it could be secured, many would be content; but nothing terrestrial can be kept at a stand. Ease, if it is not rising into pleasure, will be falling towards pain; and whatever hope the dreams of speculation may suggest of observing the proportion between nutriment and labour, and keeping the body in a healthy state by supplies exactly equal to its waste, we know that, in effect, the vital powers unexcited by motion, grow gradually languid; that as their vigour fails, obstructions are generated; and that from obstructions proceed most of those pains which wear us away slowly with periodical tortures, and which, though they sometimes suffer life to be long, condemn it to be useless, chain us down to the couch of misery, and mock us with the hopes of death.

Exercise cannot secure us from that dissolution to which we are decreed; but while the soul and body continue united, it can make the association pleasing, and give probable hopes that they shall be disjoined by an easy separation. It was a principle among the ancients, that acute diseases are from heaven, and chronical from ourselves; the dart of death indeed falls from heaven, but we poison it by our own misconduct; to die is the fate of man, but to die with lingering anguish is generally his folly.

It is necessary to that perfection of which our present state is capable, that the mind and body should both be kept in action; that neither the faculties of the one nor of the other be suffered to grow lax or torpid for want of use;

that neither health be purchased by voluntary submission to ignorance, nor knowledge cultivated at the expence of that health, which must enable it either to give pleasure to its possessor or assistance to others. It is too frequently the pride of students to despise those amusements and recreations which give to the rest of mankind strength of limbs and cheerfulness of heart. Solitude and contemplation are indeed seldom consistent with such skill in common exercises or sports as is necessary to make them practised with delight, and no man is willing to do that of which the necessity is not pressing and immediate, when he knows that his aukwardness must make him ridiculous.

●   ●   ●   ●

It is certain that any wild wish or vain imagination never takes such firm possession of the mind, as when it is found empty and unoccupied. The old peripatetick principle, that "Nature abhors a Vacuum," may be properly applied to the intellect, which will embrace any thing, however absurd or criminal, rather than be wholly without an object. Perhaps every man may date the predominance of those desires that disturb his life and contaminate his conscience, from some unhappy hour when too much leisure exposed him to their incursions; for he has lived with little observation either on himself or others, who does not know that to be idle is to be vicious.

From No. 87. Tuesday, 15 January 1751.

Invidus, iracundus, iners, vinosus, amator,
Nemo adeo ferus est, ut non mitescere possit,
Si modo culturae patientem commodet aurem.

Horace, EPISTLES, I.1.38–40.

The slave to envy, anger, wine or love,
The wretch of sloth, its excellence shall prove:
Fierceness itself shall hear its rage away,
When list'ning calmly to th' instructive lay.

Francis.

•   •   •   •

Advice, as it always gives a temporary appearance of superiority, can never be very grateful, even when it is most necessary or most judicious. But for the same reason every one is eager to instruct his neighbours. To be wise or to be virtuous, is to buy dignity and importance at a high price; but when nothing is necessary to elevation but detection of the follies or the faults of others, no man is so insensible to the voice of fame as to linger on the ground.

————*Tentanda via est, qua me quoque possim*
Tollere humo, victorque virûm volitare per ora.

Virgil, GEORGICS, III.8–9.

New ways I must attempt, my groveling name
To raise aloft, and wing my flight to fame.

Dryden.

Vanity is so frequently the apparent motive of advice, that we, for the most part, summon our powers to oppose it without any very accurate enquiry whether it is right. It is sufficient that another is growing great in his own eyes at our expence, and assumes authority over us without our permission; for many would contentedly suffer the consequences of their own mistakes, rather than the insolence of him who triumphs as their deliverer.

It is, indeed, seldom found that any advantages are enjoyed with that moderation which the uncertainty of all human good so powerfully enforces; and therefore the adviser may justly suspect, that he has inflamed the oppo-

sition which he laments by arrogance and superciliousness. He may suspect, but needs not hastily to condemn
himself, for he can rarely be certain, that the softest
language or most humble diffidence would have escaped
resentment; since scarcely any degree of circumspection
can prevent or obviate the rage with which the slothful,
the impotent, and the unsuccessful, vent their discontent
upon those that excel them. Modesty itself, if it is praised,
will be envied; and there are minds so impatient of
inferiority, that their gratitude is a species of revenge,
and they return benefits, not because recompence is a
pleasure, but because obligation is a pain.

The number of those whom the love of themselves has
thus far corrupted, is perhaps not great; but there are few
so free from vanity as not to dictate to those who will hear
their instructions with a visible sense of their own beneficence; and few to whom it is not unpleasing to receive
documents, however tenderly and cautiously delivered, or
who are not willing to raise themselves from pupillage, by
disputing the propositions of their teacher.

It was the maxim, I think, of Alphonsus of Arragon,
that "dead counsellors are safest."[1] The grave puts an end
to flattery and artifice, and the information that we receive from books is pure from interest, fear, or ambition.
Dead counsellors are likewise most instructive; because
they are heard with patience and with reverence. We are
not unwilling to believe that man wiser than ourselves,
from whose abilities we may receive advantage, without
any danger of rivalry or opposition, and who affords us
the light of his experience, without hurting our eyes by
flashes of insolence.

1. "Ninguno avia de tomar consejos con los vivos, sino con los
muertos." Melchor de Santa Cruz, *Floresta Española* (1574), II.1.25
(Madrid, 1953, p. 44).

By the consultation of books, whether of dead or living authors, many temptations to petulance and opposition, which occur in oral conferences, are avoided. An author cannot obtrude his advice unasked, nor can be often suspected of any malignant intention to insult his readers with his knowledge or his wit. Yet so prevalent is the habit of comparing ourselves with others, while they remain within the reach of our passions, that books are seldom read with complete impartiality, but by those from whom the writer is placed at such a distance that his life or death is indifferent.

We see that volumes may be perused, and perused with attention, to little effect; and that maxims of prudence, or principles of virtue, may be treasured in the memory without influencing the conduct. Of the numbers that pass their lives among books, very few read to be made wiser or better, apply any general reproof of vice to themselves, or try their own manners by axioms of justice. They purpose either to consume those hours for which they can find no other amusement; to gain or preserve that respect which learning has always obtained; or to gratify their curiosity with knowledge, which, like treasures buried and forgotten, is of no use to others or themselves.

"The preacher, (says a French author) may spend an hour in explaining and enforcing a precept of religion, without feeling any impression from his own performance, because he may have no further design than to fill up his hour." A student may easily exhaust his life in comparing divines and moralists, without any practical regard to morality or religion; he may be learning not to live, but to reason; he may regard only the elegance of stile, justness of argument, and accuracy of method; and may enable himself to criticise with judgment, and dispute with subtilty, while the chief use of his volumes is unthought of, his mind is unaffected, and his life is unreformed.

But though truth and virtue are thus frequently defeated by pride, obstinacy, or folly, we are not allowed to desert them; for whoever can furnish arms which they have not hitherto employed, may enable them to gain some hearts which would have resisted any other method of attack. Every man of genius has some arts of fixing the attention peculiar to himself, by which, honestly exerted, he may benefit mankind; for the arguments for purity of life fail of their due influence, not because they have been considered and confuted, but because they have been passed over without consideration. To the position of Tully, that if Virtue could be seen, she must be loved, may be added, that if Truth could be heard, she must be obeyed.[2]

No. 90. Saturday, 26 January 1751.

In tenui labor.

Virgil, GEORGICS, IV.6.

What toil in slender things!

It is very difficult to write on the minuter parts of literature without failing either to please or instruct. Too much nicety of detail disgusts the greatest part of readers, and to throw a multitude of particulars under general heads, and lay down rules of extensive comprehension, is to common understandings of little use. They who undertake these subjects are therefore always in danger, as one

2. *De Officiis*, I.v (par. 15). Cicero is quoting the remark, in turn, from Plato.

or other inconvenience arises to their imagination, of
frighting us with rugged science, or amusing us with
empty sound.

In criticising the work of Milton, there is, indeed,
opportunity to intersperse passages that can hardly fail to
relieve the languors of attention; and since, in examining
the variety and choice of the pauses with which he has
diversified his numbers, it will be necessary to exhibit the
lines in which they are to be found, perhaps the remarks
may be well compensated by the examples, and the
irksomeness of grammatical disquisitions somewhat
alleviated.

Milton formed his scheme of versification by the poets
of Greece and Rome, whom he proposed to himself for
his models so far as the difference of his language from
theirs would permit the imitation. There are indeed
many inconveniencies inseparable from our heroick measure compared with that of Homer and Virgil; inconveniencies, which it is no reproach to Milton not to have
overcome, because they are in their own nature insuperable; but against which he has struggled with so much art
and diligence, that he may at least be said to have deserved
success.

The hexameter of the ancients may be considered as
consisting of fifteen syllables, so melodiously disposed,
that, as every one knows who has examined the poetical
authors, very pleasing and sonorous lyrick measures are
formed from the fragments of the heroick. It is, indeed,
scarce possible to break them in such a manner but that
invenias etiam disjecti membra poetae, some harmony
will still remain, and the due proportions of sound will
always be discovered. This measure therefore allowed
great variety of pauses, and great liberties of connecting
one verse with another, because wherever the line was

interrupted, either part singly was musical. But the ancients seem to have confined this privilege to hexameters; for in their other measures, though longer than the English heroick, those who wrote after the refinements of versification venture so seldom to change their pauses, that every variation may be supposed rather a compliance with necessity than the choice of judgment.

Milton was constrained within the narrow limits of a measure not very harmonious in the utmost perfection; the single parts, therefore, into which it was to be sometimes broken by pauses, were in danger of losing the very form of verse. This has, perhaps, notwithstanding all his care, sometimes happened.

As harmony is the end of poetical measures, no part of a verse ought to be so separated from the rest as not to remain still more harmonious than prose, or to shew, by the disposition of the tones, that it is part of a verse. This rule in the old hexameter might be easily observed, but in English will very frequently be in danger of violation; for the order and regularity of accents cannot well be perceived in a succession of fewer than three syllables, which will confine the English poet to only five pauses; it being supposed, that, when he connects one line with another, he should never make a full pause at less distance than that of three syllables from the beginning or end of a verse.

That this rule should be universally and indispensably established, perhaps cannot be granted; something may be allowed to variety, and something to the adaptation of the numbers to the subject; but it will be found generally necessary, and the ear will seldom fail to suffer by its neglect.

Thus when a single syllable is cut off from the rest, it must either be united to the line with which the sense connects it, or be sounded alone. If it be united to the other line, it corrupts its harmony; if disjoined, it must stand alone and with regard to musick, be superfluous; for there is no harmony in a single sound, because it has no proportion to another.

> Hypocrites austerely talk,
> Defaming as impure what God declares
> *Pure;* and commands to some, leaves free to all.
>
> PARADISE LOST, IV.744, 746–47.

When two syllables likewise are abscinded from the rest, they evidently want some associate sounds to make them harmonious.

> ————Eyes————
> ————more wakeful than to drouze,
> Charm'd with arcadian pipe, the past'ral reed
> Of Hermes, or his opiate rod. *Meanwhile*
> To re-salute the world with sacred light
> Leucothea wak'd.
>
> XI.130, 131–35.

> He ended, and the sun gave signal high
> To the bright minister that watch'd: *he blew*
> His trumpet
>
> XI.72–74.

> First in his east the glorious lamp was seen,
> Regent of day; and all th' horizon round
> Invested with bright rays, jocund to run
> His longitude through heav'n's high road; *the gray*
> Dawn, and the pleiades, before him danc'd,
> Shedding sweet influence.
>
> VII.370–75.

The same defect is perceived in the following lines, where the pause is at the second syllable from the beginning.

> The race
> Of that wild rout that tore the Thracian bard
> In Rhodope, where woods and rocks had ears,
> To rapture, 'till the savage clamour drown'd
> Both harp and voice; nor could the muse defend
> *Her son.* So fail not thou, who thee implores.
>
> VII.33–38.

When the pause falls upon the third syllable or the seventh, the harmony is better preserved; but as the third and seventh are weak syllables, the period leaves the ear unsatisfied, and in expectation of the remaining part of the verse.

> He, with his horrid crew,
> Lay vanquish'd, rolling in the fiery gulph,
> Confounded though immor*tal.* But his doom
> Reserv'd him to more wrath; for now the thought
> Both of lost happiness and lasting pain
> Torments *him.*
>
> I.51–56.

> God,————with frequent intercourse,
> Thither will send his winged messengers
> On errands of supernal grace. So sung
> The glorious train ascend*ing.*
>
> VII.569, 571–74.

It may be, I think, established as a rule, that a pause which concludes a period should be made for the most part upon a strong syllable, as the fourth and sixth; but those pauses which only suspend the sense may be placed upon the weaker. Thus the rest in the third line of the first passage satisfies the ear better than in the fourth, and the close of the second quotation better than of the third.

> The evil soon
> Drawn back, redounded (as a flood) on those
> From whom it *sprung;* impossible to mix
> With *blessedness.*
>
> VII.56–59.

> ————What we by day
> Lop overgrown, or prune, or prop, or bind
> One night or two with wanton growth derides,
> Tending to *wild.*
>
> IX.209–12.

> The paths and bow'rs doubt not but our joint hands
> Will keep from wilderness with ease as wide
> As we need walk, till younger hands ere long
> Assist *us.*
>
> IX.244–47.

The rest in the fifth place has the same inconvenience as in the seventh and third, that the syllable is weak.

> Beast now with beast 'gan war, and fowl with fowl,
> And fish with fish, to graze the herb all leaving,
> Devour'd each *other:* Nor stood much in awe
> Of man, but fled *him,* or with countenance grim,
> Glar'd on him pass*ing.*
>
> X.710–14.

The noblest and most majestic pauses which our versification admits, are upon the fourth and sixth syllables, which are both strongly sounded in a pure and regular verse, and at either of which the line is so divided, that both members participate of harmony.

But now at last the sacred influence
Of light ap*pears,* and from the walls of heav'n
Shoots far into the bosom of dim night
A glimmering *dawn:* here nature first begins
Her farthest verge, and chaos to retire.

II.1034–38.

But far above all others, if I can give any credit to my own ear, is the rest upon the sixth syllable, which taking in a complete compass of sound, such as is sufficient to constitute one of our lyrick measures, makes a full and solemn close. Some passages which conclude at this stop, I could never read without some strong emotions of delight or admiration.

Before the hills appear'd, or fountain flow'd,
Thou with the eternal wisdom didst converse,
Wisdom thy sister; and with her didst play
In presence of the almighty father, pleas'd
With thy celestial *song.*

VII.8–12.

Or other worlds they seem'd, or happy isles,
Like those Hesperian gardens fam'd of old,
Fortunate fields, and groves, and flow'ry vales,
Thrice happy isles! But who dwelt happy there,
He staid not to in*quire.*

III.567–71.

He blew
His trumpet, heard in Oreb since, perhaps
When God descended; and, perhaps, once more
To sound at general *doom.*

XI.73–76.

If the poetry of Milton be examined, with regard to the pauses and flow of his verses into each other, it will appear, that he has performed all that our language would admit; and the comparison of his numbers with those who have cultivated the same manner of writing, will show that he excelled as much in the lower as the higher parts of his art, and that his skill in harmony was not less than his invention or his learning.

No. 93. Tuesday, 5 February 1751.

———————— Experiar quid concedatur in illos
Quorum Flaminiâ tegitur cinis atque Latinâ.

Juvenal, I.170–71.

More safely truth to urge her claim presumes,
On names now found alone on books and tombs.

There are few books on which more time is spent by young students, than on treatises which deliver the characters of authors; nor any which oftener deceive the expectation of the reader, or fill his mind with more opinions which the progress of his studies and the encrease of his knowledge oblige him to resign.

Baillet has introduced his collection of the decisions of the learned, by an enumeration of the prejudices which mislead the critick, and raise the passions in rebellion against the judgment.[1] His catalogue, though large, is imperfect; and who can hope to complete it? The beauties of writing have been observed to be often such as cannot in the present state of human knowledge be evinced by evidence, or drawn out into demonstrations; they are therefore wholly subject to the imagination, and do not force their effects upon a mind preoccupied by unfavour-

1. *Jugemens des Scavans* (1685–1686), I. pt. 2, chs. 1–14.

able sentiments, nor overcome the counteraction of a false principle or of stubborn partiality.

To convince any man against his will is hard, but to please him against his will is justly pronounced by Dryden to be above the reach of human abilities.[2] Interest and passion will hold out long against the closest siege of diagrams and syllogisms, but they are absolutely impregnable to imagery and sentiment; and will for ever bid defiance to the most powerful strains of Virgil or Homer, though they may give way in time to the batteries of Euclid or Archimedes.

In trusting therefore to the sentence of a critick, we are in danger not only from that vanity which exalts writers too often to the dignity of teaching what they are yet to learn, from that negligence which sometimes steals upon the most vigilant caution, and that fallibility to which the condition of nature has subjected every human understanding; but from a thousand extrinsick and accidental causes, from every thing which can excite kindness or malevolence, veneration or contempt.

Many of those who have determined with great boldness, upon the various degrees of literary merit, may be justly suspected of having passed sentence, as Seneca remarks of Claudius,

> *Una tantum parte audita,*
> *Saepe et nulla,*
>
> APOCOLOCYNTOSIS, XII.11–12.

without much knowledge of the cause before them; for it will not easily be imagined of Langbaine, Borrichitus or

2. See Hill's note in "Congreve," *Lives,* II.217, n. 3. Johnson is probably thinking of Congreve's lines, in the Epilogue to *The Way of the World:* "And sure he must have more than mortal skill/ Who pleases anyone against his will."

Rapin, that they had very accurately perused all the books which they praise or censure; or that, even if nature and learning had qualified them for judges, they could read for ever with the attention necessary to just criticism. Such performances, however, are not wholly without their use; for they are commonly just echoes to the voice of fame, and transmit the general suffrage of mankind when they have no particular motives to suppress it.

Criticks, like all the rest of mankind, are very frequently misled by interest. The bigotry with which editors regard the authors whom they illustrate or correct, has been generally remarked. Dryden was known to have written most of his critical dissertations only to recommend the work upon which he then happened to be employed; and Addison is suspected to have denied the expediency of poetical justice, because his own Cato was condemned to perish in a good cause.[3]

There are prejudices which authors, not otherwise weak or corrupt, have indulged without scruple; and perhaps some of them are so complicated with our natural affections, that they cannot easily be disintangled from the heart. Scarce any can hear with impartiality a comparison between the writers of his own and another country; and though it cannot, I think, be charged equally on all nations, that they are blinded with this literary patriotism, yet there are none that do not look upon their authors with the fondness of affinity, and esteem them as well for the place of their birth, as for their knowledge or their wit. There is, therefore, seldom much respect due to comparative criticism, when the competitors are of different countries, unless the judge is of a nation equally indifferent to both. The Italians could not for a long time

3. *Spectator* 40.

believe, that there was any learning beyond the mountains; and the French seem generally persuaded, that
there are no wits or reasoners equal to their own. I can
scarcely conceive that if Scaliger had not considered himself as allied to Virgil, by being born in the same country,
he would have found his works so much superior to those
of Homer, or have thought the controversy worthy of so
much zeal, vehemence, and acrimony.

There is, indeed, one prejudice, and only one, by
which it may be doubted whether it is any dishonour to be
sometimes misguided. Criticism has so often given occasion to the envious and ill-natured of gratifying their
malignity, that some have thought it necessary to recommend the virtue of candour without restriction, and to
preclude all future liberty of censure. Writers possessed
with this opinion are continually enforcing civility and
decency, recommending to criticks the proper diffidence
of themselves, and inculcating the veneration due to celebrated names.

I am not of opinion that these professed enemies of
arrogance and severity, have much more benevolence or
modesty than the rest of mankind; or that they feel in
their own hearts, any other intention than to distinguish
themselves by their softness and delicacy. Some are modest because they are timorous, and some are lavish of
praise because they hope to be repaid.

There is indeed some tenderness due to living writers,
when they attack none of those truths which are of
importance to the happiness of mankind, and have committed no other offence than that of betraying their own
ignorance or dulness. I should think it cruelty to crush
an insect who had provoked me only by buzzing in my
ear; and would not willingly interrupt the dream of
harmless stupidity, or destroy the jest which makes its

author laugh. Yet I am far from thinking this tenderness universally necessary; for he that writes may be considered as a kind of general challenger, whom every one has a right to attack; since he quits the common rank of life, steps forward beyond the lists, and offers his merit to the publick judgment. To commence author is to claim praise, and no man can justly aspire to honour, but at the hazard of disgrace.

But whatever be decided concerning contemporaries, whom he that knows the treachery of the human heart, and considers how often we gratify our own pride or envy under the appearance of contending for elegance and propriety, will find himself not much inclined to disturb; there can surely be no exemptions pleaded to secure them from criticism, who can no longer suffer by reproach, and of whom nothing now remains but their writings and their names. Upon these authors the critick is, undoubtedly, at full liberty to exercise the strictest severity, since he endangers only his own fame, and, like Æneas when he drew his sword in the infernal regions, encounters phantoms which cannot be wounded. He may indeed pay some regard to established reputation; but he can by that shew of reverence consult only his own security, for all other motives are now at an end.

The faults of a writer of acknowledged excellence are more dangerous, because the influence of his example is more extensive; and the interest of learning requires that they should be discovered and stigmatized, before they have the sanction of antiquity conferred upon them, and become precedents of indisputable authority.

It has, indeed, been advanced by Addison, as one of the characteristicks of a true critick, that he points out beauties rather than faults.[4] But it is rather natural to a man

4. *Spectator* 291.

of learning and genius, to apply himself chiefly to the
study of writers who have more beauties than faults to be
displayed: for the duty of criticism is neither to depreciate, nor dignify by partial representations, but to hold
out the light of reason, whatever it may discover; and to
promulgate the determinations of truth, whatever she
shall dictate.

No. 101. Tuesday, 5 March 1751.

Mella jubes Hyblaea tibi vel Hymettia nasci,
  Et thyma Cecropiae Corsica ponis api.

Martial, XI.42.3–4.

Alas! dear Sir, you try in vain,
Impossibilities to gain;
No bee from Corsica's rank juice,
Hyblaean honey can produce.

F. Lewis.

TO THE RAMBLER.

SIR,
  Having by several years of continual study treasured in
my mind a great number of principles and ideas, and
obtained by frequent exercise the power of applying them
with propriety, and combining them with readiness, I
resolved to quit the university, where I considered myself
as a gem hidden in the mine, and to mingle in the croud of
publick life. I was naturally attracted by the company of
those who were of the same age with myself, and finding
that my academical gravity contributed very little to my
reputation, applied my faculties to jocularity and burlesque. Thus, in a short time, I had heated my imagination to such a state of activity and ebullition, that upon

every occasion it fumed away in bursts of wit, and evaporations of gaiety. I became on a sudden the idol of the
coffee-house, was in one winter sollicited to accept the
presidentship of five clubs, was dragged by violence to
every new play, and quoted in every controversy upon
theatrical merit; was in every publick place surrounded
by a multitude of humble auditors, who retailed in other
places of resort my maxims and my jests, and was boasted
as their intimate and companion by many, who had no
other pretensions to my acquaintance, than that they had
drank chocolate in the same room.

You will not wonder, Mr. Rambler, that I mention my
success with some appearance of triumph and elevation.
Perhaps no kind of superiority is more flattering or
alluring than that which is conferred by the powers of
conversation, by extemporaneous sprightliness of fancy,
copiousness of language, and fertility of sentiment. In
other exertions of genius, the greater part of the praise is
unknown and unenjoyed; the writer, indeed, spreads his
reputation to a wider extent, but receives little pleasure
or advantage from the diffusion of his name, and only
obtains a kind of nominal sovereignty over regions which
pay no tribute. The colloquial wit has always his own
radiance reflected on himself, and enjoys all the pleasure
which he bestows; he finds his power confessed by every
one that approaches him, sees friendship kindling with
rapture, and attention swelling into praise.

The desire which every man feels of importance and
esteem, is so much gratified by finding an assembly, at
his entrance, brightened with gladness and hushed with
expectation, that the recollection of such distinctions can
scarcely fail to be pleasing whensoever it is innocent. And
my conscience does not reproach me with any mean or
criminal effects of vanity; since I always employed my

influence on the side of virtue, and never sacrificed my understanding or my religion to the pleasure of applause.

There were many whom either the desire of enjoying my pleasantry, or the pride of being thought to enjoy it, brought often into my company; but I was caressed in a particular manner by Demochares, a gentleman of a large estate, and a liberal disposition. My fortune being by no means exuberant, enclined me to be pleased with a friend who was willing to be entertained at his own charge. I became by daily invitations habituated to his table, and, as he believed my acquaintance necessary to the character of elegance, which he was desirous of establishing, I lived in all the luxury of affluence, without expence or dependence, and passed my life in a perpetual reciprocation of pleasure with men brought together by similitude of accomplishments, or desire of improvement.

But all power has its sphere of activity, beyond which it produces no effect. Demochares being called by his affairs into the country, imagined that he should encrease his popularity by coming among his neighbours accompanied by a man whose abilities were so generally allowed. The report presently spread thro' half the county that Demochares was arrived, and had brought with him the celebrated Hilarius, by whom such merriment would be excited, as had never been enjoyed or conceived before. I knew, indeed, the purpose for which I was invited, and, as men do not look diligently out for possible miscarriages, was pleased to find myself courted upon principles of interest, and considered as capable of reconciling factions, composing feuds, and uniting a whole province in social happiness.

After a few days spent in adjusting his domestick regulations, Demochares invited all the gentlemen of his neighbourhood to dinner, and did not forget to hint how much my presence was expected to heighten the pleasure of the feast. He informed me what prejudices my reputation had raised in my favour, and represented the satisfaction with which he should see me kindle up the blaze of merriment, and should remark the various effects that my fire would have upon such diversity of matter.

This declaration, by which he intended to quicken my vivacity, filled me with solicitude. I felt an ambition of shining, which I never knew before; and was therefore embarrassed with an unusual fear of disgrace.[1] I passed the night in planning out to myself the conversation of the coming day; recollected all my topicks of raillery, proposed proper subjects of ridicule, prepared smart replies to a thousand questions, accommodated answers to imaginary repartees, and formed a magazine of remarks, apophthegms, tales, and illustrations.

The morning broke at last in the midst of these busy meditations. I rose with the palpitations of a champion on the day of combat; and, notwithstanding all my efforts, found my spirits sunk under the weight of expectation. The company soon after began to drop in, and every one at his entrance was introduced to Hilarius. What conception the inhabitants of this region had formed of a wit, I cannot yet discover; but observed that they all seemed, after the regular exchange of compliments, to turn away disappointed, and that while we waited for dinner, they cast their eyes first upon me, and then upon each other, like a theatrical assembly waiting for a shew.

From the uneasiness of this situation, I was relieved by the dinner, and as every attention was taken up by the business of the hour, I sunk quietly to a level with the rest of the company. But no sooner were the dishes re-

1. Cf. *Rambler* 159.

moved, than instead of chearful confidence and familiar prattle, an universal silence again shewed their expectation of some unusual performance. My friend endeavoured to rouse them by healths and questions, but they answered him with great brevity, and immediately relapsed into their former taciturnity.

I had waited in hope of some opportunity to divert them, but could find no pass opened for a single sally; and who can be merry without an object of mirth? After a few faint efforts, which produced neither applause nor opposition, I was content to mingle with the mass, to put round the glass in silence, and solace myself with my own contemplations.

My friend looked round him; the guests stared at one another; and if now and then a few syllables were uttered with timidity and hesitation, there was none ready to make any reply. All our faculties were frozen, and every minute took away from our capacity of pleasing, and disposition to be pleased.[2] Thus passed the hours to which so much happiness was decreed; the hours which had, by a kind of open proclamation, been devoted to wit, to mirth, and to Hilarius.

At last the night came on, and the necessity of parting freed us from the persecutions of each other. I heard them as they walked along the court murmuring at the loss of the day, and enquiring whether any man would pay a second visit to a house haunted by a wit.

Demochares, whose benevolence is greater than his penetration, having flattered his hopes with the secondary honour which he was to gain by my sprightliness and elegance, and the affection with which he should be followed for a perpetual banquet of gaiety, was not able to

2. Cf. the similar account in *Idler* 58 (pars. 1–2).

conceal his vexation and resentment, nor would easily be convinced, that I had not sacrificed his interest to sullenness and caprice, had studiously endeavoured to disgust his guests, and suppressed my powers of delighting, in obstinate and premeditated silence. I am informed that the reproach of their ill reception is divided by the gentlemen of the country between us; some being of opinion that my friend is deluded by an impostor, who, though he has found some art of gaining his favour, is afraid to speak before men of more penetration; and others concluding, that I think only London the proper theatre of my abilities, and disdain to exert my genius for the praise of rusticks.

I believe, Mr. Rambler, that it has sometimes happened to others, who have the good or ill fortune to be celebrated for wits, to fall under the same censures upon the like occasions. I hope therefore that you will prevent any misrepresentations of such failures, by remarking that invention is not wholly at the command of its possessor; that the power of pleasing is very often obstructed by the desire; that all expectation lessens surprize, yet some surprize is necessary to gaiety; and that those who desire to partake of the pleasure of wit must contribute to its production, since the mind stagnates without external ventilation, and that effervescence of the fancy, which flashes into transport, can be raised only by the infusion of dissimilar ideas.

From No. 106. Saturday, 23 March 1751.

Opinionum commenta delet dies, naturae judicia confirmat.

                                   Cicero, DE NATURA DEORUM, II.2.5.

Time obliterates the fictions of opinion, and confirms
the decisions of nature.

         •   •   •   •

No place affords a more striking conviction of the vanity of human hopes, than a publick library; for who can
see the wall crouded on every side by mighty volumes,
the works of laborious meditation, and accurate enquiry,
now scarcely known but by the catalogue, and preserved
only to encrease the pomp of learning, without considering how many hours have been wasted in vain endeavours, how often imagination has anticipated the praises
of futurity, how many statues have risen to the eye of
vanity, how many ideal converts have elevated zeal, how
often wit has exulted in the eternal infamy of his antag-
onists, and dogmatism has delighted in the gradual advances of his authority, the immutability of his decrees,
and the perpetuity of his power?

   ————— *Non unquam dedit*
Documenta fors majora, quàm fragili loco
Starent superbi. —————
Seneca, TROADES, ll. 4–6.

Insulting chance ne'er call'd with louder voice,
On swelling mortals to be proud no more.

Of the innumerable authors whose performances are
thus treasured up in magnificent obscurity, most are forgotten, because they never deserved to be remembered,
and owed the honours which they once obtained, not to
judgment or to genius, to labour or to art, but to the
prejudice of faction, the stratagem of intrigue, or the
servility of adulation.

Nothing is more common than to find men whose

works are now totally neglected, mentioned with praises by their contemporaries, as the oracles of their age, and the legislators of science. Curiosity is naturally excited, their volumes after long enquiry are found, but seldom reward the labour of the search. Every period of time has produced these bubbles of artificial fame, which are kept up a while by the breath of fashion, and then break at once and are annihilated. The learned often bewail the loss of ancient writers whose characters have survived their works; but, perhaps, if we could now retrieve them, we should find them only the Granvilles, Montagues, Stepneys, and Sheffields of their time, and wonder by what infatuation or caprice they could be raised to notice.

It cannot, however, be denied, that many have sunk into oblivion, whom it were unjust to number with this despicable class. Various kinds of literary fame seem destined to various measures of duration. Some spread into exuberance with a very speedy growth, but soon wither and decay; some rise more slowly, but last long. Parnassus has its flowers of transient fragrance, as well as its oaks of towering height, and its laurels of eternal verdure.

Among those whose reputation is exhausted in a short time by its own luxuriance, are the writers who take advantage of present incidents or characters which strongly interest the passions, and engage universal attention.[1] It is not difficult to obtain readers, when we discuss a question which every one is desirous to understand, which is debated in every assembly, and has divided the nation into parties; or when we display the faults or virtues of him whose public conduct has made almost every man his enemy or his friend. To the quick circulation of such

1. Cf. Johnson's remarks on Butler's *Hudibras, Idler* 59.

productions all the motives of interest and vanity concur; the disputant enlarges his knowledge, the zealot animates his passion, and every man is desirous to inform himself concerning affairs so vehemently agitated and variously represented.

It is scarcely to be imagined, through how many subordinations of interest, the ardour of party is diffused; and what multitudes fancy themselves affected by every satire or panegyrick on a man of eminence. Whoever has, at any time, taken occasion to mention him with praise or blame, whoever happens to love or hate any of his adherents, as he wishes to confirm his opinion, and to strengthen his party, will diligently peruse every paper from which he can hope for sentiments like his own. An object, however small in itself, if placed near to the eye, will engross all the rays of light; and a transaction, however trivial, swells into importance, when it presses immediately on our attention. He that shall peruse the political pamphlets of any past reign, will wonder why they were so eagerly read, or so loudly praised. Many of the performances which had power to inflame factions, and fill a kingdom with confusion, have now very little effect upon a frigid critick, and the time is coming, when the compositions of later hirelings shall lie equally despised. In proportion, as those who write on temporary subjects, are exalted above their merit at first, they are afterwards depressed below it; nor can the brightest elegance of diction, or most artful subtilty of reasoning, hope for much esteem from those whose regard is no longer quickened by curiosity or pride.

It is, indeed, the fate of controvertists, even when they contend for philosophical or theological truth, to be soon laid aside and slighted. Either the question is decided, and there is no more place for doubt and opposition; or mankind despair of understanding it, and grow weary of disturbance, content themselves with quiet ignorance, and refuse to be harrassed with labours which they have no hopes of recompensing with knowledge.

*   *   *   *   *

There are, indeed, few kinds of composition from which an author, however learned or ingenious, can hope a long continuance of fame. He who has carefully studied human nature, and can well describe it, may with most reason flatter his ambition. Bacon, among all his pretensions to the regard of posterity, seems to have pleased himself chiefly with his essays, "which come home to men's business and bosoms," and of which, therefore, he declares his expectation, that they "will live as long as books last."[2] It may, however, satisfy an honest and benevolent mind to have been useful, though less conspicuous; nor will he that extends his hope to higher rewards, be so much anxious to obtain praise, as to discharge the duty which Providence assigns him.

No. 121. Tuesday, 14 May 1751.

O imitatores, servum pecus!
                              Horace, EPISTLES, I.19.19.

Away, ye imitators, servile herd!
                              Elphinston.

I have been informed by a letter, from one of the universities, that among the youth from whom the next swarm of reasoners is to learn philosophy, and the next flight of

2. Dedication to the *Essays.*

beauties to hear elegies and sonnets, there are many, who, instead of endeavouring by books and meditation to form their own opinions, content themselves with the secondary knowledge, which a convenient bench in a coffee-house can supply; and, without any examination or distinction, adopt the criticisms and remarks, which happen to drop from those, who have risen, by merit or fortune, to reputation and authority.

These humble retailers of knowledge my correspondent stigmatizes with the name of Echoes; and seems desirous, that they should be made ashamed of lazy submission, and animated to attempts after new discoveries, and original sentiments.

It is very natural for young men to be vehement, acrimonious, and severe. For, as they seldom comprehend at once all the consequences of a position, or perceive the difficulties by which cooler and more experienced reasoners are restrained from confidence, they form their conclusions with great precipitance. Seeing nothing that can darken or embarrass the question, they expect to find their own opinion universally prevalent, and are inclined to impute uncertainty and hesitation to want of honesty, rather than of knowledge. I may, perhaps, therefore be reproached by my lively correspondent, when it shall be found, that I have no inclination to persecute these collectors of fortuitous knowledge with the severity required; yet, as I am now too old to be much pained by hasty censure, I shall not be afraid of taking into protection those whom I think condemned without a sufficient knowledge of their cause.

He that adopts the sentiments of another, whom he has reason to believe wiser than himself, is only to be blamed, when he claims the honours which are not due but to the author, and endeavours to deceive the world into praise and veneration; for, to learn, is the proper business of youth; and whether we encrease our knowledge by books, or by conversation, we are equally indebted to foreign assistance.

The greater part of students are not born with abilities to construct systems, or advance knowledge; nor can have any hope beyond that of becoming intelligent hearers in the schools of art, of being able to comprehend what others discover, and to remember what others teach. Even those to whom Providence has allotted greater strength of understanding, can expect only to improve a single science. In every other part of learning, they must be content to follow opinions, which they are not able to examine; and, even in that which they claim as peculiarly their own, can seldom add more than some small particle of knowledge, to the hereditary stock devolved to them from ancient times, the collective labour of a thousand intellects.

In science, which being fixed and limited, admits of no other variety than such as arises from new methods of distribution, or new arts of illustration, the necessity of following the traces of our predecessors is indisputably evident; but there appears no reason, why imagination should be subject to the same restraint.[1] It might be conceived, that of those who profess to forsake the narrow paths of truth every one may deviate towards a different point, since though rectitude is uniform and fixed, obliquity may be infinitely diversified. The roads of science are narrow, so that they who travel them, must either follow or meet one another; but in the boundless regions of possibility, which fiction claims for her dominion, there are surely a thousand recesses unexplored, a thousand flowers unplucked, a thousand fountains unex-

1. Cf. *Ramblers* 23 (par. 6) and 125 (par. 2).

hausted, combinations of imagery yet unobserved, and races of ideal inhabitants not hitherto described.[2]

Yet, whatever hope may persuade, or reason evince, experience can boast of very few additions to ancient fable. The wars of Troy, and the travels of Ulysses, have furnished almost all succeeding poets with incidents, characters, and sentiments.[3] The Romans are confessed to have attempted little more than to display in their own tongue the inventions of the Greeks. There is, in all their writings, such a perpetual recurrence of allusions to the tales of the fabulous age, that they must be confessed often to want that power of giving pleasure which novelty supplies; nor can we wonder, that they excelled so much in the graces of diction, when we consider how rarely they were employed in search of new thoughts.

The warmest admirers of the great Mantuan poet can extol him for little more than the skill with which he has, by making his hero both a traveller and a warrior, united the beauties of the Iliad and Odyssey in one composition: yet his judgment was perhaps sometimes overborn by his avarice of the Homeric treasures; and, for fear of suffering a sparkling ornament to be lost, he has inserted it where it cannot shine with its original splendor.

When Ulysses visited the infernal regions, he found, among the heroes that perished at Troy, his competitor Ajax, who, when the arms of Achilles were adjudged to Ulysses, died by his own hand in the madness of disappointment. He still appeared to resent, as on earth, his loss and disgrace. Ulysses endeavoured to pacify him with praises and submission; but Ajax walked away without reply. This passage has always been considered as emi-

2. Cf. *Ramblers* 124 (par. 9), 129 (final par.), and the close of *Adventurer* 95.

3. Cf. on Homer, *Preface to Shakespeare* (par. 3).

nently beautiful; because Ajax, the haughty chief, the unlettered soldier, of unshaken courage, of immoveable constancy, but without the power of recommending his own virtues by eloquence, or enforcing his assertions by any other argument than the sword, had no way of making his anger known, but by gloomy sullenness, and dumb ferocity. His hatred of a man whom he conceived to have defeated him only by volubility of tongue, was therefore naturally shewn by silence more contemptuous and piercing than any words that so rude an orator could have found, and by which he gave his enemy no opportunity of exerting the only power in which he was superior.

When Æneas is sent by Virgil to the shades, he meets Dido the queen of Carthage, whom his perfidy had hurried to the grave; he accosts her with tenderness and excuses; but the lady turns away like Ajax in mute disdain. She turns away like Ajax, but she resembles him in none of those qualities which give either dignity or propriety to silence. She might, without any departure from the tenour of her conduct, have burst out like other injured women into clamour, reproach, and denunciation; but Virgil had his imagination full of Ajax, and therefore could not prevail on himself to teach Dido any other mode of resentment.

If Virgil could be thus seduced by imitation, there will be little hope, that common wits should escape; and accordingly we find, that besides the universal and acknowledged practice of copying the ancients, there has prevailed in every age a particular species of fiction. At one time all truth was conveyed in allegory; at another, nothing was seen but in a vision; at one period, all the poets followed sheep, and every event produced a pastoral; at another they busied themselves wholly in giving directions to a painter.

It is indeed easy to conceive why any fashion should become popular, by which idleness is favoured, and imbecillity assisted; but surely no man of genius can much applaud himself for repeating a tale with which the audience is already tired, and which could bring no honour to any but its inventor.

There are, I think, two schemes of writing, on which the laborious wits of the present time employ their faculties. One is the adaptation of sense to all the rhymes which our language can supply to some word, that makes the burden of the stanza; but this, as it has been only used in a kind of amorous burlesque, can scarcely be censured with much acrimony. The other is the imitation of Spenser, which, by the influence of some men of learning and genius, seems likely to gain upon the age, and therefore deserves to be more attentively considered.

To imitate the fictions and sentiments of Spenser can incur no reproach, for allegory is perhaps one of the most pleasing vehicles of instruction. But I am very far from extending the same respect to his diction or his stanza. His stile was in his own time allowed to be vicious, so darkened with old words and peculiarities of phrase, and so remote from common use, that Johnson [Ben Jonson] boldly pronounces him "to have written no language."[4] His stanza is at once difficult and unpleasing; tiresome to the ear by its uniformity, and to the attention by its length. It was at first formed in imitation of the Italian poets, without due regard to the genius of our language. The Italians have little variety of termination, and were forced to contrive such a stanza as might admit the greatest number of similar rhymes; but our words end with so much diversity, that it is seldom convenient for us to bring more than two of the same sound together. If it be

4. *Timber, or Discoveries,* ed. F. E. Schelling (1892), p. 57.

justly observed by Milton,[5] that rhyme obliges poets to
express their thoughts in improper terms, these impro-
prieties must always be multiplied, as the difficulty of
rhyme is encreased by long concatenations.

The imitators of Spenser are indeed not very rigid
censors of themselves, for they seem to conclude, that
when they have disfigured their lines with a few obso-
lete syllables, they have accomplished their design, without considering that they ought not only to admit old
words,[6] but to avoid new. The laws of imitation are
broken by every word introduced since the time of Spenser, as the character of Hector is violated by quoting
Aristotle in the play.[7] It would indeed be difficult to exclude from a long poem all modern phrases, though it is
easy to sprinkle it with gleanings of antiquity. Perhaps,
however, the stile of Spenser might by long labour be
justly copied; but life is surely given us for higher purposes than to gather what our ancestors have wisely
thrown away, and to learn what is of no value, but because
it has been forgotten.

No. 134. Saturday, 29 June 1751.

Quis scit, an adjiciant hodiernae crastina summae
Tempora Dî superi!

                                    Horace, ODES, IV.7.17–18.

Who knows if Heav'n, with ever-bounteous pow'r,
Shall add to-morrow to the present hour?

                                                        Francis.

5. Preface to *Paradise Lost*.
6. Cf. "Gay" and "Collins," *Lives,* II.269 (par. 4); III.341 (par. 17), and
on Thomas Warton, *Life,* III.158–59.
7. *Troilus and Cressida*, II.2.166.

I sat yesterday morning employed in deliberating on which, among the various subjects that occurred to my imagination, I should bestow the paper of to-day. After a short effort of meditation by which nothing was determined, I grew every moment more irresolute, my ideas wandered from the first intention, and I rather wished to think, than thought, upon any settled subject; till at last I was awakened from this dream of study by a summons from the press:[1] the time was come for which I had been thus negligently purposing to provide, and, however dubious or sluggish, I was now necessitated to write.

Though to a writer whose design is so comprehensive and miscellaneous, that he may accommodate himself with a topick from every scene of life, or view of nature, it is no great aggravation of his task to be obliged to a sudden composition, yet I could not forbear to reproach myself for having so long neglected what was unavoidably to be done, and of which every moment's idleness increased the difficulty. There was however some pleasure in reflecting that I, who had only trifled till diligence was necessary, might still congratulate myself upon my superiority to multitudes, who have trifled till diligence is vain; who can by no degree of activity or resolution recover the opportunities which have slipped away; and who are condemned by their own carelessness to hopeless calamity and barren sorrow.

The folly of allowing ourselves to delay what we know cannot be finally escaped, is one of the general weaknesses, which, in spite of the instruction of moralists, and the remonstrances of reason, prevail to a greater or less

1. Mrs. Thrale (Miscellanies, 1.178) states that this issue of the Rambler "on the subject of Procrastination was hastily composed, as I have heard, in Sir Joshua Reynolds's parlour, while the boy waited to carry it to the press."

degree in every mind: even they who most steadily withstand it, find it, if not the most violent, the most pertinacious of their passions, always renewing its attacks, and
though often vanquished, never destroyed.

It is indeed natural to have particular regard to the
time present, and to be most solicitous for that which is
by its nearness enabled to make the strongest impressions.
When therefore any sharp pain is to be suffered, or any
formidable danger to be incurred, we can scarcely exempt
ourselves wholly from the seducements of imagination;
we readily believe that another day will bring some support or advantage which we now want; and are easily
persuaded, that the moment of necessity which we desire
never to arrive, is at a great distance from us.

Thus life is languished away in the gloom of anxiety,
and consumed in collecting resolutions which the next
morning dissipates; in forming purposes which we
scarcely hope to keep, and reconciling ourselves to our
own cowardice by excuses, which, while we admit them,
we know to be absurd. Our firmness is by the continual
contemplation of misery hourly impaired; every submission to our fear enlarges its dominion; we not only waste
that time in which the evil we dread might have been
suffered and surmounted, but even where procrastination produces no absolute encrease of our difficulties,
make them less superable to ourselves by habitual terrors.
When evils cannot be avoided, it is wise to contract the
interval of expectation; to meet the mischiefs which will
overtake us if we fly; and suffer only their real malignity
without the conflicts of doubt and anguish of anticipation.

To act is far easier than to suffer, yet we every day see
the progress of life retarded by the *vis inertiae,* the mere
repugnance to motion, and find multitudes repining at

the want of that which nothing but idleness hinders them from enjoying. The case of Tantalus, in the region of poetick punishment, was somewhat to be pitied, because the fruits that hung about him retired from his hand; but what tenderness can be claimed by those who though perhaps they suffer the pains of Tantalus will never lift their hands for their own relief?

There is nothing more common among this torpid generation than murmurs and complaints; murmurs at uneasiness which only vacancy and suspicion expose them to feel, and complaints of distresses which it is in their own power to remove. Laziness is commonly associated with timidity. Either fear originally prohibits endeavours by infusing despair of success; or the frequent failure of irresolute struggles, and the constant desire of avoiding labour, impress by degrees false terrors on the mind. But fear, whether natural or acquired, when once it has full possession of the fancy, never fails to employ it upon visions of calamity, such as if they are not dissipated by useful employment, will soon overcast it with horrors, and imbitter life not only with those miseries by which all earthly beings are really more or less tormented, but with those which do not yet exist, and which can only be discerned by the perspicacity of cowardice.

Among all who sacrifice future advantage to present inclination, scarcely any gain so little as those that suffer themselves to freeze in idleness. Others are corrupted by some enjoyment of more or less power to gratify the passions; but to neglect our duties, merely to avoid the labour of performing them, a labour which is always punctually rewarded, is surely to sink under weak temptations. Idleness never can secure tranquillity; the call of reason and of conscience will pierce the closest pavilion of the sluggard, and, though it may not have force to drive him from his down, will be loud enough to hinder him from sleep. Those moments which he cannot resolve to make useful by devoting them to the great business of his being, will still be usurped by powers that will not leave them to his disposal; remorse and vexation will seize upon them, and forbid him to enjoy what he is so desirous to appropriate.

There are other causes of inactivity incident to more active faculties and more acute discernment. He to whom many objects of persuit arise at the same time, will frequently hesitate between different desires, till a rival has precluded him, or change his course as new attractions prevail, and harrass himself without advancing. He who sees different ways to the same end, will, unless he watches carefully over his own conduct, lay out too much of his attention upon the comparison of probabilities, and the adjustment of expedients, and pause in the choice of his road, till some accident intercepts his journey. He whose penetration extends to remote consequences, and who, whenever he applies his attention to any design, discovers new prospects of advantage, and possibilities of improvement, will not easily be persuaded that his project is ripe for execution; but will superadd one contrivance to another, endeavour to unite various purposes in one operation, multiply complications, and refine niceties, till he is entangled in his own scheme, and bewildered in the perplexity of various intentions.[2] He that resolves to unite all the beauties of situation in a new purchase, must waste his life in roving to no purpose from province to province. He that hopes in the same house to obtain every convenience, may draw plans and study Palladio, but will never lay a stone. He will attempt a treatise on some important subject, and amass materials, consult

2. Cf. *Rambler* 63.

authors, and study all the dependent and collateral parts of learning, but never conclude himself qualified to write. He that has abilities to conceive perfection, will not easily be content without it; and since perfection cannot be reached, will lose the opportunity of doing well in the vain hope of unattainable excellence.

The certainty that life cannot be long, and the probability that it will be much shorter than nature allows,, ought to awaken every man to the active prosecution of whatever he is desirous to perform. It is true that no diligence can ascertain success; death may intercept the swiftest career; but he who is cut off in the execution of an honest undertaking, has at least the honour of falling in his rank, and has fought the battle, though he missed the victory.

No. 135. Tuesday, 2 July 1751.

Coelum, non animum mutant.
Horace, EPISTLES, I.11.27.

Place may be chang'd; but who can change his mind?

It is impossible to take a view on any side, or observe any of the various classes that form the great community of the world, without discovering the influence of example; and admitting with new conviction the observation of Aristotle, that "man is an imitative being."[1] The greater, far the greater, number follow the track which others have beaten, without any curiosity after new discoveries, or ambition of trusting themselves to their own conduct. And, of those who break the ranks and disorder the uni-

1. *Poetics,* 4.1448^b 5–6.

formity of the march, most return in a short time from
their deviation, and prefer the equal and steady satisfaction of security before the frolicks of caprice and the
honours of adventure.

In questions difficult or dangerous it is indeed natural
to repose upon authority, and, when fear happens to predominate, upon the authority of those whom we do not
in general think wiser than ourselves. Very few have
abilities requisite for the discovery of abstruse truth; and
of those few some want leisure and some resolution. But
it is not so easy to find the reason of the universal submission to precedent where every man might safely judge for
himself; where no irreparable loss can be hazarded, nor
any mischief of long continuance incurred. Vanity might
be expected to operate where the more powerful passions
are not awakened; the mere pleasure of acknowledging
no superior might produce slight singularities, or the
hope of gaining some new degree of happiness awaken
the mind to invention or experiment.

If in any case the shackles of prescription could be
wholly shaken off, and the imagination left to act without
controul, on what occasion should it be expected, but in
the selection of lawful pleasure? Pleasure, of which the
essence is choice; which compulsion dissociates from
every thing to which nature has united it; and which
owes not only its vigour but its being to the smiles of
liberty. Yet we see that the senses, as well as the reason,
are regulated by credulity; and that most will feel, or say
that they feel, the gratifications which others have taught
them to expect.

At this time of universal migration, when almost every
one, considerable enough to attract regard, has retired, or
is preparing with all the earnestness of distress to retire,
into the country; when nothing is to be heard but the

hopes of speedy departure, or the complaints of involuntary delay; I have often been tempted to enquire what happiness is to be gained, or what inconvenience to be avoided, by this stated recession. Of the birds of passage, some follow the summer, and some the winter, because they live upon sustenance which only summer or winter can supply; but of the annual flight of human rovers it is much harder to assign the reason, because they do not appear either to find or seek any thing which is not equally afforded by the town and country.

I believe, that many of these fugitives may have heard of men whose continual wish was for the quiet of retirement, who watched every opportunity to steal away from observation, to forsake the croud, and delight themselves with "the society of solitude."[2] There is indeed scarcely any writer who has not celebrated the happiness of rural privacy, and delighted himself and his reader with the melody of birds, the whisper of groves, and the murmur of rivulets; nor any man eminent for extent of capacity, or greatness of exploits, that has not left behind him some memorials of lonely wisdom, and silent dignity.

But almost all absurdity of conduct arises from the imitation of those whom we cannot resemble. Those who thus testified their weariness of tumult and hurry, and hasted with so much eagerness to the leisure of retreat, were either men overwhelmed with the pressure of difficult employments, harrassed with importunities, and distracted with multiplicity; or men wholly engrossed by speculative sciences, who having no other end of life but to learn and teach, found their searches interrupted by the common commerce of civility, and their reasonings disjointed by frequent interruptions. Such men might reasonably fly to that ease and convenience which their

2. *Paradise Lost,* IX.249. Cf. the remarks on Cowley, above, *Rambler* 6.

condition allowed them to find only in the country. The statesman who devoted the greater part of his time to the publick, was desirous of keeping the remainder in his own power. The general ruffled with dangers, wearied with labours, and stunned with acclamations, gladly snatched an interval of silence and relaxation. The naturalist was unhappy where the works of providence were not always before him. The reasoner could adjust his systems only where his mind was free from the intrusion of outward objects.

Such examples of solitude very few of those who are now hastening from the town, have any pretensions to plead in their own justification, since they cannot pretend either weariness of labour, or desire of knowledge. They purpose nothing more than to quit one scene of idleness for another, and after having trifled in publick, to sleep in secrecy. The utmost that they can hope to gain is the change of ridiculousness to obscurity, and the privilege of having fewer witnesses to a life of folly. He who is not sufficiently important to be disturbed in his pursuits, but spends all his hours according to his own inclination, and has more hours than his mental faculties enable him to fill either with enjoyment or desires, can have nothing to demand of shades and valleys. As bravery is said to be a panoply, insignificancy is always a shelter.

There are however pleasures and advantages in a rural situation, which are not confined to philosophers and heroes. The freshness of the air, the verdure of the woods, the paint of the meadows, and the unexhausted variety which summer scatters upon the earth, may easily give delight to an unlearned spectator. It is not necessary that he who looks with pleasure on the colours of a flower should study the principles of vegetation, or that the Ptolemaick and Copernican system should be compared before the light of the sun can gladden, or its warmth invigorate. Novelty is itself a source of gratification, and Milton justly observes,[3] that to him who has been long pent up in cities no rural object can be presented, which will not delight or refresh some of his senses.

Yet even these easy pleasures are missed by the greater part of those who waste their summer in the country. Should any man pursue his acquaintances to their retreats, he would find few of them listening to Philomel, loitering in woods, or plucking daisies, catching the healthy gale of the morning, or watching the gentle coruscations of declining day. Some will be discovered at a window by the road side, rejoicing when a new cloud of dust gathers towards them, as at the approach of a momentary supply of conversation, and a short relief from the tediousness of unideal vacancy. Others are placed in the adjacent villages, where they look only upon houses as in the rest of the year, with no change of objects but what a remove to any new street in London might have given them. The same set of acquaintances still settle together, and the form of life is not otherwise diversified than by doing the same things in a different place. They pay and receive visits in the usual form, they frequent the walks in the morning, they deal cards at night, they attend to the same tattle, and dance with the same partners; nor can they at their return to their former habitation congratulate themselves on any other advantage, than that they have passed their time like others of the same rank; and have the same right to talk of the happiness and beauty of the country, of happiness which they never felt, and beauty which they never regarded.

To be able to procure its own entertainments, and to subsist upon its own stock, is not the prerogative of every

3. *Paradise Lost,* IX.445–51.

mind. There are indeed understandings so fertile and comprehensive, that they can always feed reflection with new supplies, and suffer nothing from the preclusion of adventitious amusements; as some cities have within their own walls enclosed ground enough to feed their inhabitants in a siege. But others live only from day to day, and must be constantly enabled, by foreign supplies, to keep out the encroachments of languor and stupidity. Such could not indeed be blamed for hovering within reach of their usual pleasures, more than any other animal for not quitting its native element, were not their faculties contracted by their own fault. But let not those who go into the country, merely because they dare not be left alone at home, boast their love of nature, or their qualifications for solitude; nor pretend that they receive instantaneous infusions of wisdom from the Dryads, and are able, when they leave smoke and noise behind, to act, or think, or reason for themselves.

No. 146. Saturday, 10 August 1751.

Sunt illic duo, tresve, qui revolvant
Nostrarum tineas ineptiarum:
Sed cum sponsio, fabulaeque lassae
De Scorpo fuerint et Incitato.

                                    Martial, XI.1.13–16.

'Tis possible that one or two
These fooleries of mine may view;
But then the bettings must be o'er,
Nor Crab or Childers[1] talk'd of more.

                                    F. Lewis.

1. Noted racing horses of the day. Childers may refer either to Lord Chedworth's Grey Childers or, more probably, the Hampton-Court Childers. Cf. *Idler* 62 (par. 10).

None of the projects or designs which exercise the mind of man, are equally subject to obstructions and disappointments with the pursuit of fame. Riches cannot easily be denied to them who have something of greater value to offer in exchange; he whose fortune is endangered by litigation, will not refuse to augment the wealth of the lawyer; he whose days are darkened by languor, or whose nerves are excruciated by pain, is compelled to pay tribute to the science of healing. But praise may be always omitted without inconvenience. When once a man has made celebrity necessary to his happiness, he has put it in the power of the weakest and most timorous malignity, if not to take away his satisfaction, at least to withhold it. His enemies may indulge their pride by airy negligence, and gratify their malice by quiet neutrality. They that could never have injured a character by invectives may combine to annihilate it by silence; as the women of Rome threatened to put an end to conquest and dominion, by supplying no children to the commonwealth.

When a writer has with long toil produced a work intended to burst upon mankind with unexpected lustre, and withdraw the attention of the learned world from every other controversy or enquiry, he is seldom contented to wait long without the enjoyment of his new praises. With an imagination full of his own importance, he walks out like a monarch in disguise, to learn the various opinions of his readers. Prepared to feast upon admiration; composed to encounter censures without emotion; and determined not to suffer his quiet to be injured by a sensibility too exquisite of praise or blame, but to laugh with equal contempt at vain objections and injudicious commendations, he enters the places of mingled conversation, sits down to his tea in an obscure corner, and while he appears to examine a file of antiquated journals, catches the conversation of the whole room. He listens, but hears no mention of his book, and therefore supposes that he has disappointed his curiosity by delay, and that as men of learning would naturally begin their conversation with such a wonderful novelty, they had digressed to other subjects before his arrival. The company disperses, and their places are supplied by others equally ignorant, or equally careless. The same expectation hurries him to another place, from which the same disappointment drives him soon away. His impatience then grows violent and tumultuous; he ranges over the town with restless curiosity, and hears in one quarter of a cricket-match, in another of a pick-pocket; is told by some of an unexpected bankrupcy, by others of a turtle feast; is sometimes provoked by importunate enquiries after the white bear, and sometimes with praises of the dancing dog; he is afterwards entreated to give his judgment upon a wager about the height of the monument; invited to see a foot race in the adjacent villages; desired to read a ludicrous advertisement; or consulted about the most effectual method of making enquiry after a favourite cat. The whole world is busied in affairs, which he thinks below the notice of reasonable creatures, and which are nevertheless sufficient to withdraw all regard from his labours and his merits.

He resolves at last to violate his own modesty, and to recal the talkers from their folly by an enquiry after himself. He finds every one provided with an answer; one has seen the work advertised, but never met with any that had read it; another has been so often imposed upon by specious titles, that he never buys a book till its character is established; a third wonders what any man can hope to produce after so many writers of greater eminence; the next has enquired after the author, but can hear no account of him, and therefore suspects the name to be fictitious; and another knows him to be a man condemned by indigence to write too frequently what he does not understand.

Many are the consolations with which the unhappy author endeavours to allay his vexation, and fortify his patience. He has written with too little indulgence to the understanding of common readers; he has fallen upon an age in which solid knowledge, and delicate refinement, have given way to low merriment and idle buffoonry, and therefore no writer can hope for distinction, who has any higher purpose than to raise laughter. He finds that his enemies, such as superiority will always raise, have been industrious, while his performance was in the press, to vilify and blast it; and that the bookseller, whom he had resolved to enrich, has rivals that obstruct the circulation of his copies. He at last reposes upon the consideration, that the noblest works of learning and genius have always made their way slowly against ignorance and prejudice; and that reputation which is never to be lost, must be gradually obtained, as animals of longest life are observed not soon to attain their full stature and strength.[2]

By such arts of voluntary delusion does every man endeavour to conceal his own unimportance from himself. It is long before we are convinced of the small proportion which every individual bears to the collective body of mankind; or learn how few can be interested in the fortune of any single man; how little vacancy is left in the world for any new object of attention; to how small extent the brightest blaze of merit can be spread amidst the mists of business and of folly; and how soon it is clouded by the intervention of other novelties. Not only the writer

2. Cf. this and the following paragraph with the fine passage, similar in phrasing, in "Savage," *Lives*, II. 379 (pars. 164–66).

of books, but the commander of armies, and the deliverer of nations, will easily outlive all noisy and popular reputation: he may be celebrated for a time by the public voice, but his actions and his name will soon be considered as remote and unaffecting, and be rarely mentioned but by those whose alliance gives them some vanity to gratify by frequent commemoration.

It seems not to be sufficiently considered how little renown can be admitted in the world. Mankind are kept perpetually busy by their fears or desires, and have not more leisure from their own affairs, than to acquaint themselves with the accidents of the current day. Engaged in contriving some refuge from calamity, or in shortening the way to some new possession, they seldom suffer their thoughts to wander to the past or future; none but a few solitary students have leisure to enquire into the claims of antient heroes or sages, and names which hoped to range over kingdoms and continents shrink at last into cloisters or colleges.

Nor is it certain, that even of these dark and narrow habitations, these last retreats of fame, the possession will be long kept. Of men devoted to literature very few extend their views beyond some particular science, and the greater part seldom enquire, even in their own profession, for any authors but those whom the present mode of study happens to force upon their notice; they desire not to fill their minds with unfashionable knowledge, but contentedly resign to oblivion those books which they now find censured or neglected.

The hope of fame is necessarily connected with such considerations as must abate the ardour of confidence, and repress the vigour of pursuit. Whoever claims renown from any kind of excellence, expects to fill the place which is now possessed by another, for there are already

names of every class sufficient to employ all that will desire to remember them; and surely he that is pushing his
predecessors into the gulph of obscurity, cannot but
sometimes suspect, that he must himself sink in like manner, and as he stands upon the same precipice, be swept
away with the same violence.

It sometimes happens, that fame begins when life is at
an end; but far the greater number of candidates for
applause have owed their reception in the world to some
favourable casualties, and have therefore immediately
sunk into neglect, when death stripped them of their
casual influence, and neither fortune nor patronage op-
erated in their favour. Among those who have better
claims to regard, the honour paid to their memory is
commonly proportionate to the reputation which they
enjoyed in their lives, though still growing fainter, as it
is at a greater distance from the first emission; and since
it is so difficult to obtain the notice of contemporaries,
how little is to be hoped from future times? What can
merit effect by its own force, when the help of art or
friendship can scarcely support it?

No. 156. Saturday, 14 September 1751.

Nunquam aliud natura, aliud sapientia dicit.
                                        Juvenal, XIV.321.

For wisdom ever echoes nature's voice.

Every government, say the politicians, is perpetually de-
generating towards corruption, from which it must be
rescued at certain periods by the resuscitation of its first
principles, and the re-establishment of its original constitution. Every animal body, according to the methodick
physicians, is, by the predominance of some exuberant

quality, continually declining towards disease and death, which must be obviated by a seasonable reduction of the peccant humour to the just equipoise which health requires.

In the same manner the studies of mankind, all at least which, not being subject to rigorous demonstration, admit the influence of fancy and caprice, are perpetually tending to error and confusion. Of the great principles of truth which the first speculatists discovered, the simplicity is embarrassed by ambitious additions, or the evidence obscured by inaccurate argumentation; and as they descend from one succession of writers to another, like light transmitted from room to room, they lose their strength and splendour, and fade at last in total evanescence.

The systems of learning therefore must be sometimes reviewed, complications analised into principles, and knowledge disentangled from opinion. It is not always possible, without a close inspection, to separate the genuine shoots of consequential reasoning, which grow out of some radical postulate, from the branches which art has engrafted on it. The accidental prescriptions of authority, when time has procured them veneration, are often confounded with the laws of nature, and those rules are supposed coeval with reason, of which the first rise cannot be discovered.[1]

Criticism has sometimes permitted fancy to dictate the laws by which fancy ought to be restrained, and fallacy to perplex the principles by which fallacy is to be detected; her superintendance of others has betrayed her to negligence of herself; and, like the antient Scythians,[2] by extending her conquests over distant regions, she has left her throne vacant to her slaves.

1. Cf. *Rambler* 158 (par. 1).
2. Herodotus, IV.1–4.

Among the laws of which the desire of extending authority, or ardour of promoting knowledge has prompted the prescription, all which writers have received, had not the same original right to our regard. Some are to be considered as fundamental and indispensable, others only as useful and convenient; some as dictated by reason and necessity, others as enacted by despotick antiquity; some as invincibly supported by their conformity to the order of nature and operations of the intellect; others as formed by accident, or instituted by example, and therefore always liable to dispute and alteration.

That many rules have been advanced without consulting nature or reason, we cannot but suspect, when we find it peremptorily decreed by the antient masters, that "only three speaking personages should appear at once upon the stage";[3] a law which, as the variety and intricacy of modern plays has made it impossible to be observed, we now violate without scruple, and, as experience proves, without inconvenience.

The original of this precept was merely accidental. Tragedy was a monody or solitary song in honour of Bacchus, improved afterwards into a dialogue by the addition of another speaker; but the antients, remembering that the tragedy was at first pronounced only by one, durst not for some time venture beyond two; at last when custom and impunity had made them daring, they extended their liberty to the admission of three, but restrained themselves by a critical edict from further exorbitance.

By what accident the number of acts was limited to five, I know not that any author has informed us; but certainly it is not determined by any necessity arising either from

3. Horace, *Ars Poetica*, 192; cf. Aristotle, *Poetics*, 4.1449ᵃ 15–19.

the nature of action or propriety of exhibition. An act is only the representation of such a part of the business of the play as proceeds in an unbroken tenor, or without any intermediate pause. Nothing is more evident than that of every real, and by consequence of every dramatick action, the intervals may be more or fewer than five; and indeed the rule is upon the English stage every day broken in effect, without any other mischief than that which arises from an absurd endeavour to observe it in appearance. Whenever the scene is shifted the act ceases, since some time is necessarily supposed to elapse while the personages of the drama change their place.

With no greater right to our obedience have the criticks confined the dramatic action to a certain number of hours.[4] Probability requires that the time of action should approach somewhat nearly to that of exhibition, and those plays will always be thought most happily conducted which croud the greatest variety into the least space. But since it will frequently happen that some delusion must be admitted, I know not where the limits of imagination can be fixed. It is rarely observed that minds not prepossessed by mechanical criticism feel any offence from the extension of the intervals between the acts; nor can I conceive it absurd or impossible, that he who can multiply three hours into twelve or twenty-four, might image with equal ease a greater number.

I know not whether he that professes to regard no other laws than those of nature, will not be inclined to receive tragi-comedy to his protection, whom, however generally condemned, her own laurels have hitherto shaded from the fulminations of criticism. For what is there in the mingled drama which impartial reason can condemn?

4. With the discussion both of the unities and of tragi-comedy (below) cf. *Preface to Shakespeare* (pars. 14–28, 42–59).

The connexion of important with trivial incidents, since it is not only common but perpetual in the world, may surely be allowed upon the stage, which pretends only to be the mirrour of life. The impropriety of suppressing passions before we have raised them to the intended agitation, and of diverting the expectation from an event which we keep suspended only to raise it, may be speciously urged. But will not experience shew this objection to be rather subtle than just? is it not certain that the tragic and comic affections have been moved alternately with equal force, and that no plays have oftner filled the eye with tears, and the breast with palpitation, than those which are variegated with interludes of mirth?

I do not however think it safe to judge of works of genius merely by the event. These resistless vicissitudes of the heart, this alternate prevalence of merriment and solemnity, may sometimes be more properly ascribed to the vigour of the writer than the justness of the design: and instead of vindicating tragi-comedy by the success of Shakespeare, we ought perhaps to pay new honours to that transcendent and unbounded genius that could preside over the passions in sport; who, to actuate the affections, needed not the slow gradation of common means, but could fill the heart with instantaneous jollity or sorrow, and vary our disposition as he changed his scenes. Perhaps the effects even of Shakespeare's poetry might have been yet greater, had he not counter-acted himself; and we might have been more interested in the distresses of his heroes had we not been so frequently diverted by the jokes of his buffoons.

There are other rules more fixed and obligatory. It is necessary that of every play the chief action should be single; for since a play represents some transaction, through its regular maturation to its final event, two actions equally important must evidently constitute two plays.

As the design of tragedy is to instruct by moving the passions, it must always have a hero, a personage apparently and incontestably superior to the rest, upon whom the attention may be fixed, and the anxiety suspended. For though of two persons opposing each other with equal abilities and equal virtue, the auditor will inevitably in time choose his favourite, yet as that choice must be without any cogency of conviction, the hopes or fears which it raises will be faint and languid. Of two heroes acting in confederacy against a common enemy, the virtues or dangers will give little emotion, because each claims our concern with the same right, and the heart lies at rest between equal motives.

It ought to be the first endeavour of a writer to distinguish nature from custom, or that which is established because it is right, from that which is right only because it is established; that he may neither violate essential principles by a desire of novelty, nor debar himself from the attainment of beauties within his view by a needless fear of breaking rules which no literary dictator had authority to enact.

No. 158. Saturday, 21 September 1751.

Grammatici certant, et adhuc sub judice lis est.
　　　　　　　　　　　　Horace, ARS POETICA, 1. 78.

——————————————Criticks yet contend,
And of their vain disputings find no end.
　　　　　　　　　　　　　　　　　　Francis.

Criticism, though dignified from the earliest ages by the labours of men eminent for knowledge and sagacity; and, since the revival of polite literature, the favourite study of European scholars, has not yet attained the certainty and stability of science. The rules hitherto received, are seldom drawn from any settled principle or self-evident postulate, or adapted to the natural and invariable constitution of things; but will be found upon examination the arbitrary edicts of legislators, authorised only by themselves, who, out of various means by which the same end may be attained, selected such as happened to occur to their own reflexion, and then by a law which idleness and timidity were too willing to obey, prohibited new experiments of wit, restrained fancy from the indulgence of her innate inclination to hazard and adventure, and condemned all future flights of genius to pursue the path of the Meonian eagle.[1]

This authority may be more justly opposed, as it is apparently derived from them whom they endeavour to controul; for we owe few of the rules of writing to the acuteness of criticks, who have generally no other merit than that, having read the works of great authors with attention, they have observed the arrangement of their matter, or the graces of their expression, and then expected honour and reverence for precepts which they never could have invented: so that practice has introduced rules, rather than rules have directed practice.

For this reason the laws of every species of writing have been settled by the ideas of him who first raised it to reputation, without enquiry whether his performances were not yet susceptible of improvement. The excellencies and faults of celebrated writers have been equally recommended to posterity; and so far has blind reverence prevailed, that even the number of their books has been thought worthy of imitation.

1. Homer (reputedly a native of Meonia—i.e. Lydia).

The imagination of the first authors of lyrick poetry was vehement and rapid, and their knowledge various and extensive. Living in an age when science had been little cultivated, and when the minds of their auditors, not being accustomed to accurate inspection, were easily dazzled by glaring ideas, they applied themselves to instruct, rather by short sentences and striking thoughts, than by regular argumentation; and finding attention more successfully excited by sudden sallies and unexpected exclamations, than by the more artful and placid beauties of methodical deduction, they loosed their genius to its own course, passed from one sentiment to another without expressing the intermediate ideas, and roved at large over the ideal world with such lightness and agility that their footsteps are scarcely to be traced.

From this accidental peculiarity of the ancient writers the criticks deduce the rules of lyrick poetry, which they have set free from all the laws by which other compositions are confined, and allow to neglect the niceties of transition, to start into remote digressions, and to wander without restraint from one scene of imagery to another.

A writer of later times has, by the vivacity of his essays, reconciled mankind to the same licentiousness in short dissertations; and he therefore who wants skill to form a plan, or diligence to pursue it, needs only entitle his performance an essay, to acquire the right of heaping together the collections of half his life, without order, coherence, or propriety.

In writing, as in life, faults are endured without disgust when they are associated with transcendent merit, and may be sometimes recommended to weak judgments by the lustre which they obtain from their union with excellence; but it is the business of those who presume to superintend the taste or morals of mankind, to separate delusive combinations, and distinguish that which may be praised from that which can only be excused. As vices never promote happiness, though when overpowered by more active and more numerous virtues, they cannot totally destroy it; so confusion and irregularity produce no beauty, though they cannot always obstruct the brightness of genius and learning. To proceed from one truth to another, and connect distant propositions by regular consequences, is the great prerogative of man. Independent and unconnected sentiments flashing upon the mind in quick succession, may, for a time, delight by their novelty, but they differ from systematical reasoning, as single notes from harmony, as glances of lightening from the radiance of the sun.

When rules are thus drawn, rather from precedents than reason, there is danger not only from the faults of an author, but from the errors of those who criticise his works; since they may often mislead their pupils by false representations, as the Ciceronians of the sixteenth century were betrayed into barbarisms by corrupt copies of their darling writer.

It is established at present, that the proemial lines of a poem, in which the general subject is proposed, must be void of glitter and embellishment. "The first lines of *Paradise Lost*," says Addison, "are perhaps as plain, simple, and unadorned as any of the whole poem, in which particular the author has conformed himself to the example of Homer and the precept of Horace."[2]

This observation seems to have been made by an implicit adoption of the common opinion, without consideration either of the precept or example. Had Horace been consulted, he would have been found to direct only what should be comprised in the proposition, not how it

2. *Spectator* 303.

should be expressed, and to have commended Homer in
opposition to a meaner poet, not for the gradual elevation
of his diction, but the judicious expansion of his plan; for
displaying unpromised events, not for producing unexpected elegancies.

———— *Speciosa dehinc miracula promit,*
Antiphaten Scyllamque, & cum Cyclope Charybdim.
                              Horace, ARS POETICA, ll. 144–45.

But from a cloud of smoke he breaks to light,
And pours his specious miracles to sight;
Antiphates his hideous feast devours,
Charybdis barks, and Polyphemus roars.
                                                              Francis.

If the exordial verses of Homer be compared with the
rest of the poem, they will not appear remarkable for
plainness or simplicity, but rather eminently adorned
and illuminated.

Ἄνδρά μοι ἔννεπε Μοῦσα πολύτροπον, ὅς μάλα πολλὰ
Πλάγχθη, ἐπεὶ Τροίης ἱερὸν πτολίεθρον ἔπερσε·
Πολλῶν δ' ἀνθρώπων ἴδεν ἄστεα, καὶ νόον ἔγνω.
Πολλὰ δ' ογ' ἐν πόντῳ πάθεν ἄλγεα ὅν κατὰ θυμόν,
Ἀρνύμενος ἥν τε ψυχὴν καὶ νόστον ἑταίρων·
Ἀλλ' οὐδ' ὣς ἑτάρους ἐρρύσσατο ἱέμενός περ·
Αὐτῶν γὰρ σφετέρῃσιν ἀτασθαλίῃσιν ὄλοντο,
Νήπιοι οἳ κατὰ βοῦς ὑπερίονος ἠελίοιο
Ἤσθιον· αὐτὰρ ὅ τοῖσιν ἀφείλετο νόστιμον ἦμαρ·
Τῶν ἁμόθεν γε, θεὰ, θύγατερ Διὸς, εἰπὲ καὶ ἡμῖν.

                                                ODYSSEY, I.1–10.

The man, for wisdom's various arts renown'd,
Long exercis'd in woes, O muse! resound.
Who, when his arms had wrought the destin'd fall

Of sacred Troy, and raz'd her heav'n-built wall,
Wand'ring from clime to clime, observant stray'd,
Their manners noted, and their states survey'd.
On stormy seas unnumber'd toils he bore,
Safe with his friends to gain his natal shore:
Vain toils! their impious folly dar'd to prey
On herds devoted to the god of day;
The god vindictive doom'd them never more
(Ah men unbless'd) to touch that natal shore.
O snatch some portion of these acts from fate,
Celestial muse! and to our world relate.

Pope.

The first verses of the *Iliad* are in like manner particularly splendid, and the proposition of the *Æneid* closes with dignity and magnificence not often to be found even in the poetry of Virgil.

The intent of the introduction is to raise expectation, and suspend it; something therefore must be discovered, and something concealed; and the poet, while the fertility of his invention is yet unknown, may properly recommend himself by the grace of his language.

He that reveals too much, or promises too little; he that never irritates the intellectual appetite, or that immediately satiates it, equally defeats his own purpose. It is necessary to the pleasure of the reader, that the events should not be anticipated, and how then can his attention be invited, but by grandeur of expression?

From No. 159. Tuesday, 24 September 1751.

Sunt verba et voces, quibus hunc lenire dolorem
Possis, et magnam morbi deponere partem.

Horace, EPISTLES, I.1.34–35.

The pow'r of words, and soothing sounds appease
The raging pain, and lessen the disease.

                                                    Francis.

·   ·   ·   ·

No cause more frequently produces bashfulness than too high an opinion of our own importance. He that imagines an assembly filled with his merit, panting with expectation, and hushed with attention, easily terrifies himself with the dread of disappointing them, and strains his imagination in pursuit of something that may vindicate the veracity of fame, and shew that his reputation was not gained by chance. He considers, that what he shall say or do will never be forgotten; that renown or infamy are suspended upon every syllable, and that nothing ought to fall from him which will not bear the test of time. Under such solicitude, who can wonder that the mind is overwhelmed, and by struggling with attempts above her strength, quickly sinks into languishment and despondency.

The most useful medicines are often unpleasing to the taste. Those who are oppressed by their own reputation, will perhaps not be comforted by hearing that their cares are unnecessary.[1] But the truth is, that no man is much regarded by the rest of the world. He that considers how little he dwells upon the condition of others, will learn how little the attention of others is attracted by himself. While we see multitudes passing before us, of whom perhaps not one appears to deserve our notice, or excites our sympathy, we should remember, that we likewise are lost in the same throng, that the eye which happens to glance upon us is turned in a moment on him that follows us,

1. Cf. the satiric sketch, in *Rambler* 16, of the young writer who considers himself "condemned to all the miseries of high reputation."

and that the utmost which we can reasonably hope or fear is to fill a vacant hour with prattle, and be forgotten.

No. 165. Tuesday, 15 October 1751.

Ἦν νέος, ἀλλὰ πένης· νῦν γηρῶν, πλούσιός εἰμι.
   Ὦ μόνος ἐκ πάντων οἰκτρὸς ἐν ἀμφοτέροις,
Ὃς τότε μὲν χρῆσθαι δυνάμην, ὁπότ' οὐδὲ ἓν εἶχον.
   Νῦν δ' ὁπότε χρῆσθαι μὴ δύναμαι, τότ' ἔχω.

GREEK ANTHOLOGY, IX.138 (Antiphilus).

Young was I once and poor, now rich and old;
A harder case than mine was never told;
Blest with the pow'r to use them —— I had none;
Loaded with *riches* now, the pow'r is gone.

F. Lewis.

TO THE RAMBLER.

SIR,

The writers who have undertaken the unpromising task of moderating desire, exert all the power of their eloquence, to shew that happiness is not the lot of man, and have by many arguments and examples proved the instability of every condition by which envy or ambition are excited. They have set before our eyes all the calamities to which we are exposed from the frailty of nature, the influence of accident, or the stratagems of malice; they have terrified greatness with conspiracies, and riches with anxieties, wit with criticism, and beauty with disease.

All the force of reason and all the charms of language are indeed necessary to support positions which every man hears with a wish to confute them. Truth finds an easy entrance into the mind when she is introduced by desire, and attended by pleasure; but when she intrudes

uncalled, and brings only fear and sorrow in her train,
the passes of the intellect are barred against her by prejudice and passion; if she sometimes forces her way by
the batteries of argument, she seldom long keeps possession of her conquests, but is ejected by some favoured
enemy, or at best obtains only a nominal sovereignty,
without influence and without authority.

That life is short we are all convinced, and yet suffer
not that conviction to repress our projects or limit our
expectations; that life is miserable we all feel, and yet we
believe that the time is near when we shall feel it no
longer. But to hope happiness and immortality is equally
vain. Our state may indeed be more or less imbittered,
as our duration may be more or less contracted; yet the
utmost felicity which we can ever attain, will be little
better than alleviation of misery, and we shall always feel
more pain from our wants than pleasure from our enjoyments. The incident which I am going to relate will shew,
that to destroy the effect of all our success, it is not necessary that any signal calamity should fall upon us, that
we should be harrassed by implacable persecution, or
excruciated by irremediable pains; the brightest hours of
prosperity have their clouds, and the stream of life, if it
is not ruffled by obstructions, will grow putrid by stag-
nation.[1]

My father resolving not to imitate the folly of his ancestors, who had hitherto left the younger sons encum-
brances on the eldest, destined me to a lucrative
profession, and I being careful to lose no opportunity of
improvement, was at the usual time in which young men
enter the world, well qualified for the exercise of the
business which I had chosen.

1. "Do not suffer life to stagnate: it will grow muddy for want of
motion" (*Rasselas,* ch. 35, par. 8).

My eagerness to distinguish myself in publick, and my impatience of the narrow scheme of life to which my indigence confined me, did not suffer me to continue long in the town where I was born. I went away as from a place of confinement, with a resolution to return no more, till I should be able to dazzle with my splendor those who now looked upon me with contempt, to reward those who had paid honours to my dawning merit, and to show all who had suffered me to glide by them unknown and neglected, how much they mistook their interest in omitting to propitiate a genius like mine.

Such were my intentions when I sallied forth into the unknown world, in quest of riches and honours, which I expected to procure in a very short time; for what could withold them from industry and knowledge? He that indulges hope will always be disappointed. Reputation I very soon obtained, but as merit is much more cheaply acknowledged than rewarded, I did not find myself yet enriched in proportion to my celebrity.

I had however in time surmounted the obstacles by which envy and competition obstruct the first attempts of a new claimant, and saw my opponents and censurers tacitly confessing their despair of success, by courting my friendship and yielding to my influence. They who once persued me, were now satisfied to escape from me; and they who had before thought me presumptuous in hoping to overtake them, had now their utmost wish, if they were permitted at no great distance quietly to follow me.

My wants were not madly multiplied as my acquisitions encreased, and the time came at length when I thought myself enabled to gratify all reasonable desires, and when, therefore, I resolved to enjoy that plenty and serenity which I had been hitherto labouring to procure, to enjoy them while I was yet neither crushed by age into infirmity, nor so habituated to a particular manner of life as to be unqualified for new studies or entertainments.

I now quitted my profession, and to set myself at once free from all importunities to resume it, changed my residence, and devoted the remaining part of my time to quiet and amusement. Amidst innumerable projects of pleasure which restless idleness incited me to form, and of which most, when they came to the moment of execution, were rejected for others of no longer continuance, some accident revived in my imagination the pleasing ideas of my native place. It was now in my power to visit those from whom I had been so long absent, in such a manner as was consistent with my former resolution, and I wondered how it could happen that I had so long delayed my own happiness.

Full of the admiration which I should excite, and the homage which I should receive, I dressed my servants in a more ostentatious livery, purchased a magnificent chariot, and resolved to dazzle the inhabitants of the little town with an unexpected blaze of greatness.

While the preparations that vanity required were made for my departure, which, as workmen will not easily be hurried beyond their ordinary rate, I thought very tedious, I solaced my impatience with imaging the various censures that my appearance would produce, the hopes which some would feel from my bounty, the terror which my power would strike on others; the aukward respect with which I should be accosted by timorous officiousness; and the distant reverence with which others less familiar to splendour and dignity would be contented to gaze upon me. I deliberated a long time, whether I should immediately descend to a level with my former acquaintances, or make my condescension more grateful by a gentle transition from haughtiness and reserve. At length

I determined to forget some of my companions, till they discovered themselves by some indubitable token, and to receive the congratulations of others upon my good fortune with indifference, to show that I always expected what I had now obtained. The acclamations of the populace I purposed to reward with six hogsheads of ale, and a roasted ox, and then recommend to them to return to their work.

At last all the trappings of grandeur were fitted, and I began the journey of triumph, which I could have wished to have ended in the same moment, but my horses felt none of their master's ardour, and I was shaken four days upon rugged roads. I then entered the town, and having graciously let fall the glasses, that my person might be seen, passed slowly through the street. The noise of the wheels brought the inhabitants to their doors, but I could not perceive that I was known by them. At last I alighted, and my name, I suppose, was told by my servants, for the barber stept from the opposite house, and seized me by the hand with honest joy in his countenance, which, according to the rule that I had prescribed to myself, I repressed with a frigid graciousness. The fellow, instead of sinking into dejection, turned away with contempt, and left me to consider how the second salutation should be received. The next friend was better treated, for I soon found that I must purchase by civility that regard which I had expected to enforce by insolence.

There was yet no smoak of bonfires, no harmony of bells, no shout of crouds, nor riot of joy; the business of the day went forward as before, and after having ordered a splendid supper, which no man came to partake, and which my chagrin hindered me from tasting, I went to bed, where the vexation of disappointment overpowered the fatigue of my journey, and kept me from sleep.

I rose so much humbled by those mortifications, as to enquire after the present state of the town, and found that I had been absent too long to obtain the triumph which had flattered my expectation. Of the friends whose compliments I expected, some had long ago moved to distant provinces, some had lost in the maladies of age all sense of another's prosperity, and some had forgotten our former intimacy amidst care and distresses. Of three whom I had resolved to punish for their former offences by a longer continuance of neglect, one was, by his own industry, raised above my scorn, and two were sheltered from it in the grave. All those whom I loved, feared, or hated, all whose envy or whose kindness I had hopes of contemplating with pleasure, were swept away, and their place was filled by a new generation with other views and other competitions; and among many proofs of the impotence of wealth, I found that it conferred upon me very few distinctions in my native place.[2]

I am, Sir, &c.
SEROTINUS.[3]

No. 176. Saturday, 23 November 1751.

———— *Naso suspendere adunco.*

Horace, SATIRES, 1.6.5.

On me you turn the nose ————

There are many vexatious accidents and uneasy situations which raise little compassion for the sufferer, and which

2. Cf. the above paragraph with the traveler's return to his native place in *Idler* 58.

3. Mrs. Thrale, probably with some exaggeration, states that Johnson himself considered the character Serotinus "as a masterpiece in the science of life and manners" *(Miscellanies,* I.179).

no man but those whom they immediately distress, can regard with seriousness. Petty mischiefs, that have no influence on futurity, nor extend their effects to the rest of life, are always seen with a kind of malicious pleasure. A mistake or embarrasment, which for the present moment fills the face with blushes, and the mind with confusion, will have no other effect upon those who observe it than that of convulsing them with irresistible laughter. Some circumstances of misery are so powerfully ridiculous, that neither kindness nor duty can withstand them; they bear down love, interest, and reverence, and force the friend, the dependent, or the child, to give way to instantaneous motions of merriment.

Among the principal of comick calamities, may be reckoned the pain which an author, not yet hardened into insensibility, feels at the onset of a furious critick, whose age, rank or fortune gives him confidence to speak without reserve; who heaps one objection upon another, and obtrudes his remarks, and enforces his corrections without tenderness or awe.

The author, full of the importance of his work, and anxious for the justification of every syllable, starts and kindles at the slightest attack; the critick, eager to establish his superiority, triumphing in every discovery of failure, and zealous to impress the cogency of his arguments, pursues him from line to line without cessation or remorse. The critick, who hazards little, proceeds with vehemence, impetuosity and fearlessness; the author, whose quiet and fame, and life and immortality are involved in the controversy, tries every art of subterfuge and defence; maintains modestly what he resolves never to yield, and yields unwillingly what cannot be maintained. The critick's purpose is to conquer, the author only hopes to escape; the critick therefore knits his brow, and raises his voice, and rejoices whenever he perceives any tokens of pain excited by the pressure of his assertions, or the point of his sarcasms. The author, whose endeavour is at once to mollify and elude his persecutor, composes his features, and softens his accent, breaks the force of assault by retreat, and rather steps aside than flies or advances.

As it very seldom happens that the rage of extemporary criticism inflicts fatal or lasting wounds, I know not that the laws of benevolence entitle this distress to much sympathy. The diversion of baiting an author has the sanction of all ages and nations, and is more lawful than the sport of teizing other animals, because for the most part he comes voluntarily to the stake, furnished, as he imagines, by the patron powers of literature, with resistless weapons, and impenetrable armour, with the mail of the boar of Erymanth, and the paws of the lion of Nemea.[1]

But the works of genius are sometimes produced by other motives than vanity; and he whom necessity or duty enforces to write, is not always so well satisfied with himself, as not to be discouraged by censorious impudence. It may therefore be necessary to consider how they whom publication lays open to the insults of such as their obscurity secures against reprisals, may extricate themselves from unexpected encounters.

Vida, a man of considerable skill in the politicks of literature, directs his pupil wholly to abandon his defence, and even when he can irrefragably refute all objections, to suffer tamely the exultations of his antagonist.[2]

This rule may perhaps be just, when advice is asked,

1. Alluding to two of the labors of Hercules.
2. *Ars Poetica*, III.469–72.

and severity solicited, because no man tells his opinion so freely as when he imagines it received with implicit veneration; and critics ought never to be consulted but while errors may yet be rectified or insipidity suppressed. But when the book has once been dismissed into the world, and can be no more retouched, I know not whether a very different conduct should not be prescribed, and whether firmness and spirit may not sometimes be of use to overpower arrogance and repel brutality. Softness, diffidence and moderation will often be mistaken for imbecility and dejection; they lure cowardice to the attack by the hopes of easy victory, and it will soon be found that he whom every man thinks he can conquer, shall never be at peace.

The animadversions of criticks are commonly such as may easily provoke the sedatest writer to some quickness of resentment and asperity of reply. A man who by long consideration has familiarised a subject to his own mind, carefully surveyed the series of his thoughts, and planned all the parts of his composition into a regular dependance on each other, will often start at the sinistrous interpretations, or absurd remarks of haste and ignorance, and wonder by what infatuation they have been led away from the obvious sense, and upon what peculiar principles of judgment they decide against him.

The eye of the intellect, like that of the body, is not equally perfect in all, nor equally adapted in any to all objects; the end of criticism is to supply its defects; rules are the instruments of mental vision, which may indeed assist our faculties when properly used, but produce confusion and obscurity by unskilful application.

Some seem always to read with the microscope of criticism, and employ their whole attention upon minute elegance, or faults scarcely visible to common observation. The dissonance of a syllable, the recurrence of the same sound, the repetition of a particle, the smallest deviation from propriety, the slightest defect in construction or arrangement, swell before their eyes into enormities. As they discern with great exactness, they comprehend but a narrow compass, and know nothing of the justness of the design, the general spirit of the performance, the artifice of connection, or the harmony of the parts; they never conceive how small a proportion that which they are busy in contemplating bears to the whole, or how the petty inaccuracies with which they are offended, are absorbed and lost in general excellence.

Others are furnished by criticism with a telescope. They see with great clearness whatever is too remote to be discovered by the rest of mankind, but are totally blind to all that lies immediately before them. They discover in every passage some secret meaning, some remote allusion, some artful allegory, or some occult imitation which no other reader ever suspected;[3] but they have no perception of the cogency of arguments, the force of pathetick sentiments, the various colours of diction, or the flowery embellishments of fancy; of all that engages the attention of others, they are totally insensible, while they pry into worlds of conjecture, and amuse themselves with phantoms in the clouds.

In criticism, as in every other art, we fail sometimes by our weakness, but more frequently by our fault. We are sometimes bewildered by ignorance, and sometimes by prejudice, but we seldom deviate far from the right, but when we deliver ourselves up to the direction of vanity.

3. Cf. the portrait of Dick Minim, *Idler* 60.

No. 183. Tuesday, 17 December 1751.

Nulla fides regni sociis, omnisque potestas
Impatiens consortis erat.

Lucan, 1.92–93.

No faith of partnership dominion owns;
Still discord hovers o'er divided thrones.

The hostility perpetually exercised between one man and another, is caused by the desire of many for that which only few can possess. Every man would be rich, powerful, and famous; yet fame, power, and riches, are only the names of relative conditions, which imply the obscurity, dependance, and poverty of greater numbers.

This universal and incessant competition, produces injury and malice by two motives, interest, and envy; the prospect of adding to our possessions what we can take from others, and the hope of alleviating the sense of our disparity by lessening others, though we gain nothing to ourselves.

Of these two malignant and destructive powers, it seems probable at the first view, that interest has the strongest and most extensive influence. It is easy to conceive that opportunities to seize what has been long wanted, may excite desires almost irresistible; but surely, the same eagerness cannot be kindled by an accidental power of destroying that which gives happiness to another. It must be more natural to rob for gain, than to ravage only for mischief.

Yet I am inclined to believe, that the great law of mutual benevolence is oftner violated by envy than by interest, and that most of the misery which the defamation of blameless actions, or the obstruction of honest endeavours brings upon the world, is inflicted by men that propose no advantage to themselves but the satisfaction of poisoning the banquet which they cannot taste, and blasting the harvest which they have no right to reap.

Interest can diffuse itself but to a narrow compass. The number is never large of those who can hope to fill the posts of degraded power, catch the fragments of shattered fortune, or succeed to the honours of depreciated beauty. But the empire of envy has no limits, as it requires to its influence very little help from external circumstances. Envy may always be produced by idleness and pride, and in what place will not they be found?

Interest requires some qualities not universally bestowed. The ruin of another will produce no profit to him, who has not discernment to mark his advantage, courage to seize, and activity to pursue it; but the cold malignity of envy may be exerted in a torpid and quiescent state, amidst the gloom of stupidity, in the coverts of cowardice. He that falls by the attacks of interest, is torn by hungry tigers; he may discover and resist his enemies. He that perishes in the ambushes of envy, is destroyed by unknown and invisible assailants, and dies like a man suffocated by a poisonous vapour, without knowledge of his danger, or possibility of contest.

Interest is seldom pursued but at some hazard. He that hopes to gain much, has commonly something to lose, and when he ventures to attack superiority, if he fails to conquer, is irrecoverably crushed. But envy may act without expence, or danger. To spread suspicion, to invent calumnies, to propagate scandal, requires neither labour nor courage. It is easy for the author of a lye, however malignant, to escape detection, and infamy needs very little industry to assist its circulation.

Envy is almost the only vice which is practicable at all times, and in every place; the only passion which can never lie quiet for want of irritation; its effects therefore are every where discoverable, and its attempts always to be dreaded.

It is impossible to mention a name which any advantageous distinction has made eminent, but some latent animosity will burst out. The wealthy trader, however he may abstract himself from publick affairs, will never want those who hint, with Shylock,[1] that ships are but boards. The beauty, adorned only with the unambitious graces of innocence and modesty, provokes, whenever she appears, a thousand murmurs of detraction. The genius, even when he endeavours only to entertain or instruct, yet suffers persecution from innumerable criticks, whose acrimony is excited merely by the pain of seeing others pleased, and of hearing applauses which another enjoys.

The frequency of envy makes it so familiar, that it escapes our notice; nor do we often reflect upon its turpitude or malignity, till we happen to feel its influence. When he that has given no provocation to malice, but by attempting to excel, finds himself pursued by multitudes whom he never saw with all the implacability of personal resentment; when he perceives clamour and malice let loose upon him as a publick enemy, and incited by every stratagem of defamation; when he hears the misfortunes of his family, or the follies of his youth exposed to the world; and every failure of conduct, or defect of nature aggravated and ridiculed; he then learns to abhor those artifices at which he only laughed before, and discovers how much the happiness of life would be advanced by the eradication of envy from the human heart.

Envy is, indeed, a stubborn weed of the mind, and

1. *Merchant of Venice,* I.30.20.

seldom yields to the culture of philosophy. There are, however, considerations, which if carefully implanted and diligently propagated, might in time overpower and repress it, since no one can nurse it for the sake of pleasure, as its effects are only shame, anguish, and perturbation.

It is above all other vices inconsistent with the character of a social being, because it sacrifices truth and kindness to very weak temptations. He that plunders a wealthy neighbour, gains as much as he takes away, and may improve his own condition in the same proportion as he impairs another's; but he that blasts a flourishing reputation, must be content with a small dividend of additional fame, so small as can afford very little consolation to balance the guilt by which it is obtained.

I have hitherto avoided that dangerous and empirical morality, which cures one vice by means of another. But envy is so base and detestable, so vile in its original, and so pernicious in its effects, that the predominance of almost any other quality is to be preferred. It is one of those lawless enemies of society, against which poisoned arrows may honestly be used. Let it, therefore, be constantly remembered, that whoever envies another, confesses his superiority, and let those be reformed by their pride who have lost their virtue.

It is no slight aggravation of the injuries which envy incites, that they are committed against those who have given no intentional provocation; and that the sufferer is often marked out for ruin, not because he has failed in any duty, but because he has dared to do more than was required.

Almost every other crime is practised by the help of some quality which might have produced esteem or love, if it had been well employed; but envy is mere unmixed and genuine evil; it pursues a hateful end by despicable means, and desires not so much its own happiness as another's misery. To avoid depravity like this, it is not necessary that any one should aspire to heroism or sanctity, but only, that he should resolve not to quit the rank which nature assigns him, and wish to maintain the dignity of a human being.

No. 188. Saturday, 4 January 1752.

———————— *Si te colo, Sexte, non amabo.*

Martial, II.55.3.

The more I honour thee, the less I love.

None of the desires dictated by vanity is more general, or less blameable, than that of being distinguished for the arts of conversation. Other accomplishments may be possessed without opportunity of exerting them, or wanted without danger that the defect can often be remarked; but as no man can live otherwise than in an hermitage, without hourly pleasure or vexation, from the fondness or neglect of those about him, the faculty of giving pleasure is of continual use. Few are more frequently envied than those who have the power of forcing attention wherever they come, whose entrance is considered as a promise of felicity, and whose departure is lamented, like the recess of the sun from northern climates, as a privation of all that enlivens fancy, or inspirits gaiety.

It is apparent, that to excellence in this valuable art, some peculiar qualifications are necessary; for every one's experience will inform him, that the pleasure which men are able to give in conversation, holds no stated proportion to their knowledge or their virtue. Many find their way to the tables and the parties of those who never consider them as of the least importance in any other place; we have all, at one time or other, been content to love those whom we could not esteem, and been persuaded to try the dangerous experiment of admitting him for a companion whom we knew to be too ignorant for a counsellor, and too treacherous for a friend.

I question whether some abatement of character is not necessary to general acceptance. Few spend their time with much satisfaction under the eye of uncontestable superiority; and therefore, among those whose presence is courted at assemblies of jollity, there are seldom found men eminently distingushed for powers or acquisitions. The wit whose vivacity condemns slower tongues to silence, the scholar whose knowledge allows no man to fancy that he instructs him, the critick who suffers no fallacy to pass undetected, and the reasoner who condemns the idle to thought, and the negligent to attention, are generally praised and feared, reverenced and avoided.

He that would please must rarely aim at such excellence as depresses his hearers in their own opinion, or debars them from the hope of contributing reciprocally to the entertainment of the company. Merriment, extorted by sallies of imagination, sprightliness of remark, or quickness of reply, is too often what the Latins call, the "Sardinian Laughter,"[1] a distortion of the face without gladness of heart.

For this reason, no stile of conversation is more extensively acceptable than the narrative. He who has stored his memory with slight anecdotes, private incidents, and personal particularities, seldom fails to find his audience favourable. Almost every man listens with eagerness to

1. See *Odyssey,* XX.302.

contemporary history; for almost every man has some real or imaginary connection with a celebrated character, some desire to advance, or oppose a rising name. Vanity often co-operates with curiosity. He that is a hearer in one place qualifies himself to become a speaker in another; for though he cannot comprehend a series of argument, or transport the volatile spirit of wit without evaporation, he yet thinks himself able to treasure up the various incidents of a story, and pleases his hopes with the information which he shall give to some inferior society.

Narratives are for the most part heard without envy, because they are not supposed to imply any intellectual qualities above the common rate. To be acquainted with facts not yet echoed by plebeian mouths, may happen to one man as well as to another, and to relate them when they are known, has in appearance so little difficulty, that every one concludes himself equal to the task.

But it is not easy, and in some situations of life not possible, to accumulate such a stock of materials as may support the expence of continual narration; and it frequently happens, that they who attempt this method of ingratiating themselves, please only at the first interview; and, for want of new supplies of intelligence, wear out their stories by continual repetition.

There would be, therefore, little hope of obtaining the praise of a good companion, were it not to be gained by more compendious methods; but such is the kindness of mankind to all, except those who aspire to real merit and rational dignity, that every understanding may find some way to excite benevolence; and whoever is not envied, may learn the art of procuring love. We are willing to be pleased, but are not willing to admire; we favour the mirth or officiousness that solicits our regard, but oppose the worth or spirit that enforces it.

The first place among those that please, because they desire only to please, is due to the "merry fellow," whose laugh is loud, and whose voice is strong; who is ready to echo every jest with obstreperous approbation, and countenance every frolick with vociferations of applause. It is not necessary to a merry fellow to have in himself any fund of jocularity, or force of conception; it is sufficient that he always appears in the highest exaltation of gladness, for the greater part of mankind are gay or serious by infection, and follow without resistance the attraction of example.

Next to the merry fellow is the "good-natured man," a being generally without benevolence, or any other virtue, than such as indolence and insensibility confer.[2] The characteristick of a good-natured man is to bear a joke; to sit unmoved and unaffected amidst noise and turbulence, profaneness and obscenity; to hear every tale without contradiction; to endure insult without reply; and to follow the stream of folly, whatever course it shall happen to take. The good-natured man is commonly the darling of the petty wits, with whom they exercise themselves in the rudiments of raillery; for he never takes advantage of failings, nor disconcerts a puny satirist with unexpected sarcasms; but while the glass continues to circulate, contentedly bears the expence of uninterrupted laughter, and retires rejoicing at his own importance.

The "modest man" is a companion of a yet lower rank, whose only power of giving pleasure is not to interrupt it. The modest man satisfies himself with peaceful silence, which all his companions are candid enough to consider as proceeding not from inability to speak, but willingness to hear.

2. See *Rambler* 72, above, n. 3.

Many, without being able to attain any general character of excellence, have some single art of entertainment
which serves them as a passport through the world. One
I have known for fifteen years[3] the darling of a weekly
club, because every night, precisely at eleven, he begins
his favourite song, and during the vocal performance by
correspondent motions of his hand, chalks out a giant
upon the wall. Another has endeared himself to a long
succession of acquaintances by sitting among them with
his wig reversed; another by contriving to smut the nose
of any stranger who was to be initiated in the club;
another by purring like a cat, and then pretending to be
frighted; and another by yelping like a hound, and calling
to the drawers to drive out the dog.[4]

Such are the arts by which cheerfulness is promoted,
and sometimes friendship established; arts, which those
who despise them should not rigorously blame, except
when they are practised at the expence of innocence; for
it is always necessary to be loved, but not always necessary
to be reverenced.

No. 196. Saturday, 1 February 1752.

Multa ferunt anni venientes commoda secum
Multa recedentes adimunt. ————
                    Horace, ARS POETICA, ll. 175–76.

The blessings flowing in with life's full tide,
Down with our ebb of life decreasing glide.
                                        Francis.

3. Approximately the time Johnson had been in London thus far.
4. For Mrs. Thrale's attempts to identify the characters in this paragraph, see *Miscellanies,* I.179.

Baxter, in the narrative of his own life, has enumerated several opinions, which, though he thought them evident and incontestable at his first entrance into the world, time and experience disposed him to change.[1]

Whoever reviews the state of his own mind from the dawn of manhood to its decline, and considers what he pursued or dreaded, slighted or esteemed at different periods of his age, will have no reason to imagine such changes of sentiment peculiar to any station or character. Every man, however careless and inattentive, has conviction forced upon him; the lectures of time obtrude themselves upon the most unwilling or dissipated auditor; and, by comparing our past with our present thoughts, we perceive that we have changed our minds, though perhaps we cannot discover when the alteration happened, or by what causes it was produced.

This revolution of sentiments occasions a perpetual contest between the old and young. They who imagine themselves entitled to veneration by the prerogative of longer life, are inclined to treat the notions of those whose conduct they superintend with superciliousness and contempt, for want of considering that the future and the past have different appearances; that the disproportion will always be great between expectation and enjoyment, between new possession and satiety; that the truth of many maxims of age, gives too little pleasure to be allowed till it is felt; and that the miseries of life would be encreased beyond all human power of endurance, if we were to enter the world with the same opinions as we carry from it.

We naturally indulge those ideas that please us. Hope will predominate in every mind, till it has been suppressed by frequent disappointments. The youth has not

1. *Reliquiae Baxterianae,* ed. Matthew Sylvester (1696), I.124–38.

yet discovered how many evils are continually hovering about us, and when he is set free from the shackles of dicipline, looks abroad into the world with rapture; he sees an elysian region open before him, so variegated with beauty, and so stored with pleasure, that his care is rather to accumulate good, than to shun evil; he stands distracted by different forms of delight, and has no other doubt than which path to follow of those which all lead equally to the bowers of happiness.

He who has seen only the superficies of life believes every thing to be what it appears, and rarely suspects that external splendor conceals any latent sorrow or vexation. He never imagines that there may be greatness without safety, affluence without content, jollity without friendship, and solitude without peace. He fancies himself permitted to cull the blessings of every condition, and to leave its inconveniencies to the idle and the ignorant. He is inclined to believe no man miserable but by his own fault, and seldom looks with much pity upon failings or miscarriages, because he thinks them willingly admitted, or negligently incurred.

It is impossible, without pity and contempt, to hear a youth of generous sentiments and warm imagination, declaring in the moment of openness and confidence his designs and expectations; because long life is possible, he considers it as certain, and therefore promises himself all the changes of happiness, and provides gratifications for every desire. He is, for a time, to give himself wholly to frolick and diversion, to range the world in search of pleasure, to delight every eye, to gain every heart, and to be celebrated equally for his pleasing levities and solid attainments, his deep reflections, and his sparkling repartees. He then elevates his views to nobler enjoyments, and finds all the scattered excellencies of the female world

united in a woman, who prefers his addresses to wealth
and titles; he is afterwards to engage in business, to
dissipate difficulty, and over-power opposition; to climb
by the mere force of merit to fame and greatness; and
reward all those who countenanced his rise, or paid due
regard to his early excellence. At last he will retire in
peace and honour; contract his views to domestick pleasures; form the manners of children like himself; observe
how every year expands the beauty of his daughters, and
how his sons catch ardour from their father's history; he
will give laws to the neighbourhood; dictate axioms to
posterity; and leave the world an example of wisdom and
of happiness.

With hopes like these, he sallies jocund into life; to
little purpose is he told, that the condition of humanity
admits no pure and unmingled happiness; that the exuberant gaiety of youth ends in poverty or disease; that uncommon qualifications and contrarieties of excellence,
produce envy equally with applause; that whatever admiration and fondness may promise him, he must marry a
wife like the wives of others, with some virtues and some
faults, and be as often disgusted by her vices, as delighted
by her elegance; that if he adventures into the circle of
action, he must expect to encounter men as artful, as
daring, as resolute as himself; that of his children, some
may be deformed, and others vicious; some may disgrace
him by their follies, some offend him by their insolence,
and some exhaust him by their profusion. He hears all
this with obstinate incredulity, and wonders by what
malignity old age is influenced, that it cannot forbear to
fill his ears with predictions of misery.

Among other pleasing errors of young minds, is the
opinion of their own importance. He that has not yet
remarked, how little attention his contemporaries can

spare from their own affairs, conceives all eyes turned upon himself, and imagines every one that approaches him to be an enemy or a follower, an admirer or a spy. He therefore considers his fame as involved in the event of every action. Many of the virtues and vices of youth proceed from this quick sense of reputation. This it is that gives firmness and constancy, fidelity and disinterestedness, and it is this that kindles resentment for slight injuries, and dictates all the principles of sanguinary honour.

But as time brings him forward into the world, he soon discovers that he only shares fame or reproach with innumerable partners; that he is left unmarked in the obscurity of the croud; and that what he does, whether good or bad, soon gives way to new objects of regard. He then easily sets himself free from the anxieties of reputation, and considers praise or censure as a transient breath, which, while he hears it, is passing away, without any lasting mischief or advantage.

In youth, it is common to measure right and wrong by the opinion of the world, and in age to act without any measure but interest, and to lose shame without substituting virtue.

Such is the condition of life, that something is always wanting to happiness. In youth we have warm hopes, which are soon blasted by rashness and negligence, and great designs which are defeated by inexperience. In age we have knowledge and prudence without spirit to exert, or motives to prompt them; we are able to plan schemes and regulate measures, but have not time remaining to bring them to completion.[2]

2. Boswell, from "a small duodecimo volume" containing "hints for essays," gives a rather full outline for the above essay and for *Adventurer* 45 (*Life*, I.204–07).

No. 207. Tuesday, 10 March 1752.

Solve senescentem mature sanus equum, ne
Peccet ad extremum ridendus.

Horace, EPISTLES, I.1.8–9.

The voice of reason cries with winning force,
Loose from the rapid car your aged horse,
Lest, in the race derided, left behind,
He drag his jaded limbs and burst his wind.

Francis.

Such is the emptiness of human enjoyment, that we are always impatient of the present. Attainment is followed by neglect, and possession by disgust; and the malicious remark of the Greek epigrammatist on marriage may be applied to every other course of life, that its two days of happiness are the first and the last.[1]

Few moments are more pleasing than those in which the mind is concerting measures for a new undertaking. From the first hint that wakens the fancy, till the hour of actual execution, all is improvement and progress, triumph and felicity. Every hour brings additions to the original scheme, suggests some new expedient to secure success, or discovers consequential advantages not hitherto foreseen. While preparations are made, and materials accumulated, day glides after day through elysian prospects, and the heart dances to the song of hope.

Such is the pleasure of projecting, that many content themselves with a succession of visionary schemes, and wear out their allotted time in the calm amusement of contriving what they never attempt or hope to execute.

Others, not able to feast their imagination with pure ideas, advance somewhat nearer to the grossness of action,

1. Palladus, *Greek Anthology*, XI.381.

with great diligence collect whatever is requisite to their design, and, after a thousand researches and consultations, are snatched away by death, as they stand *in procinctu* waiting for a proper opportunity to begin.

If there were no other end of life, than to find some adequate solace for every day, I know not whether any condition could be preferred to that of the man who involves himself in his own thoughts, and never suffers experience to shew him the vanity of speculation; for no sooner are notions reduced to practice, than tranquillity and confidence forsake the breast; every day brings its task, and often without bringing abilities to perform it: Difficulties embarrass, uncertainty perplexes, opposition retards, censure exasperates, or neglect depresses. We proceed, because we have begun; we complete our design, that the labour already spent may not be vain: but as expectation gradually dies away, the gay smile of alacrity disappears, we are compelled to implore severer powers, and trust the event to patience and constancy.

When once our labour has begun, the comfort that enables us to endure it is the prospect of its end; for though in every long work there are some joyous intervals of self-applause, when the attention is recreated by unexpected facility, and the imagination soothed by incidental excellencies; yet the toil with which performance struggles after idea, is so irksome and disgusting, and so frequent is the necessity of resting below that perfection which we imagined within our reach, that seldom any man obtains more from his endeavours than a painful conviction of his defects, and a continual resuscitation of desires which he feels himself unable to gratify.

So certainly is weariness the concomitant of our undertakings, that every man, in whatever he is engaged, consoles himself with the hope of change; if he has made his way by assiduity to publick employment, he talks among his friends of the delight of retreat; if by the necessity of solitary application he is secluded from the world, he listens with a beating heart to distant noises, longs to mingle with living beings, and resolves to take hereafter his fill of diversions, or display his abilities on the universal theatre, and enjoy the pleasure of distinction and applause.

Every desire, however innocent, grows dangerous, as by long indulgence it becomes ascendent in the mind. When we have been much accustomed to consider any thing as capable of giving happiness, it is not easy to restrain our ardour, or to forbear some precipitation in our advances, and irregularity in our persuits. He that has cultivated the tree, watched the swelling bud and opening blossom, and pleased himself with computing how much every sun and shower add to its growth, scarcely stays till the fruit has obtained its maturity, but defeats his own cares by eagerness to reward them. When we have diligently laboured for any purpose, we are willing to believe that we have attained it, and, because we have already done much, too suddenly conclude that no more is to be done.

All attraction is encreased by the approach of the attracting body. We never find ourselves so desirous to finish, as in the latter part of our work, or so impatient of delay, as when we know that delay cannot be long. This unseasonable importunity of discontent may be partly imputed to languor and weariness, which must always oppress those more whose toil has been longer continued; but the greater part usually proceeds from frequent contemplation of that ease which is now considered as within reach, and which, when it has once flattered our hopes, we cannot suffer to be withheld.

In some of the noblest compositions of wit, the conclusion falls below the vigour and spirit of the first books;
and as a genius is not to be degraded by the imputation
of human failings, the cause of this declension is commonly sought in the structure of the work, and plausible
reasons are given why in the defective part less ornament
was necessary, or less could be admitted. But, perhaps,
the author would have confessed, that his fancy was tired,
and his perseverance broken; that he knew his design
to be unfinished, but that, when he saw the end so near,
he could no longer refuse to be at rest.

Against the instillations of this frigid opiate, the heart
should be secured by all the considerations which once
concurred to kindle the ardour of enterprize. Whatever
motive first incited action, has still greater force to stimulate perseverance; since he that might have lain still at
first in blameless obscurity, cannot afterwards desist but
with infamy and reproach. He, whom a doubtful promise
of distant good, could encourage to set difficulties at defiance, ought not to remit his vigour, when he has almost
obtained his recompence. To faint or loiter, when only
the last efforts are required, is to steer the ship through
tempests, and abandon it to the winds in sight of land;
it is to break the ground and scatter the seed, and at last
to neglect the harvest.

The masters of rhetorick direct, that the most forcible
arguments be produced in the latter part of an oration,
lest they should be effaced or perplexed by supervenient
images. This precept may be justly extended to the series
of life: Nothing is ended with honour, which does not
conclude better than it begun. It is not sufficient to maintain the first vigour; for excellence loses its effect upon
the mind by custom, as light after a time ceases to dazzle.
Admiration must be continued by that novelty which first

produced it, and how much soever is given, there must always be reason to imagine that more remains.

We not only are most sensible of the last impressions, but such is the unwillingness of mankind to admit transcendent merit, that, though it be difficult to obliterate the reproach of miscarriages by any subsequent atchievement, however illustrious, yet the reputation raised by a long train of success, may be finally ruined by a single failure, for weakness or error will be always remembered by that malice and envy which it gratifies.

For the prevention of that disgrace, which lassitude and negligence may bring at last upon the greatest performances, it is necessary to proportion carefully our labour to our strength. If the design comprises many parts, equally essential, and therefore not to be separated, the only time for caution is before we engage; the powers of the mind must be then impartially estimated, and it must be remembered, that not to complete the plan, is not to have begun it; and, that nothing is done, while any thing is omitted.

But, if the task consists in the repetition of single acts, no one of which derives its efficacy from the rest, it may be attempted with less scruple, because there is always opportunity to retreat with honour. The danger is only lest we expect from the world the indulgence with which most are disposed to treat themselves; and in the hour of listlessness imagine, that the diligence of one day will atone for the idleness of another, and that applause begun by approbation will be continued by habit.

He that is himself weary will soon weary the public. Let him therefore lay down his employment, whatever it be, who can no longer exert his former activity or attention; let him not endeavour to struggle with censure, or obstinately infest the stage till a general hiss commands him to depart.

THE *ADVENTURER*

THE HOMERIDAE

From No. 45. Tuesday, 10 April 1753.[1]

Nulla fides regni sociis, omnisque potestas
Impatiens consortis erit.

Lucan, I.92–93.

No faith of partnership dominion owns;
Still discord hovers o'er divided thrones.

.   .   .   .

"There never appear," says Swift,[2] "more than five or six men of genius in an age; but if they were united, the world could not stand before them." It is happy, therefore, for mankind, that of this union there is no probability. As men take in a wider compass of intellectual survey, they are more likely to chuse different objects of pursuit; as they see more ways to the same end, they will be less easily persuaded to travel together; as each is better qualified to form an independent scheme of private greatness, he will reject with greater obstinacy the project of another; as each is more able to distinguish himself as the head of a party, he will less readily be made a follower or an associate.

The reigning philosophy informs us, that the vast

1. For what Boswell calls "the embryo" of this number, see *Life*, I.206–07.
2. "I have often endeavoured to establish a friendship among all men of genius, and would fain have it done. They are seldom above three or four contemporaries, and if they could be united, would drive the world before them." Letter to Pope, 20 Sept., 1723 (*Correspondence*, ed. Ball, III.175).

bodies which constitute the universe, are regulated in their progress through the etherial spaces, by the perpetual agency of contrary forces; by one of which they are restrained from deserting their orbits, and losing themselves in the immensity of heaven; and held off by the other from rushing together, and clustering round their centre with everlasting cohesion.

The same contrariety of impulse may be perhaps discovered in the motions of men: we are formed for society, not for combination; we are equally unqualified to live in a close connection with our fellow beings, and in total separation from them: we are attracted towards each other by general sympathy, but kept back from contact by private interests.

Some philosophers have been foolish enough to imagine, that improvements might be made in the system of the universe, by a different arrangement of the orbs of heaven; and politicians, equally ignorant and equally presumptuous, may easily be led to suppose, that the happiness of our world would be promoted by a different tendency of the human mind. It appears, indeed, to a slight and superficial observer, that many things impracticable in our present state, might be easily effected, if mankind were better disposed to union and co-operation; but a little reflection will discover, that if confederacies were easily formed, they would lose their efficacy, since numbers would be opposed to numbers, and unanimity to unanimity; and instead of the present petty competitions of individuals or single families, multitudes would be supplanting multitudes, and thousands plotting against thousands.

There is no class of the human species, of which the union seems to have been more expected, than of the learned: the rest of the world have almost always agreed, to shut scholars up together in colleges and cloisters; surely not without hope, that they would look for that happiness in concord, which they were debarred from finding in variety; and that such conjunctions of intellect would recompense the munificence of founders and patrons, by performances above the reach of any single mind.

But Discord, who found means to roll her apple into the banquetting chamber of the Goddesses, has had the address to scatter her laurels in the seminaries of learning. The friendship of students and of beauties is for the most part equally sincere, and equally durable: as both depend for happiness on the regard of others, on that of which the value arises merely from comparison, they are both exposed to perpetual jealousies, and both incessantly employed in schemes to intercept the praises of each other.

I am, however, far from intending to inculcate, that this confinement of the studious to studious companions has been wholly without advantage to the public: neighbourhood, where it does not conciliate friendship, incites competition; and he that would contentedly rest in a lower degree of excellence, where he had no rival to dread, will be urged by his impatience of inferiority to incessant endeavours after great attainments.

These stimulations of honest rivalry, are, perhaps, the chief effects of academies and societies; for whatever be the bulk of their joint labours, every single piece is always the production of an individual, that owes nothing to his colleagues but the contagion of diligence, a resolution to write because the rest are writing, and the scorn of obscurity while the rest are illustrious.

From No. 50. Saturday, 28 April 1753.

Quicunque turpi fraude semel innotuit,
Etiamsi vera dicit, amittit fidem.

Phaedrus, I.10.1–2.

The wretch that often has deceiv'd,
Though truth he speaks, is ne'er believ'd.

When Aristotle was once asked, what a man could gain by uttering falsehoods; he replied, "not to be credited when he shall tell the truth."[1]

The character of a liar is at once so hateful and contemptible, that even of those who have lost their virtue it might be expected, that from the violation of truth they should be restrained by their pride. Almost every other vice that disgraces human nature, may be kept in countenance by applause and association: the corrupter of virgin innocence sees himself envied by the men, and at least not detested by the women: the drunkard may easily unite with beings, devoted like himself to noisy merriment or silent insensibility, who will celebrate his victories over the novices of intemperance, boast themselves the companions of his prowess, and tell with rapture of the multitudes whom unsuccessful emulation has hurried to the grave: even the robber and the cut-throat have their followers, who admire their address and intrepidity, their stratagems of rapine, and their fidelity to the gang.

The liar, and only the liar, is invariably and universally despised, abandoned, and disowned; he has no domestic consolations, which he can oppose to the censure of mankind; he can retire to no fraternity where his crimes may stand in the place of virtues; but is given up

1. Diogenes Laertius, *Lives,* "Aristotle," XI.

to the hisses of the multitude, without friend and without apologist. It is the peculiar condition of falsehood, to be equally detested by the good and bad: "The devils," says Sir Thomas Brown, "do not tell lies to one another; for truth is necessary to all societies; nor can the society of hell subsist without it."[2]

It is natural to expect, that a crime thus generally detested, should be generally avoided; at least, that none should expose himself to unabated and unpitied infamy, without an adequate temptation; and that to guilt so easily detected, and so severely punished, an adequate temptation would not readily be found.

Yet so it is, that in defiance of censure and contempt, truth is frequently violated; and scarcely the most vigilant and unremitted circumspection will secure him that mixes with mankind, from being hourly deceived by men of whom it can scarcely be imagined, that they mean any injury to him, or profit to themselves; even where the subject of conversation could not have been expected to put the passions in motion, or to have excited either hope or fear, or zeal or malignity, sufficient to induce any man to put his reputation in hazard, however little he might value it, or to overpower the love of truth, however weak might be its influence.

The casuists have very diligently distinguished lyes into their several classes, according to their various degrees of malignity: but they have, I think, generally omitted that which is most common, and, perhaps, not least mischievous; which, since the moralists have not given it a name, I shall distinguish as the Lye of Vanity.

To vanity may justly be imputed most of the falsehoods, which every man perceives hourly playing upon

2. *Pseudodoxia Epidemica*, I.xi (par. 16).

his ear, and, perhaps, most of those that are propagated with success.[3] To the lye of commerce, and the lye of malice, the motive is so apparent, that they are seldom negligently or implicitly received: suspicion is always watchful over the practices of interest; and whatever the hope of gain, or desire of mischief, can prompt one man to assert, another is by reasons equally cogent incited to refute. But vanity pleases herself with such slight gratifications, and looks forward to pleasure so remotely consequential, that her practices raise no alarm, and her stratagems are not easily discovered.

Vanity is, indeed, often suffered to pass unpursued by suspicion; because he that would watch her motions, can never be at rest: fraud and malice are bounded in their influence; some opportunity of time and place is necessary to their agency; but scarce any man is abstracted one moment from his vanity; and he, to whom truth affords no gratifications, is generally inclined to seek them in falsehood.

·   ·   ·   ·

No. 84. Saturday, 25 August 1753.

—————— *Tolle periclum,*
Jam vaga prosiliet fraenis natura remotis.

Horace, SATIRES, 11.7.73–74.

But take the danger and the shame away,
And vagrant nature bounds upon her prey.

Francis.

---

3. See *Rambler* 13 (par. 5): "Most men seem rather inclined to confess the want of virtue than of importance." The sketches in *Adventurer* 84, below, are an illustration.

TO THE ADVENTURER.

SIR,

It has been observed, I think, by Sir William Temple, and after him by almost every other writer, that England affords a greater variety of characters, than the rest of the world.[1] This is ascribed to the liberty prevailing amongst us, which gives every man the privilege of being wise or foolish his own way, and preserves him from the necessity of hypocrisy, or the servility of imitation.

That the position itself is true, I am not completely satisfied. To be nearly acquainted with the people of different countries can happen to very few; and in life, as in every thing else beheld at a distance, there appears an even uniformity; the petty discriminations which diversify the natural character, are not discoverable but by a close inspection; we therefore find them most at home, because there we have most opportunities of remarking them. Much less am I convinced, that this peculiar diversification, if it be real, is the consequence of peculiar liberty: for where is the government to be found, that superintends individuals with so much vigilance, as not to leave their private conduct without restraint? Can it enter into a reasonable mind to imagine, that men of every other nation are not equally masters of their own time or houses with ourselves, and equally at liberty to be parsimonious or profuse, frolic or sullen, abstinent or luxurious? Liberty is certainly necessary to the full play of predominant humours; but such liberty is to be found alike under the government of the many or the few; in monarchies or in commonwealths.

How readily the predominant passion snatches an interval of liberty, and how fast it expands itself when the

1. In his essay "Of Poetry," *Works* (1770), III.425–26.

weight of restraint is taken away, I had lately an opportunity to discover, as I took a journey into the country in a
stage coach; which, as every journey is a kind of adventure, may be very properly related to you, though I can
display no such extraordinary assembly as Cervantes has
collected at Don Quixote's inn.[2]

In a stage coach the passengers are for the most part
wholly unknown to one another, and without expectation
of ever meeting again when their journey is at an end; one
should therefore imagine, that it was of little importance
to any of them, what conjectures the rest should form
concerning him. Yet so it is, that as all think themselves
secure from detection, all assume that character of which
they are most desirous, and on no occasion is the general
ambition of superiority more apparently indulged.

On the day of our departure, in the twilight of the
morning, I ascended the vehicle, with three men and two
women my fellow travellers. It was easy to observe the
affected elevation of mien with which every one entered,
and the supercilious civility with which they paid their
compliments to each other. When the first ceremony was
dispatched, we sat silent for a long time, all employed in
collecting importance into our faces, and endeavouring
to strike reverence and submission into our companions.

It is always observable that silence propagates itself,
and that the longer talk has been suspended, the more
difficult it is to find any thing to say. We began now to
wish for conversation; but no one seemed inclined to
descend from his dignity, or first to propose a topic of
discourse. At last a corpulent gentleman, who had
equipped himself for this expedition with a scarlet surtout, and a large hat with a broad lace, drew out his watch,
looked on it in silence, and then held it dangling at his

2. *Don Quixote*, pt. I, chs. 32–47.

finger. This was, I suppose, understood by all the company as an invitation to ask the time of the day; but no body appeared to heed his overture; and his desire to be talking so far overcame his resentment, that he let us know of his own accord that it was past five, and that in two hours we should be at breakfast.

His condescension was thrown away; we continued all obdurate: the ladies held up their heads: I amused myself with watching their behaviour; and of the other two, one seemed to employ himself in counting the trees as we drove by them, the other drew his hat over his eyes, and counterfeited a slumber. The man of benevolence, to shew that he was not depressed by our neglect, hummed a tune and beat time upon his snuff-box.

Thus universally displeased with one another, and not much delighted with ourselves, we came at last to the little inn appointed for our repast, and all began at once to recompence themselves for the constraint of silence by innumerable questions and orders to the people that attended us. At last, what every one had called for was got, or declared impossible to be got at that time, and we were persuaded to sit round the same table; when the gentleman in the red surtout looked again upon his watch, told us that we had half an hour to spare, but he was sorry to see so little merriment among us; that all fellow travellers were for the time upon the level, and that it was always his way to make himself one of the company. "I remember," says he, "it was on just such a morning as this that I and my lord Mumble and the duke of Tenterden were out upon a ramble; we called at a little house as it might be this; and my landlady, I warrant you, not suspecting to whom she was talking, was so jocular and facetious, and made so many merry answers to our questions, that we were all ready to burst with laughter. At last the good

woman happening to overhear me whisper the duke and
call him by his title, was so surprised and confounded that
we could scarcely get a word from her: and the duke never
met me from that day to this, but he talks of the little
house, and quarrels with me for terrifying the landlady."

He had scarcely had time to congratulate himself on the
veneration which this narrative must have procured him
from the company, when one of the ladies having reached
out for a plate on a distant part of the table, began to
remark "the inconveniences of travelling, and the difficulty which they who never sat at home without a great
number of attendants found in performing for themselves
such offices as the road required; but that people of quality often travelled in disguise, and might be generally
known from the vulgar by their condescension to poor
inn-keepers, and the allowance which they made for any
defect in their entertainment: that for her part, while
people were civil and meant well, it was never her custom
to find fault; for one was not to expect upon a journey all
that one enjoyed at one's own house."

A general emulation seemed now to be excited. One of
the men, who had hitherto said nothing, called for the
last news paper; and having perused it a while with deep
pensiveness, "It is impossible," says he, "for any man to
guess how to act with regard to the stocks; last week it was
the general opinion that they would fall; and I sold out
twenty thousand pounds in order to a purchase: they have
now risen unexpectedly; and I make no doubt but at my
return to London I shall risk thirty thousand pounds
amongst them again."

A young man, who had hitherto distinguished himself
only by the vivacity of his look, and a frequent diversion
of his eyes from one object to another, upon this closed his
snuff-box, and told us that "he had a hundred times talked

with the chancellor and the judges on the subject of the stocks; that for his part he did not pretend to be well acquainted with the principles on which they were established, but had always heard them reckoned pernicious to trade, uncertain in their produce, and unsolid in their foundation; and that he had been advised by three judges, his most intimate friends, never to venture his money in the funds, but to put it out upon land security, till he could light upon an estate in his own country."

It might be expected that, upon these glimpses of latent dignity, we should all have began to look around us with veneration, and have behaved like the princes of romance, when the enchantment that disguises them is dissolved, and they discover the dignity of each other: yet it happened, that none of these hints made much impression on the company; every one was apparently suspected of endeavouring to impose false appearances upon the rest; all continued their haughtiness, in hopes to enforce their claims; and all grew every hour more sullen, because they found their representations of themselves without effect.

Thus we travelled on four days wth malevolence perpetually increasing, and without any endeavour but to outvie each other in superciliousness and neglect; and when any two of us could separate ourselves for a moment, we vented our indignation at the sauciness of the rest.

At length the journey was at an end, and time and chance, that strip off all disguises, have discovered that the intimate of lords and dukes is a nobleman's butler, who has furnished a shop with the money he has saved; the man who deals so largely in the funds, is the clerk of a broker in Change-alley; the lady who so carefully concealed her quality, keeps a cookshop behind the Exchange; and the young man who is so happy in the friendship of the judges, engrosses and transcribes for bread in a garret of the Temple. Of one of the women only I could make no disadvantageous detection, because she had assumed no character, but accommodated herself to the scene before her, without any struggle for distinction or superiority.

I could not forbear to reflect on the folly of practising a fraud, which, as the event shewed, had been already practised too often to succeed, and by the success of which no advantage could have been obtained; of assuming a character, which was to end with the day; and of claiming upon false pretences honours which must perish with the breath that paid them.

But Mr. Adventurer, let not those who laugh at me and my companions, think this folly confined to a stage coach. Every man in the journey of life takes the same advantage of the ignorance of his fellow travellers, disguises himself in counterfeited merit, and hears those praises with complacency which his conscience reproaches him for accepting. Every man deceives himself while he thinks he is deceiving others; and forgets that the time is at hand when every illusion shall cease; when fictitious excellence shall be torn away; and All must be shown to All in their real state.

I am, Sir,
Your humble Servant,
VIATOR.

No. 95. Tuesday, 2 October 1753.

——— *Dulcique animos novitate tenebo.*

Ovid, METAMORPHOSES, IV.284.

And with sweet novelty your soul detain.

It is often charged upon writers, that with all their pretensions to genius and discoveries, they do little more than copy one another; and that compositions obtruded upon the world with the pomp of novelty, contain only tedious repetitions of common sentiments, or at best exhibit a transposition of known images, and give a new appearance to truth only by some slight difference of dress and decoration.

The allegation of resemblance between authors is indisputably true; but the charge of plagiarism, which is raised upon it, is not to be allowed with equal readiness. A coincidence of sentiment may easily happen without any communication, since there are many occasions in which all reasonable men will nearly think alike. Writers of all ages have had the same sentiments, because they have in all ages had the same objects of speculation; the interests and passions, the virtues and vices of mankind, have been diversified in different times, only by unessential and casual varieties; and we must, therefore, expect in the works of all those who attempt to describe them, such a likeness as we find in the pictures of the same person drawn in different periods of his life.

It is necessary, therefore, that before an author be charged with plagiarism, one of the most reproachful, though, perhaps, not the most atrocious of literary crimes, the subject on which he treats should be carefully considered. We do not wonder, that historians, relating the same facts, agree in their narration; or that authors delivering the elements of science, advance the same theorems, and lay down the same definitions: yet it is not wholly without use to mankind, that books are multiplied, and that different authors lay out their labours on the same subject; for there will always be some reason why one should on particular occasions, or to particular persons, be preferable to another; some will be clear where others are obscure, some will please by their stile and others by their method, some by their embellishments and others by their simplicity, some by closeness and others by diffusion.

The same indulgence is to be shewn to the writers of morality: right and wrong are immutable; and those, therefore, who teach us to distinguish them, if they all teach us right, must agree with one another. The relations of social life, and the duties resulting from them, must be the same at all times and in all nations: some petty differences may be, indeed, produced, by general forms of government or arbitrary customs; but the general doctrine can receive no alteration.

Yet it is not to be desired, that morality should be considered as interdicted to all future writers: men will always be tempted to deviate from their duty, and will, therefore, always want a monitor to recall them; and a new book often seizes the attention of the public, without any other claim than that it is new. There is likewise in composition, as in other things, a perpetual vicissitude of fashion; and truth is recommended at one time to regard, by appearances which at another would expose it to neglect: the author, therefore, who has judgment to discern the taste of his contemporaries, and skill to gratify it, will have always an opportunity to deserve well of mankind, by conveying instruction to them in a grateful vehicle.

There are likewise many modes of composition, by which a moralist may deserve the name of an original writer: he may familiarise his system by dialogues after the manner of the ancients, or subtilize it into a series of syllogistic arguments; he may enforce his doctrine by seriousness and solemnity, or enliven it by sprightliness and gayety; he may deliver his sentiments in naked precepts, or illustrate them by historical examples; he may detain the studious by the artful concatenation of a continued discourse, or relieve the busy by short strictures and unconnected essays.

To excel in any of these forms of writing, will require a particular cultivation of the genius; whoever can attain to excellence, will be certain to engage a set of readers, whom no other method would have equally allured; and he that communicates truth with success, must be numbered among the first benefactors to mankind.

The same observation may be extended likewise to the passions: their influence is uniform, and their effects nearly the same in every human breast:[1] a man loves and hates, desires and avoids, exactly like his neighbour; resentment and ambition, avarice and indolence, discover themselves by the same symptoms, in minds distant a thousand years from one another.

Nothing, therefore, can be more unjust, than to charge an author with plagiarism, merely because he assigns to every cause its natural effect; and makes his personages act, as others in like circumstances have always done. There are conceptions in which all men will agree, though each derives them from his own observation: whoever has been in love, will represent a lover impatient of every idea that interrupts his meditations on his mistress, retiring to shades and solitude that he may muse without disturbance on his approaching happiness, or associating himself with some friend that flatters his passion, and talking away the hours of absence upon his darling subject. Whoever has been so unhappy as to have felt the

1. Cf. *Rambler* 36 (last par.): "Poetry has to do rather with the passions of men, which are uniform, than their customs, which are changeable."

miseries of long continued hatred, will, without any assistance from antient volumes, be able to relate how the passions are kept in perpetual agitation, by the recollection of injury and meditations of revenge; how the blood boils at the name of the enemy, and life is worn away in contrivances of mischief.

Every other passion is alike simple and limited, if it be considered only with regard to the breast which it inhabits: the anatomy of the mind, as that of the body, must perpetually exhibit the same appearances; and though by the continued industry of successive inquirers, new movements will be from time to time discovered, they can affect only the minuter parts, and are commonly of more curiosity than importance.

It will now be natural to inquire, by what arts are the writers of the present and future ages to attract the notice and favour of mankind. They are to observe the alterations which time is always making in the modes of life, that they may gratify every generation with a picture of themselves. Thus love is uniform, but courtship is perpetually varying; the different arts of gallantry, which beauty has inspired, would of themselves be sufficient to fill a volume; sometimes balls and serenades, sometimes tournaments and adventures have been employed to melt the hearts of ladies, who in another century have been sensible of scarce any other merit than that of riches, and listened only to jointures and pin money. Thus the ambitious man has at all times been eager of wealth and power; but these hopes have been gratified in some countries by supplicating the people, and in others by flattering the prince: honour in some states has been only the reward of military achievements, in others it has been gained by noisy turbulence and popular clamours. Avarice has worn a different form, as she actuated the usurer of Rome, and the stock jobber of England; and idleness itself, how little soever inclined to the trouble of invention, has been forced from time to time to change its amusements, and contrive different methods of wearing out the day.

Here then is the fund, from which those who study mankind may fill their compositions with an inexhaustible variety of images and allusions; and he must be confessed to look with little attention upon scenes thus perpetually changing, who cannot catch some of the figures before they are made vulgar by reiterated descriptions.

It has been discovered by Sir Isaac Newton, that the distinct and primogenial colours are only seven; but every eye can witness, that from various mixtures in various proportions, infinite diversifications of tints may be produced.[2] In like manner, the passions of the mind, which put the world in motion, and produce all the bustle and eagerness of the busy crouds that swarm upon the earth; the passions, from whence arise all the pleasures and pains that we see and hear of, if we analize the mind of man, are very few; but those few agitated and combined, as external causes shall happen to operate, and modified by prevailing opinions and accidental caprices, make such frequent alterations on the surface of life, that the show while we are busied in delineating it, vanishes from the view, and a new set of objects succeeds, doomed to the same shortness of duration with the former: thus curiosity may always find employment, and the busy part of mankind will furnish the contemplative with the materials of speculation to the end of time.

2. First stated by Newton in *Philosophical Transactions*, No. 80 (1672), p. 3082, and later in the *Opticks* (1704), Bk. I, pt. ii, prop. 2, theor. 2, p. 88; prop. 3, exper. 7, p. 92, and *passim*.

The complaint, therefore, that all topics are preoccupied, is nothing more than the murmur of ignorance or
idleness, by which some discourage others and some themselves: the mutability of mankind will always furnish
writers with new images and the luxuriance of fancy may
always embellish them with new decorations.

No. 107. Tuesday, 13 November 1753.

———— *Sub judice lis est.*

HORACE, ART OF POETRY, l. 78.

And of their vain disputings find no end.

Francis.

It has been sometimes asked by those, who find the appearance of wisdom more easily attained by questions than
solutions, how it comes to pass, that the world is divided
by such difference of opinion; and why men, equally
reasonable, and equally lovers of truth, do not always
think in the same manner.

With regard to simple propositions, where the terms
are understood, and the whole subject is comprehended
at once, there is such an uniformity of sentiment among
all human beings, that, for many ages, a very numerous
set of notions were supposed to be innate, or necessarily
coexistent with the faculty of reason; it being imagined,
that universal agreement could proceed only from the
invariable dictates of the universal parent.

In questions diffuse and compounded, this similarity of
determination is no longer to be expected. At our first
sally into the intellectual world, we all march together
along one strait and open road; but as we proceed further,
and wider prospects open to our view, every eye fixes upon
a different scene; we divide into various paths, and, as we

move forward, are still at a greater distance from each other. As a question becomes more complicated and involved, and extends to a greater number of relations, disagreement of opinion will always be multiplied, not because we are irrational, but because we are finite beings, furnished with different kinds of knowledge, exerting different degrees of attention, one discovering consequences which escape another, none taking in the whole concatenation of causes and effects, most comprehending but a very small part; each comparing what he observes with a different criterion, and each referring it to a different purpose.

Where, then, is the wonder, that they, who see only a small part, should judge erroneously of the whole? or that they, who see different and dissimilar parts, should judge differently from each other?

Whatever has various respects, must have various appearances of good and evil, beauty or deformity: thus, the gardener tears up as a weed, the plant which the physician gathers as a medicine; and "a general," says Sir Kenelm Digby, "will look with pleasure over a plain, as a fit place on which the fate of empires might be decided in battle; which the farmer will despise as bleak and barren, neither fruitful of pasturage, nor fit for tillage."[1]

Two men examining the same question, proceed commonly like the physician and gardener in selecting herbs, or the farmer and hero looking on the plain; they bring minds impressed with different notions, and direct their inquiries to different ends; they form, therefore, contrary conclusions, and each wonders at the other's absurdity.

We have less reason to be surprised or offended when we find others differ from us in opinion, because we very often differ from ourselves; how often we alter our minds,

1. Paraphrasing Digby's *Observations upon Religio Medici* (1643), later added (5th ed., 1659) to Browne's *Religio Medici*.

we do not always remark; because the change is sometimes made imperceptibly and gradually, and the last conviction effaces all memory of the former; yet every man, accustomed from time to time to take a survey of his own notions, will by a slight retrospection be able to discover, that his mind has suffered many revolutions, that the same things have in the several parts of his life been condemned and approved, persued and shunned; and that on many occasions, even when his practice has been steddy, his mind has been wavering, and he has persisted in a scheme of action, rather because he feared the censure of inconstancy, than because he was always pleased with his own choice.

Of the different faces shewn by the same objects as they are viewed on opposite sides, and of the different inclinations which they must constantly raise in him that contemplates them, a more striking example cannot easily be found than two Greek epigrammatists will afford us in their accounts of human life, which I shall lay before the reader in English prose.

Posidippus, a comic poet, utters this complaint: "Through which of the paths of life is it eligible to pass? In public assemblies are debates and troublesome affairs; domestic privacies are haunted with anxieties; in the country is labour; on the sea is terror; in a foreign land, he that has money must live in fear, he that wants it must pine in distress; are you married? you are troubled with suspicions; are you single? you languish in solitude; children occasion toil, and a childless life is a state of destitution; the time of youth is a time of folly, and grey hairs are loaded with infirmity. This choice only, therefore, can be made, either never to receive being, or immediately to lose it."[2]

2. *Greek Anthology*, IX.359.

Such and so gloomy is the prospect, which Posidippus has laid before us. But we are not to acquiesce too hastily in his determination against the value of existence, for Metrodorus, a philosopher of Athens, has shewn, that life has pleasures as well as pains; and having exhibited the present state of man in brighter colours, draws, with equal appearance of reason, a contrary conclusion:

"You may pass well through any of the paths of life. In public assemblies are honours, and transactions of wisdom; in domestic privacy is stilness and quiet; in the country are the beauties of nature; on the sea is the hope of gain; in a foreign land, he that is rich is honoured, he that is poor may keep his poverty secret; are you married? you have a chearful house; are you single? you are unincumbered; children are objects of affection; to be without children is to be without care; the time of youth is the time of vigour; and grey hairs are made venerable by piety. It will, therefore, never be a wise man's choice, either not to obtain existence, or to lose it; for every state of life has its felicity."[3]

In these epigrams are included most of the questions, which have engaged the speculations of the enquirers after happiness; and though they will not much assist our determinations, they may, perhaps, equally promote our quiet, by shewing that no absolute determination ever can be formed.

Whether a public station, or private life be desirable, has always been debated. We see here both the allurements and discouragements of civil employments; on one side there is trouble, on the other honour; the management of affairs is vexatious and difficult, but it is the only duty in which wisdom can be conspicuously displayed: it must then still be left to every man to chuse either ease or

3. Ibid., IX.360.

glory; nor can any general precept be given, since no man can be happy by the prescription of another.

Thus what is said of children by Posidippus, "that they are occasions of fatigue," and by Metrodorus, "that they are objects of affection," is equally certain; but whether they will give most pain or pleasure, must depend on their future conduct and dispositions, on many causes over which the parent can have little influence: there is, therefore, room for all the caprices of imagination, and desire must be proportioned to the hope or fear that shall happen to predominate.

Such is the uncertainty, in which we are always likely to remain with regard to questions, wherein we have most interest, and which every day affords us fresh opportunity to examine: we may examine, indeed, but we never can decide, because our faculties are unequal to the subject: we see a little, and form an opinion; we see more, and change it.

This inconstancy and unsteadiness, to which we must so often find ourselves liable, ought certainly to teach us moderation and forbearance towards those, who cannot accommodate themselves to our sentiments: if they are deceived, we have no right to attribute their mistake to obstinacy or negligence, because we likewise have been mistaken: we may, perhaps, again change our own opinion; and what excuse shall we be able to find for aversion and malignity conceived against him, whom we shall then find to have committed no fault, and who offended us only by refusing to follow us into error.

It may likewise contribute to soften that resentment, which pride naturally raises against opposition, if we consider, that he, who differs from us, does not always contradict us; he has one view of an object, and we have another; each describes what he sees with equal fidelity, and each regulates his steps by his own eyes: one man, with Posidippus, looks on celibacy as a state of gloomy solitude, without a partner in joy or a comforter in sorrow; the other considers it, with Metrodorus, as a state free from incumbrances, in which a man is at liberty to chuse his own gratifications, to remove from place to place in quest of pleasure, and to think of nothing but merriment and diversion; full of these notions, one hastens to chuse a wife, and the other laughs at his rashness, or pities his ignorance; yet it is possible that each is right, but that each is right only for himself.

Life is not the object of science: we see a little, very little; and what is beyond we only can conjecture. If we enquire of those who have gone before us, we receive small satisfaction; some have travelled life without observation, and some willingly mislead us. The only thought, therefore, on which we can repose with comfort, is that which presents to us the care of Providence, whose eye takes in the whole of things, and under whose direction all involuntary errors will terminate in happiness.

No. 111. Tuesday, 27 November 1753.

——— *Quae non fecimus ipsi,*
Vix ea nostra voco.

Ovid, METAMORPHOSES, XIII.140–41.

The deeds of long descended ancestors
Are but by grace of imputation ours.

Dryden.

The evils inseparably annexed to the present condition of man, are so numerous and afflictive, that it has been, from age to age, the task of some to bewail, and of others to solace them: and he, therefore, will be in danger of seeming a common enemy, who shall attempt to depreciate the few pleasures and felicities which nature has allowed us.

Yet I will confess, that I have sometimes employed my thoughts in examining the pretensions that are made to happiness, by the splendid and envied conditions of life; and have not thought the hour unprofitably spent, when I have detected the imposture of counterfeit advantages, and found disquiet lurking under false appearances of gayety and greatness.

It is asserted by a tragic poet, that "est miser nemo nisi comparatus," "no man is miserable, but as he is compared with others happier than himself:"[1] this position is not strictly and philosophically true. He might have said, with rigorous propriety, that no man is happy, but as he is compared with the miserable; for such is the state of this world, that we find in it absolute misery but happiness only comparative; we may incur as much pain as we can possibly endure, though we can never obtain as much happiness as we might possibly enjoy.

Yet it is certain likewise, that many of our miseries are merely comparative: we are often made unhappy, not by the presence of any real evil, but by the absence of some fictitious good; of something which is not required by any real want of nature, which has not in itself any power of gratification, and which neither reason nor fancy would have prompted us to wish, did we not see it in the possession of others.[2]

For a mind diseased with vain longings after unattainable advantages, no medicine can be prescribed, but an impartial enquiry into the real worth of that which is so ardently desired. It is well known, how much the mind,

1. Seneca, *Troades*, l. 1023.
2. Cf. *Rambler* 49 (pars. 3–6).

as well as the eye, is deceived by distance; and, perhaps, it will be found, that of many imagined blessings it may be doubted, whether he that wants or possesses them has more reason to be satisfied with his lot.

The dignity of high birth and long extraction, no man, to whom nature has denied it, can confer upon himself; and, therefore, it deserves to be considered, whether the want of that which can never be gained, may not easily be endured. It is true, that if we consider the triumph and delight, with which most of those recount their ancestors who have ancestors to recount, and the artifices by which some who have risen to unexpected fortune endeavour to insert themselves into an honourable stem, we shall be inclined to fancy, that wisdom or virtue may be had by inheritance, or that all the excellencies of a line of progenitors are accumulated on their descendant. Reason, indeed, will soon inform us, that our estimation of birth is arbitrary and capricious, and that dead ancestors can have no influence but upon imagination: let it then be examined, whether one dream may not operate in the place of another; whether he that owes nothing to fore-fathers, may not receive equal pleasure from the consciousness of owing all to himself; whether he may not, with a little meditation, find it more honourable to found than to continue a family, and to gain dignity than transmit it; whether, if he receives no dignity from the virtues of his family, he does not likewise escape the danger of being disgraced by their crimes; and whether he that brings a new name into the world, has not the convenience of playing the game of life without a stake, an opportunity of winning much though he has nothing to lose.

There is another opinion concerning happiness, which approaches much more nearly to universality, but which may, perhaps, with equal reason, be disputed. The pretensions to ancestral honours many of the sons of earth easily see to be ill grounded; but all agree to celebrate the advantage of hereditary riches, and to consider those as the minions of fortune, who are wealthy from their cradles; whose estate is "res non parta labore sed relicta," "the acquisition of another, not of themselves;"[3] and whom a father's industry has dispensed from a laborious attention to arts or commerce, and left at liberty to dispose of life as fancy shall direct them.

If every man were wise and virtuous, capable to discern the best use of time, and resolute to practise it; it might be granted, I think, without hesitation, that total liberty would be a blessing; and that it would be desirable to be left at large to the exercise of religious and social duties, without the interruption of importunate avocations.

But since felicity is relative, and that which is the means of happiness to one man may be to another the cause of misery, we are to consider, what state is best adapted to human nature in its present degeneracy and frailty. And, surely, to far the greater number it is highly expedient, that they should by some settled scheme of duties be rescued from the tyranny of caprice, that they should be driven on by necessity through the paths of life, with their attention confined to a stated task, that they may be less at leisure to deviate into mischief at the call of folly.

When we observe the lives of those whom an ample inheritance has let loose to their own direction, what do we discover that can excite our envy? Their time seems not to pass with much applause from others, or satisfaction to themselves; many squander their exuberance of

3. Martial, X.47.3.

fortune in luxury and debauchery, and have no other use
of money than to inflame their passions, and riot in a
wider range of licentiousness; others, less criminal indeed, but, surely, not much to be praised, lie down to
sleep and rise up to trifle, are employed every morning in
finding expedients to rid themselves of the day, chase
pleasure through all the places of public resort, fly from
London to Bath and from Bath to London, without any
other reason for changing place, but that they go in quest
of company as idle and as vagrant as themselves, always endeavouring to raise some new desire that they may have
something to persue, to rekindle some hope which they
know will be disappointed, changing one amusement for
another which a few months will make equally insipid, or
sinking into languor and disease, for want of something
to actuate their bodies or exhilarate their minds.

Whoever has frequented those places, where idlers
assemble to escape from solitude, knows that this is generally the state of the wealthy; and from this state it is no
great hardship to be debarred. No man can be happy in
total idleness: he that should be condemned to lie torpid
and motionless, "would fly for recreation," says South,[4]
"to the mines and the gallies;" and it is well, when nature
or fortune find employment for those, who would not
have known how to procure it for themselves.

He, whose mind is engaged by the acquisition or improvement of a fortune, not only escapes the insipidity of
indifference, and the tediousness of inactivity; but gains

4. The quotation occurs in South's sermon on Prov. 3:17: "The most
voluptuous and loose person breathing, were he but tied to follow his
hawks and his hounds, his dice and his courtship every day, would find it
the greatest torment and calamity that could befall him; he would fly to
the mines and the galleys for his recreation, and to the spade and the mat-
tock for a diversion from the misery of a continual unintermitted pleasure." *Sermons*, 1823, I.20. Johnson quoted the passage in his Dictionary
under *Galley*.

enjoyments wholly unknown to those, who live lazily on the toil of others; for life affords no higher pleasure, than that of surmounting difficulties, passing from one step of success to another, forming new wishes and seeing them gratified. He that labours in any great or laudable under-taking, has his fatigues first supported by hope, and after-wards rewarded by joy; he is always moving to a certain end, and when he has attained it, an end more distant invites him to a new persuit.

It does not, indeed, always happen, that diligence is fortunate; the wisest schemes are broken by unexpected accidents; the most constant perseverance sometimes toils through life without a recompence; but labour, though unsuccessful, is more eligible than idleness: he that prose-cutes a lawful purpose by lawful means, acts always with the approbation of his own reason; he is animated through the course of his endeavours by an expectation which though not certain, he knows to be just; and is at last comforted in his disappointment, by the conscious-ness that he has not failed by his own fault.

That kind of life is most happy which affords us most opportunities of gaining our own esteem; and what can any man infer in his own favour from a condition to which, however prosperous, he contributed nothing, and which the vilest and weakest of the species would have obtained by the same right, had he happened to be the son of the same father?

To strive with difficulties, and to conquer them, is the highest human felicity; the next, is to strive, and deserve to conquer: but he whose life has passed without a con-test, and who can boast neither success nor merit, can survey himself only as a useless filler of existence; and if he is content with his own character, must owe his satis-faction to insensibility.

Thus it appears that the satyrist advised rightly, when he directed us to resign ourselves to the hands of Heaven, and to leave to superior powers the determination of our lot:

Permittes ipsis expendere Numinibus, quid
Conveniat nobis, rebusque sit utile nostris,
Carior est illis homo quam sibi.

Juvenal, SATIRES, X.347–48, 350.

Intrust thy fortune to the pow'rs above:
Leave them to manage for thee, and to grant
What their unerring wisdom sees thee want.
In goodness as in greatness they excell,
Ah! that we lov'd ourselves but half so well.

Dryden.

What state of life admits most happiness is uncertain; but that uncertainty ought to repress the petulance of comparison, and silence the murmurs of discontent.

No. 119. Tuesday, 25 December 1753.

Latius regnes avidum domando
Spiritum, quam si Lybiam remotis
Gadibus jungas, et uterque Paenus.
Serviat uni.

Horace, ODES, II.2.9–12.

By virtue's precepts to controul
The thirsty cravings of the soul,
Is over wider realms to reign
Unenvied monarch, than if Spain
You could to distant Lybia join,
And both the Carthages were thine.

Francis.

When Socrates was asked, "which of mortal men was to be accounted nearest to the Gods in happiness?" he answered, "that man, who is in want of the fewest things."[1]

In this answer, Socrates left it to be guessed by his auditors, whether, by the exemption from want which was to constitute happiness, he meant amplitude of possessions or contraction of desire. And, indeed, there is so little difference between them, that Alexander the Great confessed the inhabitant of a tub the next man to the master of the world; and left a declaration to future ages, that if he were not Alexander, he should wish to be Diogenes.[2]

These two states, however, though they resemble each other in their consequence, differ widely with respect to the facility with which they may be attained. To make great acquisitions, can happen to very few; and in the uncertainty of human affairs, to many it will be incident to labour without reward, and to lose what they already possess by endeavours to make it more; some will always want abilities, and others opportunities to accumulate wealth. It is, therefore, happy, that nature has allowed us a more certain and easy road to plenty; every man may grow rich by contracting his wishes, and by quiet acquiescence in what has been given him supply the absence of more.

Yet so far is almost every man from emulating the happiness of the Gods, by any other means than grasping at their power; that it seems to be the great business of life, to create wants as fast as they are satisfied.[3] It has

1. Diogenes Laertius, *Lives*, "Socrates," XI.
2. Plutarch, *Lives*, "Alexander," XIV; Diogenes Laertius, *Lives*, "Diogenes," VI.
3. Cf. *Rambler* 41 (par. 1) and *Rasselas*, ch. 32 (pars. 4–5).

been long observed by moralists, that every man squanders or loses a great part of that life, of which every man knows and deplores the shortness; and it may be remarked with equal justness, that though every man laments his own insufficiency to his happiness, and knows himself a necessitous and precarious being, incessantly soliciting the assistance of others, and feeling wants which his own art or strength cannot supply; yet there is no man, who does not, by the superaddition of unnatural cares, render himself still more dependant; who does not create an artificial poverty, and suffer himself to feel pain for the want of that, of which, when it is gained, he can have no enjoyment.

It must, indeed, be allowed, that as we lose part of our time because it steals away silent and invisible, and many an hour is passed before we recollect that it is passing; so unnatural desires insinuate themselves unobserved into the mind, and we do not perceive that they are gaining upon us, till the pain which they give us awakens us to notice. No man is sufficiently vigilant to take account of every minute of his life, or to watch every motion of his heart. Much of our time likewise is sacrificed to custom; we trifle, because we see others trifle: in the same manner, we catch from example the contagion of desire; we see all about us busied in persuit of imaginary good, and begin to bustle in the same chase, lest greater activity should triumph over us.

It is true, that to man, as a member of society, many things become necessary, which, perhaps, in a state of nature are superfluous; and that many things, not absolutely necessary, are yet so useful and convenient, that they cannot easily be spared. I will make yet a more ample and liberal concession. In opulent states and regular governments, the temptations to wealth and rank, and to the distinctions that follow them, are such as no force of understanding finds it easy to resist.

If, therefore, I saw the quiet of life disturbed only by endeavours after wealth and honour; by sollicitude, which the world, whether justly or not, considered as important; I should scarcely have had courage to inculcate any precepts of moderation and forbearance. He that is engaged in a persuit, in which all mankind profess to be his rivals, is supported by the authority of all mankind in the prosecution of his design, and will, therefore, scarcely stop to hear the lectures of a solitary philosopher. Nor am I certain, that the accumulation of honest gain ought to be hindered, or the ambition of just honours always to be repressed. Whatever can enable the possessor to confer any benefit upon others, may be desired upon virtuous principles; and we ought not too rashly to accuse any man of intending to confine the influence of his acquisitions to himself.

But if we look round upon mankind, whom shall we find among those that fortune permits to form their own manners, that is not tormenting himself with a wish for something, of which all the pleasure and all the benefit will cease at the moment of attainment? One man is beggering his posterity to build a house, which when finished he never will inhabit; another is levelling mountains to open a prospect, which, when he has once enjoyed it, he can enjoy no more; another is painting ceilings, carving wainscot, and filling his apartments with costly furniture, only that some neighbouring house may not be richer or finer than his own.

That splendor and elegance are not desireable, I am not so abstracted from life as to inculcate; but if we enquire closely into the reason for which they are esteemed, we shall find them valued principally as evidences of wealth. Nothing, therefore, can shew greater depravity of understanding, than to delight in the shew when the reality is wanting; or voluntarily to become poor, that strangers may for a time imagine us to be rich.

But there are yet minuter objects and more trifling anxieties. Men may be found, who are kept from sleep by the want of a shell particularly variegated; who are wasting their lives, in stratagems to obtain a book in a language which they do not understand; who pine with envy at the flowers of another man's parterre; who hover like vultures round the owner of a fossil, in hopes to plunder his cabinet at his death; and who would not much regret to see a street in flames, if a box of medals might be scattered in the tumult.

He that imagines me to speak of these sages in terms exaggerated and hyperbolical, has conversed but little with the race of virtuosos. A slight acquaintance with their studies, and a few visits to their assemblies, would inform him, that nothing is so worthless, but that prejudice and caprice can give it value; nor any thing of so little use, but that by indulging an idle competition, or unreasonable pride, a man may make it to himself one of the necessaries of life.

Desires like these, I may surely, without incurring the censure of moroseness, advise every man to repel when they invade his mind; or if he admits them, never to allow them any greater influence, than is necessary to give petty employments the power of pleasing, and diversify the day with slight amusements.

An ardent wish, whatever be its object, will always be able to interrupt tranquillity. What we believe ourselves to want, torments us not in proportion to its real value, but according to the estimation by which we have rated it in our own minds: in some diseases, the patient has been observed to long for food, which scarce any extremity of hunger would in health have compelled him to swallow; but while his organs were thus depraved the craving was irresistible, nor could any rest be obtained till it was appeased by compliance. Of the same nature are the irregular appetites of the mind; though they are often excited by trifles, they are equally disquieting with real wants: the Roman,[4] who wept at the death of his lamprey, felt the same degree of sorrow that extorts tears on other occasions.

Inordinate desires, of whatever kind, ought to be repressed upon yet a higher consideration; they must be considered as enemies not only to happiness but to virtue. There are men among those commonly reckoned the learned and the wise, who spare no stratagems to remove a competitor at an auction, who will sink the price of a rarity at the expence of truth, and whom it is not safe to trust alone in a library or cabinet. These are faults, which the fraternity seem to look upon as jocular mischiefs, or to think excused by the violence of the temptation: but I shall always fear that he, who accustoms himself to fraud in little things, wants only opportunity to practise it in greater; "he that has hardened himself by killing a sheep," says Pythagoras, "will with less reluctance shed the blood of a man."[5]

4. Either M. L. Crassus, the triumvir, or his contemporary Quintus Hortensius, the orator. See Plutarch (*Moralia* 89ª, 811ª, 976ª), Aelian (*De natura animal*, VIII.4), Porphyry (*De abstinentia*, III.5) and Macrobius (*Saturnaliorum*, III.15.4) for Crassus, and Pliny (*Natural History*, IX.172) for Hortensius.

5. Apparently a loose paraphrase of Iamblichus, *Life of Pythagoras*, XXX. ad fin.: "Pythagoras likewise ordained abstinence from animal food . . . because it is productive of peace. For those who are accustomed to abominate the slaughter of animals as iniquitous and preternatural, will think it to be much more unlawful to kill a man, or engage in war" (T. Taylor's trans., 1926, p. 98).

To prize every thing according to its real use, ought to be the aim of a rational being. There are few things which can much conduce to happiness, and, therefore, few things to be ardently desired. He that looks upon the business and bustle of the world, with the philosophy with which Socrates surveyed the fair at Athens, will turn away at last with his exclamation, "How many things are here which I do not want!"[6]

No. 126. Saturday, 19 January 1754.

———— *Steriles nec legit arenas*
Ut caneret paucis, mersitque hoc pulvere verum.

                                    Lucan, IX.576–77.

Canst thou believe the vast eternal mind
Was e'er to Syrts and Libyan sands confin'd?
That he would chuse this waste, this barren ground,
To teach the thin inhabitants around,
And leave his truth in wilds and desarts drown'd?

                                    Rowe.

There has always prevailed among that part of mankind that addict their minds to speculation, a propensity to talk much of the delights of retirement; and some of the most pleasing compositions produced in every age, contain descriptions of the peace and happiness of a country life.

I know not whether those who thus ambitiously repeat the praises of solitude, have always considered, how much they depreciate mankind by declaring, that whatever is excellent or desirable is to be obtained by departing from

6. Diogenes Laertius, *Lives*, "Socrates," IX.

them; that the assistance which we may derive from one another, is not equivalent to the evils which we have to fear; that the kindness of a few is overbalanced by the malice of many; and that the protection of society is too dearly purchased, by encountering its dangers and enduring its oppressions.

These specious representations of solitary happiness, however opprobrious to human nature, have so far spread their influence over the world, that almost every man delights his imagination with the hopes of obtaining some time an opportunity of retreat. Many indeed, who enjoy retreat only in imagination, content themselves with believing, that another year will transport them to rural tranquillity, and die while they talk of doing what if they had lived longer they would never have done. But many likewise there are, either of greater resolution or more credulity, who in earnest try the state which they have been taught to think thus secure from cares and dangers; and retire to privacy, either that they may improve their happiness, increase their knowledge, or exalt their virtue.

The greater part of the admirers of solitude, as of all other classes of mankind, have no higher or remoter view, than the present gratification of their passions. Of these some, haughty and impetuous, fly from society only because they cannot bear to repay to others the regard which themselves exact, and think no state of life eligible, but that which places them out of the reach of censure or controul, and affords them opportunities of living in a perpetual compliance with their own inclinations, without the necessity of regulating their actions by any other man's convenience or opinion.

There are others of minds more delicate and tender, easily offended by every deviation from rectitude, soon disgusted by ignorance or impertinence, and always expecting from the conversation of mankind, more elegance, purity and truth than the mingled mass of life will easily afford. Such men are in haste to retire from grossness, falsehood and brutality; and hope to find in private habitations at least a negative felicity, and exemption from the shocks and perturbations with which public scenes are continually distressing them.

To neither of these votaries will solitude afford that content, which she has been taught so lavishly to promise. The man of arrogance will quickly discover, that by escaping from his opponents he has lost his flatterers, that greatness is nothing where it is not seen, and power nothing where it cannot be felt: and he, whose faculties are employed in too close an observation of failings and defects, will find his condition very little mended by transferring his attention from others to himself; he will probably soon come back in quest of new objects, and be glad to keep his captiousness employed on any character rather than his own.

Others are seduced into solitude merely by the authority of great names, and expect to find those charms in tranquillity which have allured statesmen and conquerors to the shades: these likewise are apt to wonder at their disappointment, from want of considering, that those whom they aspire to imitate carried with them to their country seats minds full fraught with subjects of reflection, the consciousness of great merit, the memory of illustrious actions, the knowledge of important events, and the seeds of mighty designs to be ripened by future meditation. Solitude was to such men a release from fatigue, and an opportunity of usefulness. But what can retirement confer upon him, who having done nothing can receive no support from his own importance, who having known nothing can find no entertainment in reviewing the past, and who intending nothing can form no hopes from prospects of the future: he can, surely, take no wiser course, than that of losing himself again in the croud, and filling the vacuities of his mind[1] with the news of the day.

Others consider solitude as the parent of philosophy, and retire in expectation of greater intimacies with science, as Numa repaired to the groves when he conferred with Egeria.[2] These men have not always reason to repent. Some studies require a continued prosecution of the same train of thought, such as is too often interrupted by the petty avocations of common life: sometimes, likewise, it is necessary, that a multiplicity of objects be at once present to the mind; and every thing, therefore, must be kept at a distance, which may perplex the memory, or dissipate the attention.

But though learning may be conferred by solitude, its application must be attained by general converse. He has learned to no purpose, that is not able to teach; and he will always teach unsuccessfully, who cannot recommend his sentiments by his diction or address.

Even the acquisition of knowledge is often much fa-

1. Cf. Mrs. Thrale's remarks (Piozzi, *Anecdotes, Miscellanies,* I.251): "The vacuity of life had at some early period of his life struck so forcibly on the mind of Mr. Johnson, that it became by repeated impression his favourite hypothesis . . . One man, for example, was profligate and wild, as we call it, followed the girls, or sat still at the gaming-table. 'Why, life must be filled up (says Johnson), and the man who is not capable of intellectual pleasures must content himself with such as his senses can afford.' Another was a hoarder: 'Why, a fellow must do something; and what so easy to a narrow mind as hoarding halfpence till they turn into sixpences.' "
2. Plutarch, *Lives,* "Numa," IV; Livy, I.21.

cilitated by the advantages of society: he that never compares his notions with those of others, readily acquiesces in his first thoughts, and very seldom discovers the objections which may be raised against his opinions; he, therefore, often thinks himself in possession of truth, when he is only fondling an error long since exploded. He that has neither companions nor rivals in his studies, will always applaud his own progress, and think highly of his performances, because he knows not that others have equalled or excelled him. And I am afraid it may be added, that the student who with draws himself from the world, will soon feel that ardour extinguished which praise or emulation had enkindled, and take the advantage of secrecy to sleep rather than to labour.

There remains yet another set of recluses, whose intention intitles them to higher respect, and whose motives deserve a more serious consideration. These retire from the world, not merely to bask in ease or gratify curiosity, but that being disengaged from common cares, they may employ more time in the duties of religion, that they may regulate their actions with stricter vigilance, and purify their thoughts by more frequent meditation.

To men thus elevated above the mists of mortality, I am far from presuming myself qualified to give directions. On him that appears "to pass through things temporary," with no other care than "not to lose finally the things eternal,"[3] I look with such veneration as inclines me to approve his conduct in the whole, without a minute examination of its parts; yet I could never forbear to wish, that while vice is every day multiplying seducements, and stalking forth with more hardened effrontry, virtue,

3. Paraphrased from Corinthians, iv.18.

would not withdraw the influence of her presence, or forbear to assert her natural dignity by open and undaunted perseverance in the right. Piety practised in solitude, like the flower that blooms in the desart, may give its fragrance to the winds of heaven, and delight those unbodied spirits that survey the works of God and the actions of men; but it bestows no assistance upon earthly beings, and however free from taints of impurity, yet wants the sacred splendor of beneficence.

Our Maker, who, though he gave us such varieties of temper and such difference of powers yet designed us all for happiness, undoubtedly intended that we should obtain that happiness by different means. Some are unable to resist the temptations of importunity, or the impetuosity of their own passions incited by the force of present temptations: of these it is undoubtedly the duty, to fly from enemies which they cannot conquer, and to cultivate, in the calm of solitude, that virtue which is too tender to endure the tempests of public life. But there are others, whose passions grow more strong and irregular in privacy; and who cannot maintain an uniform tenor of virtue, but by exposing their manners to the public eye, and assisting the admonitions of conscience with the fear of infamy: for such it is dangerous to exclude all witnesses of their conduct, till they have formed strong habits of virtue, and weakened their passions by frequent victories. But there is a higher order of men so inspirited with ardour, and so fortified with resolution, that the world passes before them without influence or regard: these ought to consider themselves as appointed the guardians of mankind; they are placed in an evil world, to exhibit public examples of good life; and may be said, when they withdraw to solitude, to desert the station which Providence assigned them.

No. 137. Tuesday, 26 February 1754.

Τί δ'ἔρεξα,

                    Pythagoras, AUREA CARMINA, 42.

What have I been doing?

As man is a being very sparingly furnished with the power of prescience, he can provide for the future only by considering the past; and as futurity is all in which he has any real interest, he ought very diligently to use the only means by which he can be enabled to enjoy it, and frequently to revolve the experiments which he has hitherto made upon life, that he may gain wisdom from his mistakes and caution from his miscarriages.

Though I do not so exactly conform to the precepts of Pythagoras, as to practise every night this solemn recollection, yet I am not so lost in dissipation as wholly to omit it; nor can I forbear sometimes to enquire of myself, in what employments my life has passed away. Much of my time has sunk into nothing, and left no trace by which it can be distinguished, and of this I now only know, that it was once in my power and might once have been improved.

Of other parts of life memory can give some account: at some hours I have been gay, and at others serious; I have sometimes mingled in conversation, and sometimes mediated in solitude; one day has been spent in consulting the antient sages, and another in writing Adventurers.

At the conclusion of any undertaking, it is usual to compute the loss and profit. As I shall soon cease to write Adventurers, I could not forbear lately to consider what has been the consequence of my labours; and whether I am to reckon the hours laid out in these compositions, as applied to a good and laudable purpose, or suffered to fume away in useless evaporations.

That I have intended well, I have the attestation of my own heart; but good intentions may be frustrated, when they are executed without suitable skill, or directed to an end unattainable in itself.

Some there are, who leave writers very little room for self congratulation; some who affirm, that books have no influence upon the public, that no age was ever made better by its authors, and that to call upon mankind to correct their manners, is, like Xerxes, to scourge the wind or shackle the torrent.[1]

This opinion they pretend to support by unfailing experience. The world is full of fraud and corruption, rapine and malignity; interest is the ruling motive of mankind, and every one is endeavouring to increase his own stores of happiness by perpetual accumulation, without reflecting upon the numbers whom his superfluity condemns to want: in this state of things a book of morality is published, in which charity and benevolence are strongly enforced; and it is proved beyond opposition, that men are happy in proportion as they are virtuous, and rich as they are liberal. The book is applauded, and the author is preferred; he imagines his applause deserved, and receives less pleasure from the acquisition of reward, than the consciousness of merit. Let us look again upon mankind: interest is still the ruling motive, and the world is yet full of fraud and corruption, malevolence and rapine.

The difficulty of confuting this assertion, arises merely from its generality and comprehension: to overthrow it

1. Cf. *Vanity of Human Wishes*, l. 232, "The waves he lashes, and enchains the wind," and Preface to the *Dictionary*, *Works* (1825), V.46. See *Life*, II.227.

by a detail of distinct facts, requires a wider survey of the world than human eyes can take; the progress of reformation is gradual and silent, as the extension of evening shadows; we know that they were short at noon, and are long at sun-set, but our senses were not able to discern their increase; we know of every civil nation that it was once savage, and how was it reclaimed but by precept and admonition?[2]

Mankind are universally corrupt, but corrupt in different degrees; as they are universally ignorant, yet with greater or less irradiations of knowledge. How has knowledge or virtue been increased and preserved in one place beyond another, but by diligent inculcation and rational inforcement.

Books of morality are daily written, yet its influence is still little in the world; so the ground is annually ploughed, and yet multitudes are in want of bread. But, surely, neither the labours of the moralist nor of the husbandman are vain: let them for a while neglect their tasks, and their usefulness will be known; the wickedness that is now frequent would become universal, the bread that is now scarce would wholly fail.

The power, indeed, of every individual is small, and the consequence of his endeavours imperceptible in a general prospect of the world. Providence has given no man ability to do much, that something might be left for every man to do. The business of life is carried on by a general co-operation; in which the part of any single man can be no more distinguished, than the effect of a particular drop when the meadows are floated by a summer shower: yet every drop increases the inundation, and every hand adds to the happiness or misery of mankind.

2. Cf. Johnson's "Project for the Employment of Authors" (pars. 3–5), *Works* (1825), v.355–56.

That a writer, however zealous or eloquent, seldom works a visible effect upon cities or nations, will readily be granted. The book which is read most, is read by few, compared with those that read it not; and of those few, the greater part peruse it with dispositions that very little favour their own improvement.

It is difficult to enumerate the several motives, which procure to books the honour of perusal: spite, vanity, and curiosity, hope and fear, love and hatred, every passion which incites to any other action, serves at one time or other to stimulate a reader.

Some are fond to take a celebrated volume into their hands, because they hope to distinguish their penetration, by finding faults which have escaped the public; others eagerly buy it in the first bloom of reputation, that they may join the chorus of praise, and not lag, as Falstaff terms it, in "the rearward of the fashion."[3]

Some read for stile, and some for argument: one has little care about the sentiment, he observes only how it is expressed; another regards not the conclusion, but is diligent to mark how it is inferred: they read for other purposes, than the attainment of practical knowledge; and are no more likely to grow wise by an examination of a treatise of moral prudence, than an architect to inflame his devotion by considering attentively the proportions of a temple.

Some read that they may embellish their conversation, or shine in dispute; some that they may not be detected in ignorance, or want the reputation of literary accomplishments: but the most general and prevalent reason of study, is the impossibility of finding another amusement equally cheap or constant, equally independent on the

3. *Henry IV*, pt. II, III.2.

hour or the weather. He that wants money to follow the chace of pleasure through her yearly circuit, and is left at home when the gay world rolls to Bath or Tunbridge; he whose gout compells him to hear from his chamber, the rattle of chariots transporting happier beings to plays and assemblies, will be forced to seek in books a refuge from himself.

The author is not wholly useless, who provides innocent amusements for minds like these. There are in the present state of things so many more instigations to evil, than incitements to good, that he who keeps men in a neutral state, may be justly considered as a benefactor to life.

But, perhaps, it seldom happens, that study terminates in mere pastime. Books have always a secret influence on the understanding; we cannot at pleasure obliterate ideas; he that reads books of science, though without any fixed desire of improvement, will grow more knowing; he that entertains himself with moral or religious treatises, will imperceptibly advance in goodness; the ideas which are often offered to the mind, will at last find a lucky moment when it is disposed to receive them.

It is, therefore, urged without reason, as a discouragement to writers, that there are already books sufficient in the world; that all the topics of persuasion have been discussed, and every important question clearly stated and justly decided; and that, therefore, there is no room to hope, that pigmies should conquer where heroes have been defeated, or that the petty copiers of the present time should advance the great work of reformation, which their predecessors were forced to leave unfinished.[4]

Whatever be the present extent of human knowledge,

4. Cf. No. 95 above, esp. final three pars.

it is not only finite, and therefore in its own nature capable of increase; but so narrow, that almost every understanding may by a diligent application of its powers hope to enlarge it. It is, however, not necessary, that a man should forbear to write, till he has discovered some truth unknown before; he may be sufficiently useful, by only diversifying the surface of knowledge, and luring the mind by a new appearance to a second view of those beauties which it had passed over inattentively before. Every writer may find intellects correspondent to his own, to whom his expressions are familiar, and his thoughts congenial; and, perhaps, truth is often more successfully propagated by men of moderate abilities, who, adopting the opinions of others, have no care but to explain them clearly, than by subtile speculatists and curious searchers, who exact from their readers powers equal to their own, and if their fabrics of science be strong take no care to render them accessible.

For my part, I do not regret the hours which I have laid out on these little compositions. That the world has grown apparently better, since the publication of the Adventurer, I have not observed; but am willing to think, that many have been affected by single sentiments, of which it is their business to renew the impression; that many have caught hints of truth, which it is now their duty to persue; and that those who have received no improvement, have wanted not opportunity but intention to improve.

THE *IDLER*

No. 23. Saturday, 23 September 1758.

Life has no pleasure higher or nobler than that of friendship. It is painful to consider, that this sublime enjoyment may be impaired or destroyed by innumerable causes, and that there is no human possession of which the duration is less certain.

Many have talked, in very exalted language, of the perpetuity of friendship, of invincible constancy, and unalienable kindness; and some examples have been seen of men who have continued faithful to their earliest choice; and whose affection has predominated over changes of fortune, and contrariety of opinion.

But these instances are memorable, because they are rare. The friendship which is to be practised or expected by common mortals, must take its rise from mutual pleasure,[1] and must end when the power ceases of delighting each other.

Many accidents therefore may happen, by which the ardour of kindness will be abated, without criminal baseness or contemptible inconstancy on either part. To give pleasure is not always in our power; and little does he know himself, who believes that he can be always able to receive it.

Those who would gladly pass their days together may be separated by the different course of their affairs; and friendship, like love, is destroyed by long absence, though it may be encreased by short intermissions. What we have missed long enough to want it, we value more when it is regained; but that which has been lost till it is forgotten, will be found at last with little gladness, and with still less,

1. Cf. *Rambler* 64, above.

if a substitute has supplied the place. A man deprived of
the companion to whom he used to open his bosom, and
with whom he shared the hours of leisure and merriment,
feels the day at first hanging heavy on him; his difficulties
oppress, and his doubts distract him; he sees time come
and go without his wonted gratification, and all is sadness
within and solitude about him. But this uneasiness never
lasts long, necessity produces expedients, new amusements are discovered, and new conversation is admitted.

No expectation is more frequently disappointed, than
that which naturally arises in the mind, from the prospect
of meeting an old friend, after long separation.[2] We expect the attraction to be revived, and the coalition to be
renewed; no man considers how much alteration time has
made in himself, and very few enquire what effect it has
had upon others. The first hour convinces them, that the
pleasure, which they have formerly enjoyed, is for ever
at an end; different scenes have made different impressions, the opinions of both are changed, and that similitude of manners and sentiment is lost, which confirmed
them both in the approbation of themselves.

Friendship is often destroyed by opposition of interest,
not only by the ponderous and visible interest, which the
desire of wealth and greatness forms and maintains, but
by a thousand secret and slight competitions, scarcely
known to the mind upon which they operate. There is
scarcely any man without some favourite trifle which he
values above greater attainments, some desire of petty
praise which he cannot patiently suffer to be frustrated.
This minute ambition is sometimes crossed before it is
known, and sometimes defeated by wanton petulance;
but such attacks are seldom made without the loss of
friendship; for whoever has once found the vulnerable

2. Cf. *Idler* 58 (final two pars.) below.

part will always be feared, and the resentment will burn on in secret of which shame hinders the discovery.

This, however, is a slow malignity, which a wise man will obviate as inconsistent with quiet, and a good man will repress as contrary to virtue; but human happiness is sometimes violated by some more sudden strokes.

A dispute begun in jest, upon a subject which a moment before was on both parts regarded with careless indifference, is continued by the desire of conquest, till vanity kindles into rage, and opposition rankles into enmity. Against this hasty mischief I know not what security can be obtained; men will be sometimes surprized into quarrels, and though they might both hasten to reconciliation, as soon as their tumult has subsided, yet two minds will seldom be found together, which can at once subdue their discontent, or immediately enjoy the sweets of peace, without remembring the wounds of the conflict.

Friendship has other enemies. Suspicion is always hardening the cautious, and disgust repelling the delicate. Very slender differences will sometimes part those whom long reciprocation of civility or beneficence has united. Lonelove and Ranger retired into the county to enjoy the company of each other, and returned in six weeks cold and petulant; Ranger's pleasure was to walk in the fields, and Lonelove's to sit in a bower; each had complied with the other in his turn, and each was angry that compliance had been exacted.

The most fatal disease of friendship is gradual decay, or dislike hourly encreased by causes too slender for complaint, and too numerous for removal. Those who are angry may be reconciled; those who have been injured may receive a recompence; but when the desire of pleasing and willingness to be pleased is silently diminished, the renovation of friendship is hopeless; as, when the vital

powers sink into languor, there is no longer any use of
the physician.

No. 27. Saturday, 21 October 1758.

It has been the endeavour of all those whom the world
has reverenced for superior wisdom, to persuade man to
be acquainted with himself, to learn his own powers and
his own weakness, to observe by what evils he is most
dangerously beset, and by what temptations most easily
overcome.

This counsel has been often given with serious dignity,
and often received with appearance of convictions; but,
as very few can search deep into their own minds without
meeting what they wish to hide from themselves, scarce
any man persists in cultivating such disagreeable acquaintance, but draws the veil again between his eyes
and his heart, leaves his passions and appetites as he found
them, and advises others to look into themselves.

This is the common result of enquiry even among those
that endeavour to grow wiser or better, but this endeavour is far enough from frequency; the greater part of the
multitudes that swarm upon the earth, have never been
disturbed by such uneasy curiosity, but deliver themselves up to business or to pleasure, plunge into the current of life, whether placid or turbulent, and pass on
from one point of prospect to another, attentive rather
to any thing than the state of their minds; satisfied, at an
easy rate, with an opinion that they are no worse than
others, that every man must mind his own interest, or
that their pleasures hurt only themselves, and are therefore no proper subjects of censure.

Some, however, there are, whom the intrusion of
scruples, the recollection of better notions, or the latent

reprehension of good examples, will not suffer to live entirely contented with their own conduct; these are forced to pacify the mutiny of reason with fair promises, and quiet their thoughts with designs of calling all their actions to review, and planning a new scheme for the time to come.

There is nothing which we estimate so fallaciously as the force of our own resolutions, nor any fallacy which we so unwillingly and tardily detect. He that has resolved a thousand times, and a thousand times deserted his own purpose, yet suffers no abatement of his confidence, but still believes himself his own master, and able, by innate vigour of soul, to press forward to his end, through all the obstructions that inconveniences or delights can put in his way.

That this mistake should prevail for a time is very natural. When conviction is present, and temptation out of sight, we do not easily conceive how any reasonable being can deviate from his true interest. What ought to be done while it yet hangs only in speculation, is so plain and certain, that there is no place for doubt; the whole soul yields itself to the predominance of truth, and readily determines to do what, when the time of action comes, will be at last omitted.

I believe most men may review all the lives that have passed within their observation, without remembring one efficacious resolution, or being able to tell a single instance of a course of practice suddenly changed in consequence of a change of opinion, or an establishment of determination. Many indeed alter their conduct, and are not at fifty what they were at thirty, but they commonly varied imperceptibly from themselves, followed the train of external causes, and rather suffered reformation than made it.

It is not uncommon to charge the difference between promise and performance, between profession and reality, upon deep design and studied deceit; but the truth is, that there is very little hypocrisy in the world;[1] we do not so often endeavour or wish to impose on others as on ourselves; we resolve to do right, we hope to keep our resolutions, we declare them to confirm our own hope, and fix our own inconstancy by calling witnesses of our actions; but at last habit prevails, and those whom we invited to our triumph, laugh at our defeat.

Custom is commonly too strong for the most resolute resolver though furnished for the assault with all the weapons of philosophy. "He that endeavours to free himself from an ill habit," says Bacon, "must not change too much at a time lest he should be discouraged by difficulty; nor too little, for then he will make but slow advances."[2] This is a precept which may be applauded in a book, but will fail in the trial, in which every change will be found too great or too little. Those who have been able to conquer habit, are like those that are fabled to have returned from the realms of Pluto:

> *Pauci, quos aequus amavit*
> *Jupiter, atque ardens evexit ad aethera virtus.*[3]

AENEID, VI.129–30.

They are sufficient to give hope but not security, to animate the contest but not to promise victory.

Those who are in the power of evil habits, must conquer them as they can, and conquered they must be, or

1. Cf. *Rambler* 14 (par. 8): "Nothing is more unjust, however common, than to charge with hypocrisy him that expresses zeal for those virtues which he neglects to practise . . ."
2. In Bacon's essay "Of Nature in Men."
3. "A few, loved by the kindly Jupiter, and of ardent worth, lifted to heaven."

neither wisdom nor happiness can be attained; but those who are not yet subject to their influence, may, by timely caution, preserve their freedom, they may effectually resolve to escape the tyrant, whom they will very vainly resolve to conquer.

No. 30. Saturday, 11 November 1758.

The desires of man encrease with his acquisitions; every step which he advances brings something within his view, which he did not see before, and which, as soon as he sees it, he begins to want. Where necessity ends curiosity begins, and no sooner are we supplied with every thing that nature can demand, than we sit down to contrive artificial appetites.[1]

By this restlessness of mind, every populous and wealthy city is filled with innumerable employments, for which the greater part of mankind is without a name; with artificers whose labour is exerted in producing such petty conveniences, that many shops are furnished with instruments, of which the use can hardly be found without enquiry, but which he that once knows them, quickly learns to number among necessary things.

Such is the diligence, with which, in countries completely civilized, one part of mankind labours for another, that wants are supplied faster than they can be formed, and the idle and luxurious find life stagnate, for want of some desire to keep it in motion. This species of distress furnishes a new set of occupations, and multitudes are busied, from day to day, in finding the rich and the fortunate something to do.

1. Cf. *Rambler* 49, above (pars. 3–4), and esp. *Rasselas,* ch. 32 (pars. 4–5).

It is very common to reproach those artists as useless, who produce only such superfluities as neither accommodate the body nor improve the mind; and of which no other effect can be imagined, than that they are the occasions of spending money, and consuming time.

But this censure will be mitigated, when it is seriously considered, that money and time are the heaviest burthens of life, and that the unhappiest of all mortals are those who have more of either than they know how to use. To set himself free from these incumbrances, one hurries to New-market; another travels over Europe; one pulls down his house and calls architects about him; another buys a seat in the country, and follows his hounds over hedges and through rivers; one makes collections of shells, and another searches the world for tulips and carnations.

He is surely a public benefactor who finds employment for those to whom it is thus difficult to find it for themselves. It is true that this is seldom done merely from generosity or compassion, almost every man seeks his own advantage in helping others, and therefore it is too common for mercenary officiousness, to consider rather what is grateful than what is right.

We all know that it is more profitable to be loved than esteemed, and ministers of pleasure will always be found, who study to make themselves necessary, and to supplant those who are practising the same arts.

One of the amusements of idleness is reading without the fatigue of close attention, and the world therefore swarms with writers whose wish is not to be studied but to be read.

No species of literary men has lately been so much multiplied as the writers of news. Not many years ago the nation was content with one *Gazette;* but now we have not only in the metropolis papers for every morning and every evening, but almost every large town has its weekly historian, who regularly circulates his periodical intelligence, and fills the villages of his district with conjectures on the events of war, and with debates on the true interest of Europe.

To write news in its perfection requires such a combination of qualities, that a man completely fitted for the task is not always to be found. In Sir Henry Wotton's jocular definition, "An ambassador" is said to be "a man of virtue sent abroad to tell lies for the advantage of his country";[2] a news-writer is "a man without virtue, who writes lies at home for his own profit." To these compositions is required neither genius nor knowledge, neither industry nor sprightliness, but contempt of shame, and indifference to truth are absolutely necessary. He who by a long familiarity with infamy has obtained these qualities, may confidently tell to-day what he intends to contradict to-morrow; he may affirm fearlessly what he knows that he shall be obliged to recant, and may write letters from Amsterdam or Dresden to himself.

In a time of war the nation is always of one mind, eager to hear something good of themselves and ill of the enemy. At this time the task of news-writers is easy, they have nothing to do but to tell that a battle is expected, and afterwards that a battle has been fought, in which we and our friends, whether conquering or conquered, did all, and our enemies did nothing.

Scarce any thing awakens attention like a tale of cruelty. The writer of news never fails in the intermission of action to tell how the enemies murdered children and

2. Written by Wotton in the album of a friend, J. C. Flechammer. See Logan Pearsall Smith, *Life and Letters of Sir Henry Wotton* (1907), II.9–11.

ravished virgins; and if the scene of action be somewhat distant, scalps half the inhabitants of a province.

Among the calamities of war may be justly numbered the diminution of the love of truth, by the falshoods which interest dictates and credulity encourages. A peace will equally leave the warriour and relator of wars destitute of employment; and I know not whether more is to be dreaded from streets filled with soldiers accustomed to plunder, or from garrets filled with scribblers accustomed to lie.

No. 31. Saturday, 18 November 1758.

Many moralists have remarked, that pride has of all human vices the widest dominion, appears in the greatest multiplicity of forms, and lies hid under the greatest variety of disguises; of disguises, which, like the moon's "veil of brightness," are both its "lustre and its shade,"[1] and betray it to others, tho' they hide it from ourselves.

It is not my intention to degrade pride from this pre-eminence of mischief, yet I know not whether idleness may not maintain a very doubtful and obstinate competition.

There are some that profess idleness in its full dignity, who call themselves the "Idle," as Busiris in the play "calls himself the Proud";[2] who boast that they do nothing, and thank their stars that they have nothing to do; who sleep every night till they can sleep no longer, and rise only that exercise may enable them to sleep again; who prolong the reign of darkness by double curtains,

---

1. Samuel Butler, *Hudibras*, II.1.905–08.
2. Edward Young, *Busiris* (1719), I.1.13.

and never see the sun but to "tell him how they hate his beams";[3] whose whole labour is to vary the postures of indulgence, and whose day differs from their night but as a couch or chair differs from a bed.

These are the true and open votaries of idleness, for whom she weaves the garlands of poppies, and into whose cup she pours the waters of oblivion; who exist in a state of unruffled stupidity, forgetting and forgotten; who have long ceased to live, and at whose death the survivors can only say, that they have ceased to breathe.

But idleness predominates in many lives where it is not suspected, for being a vice which terminates in itself, it may be enjoyed without injury to others, and is therefore not watched like fraud, which endangers property, or like pride which naturally seeks its gratifications in another's inferiority. Idleness is a silent and peaceful quality, that neither raises envy by ostentation, nor hatred by opposition; and therefore no body is busy to censure or detect it.

As pride sometimes is hid under humility, idleness is often covered by turbulence and hurry.[4] He that neglects his known duty and real employment, naturally endeavours to croud his mind with something that may bar out the remembrance of his own folly, and does any thing but what he ought to do with eager diligence, that he may keep himself in his own favour.

Some are always in a state of preparation, occupied in previous measures, forming plans, accumulating materials, and providing for the main affair. These are certainly under the secret power of idleness. Nothing is to be expected from the workman whose tools are for ever to be sought. I was once told by a great master, that no man ever

3. *Paradise Lost*, IV.37.
4. Cf. *Idler* 48, below, n. 1.

excelled in painting, who was eminently curious about pencils and colours.

There are others to whom idleness dictates another expedient, by which life may be passed unprofitably away without the tediousness of many vacant hours. The art is, to fill the day with petty business, to have always something in hand which may raise curiosity, but not solicitude, and keep the mind in a state of action, but not of labour.

This art has for many years been practised by my old friend Sober, with wonderful success.[5] Sober is a man of strong desires and quick imagination, so exactly ballanced by the love of ease, that they can seldom stimulate him to any difficult undertaking; they have, however, so much power, that they will not suffer him to lie quite at rest, and though they do not make him sufficiently useful to others, they make him at least weary of himself.

Mr. Sober's chief pleasure is conversation; there is no end of his talk or his attention; to speak or to hear is equally pleasing; for he still fancies that he is teaching or learning something, and is free for the time from his own reproaches.

But there is one time at night when he must go home, that his friends may sleep; and another time in the morning, when all the world agrees to shut out interruption.[6] These are the moments of which poor Sober trembles at the thought. But the misery of these tiresome intervals, he has many means of alleviating. He has persuaded himself that the manual arts are undeservedly overlooked; he has observed in many trades the effects of close thought, and just ratiocination. From speculation he proceeded to

5. The character of Sober, according to Mrs. Thrale, was intended by Johnson "as his own portrait" (*Anecdotes* [*Miscellanies*, 1.178]).
   6. On Johnson's own fear of solitude, see esp. *Life*, I.114, n. 2; IV.427.

practice, and supplied himself with the tools of a carpenter, with which he mended his coal-box very successfully, and which he still continues to employ, as he finds occasion.

He has attempted at other times the crafts of the shoemaker, tinman, plumber, and potter; in all these arts he has failed, and resolves to qualify himself for them by better information. But his daily amusement is chemistry. He has a small furnace, which he employs in distillation, and which has long been the solace of his life. He draws oils and waters, and essences and spirits, which he knows to be of no use; sits and counts the drops as they come from his retort, and forgets that, while a drop is falling, a moment flies away.[7]

Poor Sober! I have often teaz'd him with reproof, and he has often promised reformation; for no man is so much open to conviction as the idler, but there is none on whom it operates so little. What will be the effect of this paper I know not; perhaps he will read it and laugh, and light the fire in his furnace; but my hope is that he will quit his trifles, and betake himself to rational and useful diligence.

No. 32. Saturday, 25 November 1758.

Among the innumerable mortifications that waylay human arrogance on every side may well be reckoned our ignorance of the most common objects and effects, a defect of which we become more sensible by every attempt to supply it. Vulgar and inactive minds confound familiarity with knowledge, and conceive themselves informed of the whole nature of things when they are shewn their form or told their use; but the speculatist, who is not content with

7. For Johnson's own chemical experiments, see *Life*, I.140; II.155; III.398; IV.237; and Mrs. Thrale, in *Anecdotes (Miscellanies*, I.307).

superficial views, harrasses himself with fruitless curiosity, and still as he enquires more perceives only that he knows less.

Sleep is a state in which a great part of every life is passed. No animal has been yet discovered, whose existence is not varied with intervals of insensibility; and some late philosophers have extended the empire of sleep over the vegetable world.

Yet of this change so frequent, so great, so general, and so necessary, no searcher has yet found either the efficient or final cause; or can tell by what power the mind and the body are thus chained down in irresistible stupefaction; or what benefits the animal receives from this alternate suspension of its active powers.

Whatever may be the multiplicity or contrariety of opinions upon this subject, nature has taken sufficient care that theory shall have little influence on practice. The most diligent enquirer is not able long to keep his eyes open; the most eager disputant will begin about midnight to desert his argument, and once in four and twenty hours, the gay and the gloomy, the witty and the dull, the clamorous and the silent, the busy and the idle, are all overpowered by the gentle tyrant, and all lie down in the equality of sleep.

Philosophy has often attempted to repress insolence by asserting that all conditions are levelled by death;[1] a position which, however it may deject the happy, will seldom afford much comfort to the wretched. It is far more pleasing to consider that sleep is equally a leveller with death; that the time is never at a great distance, when the balm of rest shall be effused alike upon every head,

1. Whatever other expressions of this commonplace he has in mind, Johnson, who planned a new critical edition of Claudian (*Life,* IV.381), is certainly thinking of "Omnia mors aequat" (*De raptu Proserpinae,* II.302).

when the diversities of life shall stop their operation, and the high and the low shall lie down together.[2]

It is somewhere recorded of Alexander, that in the pride of conquests, and intoxication of flattery, he declared that he only perceived himself to be a man by the necessity of sleep.[3] Whether he considered sleep as necessary to his mind or body it was indeed a sufficient evidence of human infirmity; the body which required such frequency of renovation gave but faint promises of immortality; and the mind which, from time to time, sunk gladly into insensibility had made no very near approaches to the felicity of the supreme and self-sufficient nature.

I know not what can tend more to repress all the passions that disturb the peace of the world, than the consideration that there is no height of happiness or honour, from which man does not eagerly descend to a state of unconscious repose; that the best condition of life is such, that we contentedly quit its good to be disentangled from its evils; that in a few hours splendour fades before the eye, and praise itself deadens in the ear; the senses withdraw from their objects, and reason favours the retreat.

What then are the hopes and prospects of covetousness, ambition and rapacity? Let him that desires most have all his desires gratified, he never shall attain a state, which he can, for a day and a night, contemplate with satisfaction, or from which, if he had the power of perpetual vigilance, he would not long for periodical separations.

All envy would be extinguished if it were universally known that there are none to be envied, and surely none

2. Aristotle, *Nichomachean Ethics,* I.13.

3. Plutarch, "Alexander," XXII.3–4. On the other hand, Plutarch emphasizes that Alexander was far less given to drink than was commonly supposed. Johnson's remarks about Alexander's intemperance, here and in par. 10, are probably based on Quintus Curtius (see *Idler* 51, below, n. 2).

can be much envied who are not pleased with themselves.[4] There is reason to suspect that the distinctions of mankind have more shew than value, when it is found that all agree to be weary alike of pleasures and of cares, that the powerful and the weak, the celebrated and obscure, join in one common wish, and implore from nature's hand the nectar of oblivion.

Such is our desire of abstraction from ourselves, that very few are satisfied with the quantity of stupefaction which the needs of the body force upon the mind. Alexander himself added intemperance to sleep, and solaced with the fumes of wine the sovereignty of the world. And almost every man has some art, by which he steals his thoughts away from his present state.

It is not much of life that is spent in close attention to any important duty. Many hours of every day are suffered to fly away without any traces left upon the intellects. We suffer phantoms to rise up before us, and amuse ourselves with the dance of airy images, which after a time we dismiss for ever, and know not how we have been busied.

Many have no happier moments than those that they pass in solitude, abandoned to their own imagination, which sometimes puts sceptres in their hands or mitres on their heads, shifts the scene of pleasure with endless variety, bids all the forms of beauty sparkle before them, and gluts them with every change of visionary luxury.

It is easy in these semi-slumbers to collect all the possibilities of happiness, to alter the course of the sun, to bring back the past, and anticipate the future, to unite all the beauties of all seasons, and all the blessings of all climates, to receive and bestow felicity, and forget that misery is the lot of man. All this is a voluntary dream, a

4. *Rasselas,* ch. 16 (par. 9).

temporary recession from the realities of life to airy
fictions; an habitual subjection of reason to fancy.

Others are afraid to be alone, and amuse themselves by
a perpetual succession of companions, but the difference
is not great; in solitude we have our dreams to ourselves,
and in company we agree to dream in concert. The end
sought in both is forgetfulness of ourselves.

No. 36. Saturday, 23 December 1758.

The great differences that disturb the peace of mankind,
are not about ends but means.[1] We have all the same
general desires, but how those desires shall be accomplished will for ever be disputed. The ultimate purpose of
government is temporal, and that of religion is eternal
happiness. Hitherto we agree; but here we must part, to
try, according to the endless varieties of passion and
understanding combined with one another, every possible
form of government, and every imaginable tenet of
religion.

We are told by Cumberland, that "rectitude," applied
to action or contemplation, is merely metaphorical; and
that as a "right" line describes the shortest passage from
point to point, so a "right" action effects a good design by
the fewest means; and so likewise a "right" opinion is that
which connects distant truths by the shortest train of
intermediate propositions.[2]

To find the nearest way from truth to truth, or from

1. See *Adventurer* 107 (par. 3). Cf. also *Rambler* 99 (final par.): "It
has been justly observed, that discord generally operates in little things;
it is inflamed to its utmost vehemence by contrariety of taste, oftener
than of principles."

2. Richard Cumberland, *Philosophical Inquiry into the Laws of
Nature* (1750), Prolegomena, pp. xlii–xlvi.

purpose to effect, not to use more instruments where fewer will be sufficient, not to move by wheels and levers what will give way to the naked hand, is the great proof of a healthful and vigorous mind, neither feeble with helpless ignorance, nor overburdened with unwieldy knowledge.

But there are men who seem to think nothing so much the characteristick of a genius, as to do common things in an uncommon manner; like Hudibras to "tell the clock by algebra,"[3] or like the lady in Dr. Young's satires, "to drink tea by stratagem."[4] To quit the beaten track only because it is known, and take a new path, however crooked or rough, because the strait was found out before.

Every man speaks and writes with intent to be understood, and it can seldom happen but he that understands himself might convey his notions to another, if, content to be understood, he did not seek to be admired; but when once he begins to contrive how his sentiments may be received, not with most ease to his reader, but with most advantage to himself, he then transfers his consideration from words to sounds, from sentences to periods, and as he grows more elegant becomes less intelligible.

It is difficult to enumerate every species of authors whose labours counteract themselves. The man of exuberance and copiousness, who diffuses every thought thro' so many diversities of expression, that it is lost like water in a mist. The ponderous dictator of sentences, whose notions are delivered in the lump, and are, like uncoined bullion, of more weight than use. The liberal illustrator, who shews by examples and comparisons what was clearly seen when it was first proposed; and the stately son of

3. Butler's *Hudibras*, I.1.125–26.
4. Edward Young, *Satires*, VI.188; cf. "Pope," *Lives*, III.200.

demonstration, who proves with mathematical formality what no man has yet pretended to doubt.

There is a mode of style for which I know not that the masters of oratory have yet found a name, a style by which the most evident truths are so obscured that they can no longer be perceived, and the most familiar propositions so disguised that they cannot be known. Every other kind of eloquence is the dress of sense, but this is the mask, by which a true master of his art will so effectually conceal it, that a man will as easily mistake his own positions if he meets them thus transformed, as he may pass in a masquerade his nearest acquaintance.

This style may be called the "terrifick," for its chief intention is to terrify and amaze; it may be termed the "repulsive," for its natural effect is to drive away the reader; or it may be distinguished, in plain English, by the denomination of the "bugbear style," for it has more terror than danger, and will appear less formidable, as it is more nearly approached.

A mother tells her infant, that "two and two make four," the child remembers the proposition, and is able to count four to all the purposes of life, till the course of his education brings him among philosophers, who fright him from his former knowledge, by telling him that four is a certain aggregate of unites; that all numbers being only the repetition of an unite, which, though not a number itself, is the parent, root, or original of all number, "four" is the denomination assigned to a certain number of such repetitions. The only danger is, lest, when he first hears these dreadful sounds, the pupil should run away; if he has but the courage to stay till the conclusion, he will find that, when speculation has done its worst, two and two still make four.

An illustrious example of this species of eloquence, may be found in *Letters Concerning Mind*.[5] The author begins by declaring, that "the sorts of things are things that now are, have been, and shall be, and the things that strictly Are." In this position, except the last clause, in which he uses something of the scholastick language, there is nothing but what every man has heard and imagines himself to know. But who would not believe that some wonderful novelty is presented to his intellect, when he is afterwards told, in the true "bugbear" style, that "the Ares, in the former sense, are things that lie between the Have-beens and Shall-bes. The Have-beens are things that are past; the Shall-bes are things that are to come; and the things that Are, in the latter sense, are things that have not been, nor shall be, nor stand in the midst of such as are before them or shall be after them. The things that have been, and shall be, have respect to present, past, and future. Those likewise that now Are have moreover place; that, for instance, which is here, that which is to the east, that which is to the west."

All this, my dear reader, is very strange; but though it be strange, it is not new; survey these wonderful sentences again, and they will be found to contain nothing more than very plain truths, which till this author arose had always been delivered in plain language.

No. 41. Saturday, 27 January 1759.

The following letter relates to an affliction perhaps not necessary to be imparted to the publick,[1] but I could

5. By John Petvin (1691–1745), vicar of Islington, Devon; published posthumously (1750), p. 40 (Letter VI).

1. Johnson's mother had died just a few days before this in Lichfield.

not persuade myself to suppress it, because I think I know
the sentiments to be sincere, and I feel no disposition to
provide for this day any other entertainment.

> *At tu quisquis eris, miseri qui cruda poetae*
> *Credideris fletu funera digna tuo,*
> *Haec postrema tibi sit flendi causa, fluatque*
> *Lenis inoffenso vitaque morsque gradu.*[2]

MR. IDLER,

Notwithstanding the warnings of philosophers, and
the daily examples of losses and misfortunes which life
forces upon our observation, such is the absorption of our
thoughts in the business of the present day, such the resignation of our reason to empty hopes of future felicity, or
such our unwillingness to foresee what we dread, that
every calamity comes suddenly upon us, and not only
presses us as a burthen, but crushes as a blow.

There are evils which happen out of the common
course of nature, against which it is no reproach not to
be provided. A flash of lightning intercepts the traveller
in his way. The concussion of an earthquake heaps the
ruins of cities upon their inhabitants. But other miseries
time brings, though silently yet visibly forward by its
even lapse, which yet approach us unseen because we
turn our eyes away, and seize us unresisted because we
could not arm ourselves against them, but by setting
them before us.

That it is vain to shrink from what cannot be avoided,
and to hide that from ourselves which must some time
be found, is a truth which we all know, but which all
neglect, and perhaps none more than the speculative
reasoner, whose thoughts are always from home, whose
eye wanders over life, whose fancy dances after meteors

2. Source uncertain; attributed to Ovid.

of happiness kindled by itself, and who examines every thing rather than his own state.

Nothing is more evident than that the decays of age must terminate in death; yet there is no man, says Tully, who does not believe that he may yet live another year;[3] and there is none who does not, upon the same principle, hope another year for his parent or his friend, but the fallacy will be in time detected; the last year, the last day must come. It has come and is past. The life which made my own life pleasant is at an end, and the gates of death are shut upon my prospects.

The loss of a friend upon whom the heart was fixed, to whom every wish and endeavour tended, is a state of dreary desolation in which the mind looks abroad impatient of itself, and finds nothing but emptiness and horror. The blameless life, the artless tenderness, the pious simplicity, the modest resignation, the patient sickness, and the quiet death, are remembered only to add value to the loss, to aggravate regret for what cannot be amended, to deepen sorrow for what cannot be recalled.

These are the calamities by which Providence gradually disengages us from the love of life. Other evils fortitude may repel, or hope may mitigate, but irreparable privation leaves nothing to exercise resolution or flatter expectation. The dead cannot return, and nothing is left us here but languishment and grief.

Yet such is the course of nature, that whoever lives long must outlive those whom he loves and honours. Such is the condition of our present existence, that life must one time lose its associations, and every inhabitant of the earth must walk downward to the grave alone and unregarded, without any partner of his joy or grief, without any interested witness of his misfortunes or success.

3. *De Senectute,* VI.24.

Misfortune, indeed, he may yet feel, for where is the bottom of the misery of man? But what is success to him that has none to enjoy it. Happiness is not found in self-contemplation; it is perceived only when it is reflected from another.

We know little of the state of departed souls, because such knowledge is not necessary to a good life. Reason deserts us at the brink of the grave, and can give no further intelligence. Revelation is not wholly silent: "There is joy in the angels of heaven over one sinner that repenteth";[4] and surely this joy is not incommunicable to souls disentangled from the body, and made like angels.

Let hope therefore dictate, what revelation does not confute, that the union of souls may still remain; and that we who are struggling with sin, sorrow, and infirmities, may have our part in the attention and kindness of those who have finished their course and are now receiving their reward.

These are the great occasions which force the mind to take refuge in religion: when we have no help in ourselves, what can remain but that we look up to a higher and a greater power; and to what hope may we not raise our eyes and hearts, when we consider that the greatest power is the best.

Surely there is no man who, thus afflicted, does not seek succour in the Gospel, which has brought "life and immortality to light."[5] The precepts of Epicurus, who teaches us to endure what the laws of the universe make necessary, may silence but not content us. The dictates of Zeno, who commands us to look with indifference on external things, may dispose us to conceal our sorrow,

4. Luke, xv.10.
5. II Timothy, i.10.

but cannot assuage it.[6] Real alleviation of the loss of friends, and rational tranquillity in the prospect of our own dissolution, can be received only from the promises of him in whose hands are life and death, and from the assurance of another and better state, in which all tears will be wiped from the eyes,[7] and the whole soul shall be filled with joy. Philosophy may infuse stubbornness, but religion only can give patience.

I am, &c.

No. 44. Saturday, 17 February 1759.

Memory is, among the faculties of the human mind, that of which we make the most frequent use, or rather that of which the agency is incessant or perpetual. Memory is the primary and fundamental power, without which there could be no other intellectual operation. Judgment and ratiocination suppose something already known, and draw their decisions only from experience. Imagination selects ideas from the treasures of remembrance, and produces novelty only by varied combinations. We do not even form conjectures of distant, or anticipations of future events, but by concluding what is possible from what is past.

The two offices of memory are collection and distribution; by one images are accumulated, and by the other produced for use. Collection is always the employment of our first years, and distribution commonly that of our advanced age.

To collect and reposite the various forms of things, is far the most pleasing part of mental occupation. We are

6. Cf. *Rambler* 32 (esp. pars. 1–5).
7. Revelation, xxi.4.

naturally delighted with novelty, and there is a time when all that we see is new. When first we enter into the world, whithersoever we turn our eyes, they meet knowledge with pleasure at her side; every diversity of nature pours ideas in upon the soul; neither search nor labour are necessary; we have nothing more to do than to open our eyes, and curiosity is gratified.

Much of the pleasure which the first survey of the world affords, is exhausted before we are conscious of our own felicity, or able to compare our condition with some other possible state. We have therefore few traces of the joy of our earliest discoveries; yet we all remember a time when nature had so many untasted gratifications, that every excursion gave delight which can now be found no longer, when the noise of a torrent, the rustle of a wood, the song of birds, or the play of lambs, had power to fill the attention, and suspend all perception of the course of time.

But these easy pleasures are soon at an end; we have seen in a very little time so much, that we call out for new objects of observation, and endeavour to find variety in books and life. But study is laborious, and not always satisfactory; and conversation has its pains as well as pleasures; we are willing to learn, but not willing to be taught; we are pained by ignorance, but pained yet more by another's knowledge.

From the vexation of pupillage men commonly set themselves free about the middle of life, by shutting up the avenues of intelligence, and resolving to rest in their present state; and they, whose ardour of enquiry continues longer, find themselves insensibly forsaken by their instructors. As every man advances in life, the proportion between those that are younger, and that are older than himself, is continually changing; and he that has lived half a century, finds few that do not require from him that information which he once expected from those that went before him.

Then it is that the magazines of memory are opened, and the stores of accumulated knowledge are displayed by vanity or benevolence, or in honest commerce of mutual interest. Every man wants others, and is therefore glad when he is wanted by them. And as few men will endure the labour of intense meditation without necessity, he that has learned enough for his profit or his honour seldom endeavours after further acquisitions.

The pleasure of recollecting speculative notions would not be much less than that of gaining them, if they could be kept pure and unmingled with the passages of life; but such is the necessary concatenation of our thoughts, that good and evil are linked together, and no pleasure recurs but associated with pain. Every revived idea reminds us of a time when something was enjoyed that is now lost, when some hope was yet not blasted, when some purpose had yet not languished into sluggishness or indifference.

Whether it be that life has more vexations than comforts, or, what is in the event just the same, that evil makes deeper impression than good, it is certain that few can review the time past without heaviness of heart. He remembers many calamities incurred by folly, many opportunities lost by negligence. The shades of the dead rise up before him, and he laments the companions of his youth, the partners of his amusements, the assistants of his labours, whom the hand of death has snatched away.

When an offer was made to Themistocles of teaching him the art of memory, he answered, that he would rather wish for the art of forgetfulness.[1] He felt his imagination

---

1. Simonides made the offer to him. Cicero, *De Finibus*, II.32.104.

haunted by phantoms of misery which he was unable to suppress, and would gladly have calmed his thoughts with some "oblivious antidote."[2] In this we all resemble one another; the hero and the sage are, like vulgar mortals, overburthened by the weight of life, all shrink from recollection, and all wish for an art of forgetfulness.

No. 48. Saturday, 17 March 1759.

There is no kind of idleness, by which we are so easily seduced, as that which dignifies itself by the appearance of business,[1] and by making the loiterer imagine that he has something to do which must not be neglected, keeps him in perpetual agitation, and hurries him rapidly from place to place.

He that sits still, or reposes himself upon a couch, no more deceives himself than he deceives others; he knows that he is doing nothing, and has no other solace of his insignificance than the resolution which the lazy hourly make, of changing his mode of life.

To do nothing every man is ashamed, and to do much almost every man is unwilling or afraid. Innumerable expedients have therefore been invented to produce motion without labour, and employment without solicitude. The greater part of those whom the kindness of fortune has left to their own direction, and whom want does not keep chained to the counter or the plow, play throughout

2. *Macbeth*, v.3.43. Johnson cites the passage in the *Dictionary* (under "oblivious").

1. Cf. the portrait of Jack Whirler in *Idler* 19 (esp. pars. 4–8); *Idler* 31 (par. 6), and Johnson's dislike of "bustling" ("It is getting on horseback in a ship") in *Hebrides,* 13 October, 1773.

life with the shadows of business, and know not at last what they have been doing.

These imitators of action are of all denominations. Some are seen at every auction without intention to purchase; others appear punctually at the Exchange, though they are known there only by their faces. Some are always making parties, to visit collections for which they have no taste, and some neglect every pleasure and every duty to hear questions in which they have no interest, debated in parliament.

These men never appear more ridiculous, than in the distress which they imagine themselves to feel, from some accidental interruption of those empty pursuits. A tiger newly imprisoned is indeed more formidable, but not more angry than Jack Tulip with-held from a florist's feast, or Tom Distich hindered from seeing the first representation of a play.

As political affairs are the highest and most extensive of temporal concerns, the mimick of a politician is more busy and important than any other trifler. Monsieur le Noir, a man who, without property or importance in any corner of the earth, has, in the present confusion of the world, declared himself a steady adherent to the French, is made miserable by a wind that keeps back the packet-boat, and still more miserable, by every account of a Malouin privateer[2] caught in his cruize; he knows well that nothing can be done or said by him which can produce any effect but that of laughter, that he can neither hasten nor retard good or evil, that his joys and sorrows have scarcely any partakers; yet such is his zeal, and such his curiosity, that he would run barefooted to Gravesend, for the sake of knowing first that the English had lost a

2. A privateer of St. Malo. Cf. "Thoughts . . . Respecting Falkland's Islands" (par. 14).

tender, and would ride out to meet every mail from the continent if he might be permitted to open it.

Learning is generally confessed to be desirable, and there are some who fancy themselves always busy in acquiring it. Of these ambulatory students, one of the most busy is my friend Tom Restless.[3]

Tom has long had a mind to be a man of knowledge, but he does not care to spend much time among authors, for he is of opinion that few books deserve the labour of perusal, that they give the mind an unfashionable cast, and destroy that freedom of thought and easiness of manners indispensibly requisite to acceptance in the world. Tom has therefore found another way to wisdom. When he rises he goes into a coffee-house, where he creeps so near to men whom he takes to be reasoners as to hear their discourse, and endeavours to remember something which, when it has been strained thro' Tom's head, is so near to nothing that what it once was cannot be discovered. This he carries round from friend to friend thro' a circle of visits, till hearing what each says upon the question he becomes able at dinner to say a little himself, and as every great genius relaxes himself among his inferiors, meets with some who wonder how so young a man can talk so wisely.

At night he has a new feast prepared for his intellects; he always runs to a disputing society, or a speaking club, where he half hears what, if he had heard the whole, he would but half understand; goes home pleased with the consciousness of a day well spent, lies down full of ideas, and rises in the morning empty as before.

3. According to Nichols, Johnson stated that the original of Tom Restless was Thomas Tyers, whose biographical sketch of Johnson, written for the *Gentleman's Magazine* (December 1784), Boswell disparaged (*Life*, III.308–9 and n. 3). Cf. *Idler* 47, n. 1.

No. 49. Saturday, 24 March 1759.

I supped three nights ago with my friend Will Marvel. His affairs obliged him lately to take a journey into Devonshire, from which he has just returned. He knows me to be a very patient hearer, and was glad of my company, as it gave him an opportunity of disburthening himself by a minute relation of the casualties of his expedition.

Will is not one of those who go out and return with nothing to tell. He has a story of his travels, which will strike a home-bred citizen with horror, and has in ten days suffered so often the extremes of terror and joy, that he is in doubt whether he shall ever again expose either his body or mind to such danger and fatigue.

When he left London the morning was bright, and a fair day was promised. But Will is born to struggle with difficulties. That happened to him, which has sometimes, perhaps, happened to others. Before he had gone more than ten miles it began to rain. What course was to be taken! His soul disdained to turn back. He did what the king of Prussia might have done, he flapped his hat, buttoned up his cape, and went forwards, fortifying his mind, by the stoical consolation, that whatever is violent will be short.

His constancy was not long tried; at the distance of about half a mile he saw an inn, which he entered wet and weary, and found civil treatment and proper refreshment. After a respite of about two hours he looked abroad, and seeing the sky clear, called for his horse and passed the first stage without any other memorable accident.

Will considered, that labour must be relieved by pleasure, and that the strength which great undertakings require must be maintained by copious nutriment; he therefore ordered himself an elegant supper, drank two bottles of claret, and passed the beginning of the night in sound sleep; but waking before light, was forewarned of the troubles of the next day, by a shower beating against his windows with such violence as to threaten the dissolution of nature. When he arose he found what he expected, that the country was under water. He joined himself, however, to a company that was travelling the same way, and came safely to the place of dinner, tho' every step of his horse dashed the mud into the air.

In the afternoon, having parted from his company, he set forward alone, and passed many collections of water of which it was impossible to guess the depth, and which he now cannot review without some censure of his own rashness; but what a man undertakes he must perform, and Marvel hates a coward at his heart.

Few that lie warm in their beds, think what others undergo, who have perhaps been as tenderly educated, and have as acute sensations as themselves. My friend was now to lodge the second night almost fifty miles from home, in a house which he never had seen before, among people to whom he was totally a stranger, not knowing whether the next man he should meet would prove good or bad; but seeing an inn of a good appearance, he rode resolutely into the yard, and knowing that respect is often paid in proportion as it is claimed, delivered his injunction to the hostler with spirit, and entering the house, called vigorously about him.

On the third day up rose the sun and Mr. Marvel.[1] His troubles and his dangers were now such, as he wishes no other man ever to encounter. The ways were less fre-

1. Johnson echoes the *Canterbury Tales*, l. 2273 ("Up roos the sonne, and up roose Emelye").

quented, and the country more thinly inhabited. He rode
many a lonely hour thro' mire and water, and met not a
single soul for two miles together with whom he could
exchange a word. He cannot deny that, looking round
upon the dreary region, and seeing nothing but bleak
fields and naked trees, hills obscured by fogs, and flats
covered with inundations, he did for some time suffer
melancholy to prevail upon him, and wished himself
again safe at home. One comfort he had, which was to
consider, that none of his friends were in the same distress, for whom, if they had been with him, he should
have suffered more than for himself; he could not forbear
sometimes to consider how happily the Idler is settled
in an easier condition, who, surrounded like him with
terrors, could have done nothing but lie down and die.

Amidst these reflections he came to a town and found
a dinner, which disposed him to more chearful sentiments: but the joys of life are short, and its miseries are
long; he mounted and travelled fifteen miles more thro'
dirt and desolation.

At last the sun set, and all the horrors of darkness came
upon him. He then repented the weak indulgence by
which he had gratified himself at noon with too long an
interval of rest: yet he went forward along a path which
he could no longer see, sometimes rushing suddenly into
water, and sometimes incumbered with stiff clay, ignorant
whither he was going, and uncertain whether his next
step might not be the last.

In this dismal gloom of nocturnal peregrination his
horse unexpectedly stood still. Marvel had heard many
relations of the instinct of horses, and was in doubt what
danger might be at hand. Sometimes he fancied that he
was on the bank of a river still and deep, and sometimes
that a dead body lay across the track. He sat still awhile to

recollect his thoughts; and as he was about to alight and explore the darkness, out stepped a man with a lantern, and opened the turnpike. He hired a guide to the town, arrived in safety, and slept in quiet.

The rest of his journey was nothing but danger. He climbed and descended precipices on which vulgar mortals tremble to look; he passed marshes like the "Serbonian bog, where armies whole have sunk";[2] he forded rivers where the current roared like the egre[3] of the Severn; or ventured himself on bridges that trembled under him, from which he looked down on foaming whirlpools, or dreadful abysses; he wandered over houseless heaths, amidst all the rage of the elements, with the snow driving in his face, and the tempest howling in his ears.

Such are the colours in which Marvel paints his adventures. He has accustomed himself to sounding words and hyperbolical images, till he has lost the power of true description. In a road through which the heaviest carriages pass without difficulty, and the post-boy every day and night goes and returns, he meets with hardships like those which are endured in Siberian deserts, and misses nothing of romantic danger but a giant and a dragon. When his dreadful story is told in proper terms, it is only, that the way was dirty in winter, and that he experienced the common vicissitudes of rain and sunshine.

No. 50. Saturday, 31 March 1759.

The character of Mr. Marvel has raised the merriment of some and the contempt of others, who do not sufficiently

2. *Paradise Lost*, II.592–94.

3. I.e. "eagre" (the wave of the incoming tide created by a narrowing estuary).

consider how often they hear and practise the same arts of exaggerated narration.

There is not, perhaps, among the multitudes of all conditions that swarm upon the earth, a single man who does not believe that he has something extraordinary to relate of himself; and who does not, at one time or other, summon the attention of his friends to the casualties of his adventures and the vicissitudes of his fortune; casualties and vicissitudes that happen alike in lives uniform and diversified; to the commander of armies, and the writer at a desk; to the sailor who resigns himself to the wind and water, and the farmer whose longest journey is to the market.

In the present state of the world man may pass thro' Shakespear's seven stages of life,[1] and meet nothing singular or wonderful. But such is every man's attention to himself, that what is common and unheeded when it is only seen, becomes remarkable and peculiar when we happen to feel it.

It is well enough known to be according to the usual process of nature, that men should sicken and recover, that some designs should succeed and others miscarry, that friends should be separated and meet again, that some should be made angry by endeavours to please them, and some be pleased when no care has been used to gain their approbation; that men and women should at first come together by chance, like each other so well as to commence acquaintance, improve acquaintance into fondness, increase or extinguish fondness by marriage, and have children of different degrees of intellects and virtue, some of whom die before their parents, and others survive them.

1. *As You Like It,* II.7.142–66.

Yet let any man tell his own story, and nothing of all this has ever befallen him according to the common order of things; something has always discriminated his case; some unusual concurrence of events has appeared which made him more happy or more miserable than other mortals; for in pleasures or calamities, however common, every one has comforts and afflictions of his own.

It is certain that without some artificial augmentations, many of the pleasures of life, and almost all its embellishments, would fall to the ground. If no man was to express more delight that he felt, those who felt most would raise little envy. If travellers were to describe the most laboured performances of art with the same coldness as they survey them, all expectations of happiness from change of place would cease. The pictures of Raphael would hang without spectators, and the gardens of Versailles might be inhabited by hermits. All the pleasure that is received ends in an opportunity of splendid falshood, in the power of gaining notice by the display of beauties which the eye was weary of beholding, and a history of happy moments, of which, in reality, the most happy was the last.

The ambition of superior sensibility and superior eloquence disposes the lovers of arts to receive rapture at one time, and communicate it at another; and each labours first to impose upon himself, and then to propagate the imposture.

Pain is less subject than pleasure to caprices of expression.[2] The torments of disease, and the grief for irremediable misfortunes, sometimes are such as no words can declare, and can only be signified by groans, or sobs, or inarticulate ejulations. Man has from nature a mode of utterance peculiar to pain, but he has none peculiar

2. Cf. *Adventurer* 111 (par. 3), above.

to pleasure, because he never has pleasure but in such degrees as the ordinary use of language may equal or surpass.

It is nevertheless certain, that many pains as well as pleasures are heightened by rhetorical affectation, and that the picture is, for the most part, bigger than the life.

When we describe our sensations of another's sorrows, either in friendly or ceremonious condolence, the customs of the world scarcely admit of rigid veracity. Perhaps the fondest friendship would enrage oftner than comfort, were the tongue on such occasions faithfully to represent the sentiments of the heart; and I think the strictest moralists allow forms of address to be used without much regard to their literal acceptation, when either respect or tenderness requires them, because they are universally known to denote not the degree but the species of our sentiments.

But the same indulgence cannot be allowed to him who aggravates dangers incurred or sorrow endured by himself, because he darkens the prospect of futurity, and multiplies the pains of our condition by useless terror. Those who magnify their delights are less criminal deceivers, yet they raise hopes which are sure to be disappointed. It would be undoubtedly best, if we could see and hear every thing as it is, that nothing might be too anxiously dreaded, or too ardently pursued.

No. 51. Saturday, 7 April 1759.

It has been commonly remarked,[1] that eminent men are least eminent at home, that bright characters lose much of their splendor at a nearer view, and many who fill the

1. Particularly by Johnson himself, as in *Rambler* 14 (pars. 1–8).

world with their fame, excite very little reverence among those that surround them in their domestick privacies.

To blame or to suspect is easy and natural. When the fact is evident, and the cause doubtful, some accusation is always engendered between idleness and malignity. This disparity of general and familiar esteem is therefore imputed to hidden vices, and to practices indulged in secret, but carefully covered from the publick eye.

Vice will indeed always produce contempt. The dignity of Alexander, tho' nations fell prostrate before him, was certainly held in little veneration by the partakers of his midnight revels, who had seen him, in the madness of wine, murder his friend, or set fire to the Persian palace at the instigation of a harlòt;[2] and it is well remembered among us, that the avarice of Marlborough kept him in subjection to his wife,[3] while he was dreaded by France as her conqueror, and honoured by the emperor as his deliverer.

But though where there is vice there must be want of reverence, it is not reciprocally true, that when there is want of reverence there is always vice. That awe which great actions or abilities impress will be inevitably diminished by acquaintance, tho' nothing either mean or criminal should be found.

Of men, as of every thing else, we must judge according to our knowledge. When we see of a hero only his battles, or of a writer only his books, we have nothing to allay our ideas of their greatness. We consider the one

2. Johnson is probably following the accounts by Quintus Curtius of Alexander's drunkenness, the murder of Clitus, and the burning of the palace at the instigation of Thais *(History of Alexander* v.7.1–7; VIII.1.50–52). On the other hand, Plutarch, whom he cites in *Idler* 32 (n. 3), above, states that Alexander's intemperance was much exaggerated.

3. The charge of avarice against Marlborough was common. Johnson refers to the positions held by the Duchess at Anne's court, particularly the management of the privy purse.

only as the guardian of his country, and the other only as the instructor of mankind. We have neither opportunity nor motive to examine the minuter parts of their lives, or the less apparent peculiarities of their characters; we name them with habitual respect, and forget, what we still continue to know, that they are men like other mortals.

But such is the constitution of the world, that much of life must be spent in the same manner by the wise and the ignorant, the exalted and the low. Men, however distinguished by external accidents or intrinsick qualities, have all the same wants, the same pains, and, as far as the senses are consulted, the same pleasures. The petty cares and petty duties are the same in every station to every understanding, and every hour brings some occasion on which we all sink to the common level. We are all naked till we are dressed, and hungry till we are fed; and the general's triumph, and sage's disputation, end, like the humble labours of the smith or plowman, in a dinner or in sleep.

Those notions which are to be collected by reason in opposition to the senses, will seldom stand forward in the mind, but lie treasured in the remoter repositories of memory, to be found only when they are sought. Whatever any man may have written or done, his precepts or his valour will scarcely over-ballance the unimportant uniformity which runs thro' his time. We do not easily consider him as great, whom our own eyes shew us to be little; nor labour to keep present to our thoughts the latent excellencies of him who shares with us all our weaknesses and many of our follies; who like us is delighted with slight amusements, busied with trifling employments, and disturbed by little vexations.

Great powers cannot be exerted, but when great exigencies make them necessary. Great exigencies can happen but seldom, and therefore those qualities which have a claim to the veneration of mankind, lie hid, for the most part, like subterranean treasures, over which the foot passes as on common ground, till necessity breaks open the golden cavern.

In the ancient celebrations of victory, a slave was placed on the triumphal car, by the side of the general, who reminded him by a short sentence, that he was a man.[4] Whatever danger there might be lest a leader, in his passage to the capitol, should forget the frailties of his nature, there was surely no need of such an admonition; the intoxication could not have continued long; he would have been at home but a few hours before some of his dependents would have forgot his greatness, and shewn him, that notwithstanding his laurels he was yet a man.

There are some who try to escape this domestic degradation, by labouring to appear always wise or always great; but he that strives against nature, will for ever strive in vain. To be grave of mien and slow of utterance; to look with solicitude and speak with hesitation, is attainable at will; but the shew of wisdom is ridiculous when there is nothing to cause doubt, as that of valour where there is nothing to be feared.

A man who has duly considered the condition of his being, will contentedly yield to the course of things: he will not pant for distinction where distinction would imply no merit, but tho' on great occasions he may wish to be greater than others, he will be satisfied in common occurrences not to be less.

4. See Juvenal, X.41–42.

No. 57. Saturday, 19 May 1759.

Prudence is of more frequent use than any other intellectual quality; it is exerted on slight occasions, and called into act by the cursory business of common life.

Whatever is universally necessary, has been granted to mankind on easy terms. Prudence, as it is always wanted, is without great difficulty obtained. It requires neither extensive view nor profound search, but forces itself, by spontaneous impulse, upon a mind neither great nor busy, neither ingrossed by vast designs nor distracted by multiplicity of attention.

Prudence operates on life in the same manner as rules on composition; it produces vigilance rather than elevation, rather prevents loss than procures advantages; and often escapes miscarriages, but seldom reaches either power or honour. It quenches that ardour of enterprize, by which every thing is done that can claim praise or admiration, and represses that generous temerity which often fails and often succeeds. Rules may obviate faults, but can never confer beauties;[1] and prudence keeps life safe, but does not often make it happy. The world is not amazed with prodigies of excellence, but when wit tramples upon rules, and magnanimity breaks the chains of prudence.

One of the most prudent of all that have fallen within my observation, is my old companion Sophron, who has

1. Cf. *Rambler* 158 (pars. 1–3), above, and his remark to Fanny Burney that, among the judges of her work, "the first are those who know know no rules, but pronounce entirely from their natural taste and feelings; the second are those who know and judge by rules; and the third are those who know, and are above the rules. These last are those you should wish to satisfy. Next to them rate the natural judges; but ever despise those opinions that are formed by the rules." (Fanny Burney, *Diary*, ed. Dobson [1904], I.183–84).

passed through the world in quiet, by perpetual adherence to a few plain maxims, and wonders how contention and distress can so often happen.

The first principle of Sophron is to "run no hazards." Tho' he loves money, he is of opinion, that frugality is a more certain source of riches than industry. It is to no purpose that any prospect of large profit is set before him; he believes little about futurity, and does not love to trust his money out of his sight, for nobody knows what may happen. He has a small estate which he lets at the old rent, because "it is better to have a little than nothing"; but he rigorously demands payment on the stated day, for "he that cannot pay one quarter cannot pay two." If he is told of any improvements in agriculture, he likes the old way, has observed that changes very seldom answer expectation, is of opinion that our forefathers knew how to till the ground as well as we; and concludes with an argument that nothing can overpower, that the expence of planting and fencing is immediate, and the advantage distant, and that "he is no wise man who will quit a certainty for an uncertainty."

Another of Sophron's rules is, "to mind no business but his own." In the state he is of no party; but hears and speaks of publick affairs with the same coldness as of the administration of some ancient republick. If any flagrant act of fraud or oppression is mentioned, he hopes that "all is not true that is told": if misconduct or corruption puts the nation in a flame, he hopes that "every man means well." At elections he leaves his dependents to their own choice, and declines to vote himself, for every candidate is a good man, whom he is unwilling to oppose or offend.

If disputes happen among his neighbours he observes an invariable and cold neutrality. His punctuality has gained him the reputation of honesty, and his caution that of wisdom, and few would refuse to refer their claims to his award. He might have prevented many expensive law-suits, and quenched many a feud in its first smoke, but always refuses the office of arbitration, because he must decide against one or the other.

With the affairs of other families he is always unacquainted. He sees estates bought and sold, squandered and increased, without praising the economist or censuring the spendthrift. He never courts the rising lest they should fall, nor insults the fallen lest they should rise again. His caution has the appearance of virtue, and all who do not want his help praise his benevolence; but if any man solicits his assistance, he has just sent away all his money; and when the petitioner is gone declares to his family that he is sorry for his misfortunes, has always looked upon him with particular kindness, and therefore could not lend him money, lest he should destroy their friendship by the necessity of enforcing payment.

Of domestic misfortunes he has never heard. When he is told the hundredth time of a gentleman's daughter who has married the coachman, he lifts up his hands with astonishment, for he always thought her a very sober girl. When nuptial quarrels, after having filled the country with talk and laughter, at last end in separation, he never can conceive how it happened, for he looked upon them as a happy couple.

If his advice is asked, he never gives any particular direction, because events are uncertain, and he will bring no blame upon himself; but he takes the consulter tenderly by the hand, tells him he makes his case his own, and advises him not to act rashly, but to weigh the reasons on both sides; observes that a man may be as easily too hasty as too slow, and that as many fail by doing too much as too little; that "a wise man has two ears and one tongue"; and "that little said is soon amended"; that he could tell him this and that, but that after all every man is the best judge of his own affairs.

With this some are satisfied, and go home with great reverence of Sophron's wisdom, and none are offended, because every one is left in full possession of his own opinion.

Sophron gives no characters. It is equally vain to tell him of vice and virtue, for he has remarked that no man likes to be censured, and that very few are delighted with the praises of another. He has a few terms which he uses to all alike. With respect to fortune, he believes every family to be in good circumstances; he never exalts any understanding by lavish praise; yet he meets with none but very sensible people. Every man is honest and hearty, and every woman is a good creature.

Thus Sophron creeps along, neither loved nor hated, neither favoured nor opposed; he has never attempted to grow rich for fear of growing poor, and has raised no friends for fear of making enemies.

No. 58. Saturday, 26 May 1759.

Pleasure is very seldom found where it is sought. Our brightest blazes of gladness are commonly kindled by unexpected sparks. The flowers which scatter their odours from time to time in the paths of life, grow up without culture from seeds scattered by chance.

Nothing is more hopeless than a scheme of merriment. Wits and humorists are brought together from distant quarters by preconcerted invitations; they come attended by their admirers prepared to laugh and to applaud; they gaze a-while on each other, ashamed to be silent, and afraid to speak; every man is discontented with himself, grows angry with those that give him pain, and resolves that he will contribute nothing to the merriment of such worthless company. Wine inflames the general malignity, and changes sullenness to petulance, till at last none can bear any longer the presence of the rest. They retire to vent their indignation in safer places, where they are heard with attention; their importance is restored, they recover their good humour, and gladden the night with wit and jocularity.

Merriment is always the effect of a sudden impression. The jest which is expected is already destroyed. The most active imagination will be sometimes torpid, under the frigid influence of melancholy, and sometimes occasions will be wanting to tempt the mind, however volatile, to sallies and excursions. Nothing was ever said with uncommon felicity, but by the co-operation of chance; and therefore, wit as well as valour must be content to share its honours with fortune.

All other pleasures are equally uncertain; the general remedy of uneasiness is change of place;[1] almost every one has some journey of pleasure in his mind, with which he flatters his expectation. He that travels in theory has no inconveniences; he has shade and sunshine at his disposal, and wherever he alights finds tables of plenty and looks of gaiety. These ideas are indulged till the day of departure arrives, the chaise is called, and the progress of happiness begins.

1. This is the general theme of *Rambler* 6 ("The general remedy of those, who are uneasy without knowing the cause, is change of place; they are willing to imagine that their pain is the consequence of some local inconvenience, and endeavour to fly from it . . .").

A few miles teach him the fallacies of imagination. The road is dusty, the air is sultry, the horses are sluggish, and the postilion brutal. He longs for the time of dinner that he may eat and rest. The inn is crouded, his orders are neglected, and nothing remains but that he devour in haste what the cook has spoiled, and drive on in quest of better entertainment. He finds at night a more commodious house, but the best is always worse than he expected.

He at last enters his native province, and resolves to feast his mind with the conversation of his old friends, and the recollection of juvenile frolicks. He stops at the house of his friend whom he designs to overpower with pleasure by the unexpected interview. He is not known till he tells his name, and revives the memory of himself by a gradual explanation. He is then coldly received, and ceremoniously feasted.[2] He hastes away to another whom his affairs have called to a distant place, and having seen the empty house, goes away disgusted, by a disappointment which could not be intended because it could not be foreseen. At the next house he finds every face clouded with misfortune, and is regarded with malevolence as an unreasonable intruder, who comes not to visit but to insult them.

It is seldom that we find either men or places such as we expect them. He that has pictured a prospect upon his fancy, will receive little pleasure from his eyes;[3] he that has anticipated the conversation of a wit, will wonder to what prejudice he owes his reputation. Yet it is necessary to hope, tho' hope should always be deluded, for hope itself is happiness, and its frustrations, however frequent, are yet less dreadful than its extinction.

2. Cf. the portrait of Serotinus in *Rambler* 165 (esp. the final par.).
3. Cf. Letter to Mrs. Thrale, 26 June, 1775 (*Letters*, ed. Chapman [1952], II.410).

No. 59. Saturday, 2 June 1759.

In the common enjoyments of life, we cannot very liberally indulge the present hour, but by anticipating part of the pleasure which might have relieved the tediousness of another day; and any uncommon exertion of strength, or perseverance in labour, is succeeded by a long interval of languor and weariness. Whatever advantage we snatch beyond the certain portion allotted us by nature, is like money spent before it is due, which at the time of regular payment will be missed and regretted.

Fame, like all other things which are supposed to give or to encrease happiness, is dispensed with the same equality of distribution. He that is loudly praised will be clamorously censured; he that rises hastily into fame will be in danger of sinking suddenly into oblivion.

Of many writers who filled their age with wonder, and whose names we find celebrated in the books of their contemporaries, the works are now no longer to be seen, or are seen only amidst the lumber of libraries which are seldom visited, where they lie only to shew the deceitfulness of hope, and the uncertainty of honour.

Of the decline of reputation many causes may be assigned. It is commonly lost because it never was deserved, and was conferred at first, not by the suffrage of criticism, but by the fondness of friendship, or servility of flattery. The great and popular are very freely applauded, but all soon grow weary of echoing to each other a name which has no other claim to notice, but that many mouths are pronouncing it at once.

But many have lost the final reward of their labours, because they were too hasty to enjoy it. They have laid hold on recent occurrences, and eminent names, and delighted their readers with allusions and remarks, in which all were interested, and to which all therefore were attentive. But the effect ceased with its cause; the time quickly came when new events drove the former from memory, when the vicissitudes of the world brought new hopes and fears, transferred the love and hatred of the public to other agents, and the writer whose works were no longer assisted by gratitude or resentment, was left to the cold regard of idle curiosity.

He that writes upon general principles, or delivers universal truths, may hope to be often read, because his work will be equally useful at all times and in every country, but he cannot expect it to be received with eagerness, or to spread with rapidity, because desire can have no particular stimulation; that which is to be loved long must be loved with reason rather than with passion. He that lays out his labours upon temporary subjects, easily finds readers, and quickly loses them; for what should make the book valued when its subject is no more.

These observations will shew the reason why the poem of *Hudibras* is almost forgotten however embellished with sentiments and diversified with allusions, however bright with wit, and however solid with truth. The hypocrisy which it detected, and the folly which it ridiculed, have long vanished from public notice.[1] Those who had felt the mischiefs of discord, and the tyranny of usurpation, read it with rapture, for every line brought back to memory something known, and gratified resentment, by the just censure of something hated. But the book which was once quoted by princes, and which supplied conversation to all the assemblies of the gay and witty, is now seldom mentioned, and even by those that affect to mention it, is seldom read. So vainly is wit lavished upon

1. Cf. "Butler," *Lives*, I.213–14 (pars. 41–42); and *Life*, II.369–70.

fugitive topics, so little can architecture secure duration when the ground is false.

No. 60. Saturday, 9 June 1759.

Criticism is a study by which men grow important and formidable at very small expence. The power of invention has been conferred by nature upon few, and the labour of learning those sciences which may, by mere labour, be obtained, is too great to be willingly endured; but every man can exert such judgment as he has upon the works of others; and he whom nature has made weak, and idleness keeps ignorant, may yet support his vanity by the name of a critick.

I hope it will give comfort to great numbers who are passing thro' the world in obscurity, when I inform them how easily distinction may be obtained. All the other powers of literature are coy and haughty, they must be long courted, and at last are not always gained; but criticism is a goddess easy of access and forward of advance, who will meet the slow and encourage the timorous; the want of meaning she supplies with words, and the want of spirit she recompenses with malignity.

This profession has one recommendation peculiar to itself, that it gives vent to malignity without real mischief. No genius was ever blasted by the breath of criticks.[1] The poison which, if confined, would have burst the heart, fumes away in empty hisses, and malice is set at ease with very little danger to merit. The critick is the only man whose triumph is without another's pain, and whose greatness does not rise upon another's ruin.

To a study at once so easy and so reputable, so malicious and so harmless, it cannot be necessary to invite my

1. For similar remarks, see *Life*, II.61–62, n. 4.

readers by a long or laboured exhortation; it is sufficient, since all would be criticks if they could, to shew by one eminent example that all can be criticks if they will.

Dick Minim,[2] after the common course of puerile studies, in which he was no great proficient, was put apprentice to a brewer, with whom he had lived two years, when his uncle died in the city, and left him a large fortune in the stocks. Dick had for six months before used the company of the lower players, of whom he had learned to scorn a trade, and being now at liberty to follow his genius, he resolved to be a man of wit and humour. That he might be properly initiated in his new character, he frequented the coffee-houses near the theatres, where he listened very diligently day, after day, to those who talked of language and sentiments, and unities and catastrophes, till by slow degrees he began to think that he understood something of the stage, and hoped in time to talk himself.

But he did not trust so much to natural sagacity, as wholly to neglect the help of books. When the theatres were shut, he retired to Richmond with a few select writers, whose opinions he impressed upon his memory by unwearied diligence; and when he returned with other wits to the town, was able to tell, in very proper phrases, that the chief business of art is to copy nature; that a perfect writer is not to be expected, because genius decays as judgment increases; that the great art is the art of blotting,[3] and that according to the rule of Horace every piece should be kept nine years.[4]

Of the great authors he now began to display the char-

2. From *minimus*—i.e. the least or smallest particle in size, value, or both. But this portrait is by no means wholly unfavorable.

3. Johnson is here echoing clichés from Alexander Pope's *Essay on Criticism* (ll. 68, 253-54, 56-57) and *Imitations of Horace* (II.1.281). Cf. *Rambler* 23 (par. 6).

4. *Ars poetica* l. 388.

acters, laying down as an universal position that all had
beauties and defects. His opinion was, that Shakespear,
committing himself wholly to the impulse of nature,
wanted that correctness which learning would have given
him; and that Johnson [Ben Jonson], trusting to learning, did not sufficiently cast his eye on nature. He blamed
the stanza of Spenser, and could not bear the hexameters
of Sidney. Denham and Waller he held the first reformers
of English numbers, and thought that if Waller could
have obtained the strength of Denham, or Denham the
sweetness of Waller, there had been nothing wanting
to complete a poet.[5] He often expressed his commisera-
tion of Dryden's poverty, and his indignation at the age
which suffered him to write for bread; he repeated with
rapture the first lines of *All for Love,* but wondered at
the corruption of taste which could bear any thing so
unnatural as rhyming tragedies. In Otway he found uncommon powers of moving the passions, but was disgusted
by his general negligence, and blamed him for making a
conspirator his hero; and never concluded his disquisition, without remarking how happily the sound of the
clock is made to alarm the audience. Southern would have
been his favourite, but that he mixes comick with tragick
scenes, intercepts the natural course of the passions, and
fills the mind with a wild confusion of mirth and melancholy. The versification of Rowe he thought too melodious for the stage, and too little varied in different passions.
He made it the great fault of Congreve, that all his persons were wits, and that he always wrote with more art

5. Johnson, as Hill notes, echoes consecutively here Pope's *Imitations
of Horace* (II.1.279), Collins' *Epistle to Hanmer* (l. 55), Pope's *Imitations of
Horace* (II.1.98), Dryden's *Preface to the Fables* (par. 11), and Pope's
Essay on Criticism (l. 361); in the remarks on Otway immediately below,
Imitations of Horace (II.1.278) and *Spectator* 39. The remark on the Spen-
serian stanza echoes Johnson's own opinion (*Rambler* 121, par. 14).

than nature.[6] He considered *Cato* rather as a poem than a play, and allowed Addison to be the complete master of allegory and grave humour, but paid no great deference to him as a critick. He thought the chief merit of Prior was in his easy tales and lighter poems, tho' he allowed that his *Solomon* had many noble sentiments elegantly expressed. In Swift he discovered an inimitable vein of irony, and an easiness which all would hope and few would attain. Pope he was inclined to degrade from a poet to a versifier, and thought his numbers rather luscious than sweet. He often lamented the neglect of *Phaedra and Hippolitus*,[7] and wished to see the stage under better regulations.

These assertions passed commonly uncontradicted; and if now and then an opponent started up, he was quickly repressed by the suffrages of the company, and Minim went away from every dispute with elation of heart and increase of confidence.

He now grew conscious of his abilities, and began to talk of the present state of dramatick poetry; wondered what was become of the comick genius which supplied our ancestors with wit and pleasantry, and why no writer could be found that durst now venture beyond a farce. He saw no reason for thinking that the vein of humour was exhausted, since we live in a country where liberty suffers every character to spread itself to its utmost bulk, and which therefore produces more originals than all the rest of the world together. Of tragedy he concluded business to be the soul, and yet often hinted that love predominates too much upon the modern stage.

6. Minim expresses Johnson's own sentiments. Cf. "Congreve," *Lives*, II.218–19, 228 (pars. 16 and 33).

7. *Phaedra and Hippolytus*, by Edmund Smith (1707). Cf. Johnson's discussion of it in "Smith," *Lives*, II.16 (par. 49), and Addison's belief that the play was undeservedly neglected (*Spectator* 18).

He was now an acknowledged critick, and had his own seat in the coffee-house, and headed a party in the pit. Minim has more vanity than ill-nature, and seldom desires to do much mischief; he will perhaps murmur a little in the ear of him that sits next him, but endeavours to influence the audience to favour, by clapping when an actor exclaims "ye Gods," or laments the misery of his country.

By degrees he was admitted to rehearsals, and many of his friends are of opinion, that our present poets are indebted to him for their happiest thoughts; by his contrivance the bell was rung twice in *Barbarossa*,[8] and by his persuasion the author of *Cleone*[9] concluded his play without a couplet; for what can be more absurd, said Minim, than that part of a play should be rhymed, and part written in blank verse? and by what acquisition of faculties is the speaker who never could find rhymes before, enabled to rhyme at the conclusion of an act!

He is the great investigator of hidden beauties, and is particularly delighted when he finds "the sound an echo to the sense."[10] He has read all our poets with particular attention to this delicacy of versification, and wonders at the supineness with which their works have been hitherto perused, so that no man has found the sound of a drum in this distich,

When pulpit, drum ecclesiastic,
Was beat with fist instead of a stick;[11]

8. *Barbarossa*, by Dr. John Brown (1754). Cf. Johnson's criticism that "the use of a bell is unknown to the Mahometans" *(Life,* II.131, n. 2).

9. By Robert Dodsley (1758). Cf. Johnson's remark that in it "there is more blood than brains" *(Life,* IV.20).

10. Pope, *Essay on Criticism,* l. 365, the implications of which Johnson discusses in detail in *Ramblers* 92 and 94, and "Pope," *Lives,* III.230–32 (pars. 330–34).

11. *Hudibras,* I.1.11–12.

and that the wonderful lines upon honour and a bubble
have hitherto passed without notice.

Honour is like the glassy bubble,
Which costs philosophers such trouble,
Where one part crack'd, the whole does fly,
And wits are crack'd to find out why.[12]

In these verses, says Minim, we have two striking accom-
modations of the sound to the sense. It is impossible to
utter the two lines emphatically without an act like that
which they describe; "bubble" and "trouble" causing a
momentary inflation of the cheeks by the retention of the
breath, which is afterwards forcibly emitted, as in the
practice of "blowing bubbles." But the greatest excellence
is in the third line, which is "crack'd" in the middle to
express a crack, and then shivers into monosyllables. Yet
has this diamond lain neglected with common stones,
and among the innumerable admirers of *Hudibras* the
observation of this superlative passage has been reserved
for the sagacity of Minim.

No. 61. Saturday, 16 June 1759.

Mr. Minim had now advanced himself to the zenith of
critical reputation; when he was in the pit, every eye in
the boxes was fixed upon him, when he entered his coffee-
house, he was surrounded by circles of candidates, who
passed their noviciate of literature under his tuition; his
opinion was asked by all who had no opinion of their
own, and yet loved to debate and decide; and no composition was supposed to pass in safety to posterity, till it
had been secured by Minim's approbation.

12. Ibid., II.2.385–88.

Minim professes great admiration of the wisdom and munificence by which the academies of the continent were raised, and often wishes for some standard of taste, for some tribunal, to which merit may appeal from caprice, prejudice, and malignity.[1] He has formed a plan for an academy of criticism, where every work of imagination may be read before it is printed, and which shall authoritatively direct the theatres what pieces to receive or reject, to exclude or to revive.

Such an institution would, in Dick's opinion, spread the fame of English literature over Europe, and make London the metropolis of elegance and politeness, the place to which the learned and ingenious of all countries would repair for instruction and improvement, and where nothing would any longer be applauded or endured that was not conformed to the nicest rules, and finished with the highest elegance.

Till some happy conjunction of the planets shall dispose our princes or ministers to make themselves immortal by such an academy, Minim contents himself to preside four nights in a week in a critical society elected by himself, where he is heard without contradiction, and whence his judgment is disseminated through the great vulgar and the small.[2]

When he is placed in the chair of criticism, he declares loudly for the noble simplicity of our ancestors, in opposition to the petty refinements, and ornamental luxuriance. Sometimes he is sunk in despair, and perceives false delicacy daily gaining ground, and sometimes brightens his countenance with a gleam of hope, and predicts the

1. For Johnson's antagonism to the idea of an English academy, see "Roscommon," *Lives*, I.232–33 (pars. 13–18).
2. Johnson echoes the opening of Cowley's translation of Horace's *Odes*, III.1.

revival of the true sublime. He then fulminates his loudest censures against the monkish barbarity of rhyme;[3] wonders how beings that pretend to reason can be pleased with one line always ending like another; tells how unjustly and unnaturally sense is sacrificed to sound; how often the best thoughts are mangled by the necessity of confining or extending them to the dimensions of a couplet; and rejoices that genius has, in our days, shaken off the shackles which had encumbered it so long. Yet he allows that rhyme may sometimes be borne, if the lines be often broken, and the pauses judiciously diversified.

From blank verse he makes an easy transition to Milton, whom he produces as an example of the slow advance of lasting reputation. Milton is the only writer whose books Minim can read for ever without weariness. What cause it is that exempts this pleasure from satiety he has long and diligently enquired, and believes it to consist in the perpetual variation of the numbers, by which the ear is gratified and the attention awakened. The lines that are commonly thought rugged and unmusical, he conceives to have been written to temper the melodious luxury of the rest, or to express things by a proper cadence: for he scarcely finds a verse that has not this favourite beauty; he declares that he could shiver in a hothouse when he reads that

> the ground
> Burns frore, and cold performs th' effect of fire.[4]

And that when Milton bewails his blindness, the verse

> So thick a drop serene has quench'd these orbs,[5]

3. Minim echoes Milton's Preface to *Paradise Lost* and Edmund Smith on the "constraint of monkish rhyme" ("To the Memory of Mr. John Philips," l. 68).

4. *Paradise Lost*, II.594–95.

5. Ibid., III.25.

has, he knows not how, something that strikes him with an obscure sensation like that which he fancies would be felt from the sound of darkness.

Minim is not so confident of his rules of judgment as not very eagerly to catch new light from the name of the author. He is commonly so prudent as to spare those whom he cannot resist, unless, as will sometimes happen, he finds the publick combined against them. But a fresh pretender to fame he is strongly inclined to censure, 'till his own honour requires that he commend him. 'Till he knows the success of a composition, he intrenches himself in general terms; there are some new thoughts and beautiful passages, but there is likewise much which he would have advised the author to expunge. He has several favourite epithets, of which he has never settled the meaning, but which are very commodiously applied to books which he has not read, or cannot understand. One is "manly," another is "dry," another "stiff," and another "flimzy"; sometimes he discovers delicacy of style, and sometimes meets with "strange expressions."

He is never so great, or so happy, as when a youth of promising parts is brought to receive his directions for the prosecution of his studies. He then puts on a very serious air; he advises the pupil to read none but the best authors, and, when he finds one congenial to his own mind, to study his beauties, but avoid his faults, and, when he sits down to write, to consider how his favourite author would think[6] at the present time on the present occasion. He exhorts him to catch those moments when he finds his thoughts expanded and his genius exalted, but to take care lest imagination hurry him beyond the bounds of nature. He holds diligence the mother of suc-

6. Johnson echoes Longinus, trans. William Smith (1739), pp. 38f.

cess, yet enjoins him, with great earnestness, not to read more than he can digest, and not to confuse his mind by pursuing studies of contrary tendencies. He tells him, that every man has his genius,[7] and that Cicero could never be a poet. The boy retires illuminated, resolves to follow his genius, and to think how Milton would have thought; and Minim feasts upon his own beneficence till another day brings another pupil.

No. 65. Saturday, 14 July 1759.

The sequel of Clarendon's history,[1] at last happily published, is an accession to English literature equally agreeable to the admirers of elegance and the lovers of truth; many doubtful facts may now be ascertained, and many questions, after long debate, may be determined by decisive authority. He that records transactions in which himself was engaged, has not only an opportunity of knowing innumerable particulars which escape spectators, but has his natural powers exalted by that ardour which always rises at the remembrance of our own importance, and by which every man is enabled to relate his own actions better than another's.

The difficulties thro' which this work has struggled into light, and the delays with which our hopes have been long mocked, naturally lead the mind to the consideration of the common fate of posthumous compositions.

He who sees himself surrounded by admirers, and

---

7. Cf. Johnson's frequent statements to the contrary (e.g. *Rambler* 25, above, n. 5).

1. *The Life of Edward, Earl of Clarendon . . . Being a Continuation of the History of the Grand Rebellion* (1759). The editor is still unknown.

whose vanity is hourly feasted with all the luxuries of studied praise, is easily persuaded that his influence will be extended beyond his life; that they who cringe in his presence will reverence his memory, and that those who are proud to be numbered among his friends, will endeavour to vindicate his choice by zeal for his reputation.

With hopes like these, to the executors of Swift was committed the history of the last years of Queen Anne,[2] and to those of Pope the works which remained unprinted in his closet. The performances of Pope were burnt by those whom he had perhaps selected from all mankind as most likely to publish them;[3] and the history had likewise perished, had not a straggling transcript fallen into busy hands.

The papers left in the closet of Peiresc supplied his heirs with a whole winter's fuel,[4] and many of the labours of the learned Bishop Lloyd were consumed in the kitchen of his descendants.[5]

Some works, indeed, have escaped total destruction, but yet have had reason to lament the fate of orphans exposed to the frauds of unfaithful guardians. How Hale would have borne the mutilations which his *Pleas of the Crown*

2. Recounted in the Advertisement written by Charles Lucas to Swift's *History of the Four Last Years of the Queen's Reign* (1758). Cf. "Swift," *Lives*, II.27–28 (par. 65).

3. Cf. "Pope," *Lives*, III.192 (par. 249).

4. Johnson apparently refers to the account of Gilles Ménage: "On me disoit . . . que la sottise d'une nièce de M. de Peiresc nous avoit fait perdre un très-grand nombre de ces lettres: elle en avoit un cabinet plein, et les brûloit pour allumer son feu" (*Ménagiana*, 1693, par. 1, in *Ana, ou Collection de bons mots*, ed. B. de la Monnoye, 1799, II.2). They were letters to Peiresc; according to Pierre Gassendi, Peiresc's own manuscripts were carefully catalogued and bound, partly with the help of his brother and his nephew (*Mirrour of True Nobility . . . the Life of . . . Peiresk*, 1657, pp. 294–95). See also Johnson's life of Browne (par. 42).

5. A. T. Hart (*William Lloyd*, 1952, p. 146) cites Johnson himself, who may have heard it at Lichfield, as the authority for the story.

have suffered from the editor,[6] they who know his character will easily conceive.

The original copy of Burnet's history, tho' promised to some publick[7] library, has been never given; and who then can prove the fidelity of the publication, when the authenticity of Clarendon's history, tho' printed with the sanction of one of the first universities of the world, had not an unexpected manuscript been happily discovered, would, with the help of factious credulity, have been brought into question by the two lowest of all human beings,[8] a scribbler for a party, and a commissioner of excise?

Vanity is often no less mischievous than negligence or dishonesty. He that possesses a valuable manuscript, hopes to raise its esteem by concealment, and delights in the distinction which he imagines himself to obtain by keeping the key of a treasure which he neither uses nor imparts. From him it falls to some other owner, less vain but more negligent, who considers it as useless lumber, and rids himself of the incumbrance.

Yet there are some works which the authors must consign unpublished to posterity, however uncertain be the event, however hopeless be the trust. He that writes the history of his own times, if he adheres steadily to truth, will write that which his own times will not easily endure.

6. See Gilbert Burnet, *Life and Death of Sir Matthew Hale* (1682) p. 186, on Hale's unwillingness to have his unpublished works printed after his death for fear they be changed. The mutilations of the first edition of the *Pleas of the Crown* (1678) are described in a preface to the 5th edition (1716). A correspondent in the *Gentleman's Magazine*, June 1760, comments on these publications.

7. "It would be proper to reposite, in some publick place, the manuscript of Clarendon, which has not escaped all suspicion of unfaithful publication" (Johnson's note, added in 1761).

8. John Oldmixon (1673–1742) and George Duckett (d. 1732). For details see "Smith," *Lives*, II.18–20 (pars. 57–71).

He must be content to reposite his book till all private passions shall cease, and love and hatred give way to curiosity.

But many leave the labour of half their life to their executors and to chance, because they will not send them abroad unfinished, and are unable to finish them, having prescribed to themselves such a degree of exactness as human diligence scarcely can attain. "Lloyd," says Burnet, "did not lay out his learning with the same diligence as he laid it in."[9] He was always hesitating and enquiring, raising objections and removing them, and waiting for clearer light and fuller discovery. Baker, after many years past in biography, left his manuscripts to be buried in a library, because that was imperfect which could never be perfected.[10]

Of these learned men let those who aspire to the same praise, imitate the diligence and avoid the scrupulosity. Let it be always remembered that life is short, that knowledge is endless, and that many doubts deserve not to be cleared. Let those whom nature and study have qualified to teach mankind, tell us what they have learned while they are yet able to tell it, and trust their reputations only to themselves.

No. 66. Saturday, 21 July 1759.

No complaint is more frequently repeated among the learned, than that of the waste made by time among the

9. *History of His Own Time* (1840), I.130.

10. Thomas Baker (1656–1740), who intended to write an *Athenae Cantabrigienses* similar to Anthony Wood's work relating to Oxford. Of the 42 folio volumes, 23 ended in the Harleian collection, and the rest in the university library at Cambridge. Other papers went to St. John's College. For a description see *Biographia Britannica*, 2nd ed. (1778), I.521–25 n.

labours of antiquity. Of those who once filled the civilized world with their renown nothing is now left but their names, which are left only to raise desires that never can be satisfied, and sorrow which never can be comforted.

Had all the writings of the ancients been faithfully delivered down from age to age, had the Alexandrian library been spared, and the Palatine repositories remained unimpaired, how much might we have known of which we are now doomed to be ignorant; how many laborious enquiries, and dark conjectures, how many collations of broken hints and mutilated passages might have been spared. We should have known the successions of princes, the revolutions of empire, the actions of the great, and opinions of the wise, the laws and constitutions of every state, and the arts by which public grandeur and happiness are acquired and preserved. We should have traced the progress of life, seen colonies from distant regions take possession of European deserts, and troops of savages settled into communities by the desire of keeping what they had acquired; we should have traced the gradations of civility, and travelled upward to the original of things by the light of history, till in remoter times it had glimmered in fable, and at last sunk into darkness.

If the works of imagination had been less diminished, it is likely that all future times might have been supplied with inexhaustible amusement by the fictions of antiquity. The tragedies of Sophocles and Euripides would have shewn all the stronger passions in all their diversities, and the comedies of Menander would have furnished all the maxims of domestic life. Nothing would have been necessary to moral wisdom but to have studied these great masters, whose knowledge would have guided doubt, and whose authority would have silenced cavils.

Such are the thoughts that rise in every student, when

his curiosity is eluded, and his searches are frustrated; yet it may perhaps be doubted, whether our complaints are not sometimes inconsiderate, and whether we do not imagine more evil than we feel. Of the ancients, enough remains to excite our emulation, and direct our endeavours. Many of the works which time has left us, we know to have been those that were most esteemed, and which antiquity itself considered as models; so that having the originals, we may without much regret lose the imitations. The obscurity which the want of contemporary writers often produces, only darkens single passages, and those commonly of slight importance. The general tendency of every piece may be known, and tho' that diligence deserves praise which leaves nothing unexamined, yet its miscarriages are not much to be lamented; for the most useful truths are always universal, and unconnected with accidents and customs.

Such is the general conspiracy of human nature against contemporary merit, that if we had inherited from antiquity enough to afford employment for the laborious, and amusement for the idle, I know not what room would have been left for modern genius or modern industry; almost every subject would have been preoccupied, and every style would have been fixed by a precedent from which few would have ventured to depart. Every writer would have had a rival, whose superiority was already acknowledged, and to whose fame his work would, even before it was seen, be marked out for a sacrifice.

We see how little the united experience of mankind have been unable to add to the heroic characters displayed by Homer, and how few incidents the fertile imagination of modern Italy has yet produced, which may not be found in the Iliad and Odyssey.[1] It is likely, that if all the

1. Cf. *Preface to Shakespeare* (par. 3).

works of the Athenian philosophers had been extant, Mal-
branche and Locke would have been condemned to be
silent readers of the ancient metaphysicians; and it is
apparent, that if the old writers had all remained, the
Idler could not have written a disquisition on the loss.

No. 72. Saturday, 1 September 1759.

Men complain of nothing more frequently than of deficient memory; and indeed, every one finds that many of
the ideas which he desired to retain have slipped irre-
trievably away; that the. acquisitions of the mind are
sometimes equally fugitive with the gifts of fortune; and
that a short intermission of attention more certainly lessens knowledge than impairs an estate.

To assist this weakness of our nature many methods
have been proposed, all of which may be justly suspected
of being ineffectual; for no art of memory, however its
effects.have been boasted or admired, has been ever
adopted into general use, nor have those who possessed
it, appeared to excel others in readiness of recollection
or multiplicity of attainments.

There is another art of which all have felt the want,
tho' Themistocles only confessed it.[1] We suffer equal pain
from the pertinacious adhesion of unwelcome images, as
from the evanescence of those which are pleasing and
useful; and it may be doubted whether we should be
more benefited by the art of memory or the art of forgetfulness.

Forgetfulness is necessary to remembrance. Ideas are
retained by renovation of that impression which time is

1. Cicero, *De Finibus*, II.32.104. See above, p. 306.

always wearing away, and which new images are striving to obliterate. If useless thoughts could be expelled from the mind, all the valuable parts of our knowledge would more frequently recur, and every recurrence would re-instate them in their former place.

It is impossible to consider, without some regret, how much might have been learned, or how much might have been invented by a rational and vigorous application of time, uselessly or painfully passed in the revocation of events, which have left neither good nor evil behind them, in grief for misfortunes either repaired or irrepa-rable, in resentment of injuries known only to ourselves, of which death has put the authors beyond our power.

Philosophy has accumulated precept upon precept, to warn us against the anticipation of future calamities. All useless misery is certainly folly, and he that feels evils before they come may be deservedly censured; yet surely to dread the future is more reasonable than to lament the past. The business of life is to go forwards; he who sees evil in prospect meets it in his way, but he who catches it by retrospection turns back to find it. That which is feared may sometimes be avoided, but that which is regretted to-day may be regretted again to-morrow.

Regret is indeed useful and virtuous, and not only allowable but necessary, when it tends to the amendment of life, or to admonition of error which we may be again in danger of committing. But a very small part of the moments spent in meditation on the past, produce any reasonable caution or salutary sorrow. Most of the morti-fications that we have suffered, arose from the concur-rence of local and temporary circumstances, which can never meet again; and most of our disappointments have succeeded those expectations, which life allows not to be formed a second time.

It would add much to human happiness, if an art could be taught of forgetting all of which the remembrance is at once useless and afflictive, if that pain which never can end in pleasure could be driven totally away, that the mind might perform its functions without incumbrance, and the past might no longer encroach upon the present.

Little can be done well to which the whole mind is not applied; the business of every day calls for the day to which it is assigned, and he will have no leisure to regret yesterday's vexations who resolves not to have a new subject of regret to-morrow.

But to forget or to remember at pleasure, are equally beyond the power of man. Yet as memory may be assisted by method, and the decays of knowledge repaired by stated times of recollection, so the power of forgetting is capable of improvement. Reason will, by a resolute contest, prevail over imagination, and the power may be obtained of transferring the attention as judgment shall direct.

The incursions of troublesome thoughts are often violent and importunate; and it is not easy to a mind accustomed to their inroads to expel them immediately by putting better images into motion; but this enemy of quiet is above all others weakened by every defeat; the reflection which has been once overpowered and ejected, seldom returns with any formidable vehemence.

Employment is the great instrument of intellectual dominion. The mind cannot retire from its enemy into total vacancy, or turn aside from one object but by passing to another. The gloomy and the resentful are always found among those who have nothing to do, or who do nothing. We must be busy about good or evil, and he to whom the present offers nothing will often be looking backward on the past.

No. 84. Saturday, 24 November 1759.

Biography is, of the various kinds of narrative writing, that which is most eagerly read, and most easily applied to the purpose of life.[1]

In romances, when the wild field of possibility lies open to invention, the incidents may easily be made more numerous, the vicissitudes more sudden, and the events more wonderful; but from the time of life when fancy begins to be over-ruled by reason and corrected by experience, the most artful tale raises little curiosity when it is known to be false; tho' it may, perhaps, be sometimes read as a model of a neat or elegant stile, not for the sake of knowing what it contains, but how it is written; or those that are weary of themselves, may have recourse to it as a pleasing dream, of which, when they awake, they voluntarily dismiss the images from their minds.

The examples and events of history press, indeed, upon the mind with the weight of truth; but when they are reposited in the memory, they are oftener employed for shew than use, and rather diversify conversation than regulate life. Few are engaged in such scenes as give them opportunities of growing wiser by the downfal of statesmen or the defeat of generals. The stratagems of war, and the intrigues of courts, are read by far the greater part of mankind with the same indifference as the adventures of fabled heroes, or the revolutions of a fairy region.[2] Between falsehood and useless truth there is little

---

1. With the following discussion of biography, *cf. Rambler* 60.
2. One of Johnson's favorite contentions. Cf. "The miscarriages of the great designs of princes are recorded in the histories of the world, but are of little use to the bulk of mankind, who seem very little interested in admonitions against errors which they cannot commit" *(Rambler* 17); "Histories of the downfall of kingdoms, and revolutions of empires, are read with great tranquillity; the imperial tragedy pleases common audi-

difference. As gold which he cannot spend will make no
man rich, so knowledge which he cannot apply will make
no man wise.

The mischievous consequences of vice and folly, of irregular desires and predominant passions are best discovered by those relations which are levelled with the general surface of life, which tell not how any man became
great, but how he was made happy; not how he lost the
favour of his prince, but how he became discontented
with himself.

Those relations are therefore commonly of most value
in which the writer tells his own story. He that recounts
the life of another, commonly dwells most upon conspicuous events, lessens the familiarity of his tale to increase its dignity, shews his favourite at a distance deco-
rated and magnified like the ancient actors in their tragick
dress, and endeavours to hide the man that he may produce a hero.

But if it be true which was said by a French prince,
"that no man was a hero to the servants of his chamber,"[3]
it is equally true that every man is yet less a hero to himself. He that is most elevated above the croud by the importance of his employments or the reputation of his
genius, feels himself affected by fame or business but as
they influence his domestick life. The high and low, as
they have the same faculties and the same senses, have no
less similitude in their pains and pleasures. The sensations are the same in all, tho' produced by very different
occasions. The prince feels the same pain when an in-
vader seizes a province, as the farmer when a thief drives

---

tors only by its pomp of ornament, and grandeur of ideas . . ." (*Rambler*
60).

3. Generally attributed to the Prince de Condé; also ascribed to Mme.
Cornuel in *Lettres de Mlle. Aissé*, XII (13 August, 1728).

away his cow. Men thus equal in themselves will appear equal in honest and impartial biography; and those whom fortune or nature place at the greatest distance may afford instruction to each other.

The writer of his own life has at least the first qualification of an historian, the knowledge of the truth; and though it may be plausibly objected that his temptations to disguise it are equal to his opportunities of knowing it, yet I cannot but think that impartiality may be expected with equal confidence from him that relates the passages of his own life, as from him that delivers the transactions of another.

Certainty of knowledge not only excludes mistake but fortifies veracity. What we collect by conjecture, and by conjecture only can one man judge of another's motives or sentiments, is easily modified by fancy or by desire; as objects imperfectly discerned, take forms from the hope or fear of the beholder. But that which is fully known cannot be falsified but with reluctance of understanding, and alarm of conscience; of understanding, the lover of truth; of conscience, the sentinel of virtue.

He that writes the life of another is either his friend or his enemy, and wishes either to exalt his praise or aggravate his infamy; many temptations to falsehood will occur in the disguise of passions, too specious to fear much resistance. Love of virtue will animate panegyrick, and hatred of wickedness imbitter censure. The zeal of gratitude, the ardour of patriotism, fondness for an opinion, or fidelity to a party, may easily overpower the vigilance of a mind habitually well disposed, and prevail over unassisted and unfriended veracity.

But he that speaks of himself has no motive to falshood or partiality except self-love, by which all have so often been betrayed, that all are on the watch against its artifices. He that writes an apology for a single action, to confute an accusation, or recommend himself to a favour, is indeed always to be suspected of favouring his own cause; but he that sits down calmly and voluntarily to review his life for the admonition of posterity, or to amuse himself, and leaves this account unpublished, may be commonly presumed to tell truth, since falshood cannot appease his own mind, and fame will not be heard beneath the tomb.

No. 88. Saturday, 22 December 1759.

Hodie quid egisti?[1]

When the philosophers of the last age were first congregated into the Royal Society, great expectations were raised of the sudden progress of useful arts; the time was supposed to be near when engines should turn by a perpetual motion, and health be secured by the universal medicine; when learning should be facilitated by a real character, and commerce extended by ships which could reach their ports in defiance of the tempest.

But improvement is naturally slow. The society met and parted without any visible diminution of the miseries of life. The gout and stone were still painful, the ground that was not plowed brought no harvest, and neither oranges nor grapes would grow upon the hawthorne. At last, those who were disappointed began to be angry; those likewise who hated innovation were glad to gain

1. The phrase appears in Pliny, *Epistles,* I.9.1. But Johnson is perhaps putting into Latin the question from Pythagoras's *Aurea Carmina* 42: he had used the Greek original as a motto for *Adventurer* 137 (translated "What have I been doing?").

an opportunity of ridiculing men who had depreciated, perhaps with too much arrogance, the knowledge of antiquity. And it appears from some of their earliest apologies, that the philosophers felt with great sensibility the unwelcome importunities of those who were daily asking, "What have ye done?"

The truth is, that little had been done compared with what fame had been suffered to promise; and the question could only be answered by general apologies and by new hopes, which, when they were frustrated, gave a new occasion to the same vexatious enquiry.

This fatal question has disturbed the quiet of many other minds. He that in the latter part of his life too strictly enquires what he has done, can very seldom receive from his own heart such an account as will give him satisfaction.

We do not indeed so often disappoint others as ourselves. We not only think more highly than others of our own abilities, but allow ourselves to form hopes which we never communicate, and please our thoughts with employments which none ever will allot us, and with elevations to which we are never expected to rise; and when our days and years have passed away in common business or common amusements, and we find at last that we have suffered our purposes to sleep till the time of action is past, we are reproached only by our own reflections; neither our friends nor our enemies wonder that we live and die like the rest of mankind, that we live without notice and die without memorial; they know not what task we had proposed, and therefore cannot discern whether it is finished.

He that compares what he has done with what he has left undone, will feel the effect which must always follow the comparison of imagination with reality; he will look with contempt on his own unimportance, and wonder to what purpose he came into the world; he will repine that he shall leave behind him no evidence of his having been, that he has added nothing to the system of life, but has glided from youth to age among the crowd, without any effort for distinction.

Man is seldom willing to let fall the opinion of his own dignity, or to believe that he does little only because every individual is a very little being. He is better content to want diligence than power, and sooner confesses the depravity of his will than the imbecillity of his nature.

From this mistaken notion of human greatness it proceeds, that many who pretend to have made great advances in wisdom so loudly declare that they despise themselves. If I had ever found any of the self-contemners much irritated or pained by the consciousness of their meanness, I should have given them consolation by observing, that a little more than nothing is as much as can be expected from a being who with respect to the multitudes about him is himself little more than nothing. Every man is obliged by the supreme master of the universe to improve all the opportunities of good which are afforded him, and to keep in continual activity such abilities as are bestowed upon him. But he has no reason to repine though his abilities are small and his opportunities few. He that has improved the virtue or advanced the happiness of one fellow-creature, he that has ascertained a single moral proposition, or added one useful experiment to natural knowledge, may be contented with his own performance, and, with respect to mortals like himself, may demand, like Augustus, to be dismissed at his departure with applause.[2]

2. Suetonius, *Octavius,* 99.

No. 94. Saturday, 2 February 1760.

It is common to find young men ardent and diligent in the pursuit of knowledge, but the progress of life very often produces laxity and indifference; and not only those who are at liberty to chuse their business and amusements, but those likewise whose professions engaged them in literary enquiries pass the latter part of their time without improvement, and spend the day rather in any other entertainment than that which they might find among their books.

This abatement of the vigour of curiosity is sometimes imputed to the insufficiency of learning. Men are supposed to remit their labours, because they find their labours to have been vain; and to search no longer after truth and wisdom, because they at last despair of finding them.

But this reason is for the most part very falsely assigned. Of learning, as of virtue, it may be affirmed, that it is at once honoured and neglected.[1] Whoever forsakes it will for ever look after it with longing, lament the loss which he does not endeavour to repair, and desire the good which he wants resolution to seize and keep. The idler never applauds his own idleness, nor does any man repent of the diligence of his youth.

So many hindrances may obstruct the acquisition of knowledge, that there is little reason for wondering that it is in a few hands. To the greater part of mankind the duties of life are inconsistent with much study, and the hours which they would spend upon letters must be stolen from their occupations and their families. Many suffer themselves to be lured by more spritely and luxurious

1. Juvenal, *Satire*, I.74 ("Virtue is praised but neglected").

pleasures from the shades of contemplation, where they find seldom more than a calm delight, such as, though greater than all others, if its certainty and its duration be reckoned with its power of gratification, is yet easily quitted for some extemporary joy, which the present moment offers, and another perhaps will put out of reach.

It is the great excellence of learning that it borrows very little from time or place; it is not confined to season or to climate, to cities or to the country, but may be cultivated and enjoyed where no other pleasure can be obtained. But this quality, which constitutes much of its value, is one occasion of neglect; what may be done at all times with equal propriety, is deferred from day to day, till the mind is gradually reconciled to the omission, and the attention is turned to other objects. Thus habitual idleness gains too much power to be conquered, and the soul shrinks from the idea of intellectual labour and intenseness of meditation.

That those who profess to advance learning sometimes obstruct it, cannot be denied; the continual multiplication of books not only distracts choice but disappoints enquiry. To him that has moderately stored his mind with images, few writers afford any novelty; or what little they have to add to the common stock of learning is so buried in the mass of general notions, that, like silver mingled with the oar of lead, it is too little to pay for the labour of separation; and he that has often been deceived by the promise of a title, at last grows weary of examining, and is tempted to consider all as equally fallacious.

There are indeed some repetitions always lawful, because they never deceive. He that writes the history of past times, undertakes only to decorate known facts by new beauties of method or of style, or at most to illustrate them by his own reflections. The author of a system, whether moral or physical, is obliged to nothing beyond care of selection and regularity of disposition. But there are others who claim the name of authors merely to disgrace it, and fill the world with volumes only to bury letters in their own rubbish. The traveller who tells, in a pompous folio, that he saw the Pantheon at Rome, and the Medicean Venus at Florence; the natural historian who, describing the productions of a narrow island, recounts all that it has in common with every other part of the world; the collector of antiquities, that accounts every thing a curiosity which the ruins of Herculaneum happen to emit, though an instrument already shewn in a thousand repositories, or a cup common to the ancients, the moderns, and all mankind, may be justly censured as the persecutors of students, and the thieves of that time which never can be restored.

No. 103. Saturday, 5 April 1760.

Respicere ad longae jussit spatia ultima vitae.

Juvenal, x.275.[1]

Much of the pain and pleasure of mankind arises from the conjectures which every one makes of the thoughts of others; we all enjoy praise which we do not hear, and resent contempt which we do not see. The Idler may therefore be forgiven, if he suffers his imagination to represent to him what his readers will say or think when they are informed that they have now his last paper in their hands.

1. "Bidden to look at the last lap of a long life."

Value is more frequently raised by scarcity than by use. That which lay neglected when it was common, rises in estimation as its quantity becomes less. We seldom learn the true want of what we have till it is discovered that we can have no more.

This essay will, perhaps, be read with care even by those who have not yet attended to any other; and he that finds this late attention recompensed, will not forbear to wish that he had bestowed it sooner.

Though the Idler and his readers have contracted no close friendship they are perhaps both unwilling to part. There are few things not purely evil, of which we can say, without some emotion of uneasiness, "this is the last." Those who never could agree together, shed tears when mutual discontent has determined them to final separation; of a place which has been frequently visited, tho' without pleasure, the last look is taken with heaviness of heart; and the Idler, with all his chilness of tranquillity, is not wholly unaffected by the thought that his last essay is now before him.

This secret horrour of the last is inseparable from a thinking being whose life is limited, and to whom death is dreadful.[2] We always make a secret comparison between a part and the whole; the termination of any period of life reminds us that life itself has likewise its termination; when we have done any thing for the last time, we involuntarily reflect that a part of the days allotted us is past, and that as more is past there is less remaining.

It is very happily and kindly provided, that in every life there are certain pauses and interruptions, which force consideration upon the careless, and seriousness

2. "The whole of life is but keeping away the thoughts of it" (*Life*, II.93); cf. III.153, 188, 294–95. Boswell referred specifically to this number of the *Idler* in his journal (*London Journal* [1951], pp. 67–68).

upon the light; points of time where one course of action ends and another begins; and by vicissitude of fortune, or alteration of employment, by change of place, or loss of friendship, we are forced to say of something, "this is the last."

An even and unvaried tenour of life always hides from our apprehension the approach of its end. Succession is not perceived but by variation; he that lives to-day as he lived yesterday, and expects that, as the present day is, such will be the morrow, easily conceives time as running in a circle and returning to itself. The uncertainty of our duration is impressed commonly by dissimilitude of condition; it is only by finding life changeable that we are reminded of its shortness.

This conviction, however forcible at every new impression, is every moment fading from the mind; and partly by the inevitable incursion of new images, and partly by voluntary exclusion of unwelcome thoughts, we are again exposed to the universal fallacy; and we must do another thing for the last time, before we consider that the time is nigh when we shall do no more.

As the last *Idler* is published in that solemn week[3] which the Christian world has always set apart for the examination of the conscience, the review of life, the extinction of earthly desires and the renovation of holy purposes, I hope that my readers are already disposed to view every incident with seriousness, and improve it by meditation; and that when they see this series of trifles brought to a conclusion, they will consider that by outliving the *Idler*, they have past weeks, months, and years which are now no longer in their power; that an end must in time be put to every thing great as to every thing little;

3. On Holy Saturday of Easter Week.

that to life must come its last hour, and to this system of being its last day, the hour at which probation ceases, and repentance will be vain; the day in which every work of the hand, and imagination of the heart shall be brought to judgment, and an everlasting futurity shall be determined by the past.

INDEX

DEMCO